MISINFORMATION

Michael then flipped to the last tab of the file that contained copies of the corporate charter documents for Trinity Corporation. Surely there would be copies of the resolutions issuing the stock and establishing a managing director with the power to control the corporation and sign on its behalf. Just past the memorandum of association and bylaws, he found what he was looking for. When he got to the second page of the resolutions, his body froze. Next to the title Managing Director was the name

Michael Elliot

BREACH OF CONFIDENCE

Eben Paul Perison

AN ONYX BOOK

ONYX
Published by New American Library, a division of
Penguin Putnam Inc., 375 Hudson Street,
New York, New York 10014, U.S.A.
Penguin Books Ltd, 80 Strand,
London WC2R 0RL, England
Penguin Books Australia Ltd, Ringwood,
Victoria, Australia
Penguin Books Canada Ltd, 10 Alcorn Avenue,
Toronto, Ontario, Canada M4V 3B2
Penguin Books (N.Z.) Ltd, 182–190 Wairau Road,
Auckland 10, New Zealand

Penguin Books Ltd, Registered Offices:
Harmondsworth, Middlesex, England

First published by Onyx, an imprint of New American Library,
a division of Penguin Putnam Inc.

First Printing, May 2002
10 9 8 7 6 5 4 3 2 1

To Armando,
You were my father and my closest friend
and I will miss you very, very much

Prologue

Fifty-eight floors above downtown Manhattan, Richard Montague sat alone in his large corner office watching as the second hand on his clock quickly passed by. Time was running out. Outside his building the cars were caught in early-evening gridlock. On any other day he would have been out there with them, fighting his way to the Harvard Club to pound gin and tonics like they were water. But tonight he found himself trapped in the confines of his darkened office, the only light coming from an antique desk lamp, which cast a pale triangular shroud over him. On most occasions he played the part of a managing partner impeccably. His silvery hair and crow's-feet seemed to naturally inspire confidence and gave the impression of his being an elder statesman. The cool and collected demeanor that had been his trademark for so long now, however, was gone. Instead he was hunched over his desk desperately evaluating his options.

It was all slipping away from him. He should never have let it get this far, but it was too late to second-guess himself. What was done was done. Now there was only one way to stop it. In the little time he had left, he began furiously to scrawl instructions on the legal pad in front of him.

Desperate situations often required desperate measures, and he was no stranger to this truth. In his ten-year career as managing partner, he had built Davis & White from a handful of attorneys to one of the nation's most prominent and powerful law firms. Over his career he had been presented with hundreds of problems, each of which he had been able to surmount. This one, however, was different. For the first time in his life, he found himself at a complete and utter loss.

His competition, the powerful "white-shoe" Wall Street law firms, would love to see him in this condition. They were all vultures at heart. It would be just a matter of time before they began to steal the firm's clients, peeling them away like layers of skin from a carcass. Once they had finished that, they would begin to prey upon the firm's own ranks, stealing the oldest and most loyal partners with offers that a month ago these men would have shunned. The ungrateful bastards, he thought. He had built this firm attorney by attorney and client by client, but it was just a matter of time before they would all turn their backs on him. People never remembered what you had done for them in the past but only what you could do for them in the future. In the end they would view this as his fault. After all, it had occurred on his watch. He was the managing partner. He had become lazy with success and had spent too long resting on his laurels. From the top, there was only one place to go. Now all he could do was watch as the firm he had built from the ground up teetered on the edge of ruin.

It was ironic that so much now depended on an attorney to whom a few weeks ago he would have never given a second thought. Hell, he hadn't even known the young man's name, nor would he have been able to pick him out of a crowd. With more than five hundred attorneys working at the firm, it wasn't uncommon. But now his own fate and the fate of the firm rested with this one associate. This was his last chance. With him, Montague would struggle to hold things together. They would have to pry that wretched pen from his hands and take him out of his office in restraints if need be, but he wasn't going to be brought down.

A voice came out of the darkness. "Mr. Montague . . ." It was Rose, his secretary. She had been with him almost twenty-five years, and on any other night her voice would have calmed him. "The messenger just brought me this," she said, holding an envelope.

Montague looked up and scowled. "What is it?"

"It's a letter. I thought you'd want to see it immediately," she said, hesitating. "I think it's from him."

Montague winced as if he were in pain. He reached up until his hand disappeared in the darkness. With trepidation, he took the envelope from her and set it down on his desk. Through narrowed eyes he could read the words *PERSONAL AND CONFIDENTIAL* written by hand on the front of the envelope. Below them, a single word was written in large block letters:

TRINITY

He found few things unsettling at his age, but this one word created a wave of anxiety that started deep in the base of his stomach and radiated up through his rigid spine. If he had believed in such things, he would surely have seen this as some kind of dire sign or omen. No matter how hard he tried to dispel it, this word echoed through his head again and again— TRINITY . . . TRINITY . . . TRINITY—taunting him until he could no longer sit still.

Montague moved his arthritic fingers awkwardly to the top of the thin envelope, and the noise of tearing paper soon filled his large corner office. With his teeth clenched, he unfolded the single sheet of letterhead.

To Richard Montague, Esq.
Managing Partner, Davis & White
New York, New York

Dear Richard:

It is with great misgiving that I now find myself compelled to write you this letter. After all that has happened, you must believe me when I tell you that this is a decision I have given great thought to and it is one that I have not made lightly. In the time I have spent with this firm, I have been given an opportunity to work with some of the brightest and most talented lawyers in the country. All of the time I believed this firm was composed of men with the highest integrity and unquestionable moral character.

It was my sole ambition to one day become a partner with Davis & White. However, the events of the last month have forced me to question my commitment to the firm and the men within it. It is for this reason that I am now forced to resign. I can only hope that my actions have not caused harm to those who were equally naïve. This I find the most troubling effect of my actions, and it will always weigh heavy upon my soul. Still, I am forced to follow a different path. You will forgive me for not leaving my forwarding address.

Michael Elliot

PART I

PART 1

Chapter 1

The conference room on the forty-second floor of the First Interstate Bank Building was littered with closing documents. Dozens of stacks of paper ran neatly down the long narrow table in the center of the room, and steel accordion racks filled with file folders rose from either side of them. The merger agreement had been executed hours ago, and the wire transfer had been initiated immediately thereafter. Once the federal reference number for the funds had been received by the client's bank, everyone had gone immediately to a bar to celebrate, leaving only one person behind.

Michael Elliot sat quietly in the deep leather chair, staring down on the city lights. Every closing was the same, he thought. An hour of raw terror immediately before the money changed hands, followed by a strange sense of calm shortly thereafter. For the last two weeks, the Global Network merger had become his life. Looking back on it from the sanctity of the now quiet closing room, however, he didn't really believe it had been more difficult than any of the deals before it. He tried to remember the number of deals he had closed since he started with the firm six years ago. Somewhere between seventy-five and a hundred, he guessed, but it was almost impossible to be sure anymore. They all seemed to blend together.

Michael shuddered. From the hallway behind him, he could hear the familiar sound of Peter Raven yelling into the phone in his office, indifferent to the disturbance he was creating for those around him. The man was a walking stick of dynamite, just waiting for the smallest spark to set him off. Michael knew this; he had witnessed Raven's volatility on numerous occasions. In fact, this was why most of the other associates at the firm avoided working for the man at all costs. Still, at forty-three Raven had become one of the most powerful partners in the firm. Michael knew this was largely because his life was predicated on the pursuit of just two things, more money and more power. He was a man who measured himself solely by his book of business, and his contempt for those who were not equally adept at generating clients was never silent. It was primarily for this reason that he was feared even by his fellow partners.

Michael couldn't understand what made Raven so angry. As far as he could tell, the man had achieved everything an attorney could want in his professional life. He was a top rainmaker at one of the most prestigious law firms in the country and pulled down seven figures a year. He was also respected by his clients and his peers, but none of this seemed to be enough for him. Raven's insatiable need for money and power had practically consumed his life. Often Michael envied the man's drive, but he knew Raven's professional success had not come without grave personal sacrifice. He had heard that Raven's second wife had threatened to leave him earlier this year, and rumors of his indiscretions with the more attractive female associates ran rampant through the office.

Michael was again distracted by the rough sound of Raven's voice. It was becoming louder. Damn it, he thought. Raven was yelling his name as he made his way toward the conference room. He must have lost track of the time. As he turned around, he saw Raven in the doorway with his jacket on and briefcase in hand. "What in the hell are you doing? You didn't hear me in here?" Michael shook his head and tried to formulate an excuse, but before he could respond Raven interrupted him. "Never mind, it's not important."

For a moment Michael just stared at the man in front of him. Peter Raven was an anomaly. He hadn't shown signs of aging like the other partners in his class; he had remained thin and fit, and his expensive Italian suits always fell neatly over his frame. There wasn't the slightest hint of gray in his thick, slicked-back hair, and his skin, unnaturally bronze from the hours he spent each week in the tanning booth, had remained devoid of wrinkles. It was no secret to Michael why Raven looked younger than his counterparts; mostly it was thanks to his habit of shifting his work to others, usually Michael or some equally unfortunate associate.

Come Friday night at six o'clock, Raven would go through the list of corporate associates, calling them one by one and passing off projects he had accumulated over the week. This was his sadistic ritual. Although the projects had often sat on his desk for two or three days, he wouldn't begin to pass them out until Friday evening. It was almost as if the thought that all the associates would be in the office over the weekend put his own mind at ease. Over the last few years, however, the environment Raven created had resulted in unusually high attrition in the corporate department, even compared with those of other New York–based law firms.

The Global Network merger had been no different. For the past week Raven had worked Michael relentlessly, putting him in far over his head. Michael had no misconception about why Raven gave him responsibility for the billion-dollar high-tech transaction. The firm was representing the seller, and once the deal was done the buyer would inevitably bring in their own lawyers. Raven knew that any effort he devoted to the transaction would gain him little monetary benefit. He had been focusing on finding a new client to replace the old one, leaving Michael alone to agonize over the deal.

"This closing was a bitch, wasn't it?" Raven said. His arrogance was almost intolerable, but Michael just nodded and watched as Raven took the gold pack of Benson & Hedges from his pocket and placed a cigarette into his mouth. Tension filled Raven's face as he reached instinctively for his lighter but refrained from striking it. Ever since the building had become nonsmoking, he had been relegated to smoking outside the lobby or in his car in the downstairs parking garage. Accordingly, Michael knew their conversation was coming to an end. Raven would be able to refrain from the temptation only so long. "I'm going downstairs to have a drink with the client. You'll take care of things up here?"

Michael paused. As usual, his invitation to the post-closing festivities had been omitted. "Sure," he said reluctantly as he looked back down at the papers strewn over the table.

"Just make sure you don't leave the closing papers lying around," Raven said, shaking his head. "We aren't going to announce the transaction until Thursday, after we file the merger agreement."

"I know," Michael replied. "I'll lock them up in my office."

Raven grunted in satisfaction. "You know, I'm going to New York tomorrow afternoon for client meetings. Don't fuck things up when I'm gone."

"For God's sake, when are you going to trust me?"

Raven sneered. "Look, I don't trust anyone. Besides, I'm just watching out for your interests. It won't be long before you come up for partnership. Don't forget that. I want to make sure you don't screw things up for yourself, that's all."

Michael was silent.

"Remember, I had the originals of the merger agreement sent by overnight courier to Jonathan Gage in New York. Follow up with him tomorrow to make sure he got it and is set up to have it filed on Thursday," Raven mumbled, walking away with the cigarette hanging loosely from his mouth.

Michael spent the next thirty minutes packing up the closing documents. Then the ring of the telephone echoed loudly through the room. For a moment he hesitated. Who in the hell would be calling this late, he thought. Maybe it was Raven. Perhaps he'd had a change of conscience and wanted to invite him down for a drink with the client after all. Michael walked quickly over to the credenza and picked up the phone. "Conference room. . . ."

There was a long moment of silence before he heard the voice. "Who is this?" he asked nervously.

"It's Michael Elliot. . . . Who's this?"

"It's Jonathan Gage in the New York office," he said, pausing.

Michael had probably spoken with Gage a hundred times before this, but there was something strange in his voice that night, an unmistakable level of distress in the otherwise self-confident young partner. It was almost as if he could sense that something was wrong. "Jesus Christ, it's got to be two in the morning there. What are you still doing in the office?"

Gage paused. "I'm just taking care of a few things," he said. For a moment Michael thought about asking him if everything was all right, but he knew it wasn't his place to question him. Most partners at the firm provided associates with information only on a need-to-know basis. Gage was no exception. Besides, it was late in New York. Perhaps he was just tired. Michael quickly decided to dismiss his concern.

"Is Raven there?" Gage asked.

"No, he went downstairs with the client for a drink. Is there something I can help you with?"

Gage hesitated. "No, that's all right," he said. The dial tone quickly came over the line.

The only light in the office came from the Manhattan skyline. As Jonathan Gage sat alone in the darkness, he tried to remember how things had become so complicated. It had been one lapse of judgment, one grievous mistake so many years ago that had led to this. He'd been a young attorney fresh out of law school when they approached him. At the time it had seemed so glamorous and intriguing. Besides, he didn't have a family to consider, and the thought that he would one day make partner at Davis & White was almost unfathomable to him. If he'd known where his life was going to end up, he would never have done it. Now it seemed cruel that a single lapse of judgment would destroy him.

Gage rested his head wearily on his hand and cursed himself for being so naïve. He'd thought it would be a single occurrence. He knew he wasn't the only one at the firm. After it was over he had buried himself in his work and tried to forget it, but they found him. It was never very long. A late-night call placed to his office or a cleverly disguised note left on his car. As he began to rise through the ranks, the stakes just increased. They even fostered his career in ways that he would never know about. When he was barely thirty years old, he was nominated for partnership and an article about him appeared in *The Wall Street Journal* titled "New York Firm Breaks Traditional Partnership Track for Rising Star." After only five years practicing law, Jonathan Gage was the youngest man ever made partner in a prominent Wall Street law firm. Three years later he had become one of the most highly regarded takeover lawyers in the country. Now all that was about to end.

On the left-hand corner of his desk he could see the familiar picture of his wife and his children staring solemnly back at him. It had been taken last year at Christmas, and they were all in front of the fireplace. His son was holding a remote-controlled car, which he had assembled the night before, and his daughter was hugging a small stuffed bear with a bright red ribbon around its neck. In the background his wife was smiling with her arms around them. Her soft brown hair fell gently over her innocent face. She was a beautiful woman who deserved so much more than this. A tear broke from the corner of his eye as he reached over and touched the picture. In twenty-four hours he would be gone from their lives. He would miss her. He would miss them all more than they could imagine, but there was no other choice. It was just a matter of time before they found him. He knew that now. His options had been foreclosed long ago, and it would soon be time to put this all behind him.

Chapter 2

It was late by the time Michael made it back to his small apartment in Hancock Park. Although most of the other associates at the firm commuted downtown from the West Side, Michael had chosen to return to the old neighborhood where he had grown up. There was something comforting in the tree-lined streets and the old, familiar houses. The Spanish-style two-story home on Third Street where he lived had been converted into apartments, but you could barely tell this from the street. From the outside, the old house with its red tiled roof had remained largely the same. On the inside, however, it had been divided into four apartments, with two on each floor. Each was accessed through a small enclosed entry off the front door, with a narrow flight of wooden stairs leading up to his and his neighbors' apartments.

Hancock Park was only ten minutes from downtown Los Angeles, and over the years the small neighborhood had struggled to retain its character as the city grew around it. When people found out he lived there, they would ask Michael about the crime and the gang problems, neither of which he had ever encountered. More than anything, he thought that people living on the West Side perpetuated such myths to rationalize their own long commutes. Michael wasn't sure why he had come back to live in Hancock Park. There wasn't really anything left for him there anymore. The small house on the other side of Olympic Boulevard where he had grown up had been torn down years ago, and the people he remembered were pretty much gone. Only memories were left for him.

Although his grandmother had raised him by herself, Michael never thought of himself as having had a particularly hard childhood. After all, his grandmother seemed to give more of herself to him than most of the mothers and fathers in the neighborhood gave to their own children. Besides, he had never spent enough time with his mother to really miss her. All he knew about her was what his grandmother had told him and what he had seen in pictures. She was tall and thin, much like himself, with dark hair and complexion, but their physical features were where the similarities ended. Michael's grandmother told him that his mother was wild and uncontrollable, so it wasn't surprising that she became pregnant with him when she was barely seventeen. What his grandmother found most disturbing, however, was that she would never reveal who the father was. It was almost as if the girl didn't care, despite the fact that Michael's grandmother raised the issue with her every day for the first three months of her pregnancy. Finally, her daughter threatened to have the pregnancy terminated if she didn't stop. She said she would go to Nevada or some other state where such things were legal at the time. A devout Catholic, Michael's grandmother never raised the subject again.

From the moment Michael's grandmother found out about her daughter's pregnancy, she was determined that the unborn child would never be forced to bear the consequences of his mother's poor decisions. After Michael was born, however, she knew this was not destined to be the case. She could see the sad expression in the doctor's eyes when he took Michael from his mother's womb. She knew immediately something was wrong and moved around the delivery table to where the doctor was examining the newborn. Her breath quickly left her body, and her heart was still. When she saw that the baby was missing the third finger on his left hand, she couldn't help but feel that it was some kind of sign, a penance that Michael would have to pay for the sins of his mother.

The doctor told them that the absence of the ring finger would have limited functional effect. After all, the deformity was isolated to one hand, and it was the left one. He explained that children were often born with extra fingers or toes that were simply removed. Unfortunately, for Michael's opposite problem there was little he could do. However, the doctor seemed convinced that Michael was otherwise a perfectly healthy boy. Just look at him, the doctor said, smiling. Michael had been blessed with thick, curly black hair and eyes the same deep brown as those of his grandfather. Despite the doctor's consolations, Michael's mother couldn't stop crying after seeing the baby and refused to hold him. His grandmother just looked at her sternly, then took the baby and rocked him gently in her arms. She swore to herself that she would not make the same mistakes with him that she had made with her own daughter. Yes, she thought, this child would be her second chance.

When they came home from the hospital, Michael's mother seemed to have little interest in him. She spent the days inside with the shades drawn and rarely took him out. After weeks of scolding, Michael's grandmother finally wrapped the baby up in a blanket and took him to the park for some air. When they came home, Michael's mother was gone. Three days later she came back to try again, but it wasn't long before she began spending the evenings drinking with the same degenerates who had gotten her into this predicament. One day Michael's grandmother came back from the park with the baby and found a note on the door with only two words: *"Forgive me."* Neither Michael nor his grandmother ever saw Michael's mother again.

Michael's grandmother knew this was probably for the best. A strong woman, she was convinced she could raise him on her own. After all, she had raised her daughter by herself after her husband died. From the very beginning, she was determined to have the boy grow up just like any of the other kids in the neighborhood, despite his deformity. She was convinced that he could play baseball and basketball just like the others; however, when it came to teaching him such sports, she realized she couldn't do this on her own and solicited the help of Carl Ford, their next-door neighbor. Quite coincidentally, Carl was also a widower. His wife had died of cancer shortly after they were

Eben Paul Perison

married and he hadn't remarried. As far back as Michael could remember, Carl had watched over Michael and his grand-mother. Carl was a quiet man who practiced law downtown and was the closest thing Michael had to a father. He was the one who fixed things in the house when they were broken. He was also the one who taught Michael how to throw a curveball and a split-finger fastball and took him to Dodger games on Sunday afternoons. On Thanksgiving and Christmas he was a fixture in their house. Michael's grandmother would often do Carl's laun-dry and make him dinner, but Carl clearly would have spent time with Michael regardless of such gestures. In time they all had adopted one another as a kind of extended family.

As Michael grew older, the angular features that looked awkward on a boy became quite handsome. His hair remained dark and curly, yet he kept it cut short in what Carl called an Ivy League style. He had grown tall, with an athletic frame that women found attractive, but it was the look on people's faces when they first saw his hand that stole his confidence. What Michael lacked in social skills, however, he was able to make up for in other ways. From an early age it was clear that he was bright. He applied himself diligently to his studies and spent evenings reading books his grandmother would give him. He received a full scholarship to Yale, where Carl had gone. Michael could still remember his grandmother's response when he told her the news. She hugged him hard and couldn't stop crying. His success had somehow washed away the mistakes she had made with her daughter.

Michael was in his first year of college when his grand-mother passed away. When he came home for the funeral, Carl was sitting on the front porch waiting for him. There were tears running down his face, and his eyes were swollen and red. Carl told him he was sorry, as if somehow he was responsible for the stroke she had suffered. For the first time in his life, Michael felt empty and alone. Two days later they buried his grand-mother in a small cemetery in midtown Los Angeles. When the service was over, Carl gave Michael a small envelope with her will inside. The instructions were simple. The house and everything of value she owned were to be sold and the proceeds placed in a trust for Michael's law school education. Also included was a brief note. In it she told Michael that she loved him more than anything in the world and that he had given her far more than she could ever give back to him. Michael cried for hours after reading it, and not a day had gone by since that he didn't think of her. Yes, he thought, there were nothing but memories left for him here.

As he pulled into the narrow driveway on the side of the house, Michael turned off his lights and coasted into the detached garage so as not to disturb his neighbors. He always felt self-conscious about coming home this late at night, but no one seemed to care. Besides, this was the earliest he had made it home in the last two weeks. He reached for the suit jacket on the seat next to him. As he got out of his car, he could feel the warm air, and the sweet scent from the neighbor's blooming jasmine filled the backyard. He slowly reached up to close the garage door. Its creaking broke the silence as he struggled to pull it down.

Michael didn't notice the dark gray van with tinted windows parked on the opposite side of the street. Inside a man wearing night-vision goggles sat watching him. "He's going inside," he whispered to his partner, who was sitting in the back. He quickly activated the surveillance equipment. One tap on the phone and another in the bedroom. It had been too easy, he thought, far too easy.

Chapter 3

Staring out his office window the following morning, Michael could see the cars on the Harbor Freeway slowly fighting their way toward the Ninth Street exit. Behind them stood the gray sprawl of a city that had grown uncontrollably over the last thirty years. There were no natural barriers to confine the growth. All he could see was an endless stream of warehouses and factories extending south of Los Angeles, a legacy from the time the city had been a major industrial center. The smoke they emitted now just blended with the exhaust from the morning traffic, creating a layer of pinkish brown haze that hung low over the basin. The dull pounding on his door distracted him. As he turned around, Art Rollins awkwardly poked his head inside. Art, nicknamed Arturo by the other associates, was tall and rounded, with the appearance of an overgrown schoolboy. His wrinkled white shirts were always slightly untucked in the back and fit tightly around his protruding midsection. His sandy brown hair constantly fell over his eyes, making him look like a sheepdog, and the striped neckties he wore seemed to have come from a bad prep-school uniform.

While Michael and the other associates had earned their jobs at the firm mostly through their law school grades, it was widely rumored though never confirmed that Arturo had gotten his job solely as a result of his father's connections. His father was chairman of one of the largest investment houses in New York and, quite coincidentally, one of the closest friends of Richard Montague, the managing partner of Davis & White.

Needless to say, Arturo was the only attorney the firm had ever hired from Emory, a small private law school in Atlanta, where it was assumed quite accurately he had performed well below average. No matter what was speculated about his academic record, one thing about Arturo was abundantly clear: The genes that had made his father such a shrewd investment banker had skipped a generation.

What was most unusual about Arturo, however, wasn't his awkward personal appearance or his prominent background, but rather his rare ability to lose everything he touched. All objects he came into contact with, no matter how big or small, would end up missing. Michael had never seen anything like it. It was like working with David Copperfield's dysfunctional brother. Whenever people in the Los Angeles office couldn't find a file, they simply blamed it on Arturo. In response to the jesting, Arturo would simply shrug his shoulders and look at the ground, as if it was all outside his control. But he was good-natured and loyal, and in this cutthroat competitive environment those qualities clearly outweighed his faults. Over time, Arturo and Michael had become close friends.

As Arturo sat down in the chair opposite him, Michael could tell something was wrong. His friend's eyes moved quickly around the office, focusing on every inanimate object before coming to rest on his own. Michael waited, knowing that whatever was bothering Arturo would soon be revealed, and, indeed, Arturo quickly broke the silence. "Did you hear about Monehan?"

His question caught Michael off guard. James Monehan was Michael's senior and clearly one of the best lawyers in his class. In addition, he was one of the few attorneys at the firm that the associates would come to with questions they didn't want to ask the partners for fear of looking stupid. Monehan was up for partner this year, and it was rumored that he had the vote locked up. "No, I didn't," Michael replied. "What happened?"

Arturo paused. "The firm told him they were passing him

over," he said, shaking his head. "After eight years, can you believe it? I mean, the guy just had another kid."

Partnership was highly coveted in any law firm, but nowhere more than in Davis & White. Those who attained such status could look forward to a lifetime of substantial monetary reward, and partnership was rarely taken away. But those passed over were forever tainted. If anyone else had been conveying this news, Michael would have thought it was some kind of joke. Arturo, however, wouldn't find humor in such things. They both knew this was far too important to Monehan.

"Jesus Christ, did they tell him why?"

"They said it was a matter of economics. You know, if he'd been able to generate more business things might have been different," Arturo said hesitantly. "How in the hell was he supposed to generate business when they had him in here working all the time? The whole thing is screwed, if you ask me. You know how hard it's going to be for an eighth-year associate to find a job in this legal market, especially one who's been passed over for partner."

"Damn it," Michael said. "How much time did they give him?"

"I don't know, a few months."

Michael suddenly stood up. "I should go talk to him. . . . Is he still around the office?"

Arturo shook his head. "No, he canceled his meetings and left for the day. The firm told him it would be better if he took some time off before coming back to wind things up. You know, a week or two forced vacation," he said, looking down at his watch. "Damn, I was supposed to get something to Raven ten minutes ago. I better go. Are you going to be around later tonight?"

"Yeah, stop by before you leave," Michael said as he watched Arturo depart.

For the rest of the morning, Michael tried to occupy himself, but the news about Monehan kept coming back to him. The more he thought about it, the less sense it seemed to make. Other than himself, Monehan was Raven's prized associate. He had carefully moved from deal to deal, winning the praise of partners and clients. He was clearly the best lawyer in his class in Los Angeles or New York. If Monehan had been passed over, what hope was there for any of the other associates, not to mention himself? Even more disturbing was the fact that Raven hadn't told Michael about this the night before. He must have known.

There was only one way to deal with this. Michael would have to confront Raven before he left for New York. He repeatedly called Raven's office that morning, but each time the secretary would rebuff him with excuses. The first time she told him Raven was on an important conference call and couldn't be disturbed. Michael left a message, but by eleven o'clock he still hadn't heard, so he called again. This time the woman said Raven was meeting with clients and would get back to him when he was finished. It wasn't until lunchtime that Michael finally cornered Raven. He was standing in front of the mirror in the men's room straightening his silk tie and pressing down the collar of his shirt. Such displays of vanity were among the man's trademarks.

Raven quickly looked up at him. "Good afternoon, Michael," he said calmly. "My secretary told me you were trying to reach me. What's on your mind?"

Michael could feel himself shaking. "Did you know, Peter? . . . Did you know they were going to do this?"

Raven's face quickly filled with tension. "Jesus Christ, you heard about Monehan already? The gossip mill must be working overtime. I can't believe the associates have that much free time on their hands."

Michael knew this was just an attempt to dodge the subject, but he wouldn't relent. "How could you let this happen?"

Raven paused for a moment, then checked the stalls to make sure they weren't occupied. He turned back to Michael. "Look, I did the best I could for him. We're in a branch office. You know as well as I do that all the power resides in New York. They make all the damn decisions."

"For God's sake, you're on the executive committee. If anyone had the pull to make him a partner, you did."

Raven studied Michael's expression and decided to change strategy. "I went back to the partnership meeting last week and lobbied for him. I lobbied hard, but it's a numbers game, can't you see that?" he said, lowering his voice. "They told me I could only choose one of you. The corporate department couldn't support two new partners. If I put him up this year, I wouldn't be able to put you up next year." Raven placed his hand on Michael's shoulder, and suddenly Michael felt sick. "I had to pick my battles. This was one I couldn't win. I want to have the ability to make you partner when your time comes. Can't you see that? You will be the next partner we make in the corporate department."

Michael felt both ashamed and disgusted. More than anything in his life he wanted to make partner at Davis & White. He had worked hard for it, first in law school, then when he joined the firm, but never had he thought it would come down to this. He no longer knew what to say. He wished he had never confronted Raven. Maybe he would have been better off not knowing any of this.

Raven quickly looked down at his watch. "Damn it, I've got less than an hour to make it to the airport. Look, we can talk more about this when I get back. Just keep doing what you're doing and make sure everything goes smoothly on the Global Network merger. Remember, coordinate with Gage in New York," he said as he walked out, leaving Michael alone in front of the mirror, staring at his own reflection.

Chapter 4

At noon the doors to the office buildings lining Bunker Hill opened, and the workers fled like lab rats being let out of their cages. They scurried down the maze of stairs and walkways to dozens of fast-food restaurants and street vendors lying in wait for them. It was a heart surgeon's nightmare, hundreds of people standing in line to saturate their arteries with cholesterol before returning to the high-stress environments from which they came. From the StairMaster behind the gym windows, Karen Bauer could see it all. Attorneys and accountants started out thin and full of life, but soon they fell into the same rut— five pounds the first year and ten pounds the next. Before they knew it the men had small paunches that hung over their belts and the beginnings of double chins. For the women it was worse, the weight falling straight to their hips and backsides. Not me, she thought.

This had become her daily ritual: She would leave the office at eleven-thirty to beat the rush, then change in the women's locker room into a pair of running tights and a half tank exposing her thin, muscular arms and tight stomach. This outfit was her favorite and by far the most comfortable. However, after constant stares from the men working out next to her, she began to cover herself with a Duke sweatshirt. When she worked out, she wanted to sweat. She liked the feel of the cotton fleece becoming damp and her muscles becoming taut. Working out and sex were the only two ways she had found to release the stress of her job.

She was a litigator by training, which meant she spent most

of her time dealing with other people's problems. In litigation people were never happy. They were either upset about being dragged into court or, if they were the plaintiffs, upset about how much money their attorneys were charging them. After five years she had come to realize that she was nothing more than a gladiator, paid by the hour to tear her opponents apart or throw as many obstacles as possible in their paths so they wouldn't do the same to her client. Over time the trial lawyers she worked with all became angry and bitter. They couldn't divorce themselves from their work. Rather than vent her frustrations on her coworkers or the few men in her life, she decided to take them out here—thirty minutes on level eight, another ten minutes on level ten. When she was done she went over to the stationary bikes to cool down with five minutes of cycling.

The rest of her workout depended on the day of the week. On Mondays and Thursdays she did weights to keep her body toned. The other days she brought a pair of gloves and boxed. There was something cathartic about punching the heavy bag. In college she had dated a boxer who taught her the combinations—jab, cross, hook, uppercut . . . jab, cross, hook, uppercut. She practiced them over and over, faster each time, until the bag rocked. Her old boyfriend had been a good teacher. He had even shown her how to throw punches with the weight of her body behind them and how to keep her hands straight. Once she had seen him uppercut with such force that he had taken the bag clear off its hook. Now she tried to replicate that feat.

When she was done with her workout, she showered. It never took her long to get ready. She wore very little makeup; she didn't need it. Her skin was soft and smooth and her lips full. She had inherited her mother's fair Welsh features. She had also gotten her mother's eyes—large blue teardrops with long lashes that required little mascara to draw attention to them. The only thing that took time was her shoulder-length brown hair, which she toweled then brushed as she blew it dry. She often thought about cutting it short, but she couldn't force herself to do it. With her blue double-breasted suit clinging to her well-contoured body and her silk blouse open just enough to reveal a hint of cleavage, she could have been a model or an actress.

Although she had practiced law for four years, Karen had joined Davis & White only a year ago. The first three years of her career had been spent with the U.S. Attorney's Office in Los Angeles. It wasn't surprising that she was a good trial attorney. Someone with her features was bound to win favor from the judges, most of whom were male, but her success came from more than her physical appearance. She had taken hundreds of depositions, examined and defended dozens of witnesses, and even tried several of her own cases, a rarity among big firm associates. She was also well versed in the rules of evidence and knew trial procedure cold.

As much as the other attorneys in the office didn't want to admit it, she was as smart as she was gorgeous. This made her a threat, especially to the attorneys of her own gender. For the most part, however, Karen didn't associate with the other women attorneys. She didn't even attend their weekly meetings to discuss "women's issues in the law." Among the male partners these meetings were rumored to be "bitch" sessions, in which the women complained about glass ceilings. It wasn't that these things didn't exist, but clearly such limitations didn't apply to Karen Bauer. It was for this reason and the attention that she got from every male partner that she was hated by her female colleagues, not that she really cared. In the end none of them had any power over her career.

She stopped at the juice bar for a protein shake. Then, after she had restored the fluids to her body, she returned to the office to pick up her messages and prepare for battle. She usually started off by answering the messages from opposing counsel in New York or Washington. Once that was finished she would move to the messages from the West Coast, where the time difference didn't work against her. When she got back today her secretary was at lunch. She pulled the messages from the rack, walked into her office, and threw her gym bag on the floor. There were four messages. Three she recognized as being from opposing counsel, but the fourth surprised her. She looked at the time. It was stamped 12:15, more than an hour ago.

Karen stood at her desk staring at the small piece of paper. She had spoken to Richard Montague only once before, at a client reception more than a year ago. He had stared her down from across the room for a good ten minutes before making his way over. She remembered him being physically repulsive, with small black eyes and thin, pursed lips. He was in his early sixties, as best she could tell; his hair was a silvery gray and his skin weathered from too much time in the Hamptons.

He had introduced himself as the firm's managing partner, then placed his hand on her shoulder and left it there for an uncomfortable amount of time. The gin was heavy on his breath, and he went on and on about himself. This wasn't uncommon for a man of his age and stature. Most senior partners at the firm were egotistical, looking for young women to hang on their every word. Fortunately, a client interrupted them, giving her the chance to escape. She hadn't seen or heard from Montague since.

Karen ruffled the message in her fingers. She doubted whether the son of a bitch even remembered. She picked up the phone and dialed his number. An elderly woman answered. "Hello, this is Karen Bauer from the Los Angeles office for Richard Montague. I'm returning his phone call." She waited while Montague's secretary got him on the line.

"Hello, Karen," he said, pausing to clear his throat. "How are you?"

"Good," she lied. She would rather have been talking to anyone but him. "We're incredibly busy out here. For the most part I'm just trying to keep my head above water."

"Well, I hope you're not too busy. I have a matter that needs someone with your special qualifications and talent."

Here it comes, she thought. He was setting her up. This wasn't the first time she'd gotten this kind of call.

"Is your door closed?" he asked.

The question caught her off guard. She always kept her door closed to avoid associates walking by and trying to make small talk. "Yes, it's closed."

Montague took a deep breath. "Once again, let me stress the sensitivity of what I'm about to tell you. You're to talk about this case with no one, not even the head of the litigation department. Do you understand?"

"Sure," she said, rolling her eyes. It was getting worse. She reached for a pen and pad.

"The client in question is a man named Mohammed Faud. Are you familiar with him?"

Mohammed Faud, Karen thought. She had read about him once or twice in the papers, and it was never very flattering. He was a shadowy figure, an international financier with a sprawling mansion in Beverly Hills. He was reported to be involved in everything from real estate to securities arbitrage. However, what he was most known for was being an arms dealer. Over the years he had regularly advised the Arabs in their negotiations with U.S. defense contractors, many of which were based in Los Angeles. Whether it was F-16s to Saudi Arabia or SCUD missiles to Kuwait, he was always close at hand. Karen had never seen his name on an open matter but this didn't surprise her. The Arabs liked to maintain their secrecy. Besides, the firm had extensive ties in the Middle East. It was rumored that they even represented several members of the royal family, as well as numerous Arab investment banks and offshore portfolios. "Yes," she said. "I know who he is."

"This whole thing appears to be a misunderstanding," Montague went on. "Apparently, several years ago Mr. Faud was involved in negotiating the sale of two satellites to our friends in the Middle East. They were to be used solely for remote sensing and weather forecasting. The defense contractor procured all the proper export licenses and security clearances well in advance of shipment. The birds cost over two hundred forty million dollars apiece. Now, however, the U.S. Attorney's Office has some crazy idea that the satellites were modified to include advanced imaging capabilities. It's all so technical."

"What do you mean?" Karen asked.

"They think they were converted into spy satellites. Apparently, Israeli intelligence has determined that the Arabs now

have advanced satellite reconnaissance regarding troop move-
ment in the region. Until now the Defense Department liked to
believe it had a monopoly on such information. They think that
these two satellites were modified with either Russian or
French technology prior to being launched."

Jesus Christ, she thought. She set her pencil down and began
to rub her temples.

"They've already brought Mr. Faud in for questioning once.
He explained that he had no knowledge that the satellites were
modified. For God's sake, he was just a consultant assisting in
the negotiations and the procurement. Now they're digging
deeper. They requested that Mr. Faud provide them with the financial statements and bank records for his offshore management company, which we set up several years ago."

"What are they looking for?" Karen asked.

"Between you and me, I think they're looking for evidence
of payoffs. Brokers and consultants in these transactions can
make up to ten percent of the purchase price. Although Mr. Faud
hasn't disclosed the exact amount he was paid, it wouldn't surprise me if it approached forty-five million dollars. I've heard
rumors that several congressmen and senators lobbied hard to
the National Security Agency to get the export licenses for these
two satellites cleared. It's my guess that they're now looking to
see if Mr. Faud used any of his commissions to make illegal
campaign contributions to facilitate the process. Of course there
are no such questionable payments. This is just a witch-hunt."

"Then why not provide the records?" Karen asked.

Montague paused. "It's not quite that simple. The Arabs are
very concerned about their privacy. Mr. Faud believes this is
just a pretext to delve into his personal financial dealings.
Maybe once they start digging they'll find other things that
could be embarrassing for him. He just doesn't want to take the
chance. Mr. Faud has been a good client to the firm for a very
long time. He's brought in millions of dollars of business. I'd
like you to meet with him this evening. You can go into more
detail then. My secretary will give you directions."

Chapter 5

The rest of the afternoon and a good part of the evening were lost back in the conference room going over post-closing matters for the Global Network transaction. For the most part Michael didn't mind. The otherwise tedious work was all that kept his mind off his conversation with Raven. By the time Michael made it back to his office, it was almost seven o'clock. There were just two things left to do: dictate a quick closing letter and clear off his desk. As he entered the office, however, something seemed strange. His eyes studied the small room, but nothing looked out of place. The papers that cluttered his desk were exactly as he had left them, and the Lucite cubes given to him as trophies for the deals he had closed remained untouched on the bookshelf. Still, an unsettling feeling moved through him, as if someone had been there. He carefully surveyed the office one last time, but there was no visible evidence of intrusion. Just when he was about to give up, it struck him.

Michael walked over to the long thin vertical blinds covering the window. How could he have missed it? It was so obvious. Someone must have closed them, but why? It was too early for the cleaning crew to have come by. Most of the time they didn't even start vacuuming the floors or emptying trash cans until ten. Maybe they had come earlier, but why shut the blinds? They never shut the blinds.

Arturo's voice suddenly distracted him. "I was just going to head out. Do you want to have a drink?"

For a moment, preoccupied with the blinds, Michael ignored

him. Slowly he reached for the cord and pulled it until he could again see the lights of Los Angeles. "Was the cleaning crew down on your side of the building?"

The question caught Arturo by surprise. "Well . . . I don't know . . . maybe," he replied. "Why?"

"Never mind," Michael said. "It's probably nothing."

"If you have to work, we can do this another time."

"No," Michael said as he moved around to the chair behind his desk. "I can finish it later. Besides, I really need a drink after a day like this."

For the past few months this had been their ritual. Each night before they went home, Arturo would stop by Michael's office and close the door behind him. He would slouch in the chair and wait for Michael to take out the bottle of Scotch he kept locked in a desk drawer. Tonight was no different. Michael removed the pencils from the coffee cup on top of his credenza and reached for the small metal key ring hidden at the bottom. He unlocked the bottom drawer of his desk and pulled it open. Inside he could see the closing documents that Raven had asked him to keep locked up in his office. Soon there would be no more need to keep them here, he thought. The deal would be announced at a press conference Thursday in New York, and then Michael would be able to send the documents to the file room. He quickly pushed them aside and felt for the bottle of Scotch underneath.

Strangely enough, the bottle of Dewar's had been part of Michael's inheritance from his grandmother. For as long as he could remember, every Saturday night she played bingo at the Third Street Divinity Church, two blocks from their house. It was her one obsession. Although the games didn't start until seven o'clock, she would always leave half an hour early to make sure she got a seat in the front row and to buy at least six cards, which she played simultaneously. She even had her own blotter, a strange hybrid between a large pen and a sponge that she used to mark out the squares. She had accumulated a wide assortment of prizes, mostly ceramic objects that cluttered the mantel and coffee table. But there were also bottles of liquor, dozens of them in fact. His grandmother rarely drank, but the cabinet beneath her kitchen sink had been filled with enough booze to put an alcoholic to shame.

This old bottle of Dewar's was the last remaining bingo prize. Michael lifted it out and placed it on top of his desk. He then took out two glass tumblers and began to pour the deep auburn liquor into each of them. Out of the corner of his eye, he could see Arturo awkwardly brush the hair away from his rounded face. His friend would repeat this gesture again and again. Michael ignored it and handed him a glass. Arturo suddenly became animated. "Here's to Monehan," he said, lifting the glass.

Michael paused. Suddenly the waves of guilt came back to him. For a second he thought about telling Arturo what Raven had said, but he knew it would be a mistake. Arturo could never keep a secret. And if it ever got back to Raven that Michael had violated his trust, it would be the end of his career. "Yes," he said hesitantly. "Here's to Monehan."

For a moment there was only silence in the room as they sipped their Scotch. It was almost as if they were paying respect to the dead. Finally, Arturo spoke. "I better not stay too long. I have to meet Laura back at her apartment."

Laura had been Arturo's girlfriend for more than two years, and as far as Michael could tell they were a perfect match. While Arturo had a habit of losing everything he touched, Laura had the equally rare affliction of having things constantly stolen from her. In the time Michael had known her, Laura's apartment in Santa Monica had been broken into twice, and her purse had been stolen on several other occasions. Otherwise, however, Laura was a normal woman who looked after Arturo like a mother. Although she was more ample in build than most of the women Arturo had dated, her curves were flattering and her face quite beautiful. On the whole she was much better looking than Michael ever thought Arturo could do for himself. For the last few months Laura had been pressuring Arturo to marry her, but he had resisted, although Michael wasn't quite sure why.

"When are you going to find someone?" Arturo asked. "You know, Laura has a friend she could set you up with."

"That's quite all right," Michael said. The last time he let Arturo set him up on a date, it had been a disaster. The woman had been another one of Laura's friends. Although she was on the rebound, the date went okay initially. She was attractive, not turn-your-head good-looking, but he didn't need someone like that. They had even seemed to have a lot in common. She was an accountant with a large auditing firm downtown and was one of the few women who could understand what he did for a living and even find it interesting. Michael asked her out a second time, and she said yes. He thought there were possibilities. When he got home, however, there was a message on his answering machine from her old boyfriend, who threatened to kill Michael if he ever got near her again. When Michael called the woman to warn her about the threat, she was ecstatic. She'd never realized her boyfriend cared so much about her, and the next day they got back together. The two lunatics probably deserved each other, Michael thought. Needless to say, he was not going to let Arturo set him up on any more blind dates.

"You're still not holding out hope for that new attorney in litigation, are you? . . . What's her name?"

Michael spoke up reluctantly. "Karen . . . Karen Bauer."

"Yeah, that's her," Arturo said, shaking his head. "When are you going to give that up. She's way out of your league," he said. "I heard she only dates professional athletes and millionaires. Someone like you and I wouldn't even have a chance."

"You don't know that," Michael said defensively.

"Believe me, my friend, I know that. You've been talking about her for months, and you still haven't even approached her. You got no chance."

Michael knew he was probably right. "I'm just choosing my moment, that's all."

"Well, you've been choosing your moment for an awfully long time. You should just let Laura set you up again. The last girl wasn't that bad."

"The one with the homicidal boyfriend," Michael sneered. "I'll pass."

"Well, I'll concede that one," Arturo said, raising his glass.

The two made small talk for another half hour as they slowly drank their Scotch. Once they had finished Michael returned the bottle to the drawer on top of the closing documents. It was then that he noticed it. At first he had to squint to see it, and the sight nearly made him wince. In the upper-left-hand corner of the merger agreement there were two small perforations above the line of the staple. They were unmistakable. He quickly pushed the bottle of Scotch aside and removed the documents. Arturo was staring at him, wondering what he was doing, but Michael just flipped through the papers, checking to see if they all had such perforations.

"What are you doing?" Arturo asked.

"These are the closing documents for the deal I just finished. I put them in here last night," Michael said.

"What about them?"

"These are the originals. . . . Someone must have taken them out of my desk and made copies."

"What do you mean?"

"I stapled them in the closing room. Someone must have unfastened them to make copies and then restapled them. That's the only reason there could be another set of staple marks."

Arturo shook his head. "Are you sure you didn't just undo them yourself?"

Michael tried to remember whether he had made another set of copies that night. He knew it had been late, but he could swear he made only one set. "I'm almost positive."

Arturo shrugged. "I think you're just being paranoid. If anything, Raven probably came in and made copies. He knows where you keep the key."

Michael shook his head. "You're probably right," he said. "I've been stressing out about this ever since Raven told me to keep them locked in my office. Besides, we're announcing the deal this Thursday."

"So quit stressing out about it," Arturo admonished him.

Michael smiled. "You're right, I've just been working too much," he said, placing the documents back in the drawer.

Chapter 6

The headlights on her black convertible Saab cut through the fog as Karen made her way through the west gate of the exclusive community of Bel Air. She had written down the directions that afternoon, but in the darkness she found it difficult to read them. As she made her way up Bellagio Road, she could see the mansions behind their iron gates. There were few streetlights to guide her, but when she finally saw the turnoff, she veered to the right and followed it up a hill to where it ended. In front of her was a large gate surrounded by a wall of twenty-foot hedges. It was just as Montague's secretary had described. A security camera mounted on a pillar turned its eye toward her and stopped. Next to the gate was a small intercom box, and she pulled up to it and rolled down her window. She pressed the button below the speaker and waited until she heard a phone ringing.

"Yes," a man answered in a thick Arabic accent.

"My name is Karen Bauer. I'm an attorney with Davis and White. I have an appointment at eight o'clock with Mr. Faud."

There was a long moment of silence before the man responded. "Please pull inside the gate and stop."

Karen heard the sound of the gates electronically open. When she was inside she pulled over and turned off the ignition. In the rearview mirror she could see the gates automatically close behind her, and two large men just inside the periphery approached her car. Armed bodyguards, she thought. This was going to be interesting.

"Hello," she said calmly. "I'm here for an appointment with

Mr. Faud." The two men ignored her as they went through their security check. The first began walking around her car with a long pole and lighted mirror that he slid underneath the car. They were looking for explosives. The other shone his flashlight inside for a quick inspection. Seeing nothing suspicious, he asked her to open the trunk. There was something invasive about the search, but there seemed to be little use in protesting. She reached down and pulled the release.

After a moment he returned and opened the passenger-side door without asking. For a moment she thought he was going to get inside, but instead he waved a small handheld device through the air and took a swipe over the dash. She had seen airport police use a similar device on suspicious baggage to detect the chemical particles in ammunition and explosives. Clearly they weren't taking any chances. After the two men were done, they spoke briefly in a language she couldn't understand; then they waved her on.

Karen started the car and followed the driveway up the hill. The three-story Mediterranean mansion was larger than any house she had ever seen. She parked at the end of the circular driveway and walked up the stone steps to two large wooden doors. Just to the right was a doorbell, and she pressed it. In a house this large she wondered whether anyone would hear her. She listened for footsteps, but there were none. She pressed the doorbell again and waited.

She had dressed formally. Her hair was pulled conservatively away from her face, and her Coach briefcase hung loosely off her shoulder. She hadn't given a second thought to meeting the client at his home, although it was quite unusual. Mr. Faud, however, clearly traveled with a lot of security. Besides, the firm downplayed its involvement with him, and a meeting in the office was clearly out of the question. Within moments the electronic dead-bolt lock released and the doors swung open.

Inside she saw a handsome older man standing at attention. Although he wasn't as big as the other two bodyguards, something about him seemed far more dangerous. He was lean and muscular, with a body that looked hardened from years of military service. His skin was dark and leathered, and along the right side of his face a scar ran from the base of his chin to his eyelid. It was from when he was a child in Lebanon. A car bomb had exploded, and shards of glass had torn through the side of his face. As strange as it seemed, he considered himself lucky. A few millimeters in the other direction and he would have been dead.

"I'm here to see Mr. Faud," she said, reaching into her brief-case and taking out a business card. "I'm an attorney with Davis and White."

"Please follow me," the man said in perfect English.

She followed him past a winding staircase and through a sitting room with cathedral windows. She could see a large rectangular swimming pool with marble statues lining either side. The lights inside had turned the water aqua, and at the bottom she could see an ornate mosaic crest. Beyond the pool a rolling lawn disappeared into the darkness. The grounds and exterior of the house were incredible. But the interior was strangely stark. The sitting room was largely empty, and the walls were completely devoid of artwork. It was almost as if no one lived there.

Karen followed the man down a long hallway until he stopped at a large door. As he reached to open it, anxiety filled her. Mr. Faud was a mystery to her. What would he look like? Would he be wearing flowing white robes and a thick black beard, or would he have on an Armani suit? When the man opened the door, however, the wood-paneled library was empty. She stood in confusion while the man took a seat behind the desk and motioned for her to sit in the leather chair opposite him. He studied her. Any moment she expected him to leave her and retrieve Mr. Faud, but he remained still.

"Will Mr. Faud be joining us shortly?" she asked, trying to break his stare.

He smiled. "I am Mr. Faud," he said.

His response caught her by surprise. "I apologize, Mr. Faud. I didn't realize."

"That's quite all right," he replied, waving it off. "To be quite honest, I wasn't expecting a woman."

Her embarrassment suddenly turned to anger. "I can assure you that I'm very good at my job."

"I don't doubt that you are. Montague wouldn't have sent you if you weren't."

Silence filled the air between them.

He tried to put her at ease. "Richard and I go way back. Did he tell you that?"

"Yes," she said, lying. "He told me you've been a client with the firm for a very long time."

"More than that, I was his first client."

"Really," she said.

"He was a young associate at the time working in Riyadh, mostly doing joint ventures for the major oil companies. It was back in the early seventies, and we were relatively unsophisticated in matters of international business. The Middle East was just coming into its wealth and power. I was negotiating a deal for the government, and he was on the other side of the table. I quickly realized I was out of my element. On the next deal I hired him to represent our interests. Soon his business with us grew, and he eventually became a partner. Over the years he transitioned the work to other attorneys, but he always remained accountable.

"Our level of business sophistication grew quickly. Eventually we began to make investments abroad. Our relationship with Montague and your firm grew even stronger. He taught us how to structure our transactions and use offshore entities to minimize taxes and maintain our anonymity. As you probably already know, that's largely the reason you are here."

For a moment Karen wondered why he was telling her all this, but then she realized he was simply laying down the ground rules. He wanted her to know exactly how much power he had at the firm. She reached into her briefcase and took out a notebook with a legal pad inside. "The firm values the relationship greatly. Now, Mr. Faud, why don't you tell me about the investigation?"

He looked down at the notepad. "I'd prefer if you don't take notes," he said calmly.

Karen paused. "Sure," she said, closing her binder and putting it back into her briefcase.

"As Richard may have told you, from time to time I've represented sovereigns in a wide variety of matters. Sometimes they have involved negotiating the development of large-scale infrastructure projects such as power plants, refineries, or airports with U.S. contractors. Other times they've been projects of a military nature, such as the procurement of armaments, tanks, aircraft, artillery, and satellites. Three years ago I was asked to assist in connection with the procurement of two imaging satellites. They were to be used for remote sensing. As is typical in such matters, the defense contractor in question obtained all proper export licenses prior to sale. However, your government now has some idea that the satellites were modified to provide military reconnaissance. I have already explained to them that I had no knowledge the satellites were modified to include any such technology. I acted purely as a consultant assisting in the negotiations."

"But the investigation hasn't ended there, has it?"

"No," Faud said. "They have asked me to supply the financial statements and bank records for my offshore management company. Most of my consulting fees and private investments are made through this entity. I told them I would take it under advisement. That was when I called Richard. The U.S. attorney has requested I meet with them next week to discuss the matter further. I will do what I can to cooperate, but under no circumstances am I prepared to disclose my personal financial statements or those of my management company. I want you to meet with them and explain the situation. It would be my sincerest hope that we can dissuade them from pursuing this any further. I trust that will give you enough time to prepare?"

"Yes," she said. "That should be fine."

She rose and threw her briefcase over her shoulder. As she turned to leave, his voice stopped her. "Ms. Bauer, my business depends on secrecy. I trust that you will not let me down."

There was something unsettling in his tone, and Karen paused. "Mr. Faud, I can assure you that the firm will do everything legally within its power to help you. You should have nothing to worry about."

Outside she could feel the cold air surrounding her. She walked quickly down the steps and over to her car. She was reaching into her briefcase for her keys when a pair of headlights came slowly up the driveway. As it got closer she could see it was a large black limousine with tinted windows. It pulled to a stop right behind her, and the driver came out and opened the door. The first thing she saw was a pair of long slender legs in high heels. Then a head of soft blonde hair emerged. The young woman was wearing a skintight dress and giggled as she stumbled out of the car. "Whoops," she said, trying to regain her balance. The driver held her arm to steady her. Another girl inside the limousine handed her a sable coat that the driver helped her put on.

Karen wondered what the woman had looked like before the plastic surgeons got to her. After they were done they always looked the same—collagen-injected lips and huge fake tits that resembled body armor more than anything else. The next woman out of the limousine was brunette, with the same lips and bust. The two were like Barbie dolls—with identical features but different-colored hair and different hooker attire. As she lifted her legs, her skirt hiked up to her waist, and Karen could see she wasn't wearing anything underneath. She shook her head in disgust.

The brunette seemed surprised to find a woman staring at her. "Hi," she said, smiling. She then sized Karen up as if she were also a hooker. "You don't have to leave on our account," she said.

The driver turned around. "Quiet," he shouted, pulling each of the women by the hand up the stairs.

Mohammed Faud sat at his desk watching all this on the monitor in front of him. There were thirty-six cameras hidden on the estate, and each could be activated with a keystroke and viewed on his personal computer. The guards at the gate should have waited until she was gone before letting the limousine inside, but it really didn't matter. The women weren't for him anyway, but rather for the congressman and executive from the defense contractor who were scheduled to arrive later. When she was finally out the front gate, he dialed the private number for Montague's home study. He knew Montague would be waiting. He also knew he would be drunk.

When Montague had started with the firm, he was a talented attorney, full of fervor and intensity. He had climbed the ranks, like most of the other attorneys before him, by keeping his lips permanently welded to the ass of anyone more senior than himself and by stepping one by one over the bodies of his peers. When he was coming up, however, the practice of law was different. It wasn't how hard you worked as much as who you knew. Fortunately, he had a pedigree most lawyers would envy: Phillips Exeter prep, Princeton undergraduate, and Harvard Law School. With his background and growing book of Middle East business, it was no surprise that he made partner right on schedule. But it had been easier back then, and he knew it. There were no such things as fax machines or twenty-four-hour word processing. Attorneys weren't expected to be accessible at all hours of the night like they were now. Hell, they rarely even had to give out their home phone numbers.

But times had changed. Clients now worked their attorneys relentlessly and expected them always to be at their beck and call. Unfortunately he had no escape. Like most attorneys, he had managed over the years to spend far more than he made. Leveraging himself to the hilt, he had tried to maintain a lifestyle akin to that of his clients. While most of his clients were able to retire in their forties and fifties, he had been forced to stay on just to pay the bills. Fortunately, he had those qualities that screamed out "upper management." He could lie through his teeth without detection. He could feign sympathy at will. He could pat you on the back as if he was your best friend and at the same time have the other hand on your wallet. Most important, he never second-guessed himself and acted solely in his own interest at all times.

As a result, it wasn't long before he assumed the role of managing partner. Although this was a highly coveted position at Davis & White, when he took it over Montague quickly realized that his responsibilities were generally menial—monitoring firm collections, prodding partnership productivity, massaging clients' bruised egos, and arbitrating trivial staff disputes. His talents were wasted on such nonsense. But the job commanded one of the highest salaries at the firm, and God knew he could use the money. It was a con of grand proportion, but one he quickly learned to perpetrate. If any of the other partners ever found out what he did from day to day, they would surely have him tarred and feathered. But no one did know what he did, and that was the beauty of the job.

His mornings were spent looking forward to his two-hour lunches at the club, drinking martinis until his mind and body became sufficiently numb. At lunch he always chose vodka over gin so there would be no smell on his breath. Then he would return to the office for another few hours to shuffle papers on his desk. Like the Romans who would have their horses drag shrubs behind them to kick up dirt and create the illusion of armies much greater than their actual size, Montague would stack papers on his desk and move them around to look busy. He would schedule meetings among partners, then cancel because of "urgent matters." He would spend time out of the office at "important" roundtables with other managing partners and report back to the executive committee, most of whom were as pathetic as he was.

It wasn't surprising that Montague had grown to hate his life. His frigid wife spent her days and nights climbing New York's social ladder. The damn woman no longer gave it up for him, or anyone else, for that matter; it was probably for the best, because most of the time he was flaccid from the booze. His one son had grown up to be a pathetic disappointment, which just made Montague more bitter. But he was careful to never let the dismal state of his personal life show, especially in front of Mohammed Faud. After all, Faud was his lifeline, the spigot from which all money flowed. "Mohammed," he said. "How did it go?"

"You didn't tell me you were sending a woman," Faud said abruptly.

Montague laughed. "Well, she comes well recommended. Besides, when did you ever feel shy about being around a pretty woman?"

"Still, you should have told me. I don't like surprises. Don't forget, this is important to both of us."

"I understand," Montague said reassuringly. "But there's a reason why I chose her. You're going to have to trust me."

"Just don't mess this up, or the consequences will be severe for both of us."

Chapter 7

Like clockwork, at precisely two in the afternoon Michael grabbed his jacket and headed for the elevator. Although the plan seemed poorly conceived, it was the only one he had been able to come up with, and time was quickly passing. Over the past few months he had been looking for ways to talk to her, but she was a litigator and he was a corporate attorney and there was rarely any overlap between their worlds. As far as he could tell, Karen Bauer largely kept to herself. Initially he had hoped to run into her at the attorney dining room or one of the other venues that people frequented for lunch, but he never saw her there. He'd practically given up hope until he caught a glimpse of her at the Starbucks downstairs. From then on he had gone there at the same time each day, hoping to "inadvertently" run into her. He rehearsed a hundred times the things he would say when they met, but the opportunity continued to elude him.

After waiting in line for a tall regular, he went over to the counter for a lid. He'd moved as slowly as possible to increase his chances of running into her, but no luck. Maybe Arturo was right. He should try to settle for someone more in reach. Arturo's girlfriend had friends, but he wasn't about to do that again. Although he really couldn't see a woman like Karen dating a corporate associate, something inside made him want to keep on trying.

When Michael got back to his office, he couldn't believe it. Standing in the doorway was Karen Bauer. Suddenly all his plans evaporated. He could barely remember his own name, let alone the script he had memorized.

Reading his surprised look, she said, "Hi, I'm Karen Bauer," extending her hand. "You're Michael Elliot, aren't you?"

"Uh . . . yes . . . I am," he said, shifting the cup of coffee so he could shake her hand.

"I was hoping I could have a few moments of your time. I'm working on a matter for Richard Montague. When I went through the files this morning, I came upon some documents you worked on. I was hoping I could ask you a few questions."

Michael walked back into his office. "Please, sit down," he said, motioning to one of two chairs. Both were covered with stacks of manila folders. "Oh, you can just put them on the floor."

"Sure," she said, clearing a space. "Do you mind if I shut the door? This is extremely sensitive."

Michael looked perplexed. "No," he said. He removed the lid from his coffee and waited for it to cool down.

"That's what I need," she said, taking a seat. "I should have gotten one from downstairs."

"Here, why don't we share it?"

Before she could protest, Michael took an empty coffee mug off his desk and poured half the contents into it. He then handed her the original cup. Suddenly he stopped. What was he thinking? The gesture was completely absurd, as if she would drink out of his cup. "I haven't touched it yet," he said.

Karen smiled. "Thank you," she said, taking the cup from him and sipping lightly. "I'm doing some work on a case for Mohammed Faud. The Justice Department has subpoenaed certain documents pertaining to one of his management companies, Trade Wind Offshore Holdings. Apparently you're one of the lawyers who helped set it up several years back."

Michael began racking his brain. There were so many deals and so many projects it was hard to remember one that far back. "I think I remember. We set up an offshore holding company for Mr. Faud largely for tax purposes. I didn't even realize Montague was involved."

Karen set down the coffee and began to take notes. "Forgive me for asking this question, but do you recall why he set up the offshore corporation?"

"If I remember correctly, he was involved in international finance and consulting. Oftentimes profits derived from offshore activities have favorable tax treatment if they are structured correctly. Other times people set up offshore corporations to preserve secrecy or anonymity."

"How so?" she asked.

"Well, for one thing, the bank secrecy laws are a lot more restrictive in certain jurisdictions outside the U.S. It's harder for people to obtain information about your financial dealings. These offshore corporations are relatively easy to set up. There are international services that will file the charter and bylaws and even set up trustees if you'd like. It's a whole industry down there, and client confidence is well protected by the courts."

"Is this common?" she asked.

"Absolutely, at least that's what the tax attorneys tell me. He's not in any trouble, is he?"

Karen suddenly remembered Montague's earlier admonition. She was to share the details of this matter with no one. "No," she said, trying to wave it off. "It's just a routine matter. Anyway, I pulled the files this morning and started going through them. That's when I saw a piece of correspondence with your name on it and thought you might have some background that would be helpful. I may have other questions for you when I'm done." She stood up and straightened her skirt, then took the cup off the desk and smiled. "Thanks for the coffee."

"Sure," he said, watching her leave.

When she got to the door, however, she stopped. "Did you ever meet Mr. Faud?"

Michael paused. "Once," he said. "I went to his house to have him sign some documents. Originally I was going to send a paralegal, but Jonathan cautioned me against it. He wanted me to do it personally."

"Jonathan who?"

"Jonathan Gage," Michael replied. "He's a corporate partner in New York. He was the partner in charge."

Karen let her curiosity get the better of her. "Did Jonathan do all of Faud's corporate work?"

"I believe so," he said. "The funny thing was that this was the only project I did for Mr. Faud. For some reason Gage was very sensitive about this client."

"What do you mean?"

"Well, I was usually Gage's point man in Los Angeles for corporate projects. He used me for all his clients, but with Faud it was different. He would parcel the work out. I did one project. I think Art Rollins did another. Sometimes partners do that to protect themselves."

"I'm not following you," she said.

"Sometimes they don't want an associate getting too close to their client. It makes them afraid that if the associate leaves he or she might take the client with them. Other times they like to give an associate only a specific piece of a project. That way the associate can't put the whole picture together. It was probably the latter in this case. Faud seemed to enjoy his secrecy. He probably didn't want one person knowing too much about his business. Anyway, Faud seemed fine when I met him. I remember the house was something else, but he was all business. I was in and out in five minutes."

"Did he tell you he had a close relationship with Montague?"

Michael shook his head. "No, I thought he was Gage's client, but that isn't surprising either. When Montague became managing partner, he probably turned the client over to Gage."

"Oh," she said, nodding in agreement. It all seemed to make perfect sense on the face of it, but there was still something strange that she couldn't quite put her finger on. "Well, I'm sure we'll be talking again."

The forty-second floor was quiet that night and the hallways dark. Arturo and most of the other associates had gone home long ago, and Michael's only solace was the knowledge that he would be joining them shortly. He quickly dictated a post-closing letter for the Global Network transaction and left it on his secretary's chair. Then he made his way one more time through the list of open items in his day planner, crossing off each of the tasks he had completed. At the bottom of the list his eyes stopped. One item had completely slipped his mind. He had forgotten to follow up with Jonathan Gage to make sure the merger agreement was ready to be filed. Suddenly he remembered Raven's earlier admonition. His instructions had been simple: "Don't fuck things up when I'm gone." How could he have forgotten to do this?

Fortunately, he still had time. He hated waiting until the last minute—it left no room for mistakes. But he couldn't help it. Michael made a note to follow up with Gage first thing in the morning. He then shoved his day planner into his briefcase, turned off the lights, and locked his office door behind him.

As he made his way out, he was surprised to see Karen Bauer standing by the elevator with her back to him. Her long brown hair had been freed from the braid she wore it in earlier that afternoon, and it now fell gently past her shoulders. He could tell she was leaving. Her jacket was on, and her slender briefcase was hanging loosely off her shoulder by its thin leather strap. Hearing his footsteps, she turned around. "It's good to see I'm not the only one here this late," she said, smiling.

"No," he stammered. "It looks like we both got stuck here tonight." He nervously reached over and pressed the elevator button that was already lit.

"What's got you here so late?"

Michael paused. "I'm working on a deal for Raven."

"Oh," she said, raising her eyebrows and clenching her teeth. "The venerable Peter Raven."

Michael could tell from her tone that there was a derogatory remark on the tip of her tongue, but she was doing her best to hold it back. Such reactions weren't uncommon among the female associates, and Michael decided to change the subject. "What about you?" he asked. "What's keeping you here?"

"This matter for Mohammed Faud. I've spent the last eight hours reading through the files, and it's been driving me crazy." She pulled her fingers through her hair and sighed. "God, I could really use a drink."

Her words seemed to hang in the air, and Michael froze. Did she mean the two of them? Anyone else and he would have thought it was a clear invitation, but things like this just didn't happen, at least not to him. Why would a woman as perfect as Karen Bauer want to spend time with someone like him? Still, she had said it. He knew he would hate himself forever if he didn't take the chance.

"We could go downstairs," he said. "I mean, if you want to get a drink." As soon as the words left his mouth, he began to panic. What in the hell was he doing? His heart was racing, and he felt dizzy. Time seemed to stop. He wished he could take it back, but it was too late.

Karen frowned. "I hate the bar downstairs. It's always filled with attorneys from the office, and it will just make me think about work."

Michael felt as if she had stabbed him in the heart. He had taken the chance, and she had turned him down. He tried his best to muster a smile. "Sure . . . I understand."

The muted tone of the elevator saved him further embarrassment. He got inside and held the door open for her. He wished he could disappear. After pushing the button for the lobby, he moved back against the wall. The doors closed, and he watched the numbers go down.

Karen's voice broke the silence. "We could go to my place," she said, staring up at him. "I live in the Promenade. It's not far. We can walk there if you want."

Michael looked at her in amazement. He had gone from zero to eighty and then back down again in less than five seconds. "Sure" was the only word he could get out of his mouth.

The Santa Ana wind was moving slowly through the trees that sporadically lined the downtown streets, and Michael could feel its warmth against his face as he walked beside her. The dry desert wind had an almost mystical quality. Without warning it would come into the city, drawing the moisture from your skin as soon as it touched you, then turning so forceful it caused the tallest buildings to sway. What was most unusual about the Santa Ana wind, however, was its effect on people's emotional states. Whenever it came into the basin, people seemed to act differently; it felt like anything could happen. Karen's invitation was just another example.

As they made their way over the Second Street Bridge, he could see her building. The Promenade was one of the few residential high-rises downtown. Most people who worked in the city commuted from the suburbs, and the few who lived downtown didn't stay long. Apartments in these residential buildings were usually rented for a couple of months by visiting attorneys or professionals who had to be near the courts or corporate headquarters. At night and on the weekends, downtown Los Angeles became a virtual ghost town.

Michael watched as Karen used her security card to gain access to the building. As they walked through the lobby, he was somewhat surprised. It was much nicer than he had imagined. The marble floors looked new, and the interior was well taken care of. When they entered the elevator, Karen pressed the button for the top floor. Any doubt in his mind that she came from an affluent background was immediately dispelled when he entered her apartment. Rent on the two-bedroom penthouse must have been two or three times his salary. It was decorated impeccably, with contemporary furniture and original abstract oil paintings. Through the wall of windows in the living room, the lights of Los Angeles were sparkling like the contents of a jewelry box. Karen kicked off her shoes and threw her jacket on the couch.

"What would you like?" she asked as she walked over to the granite wet bar adjacent to the kitchen. "I have a bottle of Chardonnay I can open."

"That sounds great," he said.

Within moments she returned with two well-filled glasses

and handed him one. He could have sworn that the button on her blouse had fallen a notch, and he could see the outline of her lace bra through the opening. He felt the blood rushing to his head and to other, lower parts of his body. He forced himself to turn his attention back to the window. "The view's beautiful from up here."

Karen smiled. "It's really the same as from the office."

"Yeah, but it looks different from here. I mean, it's hard to really enjoy anything when you're in that pressure cooker." He took a long sip from his glass.

Karen could tell he was nervous, but she found it charming. Although he was quite handsome, he wasn't like the others she had been with, men who were either so vain that they spent most of their time looking at themselves or so arrogant that they viewed her as merely a showpiece or accessory. Yes, she thought, he was different. As she stared at him, she could see something in his soft brown eyes that she hadn't noticed before. A pain that seemed to swallow her whole. When he reached for the glass of wine, she suddenly understood why. She was surprised she hadn't noticed it before. "What happened to your hand?" she asked.

"Oh," he said, recoiling. "It's been like this from birth. I'm missing my ring finger."

She reached over and touched his hand, as if to let him know it didn't bother her in the slightest. Her question had been solely one of curiosity. "You can barely notice it," she said, sitting down and leaning back. "So, more important, tell me, why did you decide to become a lawyer? You're not one of those idealists who went to law school because they wanted to defend the poor and unfortunate but somehow found themselves trapped working for a big law firm."

"No," Michael said, pausing. "It wasn't that."

"So why then . . . was it the money?"

"No, it was never the money," he replied. "You'd probably think it was ridiculous."

"Believe me, I'm the last person to pass judgment. Come on,

tell me," she said. "Why did Mr. Elliot decide to become a big corporate attorney?"

Michael hesitated. "If you really want to know, it was because of my grandmother. She raised me by herself, and when I was old enough to go to school, she took a secretarial job for a partner at one of the big law firms downtown. Here this woman was fifty, and she was working from eight in the morning until almost seven at night just to support us. I didn't really appreciate what she was doing at the time. I guess I was just too young. You know, the funny thing was that she didn't mind the work. What she hated was the partner she worked for. He was this wiry old man who looked like he had cheated death a hundred times. I remember the few occasions I saw him he was always dressed to a tee, dark gray pin-striped suits and shiny black wing tips. He even had those French monogrammed shirts with the gold cuff links. Anytime you got near him, he smelled like cigars.

"Anyway, the old prick had this condescending attitude, thought he was so much better than she was. Sometimes I think he beat her down so much that she started to believe it herself, but she never lost faith in me. She always thought that one day I would vindicate her. I would come back to Los Angeles and become a partner with one of the big law firms downtown and prove that the son of a bitch really wasn't any better than we were."

Karen smiled. "I bet she's proud of you now."

Michael paused. "Unfortunately, she passed away when I was still in college."

For a moment Karen didn't know what to say. She placed her hand on his. "I'm sorry, Michael . . . I'm so sorry."

Michael shrugged. "It's okay, it was a long time ago," he said. Suddenly he felt embarrassed about telling her all this. But she didn't say a word. They just looked at each other. There wasn't the slightest hint of judgment in her eyes.

He realized that her hand was still resting on his. For a moment Michael sat still, listening to himself breathing. She was so beautiful, and the smell of her perfume was everywhere. The sweet scent made him forget everything; all he could think about was what it would be like to have her body pressed against his. He reached forward and brushed her hair gently away from her face, then pulled her to him until he felt her soft, warm lips on his own. She opened her mouth willingly for him. This couldn't be happening, he thought. It just couldn't be happening.

They kissed long and hard, and soon the passion consumed both of them. Before he knew it he was making his way down her neck, pulling her body tightly against his. He could no longer control himself. Their bodies had become fused. As he ran his fingers through her long brown hair, she let out a soft but encouraging moan. He began to unbutton her blouse and remove her bra. Her breasts were firm and her nipples erect. She was breathing heavily. Any moment he expected her to stop him, but she didn't. Instead she rose and reached her hands around the back of her skirt. In a sweeping motion she unzipped it and let it fall to the floor. She was wearing black lace panties, and the sight of her standing almost naked in front of him was more than he could take. He made his way down her body and pulled the lace aside, revealing a narrow line of hair that he followed. She told him not to stop.

They were on the couch now, her eyes closed and her hands on the back of his head pulling him toward her. She was wet, and his fingers slid freely into her. She was writhing beneath him. He pressed his mouth against her, kissing her gently and working her with his tongue. When she could no longer stand it, she stood, pulled him up, and quickly undid his pants. Then she pushed him down on the couch and took him into her mouth. It was all he could do to hold on. Every muscle in his body began to shudder.

As if she could sense he was going to climax, she stopped and led him into the bedroom. They kissed on the edge of the bed before she reached into the nightstand and took out a condom. She slid it over to him. He was rock hard now, and she pulled him on top of her. He took her in his arms and looked down into her eyes one more time. He needed her to reassure him. She let him know it was okay, and he slid himself deep inside. She exhaled loudly. He was younger and much more animated than the other men she had been with. He went slowly at first, with long, deep strokes, but then began to move faster and faster. When she could tell he was about to come, she stopped and threw him onto his back. She kissed him softly and got on top of him. As she slid herself down, he watched her hair falling over her shoulders and her beautiful breasts moving back and forth. She was grinding as far as she could and began to whisper, "Please don't stop . . . please don't stop."

He grabbed her by the waist and pulled her down. It was as if she no longer had control of her legs; he could feel her quivering. He tried to think of other things, anything to stop himself. She was screaming now, her voice and breathing heavy. Her body was shaking, and she let out one final cry. He held her down on top of him until she stopped moving and her breathing slowed again. He held her close, not wanting to move. She kissed him again, and he tasted the sweat as he tugged gently on her lower lip with his teeth.

She sighed, then reached down, took off the condom, and threw it on the floor. She worked her way down until her tongue reached the base of his shaft. With one hand she began to stroke him while her mouth moved slowly up and down. She pushed him inside of her, and he became even harder than before. He was moaning, and she began to move slowly, working her hands and mouth, feeling him pulsing. He arched back, and she took him deeper. He had never felt anything so intense in his life. He clenched his fists tightly, and every muscle in his body filled with tension. She continued, slowly increasing the pace until he couldn't take it any longer. His legs seemed to buckle, and he could feel himself letting go. She held him deep inside her mouth until she felt him stop. Then she came back up and laid her head against his chest. He began to brush her hair gently while they both caught their breath. She reached back down and played gently with him. She was surprised to find that he was still aroused. "Oh," she mumbled.

They explored each other like young lovers, kissing and

touching every inch of each other's bodies. She was like no other woman he had ever been with. She seemed to recoil with his touch responsively, their bodies fitting seamlessly together. He took her in as she lay on the bed. It couldn't be real, he thought. He had to kiss her constantly to reassure himself. But this wasn't his imagination. Her body was pressed against his. He was in another world, his mind and body numb. They made love another time before collapsing in each other's arms.

The light coming through the long vertical blinds awakened him. He ran his tongue over his lips and wiped the sleep from his eyes. As his pupils adjusted to the morning light, he could see her hair rising from the smooth white sheets. Thoughts of their night together kept running through his mind. He remembered the way her soft skin felt against his and how sweet she had smelled. He remembered holding her after they made love and how she had fallen asleep with her head resting on his chest. Nothing had escaped him. He would remember it all. He reached over her and began to run his fingers gently through the long brown strands. Then he brushed them away and gave her one last kiss on the back of the neck before slipping out of bed.

Chapter 8

The sun was just coming over the horizon, and its reflection had begun to turn the mirrored buildings downtown beautiful shades of red and violet. There was no traffic this early, and Michael made it home quickly. By the time he had showered, shaved, and gotten back to the office, it was barely ten minutes to eight. As he walked through the quiet lobby, he could tell that the receptionist hadn't arrived yet. The lights in the hallway were off, and the copies of the morning's *Wall Street Journal* were resting neatly on top of her desk.

Michael took one from the stack. He then felt for the switch along the wall and watched the hallway lights come on like a line of dominoes quickly falling. The lobby was decorated starkly. Two modern black leather couches and a thick glass coffee table rested on a dark slate floor. Large black-and-white Ansel Adams photographs hung on the walls. The whole room looked too much like a mausoleum for his taste. It had been decorated by Peter Raven's first wife and, oddly, the austerity of her design continued to affect the firm, though she was long gone. It was further evidence of the way Raven's personal problems permeated the office. Michael ignored it and continued on.

After grabbing a cup of coffee from the break room, he made his way to his office and hung his jacket on the hook behind the door. He sat down at his desk and reached instinctively for his day planner but realized it wasn't there. Damn it, he thought, he had left his briefcase at Karen's apartment, and his day planner was in it. He thought about calling her but quickly dismissed the idea. He couldn't have her bring it into the office. What if someone saw her? He would just stop by her apartment that evening to pick it up. Besides, it would give him another excuse to see her.

He settled into the work piled on his desk. The first few hours of the morning were always the most productive part of his day. The phone rarely seemed to ring, and the office was quiet. But around twelve o'clock Michael knew he was just moving from project to project without really accomplishing anything. His thoughts were back at Karen's apartment. He just couldn't get his mind off last night, and he hadn't finished anything he was supposed to. The sound of his office door opening distracted him. He looked up to see Arturo awkwardly enter and take the chair opposite him. There were no morning salutations. He just stared at Michael with the same look of consternation he had exhibited the day before. "Did you get the E-mail from New York?" he asked abruptly.

Michael shook his head. "What E-mail?"

"It came in a few minutes ago. Apparently, one of the partners in the New York office is missing."

"What do you mean missing?"

"I mean, no one knows where he is . . ."

Michael paused. Nothing like this had ever happened before. "Who?" he asked.

"I think you know him," Arturo replied. "His name is Jonathan Gage."

"Jonathan Gage?" Michael asked, as if he had little faith in Arturo's recollection. "Are you sure?"

"Check it out yourself if you don't believe me."

Michael turned around to his computer and searched through his E-mail messages until he came to a single envelope addressed to all attorneys and staff from Richard Montague. He knew this must be it and opened the envelope. A brief message appeared on the screen:

To: All Attorneys and Staff
From: Richard Montague

I have been informed by his family that Jonathan Gage
is apparently missing. This is highly unusual for
Jonathan, and his family is deeply concerned. They
have asked that we send out an E-mail to all attorneys
who might know of his whereabouts. If you have seen
or talked to Jonathan Gage within the last forty-eight
hours, please contact Richard Montague's secretary im-
mediately.

Trepidation moved through Michael's body as he read the
message. It was as if he knew, without understanding why, that
this would have an unalterable effect on him. In his six years
with the firm, Michael had never seen a message like this. It
didn't make any sense. Sure, it was possible that a partner forgot to tell his wife and his secretary he was going out of town,
but Jonathan Gage was far too responsible to do something like
that. Besides, he knew that too many people relied upon him.

"Who is Jonathan Gage anyway?" Arturo asked.

Michael looked up at him in disbelief. Only someone as ignorant of law firm politics as Arturo could have asked such a
question. Jonathan Gage was legendary at Davis & White.
Some people said that he was destined for partnership from the
moment he was hired from law school. He surely had the pedigree, a magna cum laude undergraduate degree in business
from the University of Pennsylvania and a juris doctorate
summa cum laude from Harvard, where he was an editor of the
law review. But Gage had something more, an intensity that
was unparalleled, a need to be better and work harder than all
the other attorneys in his starting class, no matter what the cost.
Maybe it was his family's working-class background that drove
him to work hundreds of hours each month. Maybe it was the
work ethic instilled in him by the Jesuits in the Catholic schools
where he spent the younger part of his life. Whatever it was that
motivated him, it had clearly paid off.

"You knew him, didn't you?"

"Yeah," Michael replied. "I was just talking to him on Monday night. We were working on—Oh shit."

"What is it?"

"My God, I just realized, Gage was supposed to file the merger agreement today on the Global Network transaction. What time is it?"

"It's almost noon," Arturo replied. "Why?"

"Damn it, that means it's three in New York. I've got only two hours to get the merger agreement filed."

Arturo shook his head. "So, that's plenty of time."

"Can't you see? It has to be filed in Albany. That's a hundred and fifty miles outside the city. I'm never going to make it!" Michael exclaimed.

A wall of thick gray clouds was coming in over the Hudson River that afternoon, but Richard Montague was oblivious to it. He was locked behind closed doors, reading the firm's weekly statement of attorney billable hours, determining which partners and associates were being underutilized. The business of Davis & White was simple—the more time the firm billed, the more profits it made. Since overhead was relatively fixed, it was critical that no attorney sat idle. His role as managing partner was no different from that of a master on a slave ship—through fear and intimidation he kept the associates working and the partners generating business. Fortunately, his job had been relatively easy this year. Business had been good, very good. Associates were on a run rate of close to twenty-six hundred hours a year, and if it continued the profits per partner would be at an all-time high. Clearly this was the product of a long bull market and an overfueled economy, but none of that really mattered.

The door to his office opened. "Excuse me, Mr. Montague," Rose, his secretary, said softly.

"Yes," he replied, marking his place on the page.

"There's a Michael Elliot from the Los Angeles office on the phone for you. He says it's an emergency . . . something about Jonathan Gage."

Montague winced. He rarely got calls from associates, and when he did they were rarely pleasant. Besides, the name Michael Elliot wasn't immediately familiar to him, although this wasn't surprising. He often had trouble keeping track of his fellow partners, let alone the firm's associates. He reached for the thick black notebook containing attorney biographies and flipped through it until he reached the brief description for Michael Elliot. His academic background included an undergraduate degree in economics magna cum laude from Yale and a law degree cum laude from the University of Chicago. While to most people this would have been impressive, to Montague, an Ivy League Rhodes Scholar, it seemed merely adequate, and he quickly moved on. As he continued, he discovered why the name wasn't familiar to him. Michael Elliot had worked exclusively in the Los Angeles office. Before closing the book Montague glanced at the last item on the page. The space for family description was blank, no wife or children, or for that matter anyone else. He shook his head. It was strange, but it didn't matter much. He had all the information he needed. The red light on his phone was still blinking, and he picked up the line.

"Yes," he said abruptly.

"Mr. Montague, it's Michael Elliot in the Los Angeles office. I just got your message about Jonathan Gage, and I was curious whether he had shown up."

Montague paused. He had little time for such curiosity. "No, he's still missing," he replied. The frustration was evident in his voice. "My secretary said you had some kind of emergency?"

"Yes, I'm working on the Global Network merger with Jonathan, and he was supposed to make a filing with the secretary of state in New York this morning. . . ."

Montague exhaled. "So, can't you just file it tomorrow?" he asked.

"It's the merger agreement," Michael said. "Today is the last day of their fiscal year. If it doesn't get filed by five o'clock, it could cost the client millions of dollars."

"What do you mean?" Montague asked.

"Peter Raven told me that the transaction has to occur this fiscal year for tax purposes. That means the merger agreement has to be filed today. There's no other choice."

"Damn it. How can something like this happen?" Montague shouted as he pounded his fist on his desk. He knew he was far too old for this kind of thing. He hadn't really practiced law since he became managing partner ten years ago, but there was no time to drag in one of the other partners. By the time he found someone and explained it, the window would be lost. "Where's the merger agreement?"

"I don't know. It was sent to him by Federal Express. It's probably still in his office somewhere. . . ."

Montague was silent, and Michael continued. "I have an idea. I don't know if it's going to work, but I think it's our only shot," he said, pausing. "If we can find the merger agreement in Gage's office, we can get a paralegal to take it to La Guardia. We don't have time to drive it to Albany, but we can fly it there. We'll have to charter a plane, have a courier pick it up at the Albany airport and take it straight to the secretary of state. It's going to be tight, but it's our only real chance. I just hope Gage didn't take the merger agreement with him wherever he went. . . ."

The next half hour seemed to race by. After getting off the phone with Montague, Michael called Gage's secretary, Gloria, and explained the situation to her. He waited as she searched the office for the FedEx package, but after five minutes of sifting through stacks of paper, she still hadn't found it. Michael pleaded with her to continue searching and waited as she put him on the speakerphone in the office. All he could hear was the old woman talking to herself and shuffling papers. He looked at his watch. Another five minutes had passed. Finally she told him she had made it through everything, but it simply wasn't there. A numbness moved through his body. It was like being on a train and watching an opposing railcar come screeching toward him, knowing there was nothing he could do to stop it.

Suddenly he had an idea. Gage would never have left a sensitive document lying around. Surely he would have locked it up in one of his desk drawers, as Michael had done. He asked Gloria whether any of the drawers to Gage's desk were locked. There was only one, the second drawer on the right-hand side, but the key was nowhere to be found. He told her to pry it open. At first she was reluctant, but he pleaded with her. Finally, she took a pair of steel scissors off the desk and pounded it through the crack until he could hear the wood tearing around the small lock. When Gloria pulled open the drawer, she could see a small stack of documents inside. She picked them up and read the first page out loud. They had found the Global Network merger agreement.

Fortunately, the paralegal arrived just moments later with a motorcycle helmet under his arm. His instructions from Montague were simple. Proceed with the package directly to the commuter landing field adjacent to La Guardia Airport. A helicopter would meet him there. In such a short time, Montague had been unable to charter a plane; this would have to suffice. At three-thirty the helicopter picked up the package, and that was the last Michael heard of it. For the next hour and a half he waited silently in his office.

He knew this was all his fault. Raven had told him the importance of the Global Network filing. He had even told him twice to coordinate with Gage and make sure it got done. He should have called Gage's office first thing that morning. At least that way he would have found out about what happened earlier and been able to make alternative arrangements. Now all he could do was play back Raven's words again and again in his mind. "Don't fuck things up . . . don't fuck things up . . . don't fuck things up." The closer it got to five o'clock East Coast time, the more his anxiety built. He placed another call to Gloria, but she still hadn't heard from the courier. He knew this wasn't good news, but he continued to wait. When it reached half past five East Coast time, however, he had lost all hope. Surely if the agreement had been filed in time they would have heard by now. He knew it was over. His career would end today.

Then the phone rang. Michael quickly picked it up but found himself unable to speak.

"Michael," Gloria said. A deafening silence filled the line as he braced himself for the bad news. "There was a line at the secretary of state . . . but we made it, Michael . . . we made it. It was filed at 4:55 p.m."

The executive committee of Davis & White met secretly that night in the small boardroom on the fiftieth floor of the Chase Manhattan Bank Building. Behind the thick wooden doors, Richard Montague updated them on the disappearance of Jonathan Gage and recounted the catastrophe that had been narrowly averted through his own efforts and those of a young associate in the Los Angeles office. Still, the concern that similar problems would come up haunted each of them. Failure to file the Global Network merger agreement would have cost the firm millions in malpractice liability. After an hour of discussion, a decision was reached. Someone must investigate all open matters Jonathan Gage was working on to make sure no other deadlines were missed. However, choosing that person was not so easy. Clearly it would have to be someone in the corporate department, but with the firm's intense workload each of the partners considered was far too overburdened to undertake such a project.

Then a scratchy voice came from the end of the long table. "What about the young associate who helped you out earlier?"

"Yeah," another partner responded. "He's senior enough to identify any problems. Besides, he just finished the Global Network transaction. He should have time."

"But can he be trusted?" another partner responded.

"My God, he's up for partner next year. He should be easy to manipulate. Besides, Raven will vouch for him."

"But are you sure he's good enough?" the skeptical partner asked.

"I think you're overthinking this," Montague responded.

"Jonathan Gage rarely worked alone. Besides, we can minimize the risk by alerting the corporate partners to the problem we had today and have each of them keep an eye out for new ones. This way Michael Elliot will just be our backup. If anything falls through the cracks, which I doubt will happen, he'll be there to catch it. He will be our fail-safe," he said, looking around the table. Each of the partners silently shook his head in agreement.

Chapter 9

The apartment was quiet save only for the sound of his wife in the next room reading their son a chapter from the latest Harry Potter book. His daughter was already asleep, and he knew it would only be a few minutes before his wife turned off the lights and joined him. This was the only time they had together, the few hours between the time the children were put to bed and that inevitable point in the middle of the night when they came running and jumped into bed with them. Every night started out the same. Nico would wake to the thud of either his son or daughter jumping off their bed, then hear the short shuffling of little feet until they stopped in front of their door. The handle would turn, and the door would slowly creak open. "Mommy . . . Daddy . . . I'm scared." Then they would run full speed and dive headfirst into the bed.

Within moments his wife's voice had trailed off, and she tiptoed into the bedroom. Closing the door behind her, she let out a sigh of relief. He smiled and motioned for her to join him on the bed. As she began to take off her clothes, the sound of the pager distracted him. Damn it, he thought. He rolled over and reached for the small black box on top of the nightstand. As he pressed down the button, a seven-digit number flashed across the screen. He didn't need to write it down. The number had been etched into his brain years ago. He paused for a moment and looked back up at his wife. Her blouse was already off, and she was reaching for the clasp on her bra. He shrugged. "I've got to take this. It will only take a second." Before she could respond, he reached back over to the nightstand for the phone. He dialed the number from memory and waited for someone to answer.

The phone rang twice before a rough voice came over the line. "Special Investigative Unit. . . ."

"It's Nico, I got the page. What's going on?"

"We need you to investigate a missing-persons report."

Nico paused. "You've got to be kidding me. You're calling me at this hour to follow up on a missing-persons report?"

"This is different. I just got a call from Justice. Apparently, this guy is some big-shot attorney with one of the Wall Street law firms. I mean, he must have some serious pull," the voice said. "There's all kinds of people asking questions about this. . . ."

Nico was silent. He could see his wife shaking her head and reaching down for her blouse as he continued to argue.

"I wouldn't have called you if it wasn't important. Besides, they specifically asked for you."

Nico hesitated. "Look, give me ten minutes and I'll call you from the car." As he hung up the phone, he went over to his wife and began to kiss her softly.

"Don't even try to suck up," she said flatly. Nico smiled and patted her ass, but she didn't respond. He knew it was time to go. "I'll be back in the morning to make the kids' lunches and take them to school," he whispered.

"You better be. I've got to be at the hospital by seven-thirty for pre-op."

Nico didn't mind making the kids' lunches or taking them to school. It gave him a chance to be a part of their life. They were a captive audience in his dark blue Crown Victoria, the blue and red lights visible in the back window. On the way he would find out what had happened the day before and what fears, anxieties, and troubles currently plagued them. It was never anything serious, just the typical playground squabbles. There were the ball hogs, hair pullers, sand eaters, glue munchers, projectile vomiters, and, his favorites, the kids who could fart at will.

His children attended an exclusive private school on the

Upper West Side. Most of the parents were investment bankers, lawyers, or executives. As far as Nico could tell, however, his kids were the only ones who came to school with a police escort. He was probably the only father there who had a blue-collar job, not that he cared much. He had seen some of the public schools in Manhattan and was glad he didn't have to worry about his kids running into drugs, violence, and gangs. With his wife's income as the chief cardiothoracic surgeon at New York Presbyterian, they were able to afford to send their children to school with the rich and famous. Still, it was a little awkward for him at school functions, not that they socialized much with the other parents. Frankly, most of the other parents bored him. Whenever they found out he was a lieutenant in the NYPD, they would start in on him to take care of some tickets or resolve a small problem a "friend" had because of soliciting a prostitute. Of course, Nico never did.

The one thing about the school that Nico did enjoy was career day, when the fathers and mothers would come and talk about what they did for a living. He was always the favorite speaker. Everyone else bored the kids with talk about stocks and bonds, risk arbitrage, debt underwriting, or the subtleties of antitrust litigation. They were all so full of themselves it was nauseating. But Nico let the kids ride in his police car, turn on the siren, listen to the dispatcher on the radio, handcuff each other, pat each other down for weapons, and practice reading suspects their Miranda rights. Every kid went home wanting to be a policeman or fireman, and it drove their fathers crazy. With the women his job often had a different effect. He was always getting come-ons from the divorcees or neglected housewives. Once an attractive young teacher even volunteered to let him handcuff her after hours if he needed the practice. Nico never took her up on it. He wasn't the wandering type. Nico leaned over and kissed his wife one more time before heading for the door.

Brooklyn Heights, just across the East River from downtown Manhattan, was one of New York's first suburbs. Although it had originally been a middle-class neighborhood, over the years it had become filled with young and successful professionals looking for more affordable housing. They moved out to Cobble Hill and Carroll Gardens, where they bought nineteenth-century brownstones and town houses and had them renovated. Over time these quiet neighborhoods had been revived by the new families moving in, and one could regularly see young couples pushing strollers or walking their dogs along the tree-lined streets. While these neighborhoods didn't have the prestige or the close proximity to the restaurants and entertainment of Manhattan, they had a character and charm of their own.

As Nico got off the two-lane Brooklyn–Queens Expressway at Pierrepont Street, he could see the Brooklyn Heights Promenade off to his left. The narrow park ran along the ferry district for about a third of a mile, and from it he could see the Manhattan skyline and the boats and barges moving slowly along the East River. Farther up, the base of the Brooklyn Bridge rose eerily from the dark water. Columbia Heights ran just along the other side of the park, and he looked back at the address he had written down earlier.

Nico took the first left and slowly made his way down the street until he reached 214 Columbia Heights. It was in the middle of a group of beautifully maintained brownstones, and he knew it must have cost a small fortune, even outside the city. He pulled the car to a stop. It was just past midnight, but the lights on the first floor were still on. He knew she was inside waiting for him. As he drew his hand over the rough skin of his face, he realized he was in need of a shave. He pulled down the rearview mirror and quickly looked himself over. It wasn't as bad as he thought.

Although Nico was in his early forties, he looked relatively young. His face was thin, barely showing wrinkles around the corners of his eyes, and his hair was just starting to get hints of gray. He thought the job would have aged him more than this. For the last five years he had been in charge of the Special Investigative Unit, responsible for coordinating joint investigations between the NYPD and federal agencies. But the job hadn't worn on him like it had on those who'd held it before. He attributed this fact to his adoption of eastern philosophy. He had long ago forsaken his Catholic upbringing for a religion that didn't impose guilt. The dull horn of a tugboat moving up the East River reminded him why he had come. It was time to get it over with. He slowly got out of his car, walked up the stairs to the front door of the brownstone, and knocked gently. A soft shuffling sound came from inside.

"Mrs. Gage?" Nico asked, staring at her through the narrow gap that the chain on the door permitted. "I'm Detective Nico Fiori with the NYPD. I was asked to respond to a missing-persons report." He waited for some response, but she hesitated. "Oh," he said, suddenly realizing why she hadn't opened the door. He reached into his pocket for the small leather case and held up his detective's badge. "You can call downtown to verify it if you'd like. . . ."

"No, that's okay," the woman responded.

She closed the door, unfastened the chain, and fully reopened it. It was then that Nico got his first look at Jonathan Gage's wife, and it was a picture that would stay with him. She had long brown hair and pleasant features not much different from those of his own wife, but there were deep signs of anguish on the young woman's face. Her brown eyes were swollen and purged of makeup, and her hands seemed to shake uncontrollably. Most of all, she had a look that he had seen often before. It was the terrified expression of a child lost in an amusement park.

"I finally got the children to sleep. They've been asking where their dad is all night," she said, motioning for him to come in. "We should go down to the kitchen. I don't want them to wake up."

Nico shook his head in agreement and followed her down the hallway. When they reached the kitchen, she pulled one of the chairs out from under the old wooden table and motioned for him to sit. She took the chair opposite him. As she rested her hands on the table, he could see they were still shaking. Despite how long he had been a detective, certain things always disturbed him. While others just became numb to the human suffering around them, his pain had seemed to amplify over time.

"Mrs. Gage, they told me that your husband has been missing for the last forty-eight hours, is that right?"

"Yes, he didn't come home Tuesday night, and he hasn't called since then. He's never done anything like this before," she said. "At first I just thought he might have worked late and stayed in the city, but I called the office and talked to his secretary Wednesday morning. She told me that he hadn't shown up for work. I just hope something terrible hasn't happened to him. . . ."

Nico didn't respond. He had seen this too many times when he was a patrolman. A wife would call in to the station complaining that her husband was missing. Usually it turned out that he had just gotten drunk the night before at the local bar and passed out in the park or at a friend's house. Other times the wife would find out that her husband had moved in with his mistress, not calling home until he had emptied the bank accounts and served her with divorce papers. It wasn't as uncommon as people believed, and Nico tried not to let his skepticism show. "When was the last time you talked to him?"

"At about eight o'clock Tuesday night. He told me he had some things to take care of at work and that he'd be home late. I didn't think anything of it until I woke up at three o'clock in the morning and he still wasn't home. That's when I started to worry."

"Have you called his friends?"

She nodded. "I even called Richard Montague, the managing partner at the firm where he works, earlier today and asked if he could check around the office to see if anyone knew where he was. They circulated a notice, but no one responded," she said. Her eyes started to tear up, and she took a wadded ball of facial tissue from her fist and ran it across the base of her nose. "This isn't like him. . . ."

"I'm sorry," Nico said softly, and Mrs. Gage just inhaled deeply and tried to regain her composure.

"I called the police, but they said there wasn't anything they could do for forty-eight hours. That's when Mr. Montague got the mayor's office involved. I just pray to God nothing happened to him. . . ."

"Was he acting strangely?" Nico said.

"What do you mean?"

"Did you have a fight or any marital problems?"

"My God, I know what you're thinking. You're thinking that he left us. . . . That's not like him. . . . He would never have done something like that. He was a good husband. He was a good father," she said, starting to cry again.

Nico quickly put his hand over hers. "I'm sorry. It's just a question I have to ask," he said. He tried to change the subject. "Mrs. Gage, I'm going to need you to write down your credit card information, as well as a list of your bank accounts. I'm also going to need the numbers for any of your husband's calling cards. Then I can run a trace to see if there's been any unusual activity. Oftentimes if there's been a kidnapping or mugging, the perpetrator will make the victim withdraw cash from his bank account or try to use the credit cards. By running a check we should be able to tell if there's been any foul play."

Mrs. Gage just looked away and began to shake her head.

"I'd also like to get a recent photograph for circulation. By the way, did he have any medical conditions I should be aware of?"

"What do you mean?"

"Like a heart condition or a recent head injury. Something that might have temporarily incapacitated him or left him with memory loss?"

"Oh, my God," she said, pausing. "He's never had anything like that before."

Nico closed his black leather notepad. "Mrs. Gage, I know this must be incredibly difficult for you, but you shouldn't assume the worst has happened until we eliminate all other possibilities. For all we know, he could be away on business or there's some other kind of innocent explanation for this," he said, trying his best to smile. He was interrupted by the sound of the kitchen door opening. For a split second Nico thought he would see Jonathan Gage walk in, put his arms around his wife, and explain that this was all an innocent mistake. But no such luck. In the doorway was a boy with curly brown hair and brightly colored pajamas who couldn't have been older than three or four. One of his eyes was closed and the other was half open as he walked toward his mother. "Mom, I had a bad dream. . . . Where's Daddy?"

Mrs. Gage rose from her chair, picked the boy up, and held him close. "Your father is away on business. He'll be back soon," she said, looking over to Nico. "He'll be back soon. . . ."

Chapter 10

The events of the day weighed heavily on Michael's conscience. His body felt worn, and his mind was tired. He could no longer concentrate. On top of everything, his head was throbbing with what promised to be a brutal headache. All Michael wanted to do was go home when he heard the telephone ringing. He looked down at his watch, then hesitated. He had long ago learned the dangers of answering the phone this late. Almost invariably it would be one of the senior partners who had forgotten to do something and was calling associates from his Rolodex trying to find someone to finish the work. In the last six years Michael had lost countless nights of sleep by making this mistake. Still, he couldn't help staring at the phone as it rang for the second time. It was as if it were taunting him.

Damn it, he thought. Maybe he was being paranoid. It was probably just Arturo calling to see if he wanted to get a drink, or maybe it was Karen. God, he hoped it was Karen, but answering the phone would be playing Russian roulette. Still, when it rang for the third time, he picked up. "Hello, Michael Elliot. . . ."

There was a brief moment of silence before a scratchy voice came over the line, and Michael instantly knew he had drawn the chamber with the bullet. "It's Raven. I just got out of an emergency meeting of the executive committee. They want you to come back to New York. . . ."

"I thought you were meeting with a client today."

"I was, but after the screwup this afternoon with the Global

Network merger, they called an emergency session of the executive committee and pulled me out of my meeting." Raven hesitated, and Michael instantly knew what was coming next. "Look, I covered for you. You and I both know that if you'd been on top of things this whole mess would never have happened. You should have tried to coordinate with Gage earlier. You would've found out he was missing and been able to make alternative arrangements. But that's just going to be our little secret. . . ."

Michael was silent. As much as he wanted to believe otherwise, he knew Raven was right.

"Look, it doesn't matter anymore. The important thing was that you were able to fix it. Now they think you're some kind of star. They want you to come back to New York and cover for Gage until they figure out what happened to him. They made arrangements for you to take the red-eye out of LAX tonight. If you leave now, you'll have just enough time to get home and pack."

"Tonight?" Michael asked. His thoughts went back to Karen. If he was going to be anywhere other than home, it would be at her apartment. And he still needed to get his briefcase. For a moment he imagined her waiting for him with her long brown hair and soft full lips. "I made plans," he said. "Besides, I haven't gotten a good night's sleep in weeks." As soon as the words left his mouth, he knew they had fallen on deaf ears.

"Look, Michael, you're coming up for partner shortly. This is your chance to prove yourself to the power players in New York. The executive committee remembers things like this," Raven said. "Do you really want me to tell them you couldn't make it because you had a date?"

Michael knew he didn't have any choice. "No," he said grudgingly. "I'll be there. . . . You know I'll be there."

Michael hung up the phone and began to pull his fingers nervously through his short brown hair. Damn it, he thought. He had hoped to call Karen and thank her for last night, maybe even ask her out for a late dinner. He wanted desperately to see her again and tell her how much he had been thinking about her. There had been something between them that night that went beyond the pure physical aspects of their encounter. He was sure of it. Michael took out the firm directory and looked up her home phone number. It was still relatively early, and he hoped she would be there. This wasn't the kind of message he wanted to leave on her answering machine. After the phone rang three times, he heard her familiar voice. "Hello. . . ."

"Karen, it's Michael," he said, hesitating.

"Oh, hi," she said eagerly. "I just got in the door."

"I just wanted to call and thank you for last night. I mean . . . I guess I wanted to . . . well . . ."

She interrupted him. "Don't be silly, you don't have to thank me."

"What I mean is that I really enjoyed being with you."

"I could tell," she said, laughing. "If it makes you feel better, the feeling was mutual."

"Well I hoped so, but more than that, I want to see you again."

The words hung in the air as he waited for her response. "Do you mean tonight?" she said, laughing.

"Well, unfortunately I have to catch the red-eye back to New York, but I was hoping that maybe we could see each other when I get back. You know, maybe go out for dinner."

Karen paused. "Well, why don't we talk about it when you get back," she said.

"Promise me you'll think about it."

"Oh, I will," she said playfully. "I will."

The United Airlines flight left Los Angeles at eleven o'clock that night and arrived in New York at approximately seven o'clock the following morning. Although Michael had flown it only a few times before, he could still remember the toll that it had taken on his body. It was almost worse than pulling an all-nighter. Someone had once told him that you got only a certain number of red-eye flights in your lifetime. After you reached that number, you either died or retired. Seeing the ragged group of investment bankers, lawyers, and other professionals shuffling onto the plane that night made that proposition a lot more real to him.

Michael watched curiously as they revealed the tricks they had developed to minimize the impact of the flight. Some would look for an empty row of seats and, after lifting the armrests, would lay down across it with their feet dangling in the aisle as if on a makeshift cot. Others washed down brightly colored sleeping pills with a double from the bar cart and drifted into unconsciousness. A brave few pumped their bodies full of caffeine like speed junkies and worked intensely through the flight. None of these options seemed overly appealing to Michael.

Just when he was about to turn his attention to the *Los Angeles Times* sports page, his eyes froze. Walking down the aisle with a large carry-on bag over his shoulder was the last person Michael expected to see on the red-eye. What was James Monehan doing on a flight to New York in the middle of the night? Michael called his name. At first Monehan looked up blankly, trying to figure out where the voice was coming from. Michael called again and this time raised his hand until Monehan saw him and began making his way toward Michael, his large bag bouncing off seated passengers' arms and shoulders. Monehan, oblivious to the disturbance he had created, stuffed his carry-on into the overhead compartment.

"Is anyone sitting here?"

"No," Michael responded. "Even if someone does have the seat, they're not going to have a hard time finding another."

Monehan looked over the sparsely filled cabin and nodded.

"What are you doing taking the red-eye to New York anyway?" Michael asked.

"I'm sure you heard about the partnership decision by now . . ." Michael just nodded his head. There was no point in denying it. "Well, they told me to take some time off before I came back, so that's what I'm doing. My wife took the kids to visit their grandparents in New York yesterday. I still had a few things to take care of at home, so I told her I'd take a later flight. With my frequent flyer miles, this was the only flight I could get."

The two of them made small talk until the plane took off. When the flight attendant came around an hour later with the drink cart, they were somewhere over the New Mexico desert, and Monehan ordered each of them a double gin and tonic. Gin was an acquired taste that Michael had never developed and the tonic water always seemed to amplify the flavor of the quinine, but since it had been ordered, he went along for the ride. Occasionally he looked down at the drink to check his progress, taking small sips as if it were some kind of bad medicine. After a while he could feel his forehead beginning to burn and his face become flush. No other alcohol had this effect on him. Eventually his taste buds deadened, and his sips got larger, giving him the courage to speak directly. "Do you know what you're going to do?" he asked.

Monehan just looked away and pulled at the skin at the base of his neck. After a few moments he looked back at Michael. "They told me they would arrange an in-house counsel job for me with one of the firm's clients if I wanted it," he said. "You know what's funny. A year ago I would've never considered a job like that. I always told myself I would never be one of those in-house lawyers working nine to five. I always thought they were selling out, but the strange thing is, that job doesn't seem half bad to me now." He took another sip from the gin and tonic.

For a moment, Michael was silent. He realized Monehan had been broken. All he could do was stare at him while Raven's words kept repeating in his head: "I could only choose one of you. . . . I could only choose one of you." Michael's guilt was almost intolerable. He felt the need to say something, anything. "You could always go work for another firm," he said, but he realized immediately the words were intended not to lift his friend's spirits but to ease his own conscience.

Monehan just smiled at him. "Come on, no other firm is going to want an eighth-year associate who's been passed over. You know that as well as I do. I'm tainted now, no matter how good a lawyer I am." He looked out the small window. "Anyway, it doesn't matter much anymore. If there's one thing I've learned from this, it's that all these law firms are the same. They're one giant pyramid scheme.

"They go to the top law schools and lure in young associates with stories of big salaries and big profits. Those schools are filled with men and women who've been overachievers all their damn lives. Hell, they were the ones who got the highest grades and succeeded at everything they did. Can't you see, they're the perfect marks. They all think they're going to be the one who makes it, they've been beating the odds all their lives. So the firms just play to their egos.

"For years they tell them exactly what they want to hear. . . . Monehan, you're a star . . . you're just where you want to be . . . you're a shoo-in for partner . . . you're doing all the right things. They'll tell you anything just to keep you around. We all know the firm makes most of its money off associates in their last few years before partnership. My God, you've probably been hearing it too," he said as he took the final sip from the thin plastic glass.

He paused for a moment and surveyed the men sprawled out over the seats. "Look at this, Michael. All this can be yours someday," he said, starting to laugh, but Michael failed to see the humor in his remark. Monehan suddenly became serious. "You know what happened to me last month? My son came back from preschool with a picture. Apparently, the teacher told him to draw his family. So my wife shows it to me, and there are these stick-figure drawings of him and his mom and his new sister. Then there's this blank space in the middle. Can you believe it? I was a blank space."

Michael didn't know what to say. It felt as if the air in the cabin was scathing his nostrils as he struggled to breathe. He thought about telling Monehan. At least that way he would be able to put his own mind at ease. But at what cost? It would only take Monehan further down his spiral of depression. Before he could say anything, however, Monehan spoke again.

"Do you remember Steven Nichols?"

"What?" Michael asked. "Oh, yeah, I think so. He was in our department when I started, right?"

"Yeah, he was one of the best lawyers I ever worked with. The partners loved him. He worked all the fucking time. He didn't have a wife or kids, and the firm always sent him when they had a deal out of town they needed covered, not that they care much if you have a family. If I had a question, I could always go to him. Nine times out of ten he knew the answer right off the top of his head. It was absolutely amazing. The other time he knew exactly where to find it, not like some of the partners at the firm now, who couldn't find their ass with two hands.

"I'll never forget when he came up for partner. Everybody thought he was going to make it. But when the list of all the new partners came out in the *New York Law Journal*, his name wasn't on it. I remember the firm just told him there were too many qualified candidates that year to select from. They said they wished they could make everybody a partner, but they had to make a hard decision. It was fucking amazing," he said, shaking his head. "I swear to God, I thought I was going to quit right then and there. . . . That's when Raven came by the office to talk to me. He shuts the door like he's my best friend, and then he gives me this story that it was all some kind of numbers game."

Michael stared at him with new intensity. He wanted Monehan to just shut up, but he wouldn't.

"Raven knew exactly what to do. He played me just right. So he tells me that over the next couple of years they could only make one new partner. He told me if they made Steven Nichols a partner, there wouldn't be room for me when I came up. You know, right up to this week I felt guilty about it," he said, laughing. "They'll tell you anything you want to hear. . . ."

Chapter 11

Friday Morning, December 1

A blanket of fog had moved slowly over downtown Manhattan, and Nico could see only the first ten or eleven stories of the high-rise buildings before they disappeared into the dark gray sky. For as long as he could remember he had disliked the modern glass skyscrapers that filled the city. To him they had none of the character of the more ornate stone buildings that had been erected decades before them. What these new buildings lacked in physical beauty they tried to compensate for in height, each one taller than its neighbor until they made the streets below them dark and cold. Nico remembered the story of the Tower of Babel that the Catholic priest had taught his communion class. It had been meant to illustrate the catastrophic consequences when men tried to emulate God, and he could still hear Father Anastasio's loud voice admonishing him that mere mortals were not meant to view earth from heaven. At least not until they were dead. Nico paused. If ever there was a time and a place when humanity's vanity and ego were blatantly apparent, it was right now in downtown Manhattan. He continued on.

The revolving doors of the Chase Manhattan Bank Building weren't much farther, and Nico could see the swarms of people blending indistinguishably as they made their way in from the street to the enormous marble lobby. He followed them blindly like a pack dog following the lead through a snowstorm. He passed the two guards at the front entry and stood in the center of the lobby, confronted by banks of elevators, each going to a different portion of the building. He looked down at the address he had written in his leather notebook, then walked over to the elevator reserved for the top ten floors.

A number of people were waiting in front of the large steel doors, men in neatly pressed suits with colorful silk ties and several plainly dressed women he guessed were secretaries or word processors. New York was a strange dichotomy. There were lawyers and investment bankers making seven-figure salaries, and there were secretaries and day laborers, who, along with himself, made a small fraction of that amount. There was no longer any middle class. To compound matters, the city was becoming more expensive by the day. If it wasn't for his wife's salary, Nico knew he would never have been able to afford to live in the city, let alone pay the mortgage on the remodeled brownstone on West Fifty-seventh Street in which they now lived.

As a surgeon Nico's wife made almost ten times what he did. Although the demands of her job often meant he had to spend more than his share of time taking care of their two children, this was a small price to pay. Besides, truth be told, he rather enjoyed being with the kids. All he had to do was tolerate the other detectives' jabs about "not wearing the pants in the family" and the constant questions about whether he was "sport-fucking the other soccer moms." For the most part Nico had developed a thick skin. He knew that any one of them would trade places with him in a heartbeat. Besides, he had never really cared much about what other people thought. Nico had always lived in a world unto himself, and he wasn't about to let anyone else's preconceived notions start dictating his life now.

The sound of the arriving elevator returned him to his surroundings, and he shuffled on with the others. Within moments he felt the pull of acceleration like a twenty-pound weight tied around his stomach. He looked at the faces around him, but they all seemed strangely oblivious to it. They must have ridden this rocket a thousand times before, he thought. He turned his attention to the panel of buttons and pressed the top one.

The elevator stopped at several floors before leaving Nico alone. Suddenly an uneasiness overcame him, as if something unpleasant from his past had come back to him. This would be one of many premonitions that would overcome him during his investigation of Jonathan Gage's disappearance. In retrospect it would all seem crystal clear, but at the time the signs were as opaque as the fog that had moved over the city that morning. Nico pushed the button again and breathed deeply until the feeling passed.

When the elevator doors opened onto the fifty-eighth-floor offices of Davis & White, Nico couldn't help but pause. In front of him was a two-story wall of windows looking over the city. He could see all the way from Ellis Island to the East River. This was one of the most commanding views of Manhattan he had ever seen, and his anxiety was quickly replaced with awe. So this was what it was like to witness earth from the heavens, he thought. The sharp voice of the young woman behind the reception desk, however, quickly brought him back to earth. "Excuse me, can I help you?" she asked, as if Nico was some tourist who thought he was getting off on the viewing deck of the Empire State Building.

He turned toward her. She was wearing a headset that was barely visible beneath her long hair, and the digital panel on her desk was filled with blinking lights. "Yes, my name is Nico Fiori. I'm a detective with the New York Police Department," he said, waiting for some acknowledgment, but there was none in her empty eyes. "I'm here to see Mr. Montague. I have an appointment at eight o'clock."

The woman hesitated. "Hold on."

Nico watched as she pressed a small button on the panel and began to talk. "Hello, I have a Detective Fiori here to see Mr. Montague," she said, sizing him up. "Uh-huh. . . . Sure, I'll tell him." She pressed another button and looked back at Nico. "Mr. Montague's secretary will be right down. Please have a seat, Detective Fiori."

Nico nodded and walked over to the large window. The fog was beginning to dissipate. Patches of street were becoming visible through the river of gray. There were even small, dark circles moving below him, but he couldn't tell if they were people or cars. If there really was a God looking down on earth, he just hoped that everyone didn't look quite so small and insignificant. Everything was trivial from this height, but maybe that was why there were wars, plagues, pestilence, and, of course, death. After all, that was what kept him in business.

"Excuse me, Detective Fiori. . . ."

Nico turned around to see an elderly woman wearing a dark wool skirt that fell well past her knees and a silk blouse buttoned up to her neck. She was wound so tight that the sight of her made Nico feel the need to correct his posture. He guessed she must have been over sixty, but it was hard to tell. The city often wore differently on people, and her old-fashioned schoolteacher wardrobe didn't help. "I'm Mr. Montague's secretary," the woman said. "Please follow me, Detective Fiori. Mr. Montague is expecting you."

She abruptly turned, and Nico followed her down a long hallway until she reached two imposing wooden doors. First she knocked, then pushed both doors open, revealing a large and ornate corner office. Montague was working at his desk, making copious notes on a dingy yellow legal pad. After what seemed like an eternity, he shifted his attention from his work and rose.

"Hello, Detective Fiori, my name is Richard Montague. I'm the managing partner at Davis and White," he said, reaching out to shake his hand. Nico swore he could feel the bones in the old man's fingers as he gripped his hand firmly. They were cold as stone. "I had my secretary compile the information you asked for when you called earlier," Montague said, handing Nico a thin manila folder. "There's a list of the phone calls made from Jonathan Gage's office on Tuesday, the day he disappeared. I also had our office manager provide a list of calls made from his calling cards. As you can see, there were no calls made after he left the office." Montague hesitated, as if desperate to change the subject. "Have there been any new developments?"

Nico paused. "Not yet, but I did meet with Mr. Gage's wife last night. She gave me a picture that we circulated to the hospitals and the morgues. Fortunately, no one fitting Jonathan Gage's description has been identified."

Montague sighed loudly. "Well, that's a relief," he said. "I'm afraid, however, that still doesn't explain things."

"No, it doesn't," Nico replied. For a moment he stared into Montague's eyes. There was something unusual about the old man's stare. Nico recognized it, but what exactly it was escaped him. "Do you mind if I ask you a few questions?"

Montague shook his head. "No, of course not."

Nico opened his leather notebook. "Was Mr. Gage acting strangely or unusually before his disappearance?"

"What do you mean?" Montague asked, as if surprised by the question.

"I mean, did you notice any change in his behavior? . . . Mood swings, drinking, depression . . . you know, things like that. . . ."

"No, not at all," he said. "Jonathan Gage was a fine young man and a good partner. I just hope something awful hasn't happened to him. You hear about these things all the time, but they always involve people you don't know. In all my years I've never had anything like this happen to one of our attorneys. It's very disturbing," he said.

The sympathy was about as transparent as the glass windows that lined his office. Montague didn't give a damn about Jonathan Gage. Nico doubted that the old man had ever felt a real emotion in his life. There was nothing but ice water moving through his veins. "Mr. Montague, would it be possible for me to see his office? You know, maybe if I looked around a little, it could give me some kind of insight into what happened. . . ."

There was a long silence as Montague stared through him. His eyes were still and unrevealing, like those of the corpses Nico had seen in the city morgue. He knew the answer before he heard it.

"Unfortunately, it's not quite that easy, Detective. To be

honest with you, I don't think there would be any harm in it, and I do want to help out as much as possible. However, this law firm is bound by certain obligations of confidentiality to our clients. By having you go through his office, we would be violating canons of ethics that have governed our profession for hundreds of years. I just wish there was some way to get around this."

Nico smiled and closed the notebook. "That's all right. I understand. I knew it was a long shot."

Montague hesitated. "Wait a second, I just remembered something. There's a young associate coming in from Los Angeles this morning to take over Jonathan's open matters. In fact, I'm expecting him shortly. His name is Michael Elliot, and he will be working out of Jonathan's office. I'll give him your card. If he finds anything unusual, I will make sure he passes it on to you." Montague stood up.

Nico took out a business card and handed it to him. Maybe he had misjudged the man. "That would be great. If he finds anything that might be useful, just tell him to call me. Once again, thank you for your help." He shook Montague's hand one more time before standing up to leave.

Montague's secretary was waiting for Nico by the doorway and walked him back to the elevator. When she returned to the corner office, Montague was still sitting at his desk, staring at the card Nico had given him.

"Do you want me to give Detective Fiori's card to Michael when he arrives this morning?" she asked.

Montague just looked up at her coldly. "No, that's all right. I think I've changed my mind. I'll handle this one," he said, slowly tearing the card in half and throwing the pieces into the wastebasket.

Chapter 12

The Boeing 767 touched down on the damp tarmac of Kennedy Airport at close to seven-forty in the morning, and the mad shuffle to depart the aircraft ensued immediately. Even before the plane had taxied to the gate, the haggard passengers were scrounging in the overhead compartments like a pack of field mice searching a cupboard for crumbs. Those who had checked their luggage were dialing their cellular phones, making sure drivers would be there to pick them up. As Michael waited for the plane to empty, his mind kept returning to his conversation with Monehan. The words kept coming back to him like a recurring nightmare: "They'll tell you anything you want to hear . . . they'll tell you anything you want to hear. . . ."

As much as he suspected Monehan's story was true, he couldn't force himself to believe it. He had given Davis & White the last six years of his life. Besides, why would Raven have brought him to New York to take over for Jonathan Gage if he wasn't grooming Michael for partnership? There just had to be another explanation. Perhaps Monehan had found out that the firm was choosing Michael over him and was jealous. But that was totally out of character for Monehan. Besides, he knew Michael didn't have any family. The firm and this job were all Michael had. What could possibly have been Monehan's motivation to lie?

Michael bid his friend farewell at the baggage claim. He tried to think of other things on the cab ride downtown, but his mind kept coming back to it. Driving on the Van Wyck at eight o'clock in the morning was like trying to fit a square peg in a round hole. To make matters worse, a sixteen-wheeler had jack-knifed on the Long Island Expressway, blocking traffic for miles.

For the next hour and a half, Michael kept looking at the 1960 Rolex hanging loosely on his wrist. The watch had been a gift from Carl when he graduated from law school. In fact, it was the watch Carl's father had given to him some thirty years earlier, when Carl graduated from the University of Chicago Law School. Carl had told Michael about how his father, a carpenter by trade, worked over six months of overtime just to afford the watch. Now Carl had wanted him to have it. Michael brushed the old leather band with his fingers. The watch had come in the mail the day before commencement, not that Michael had been planning on attending. Graduation was a time for families, and he didn't want to be there alone. He could still remember the note that accompanied the watch, only seven words: *"She would have been proud of you."* Michael shook his head. He often wondered where Carl was now, somewhere on Lake Arrowhead in his motorboat fishing for trout, he guessed.

"That will be thirty-five," the cabdriver said in a Nigerian accent.

Michael looked up to see the dark eyes staring at him from the rearview mirror like an owl's. "Sure," he said. "I'm going to need a receipt."

By the time Michael had paid the driver and arrived at the offices of Davis & White, it was nine-thirty. Detective Nico Fiori was long gone. Richard Montague had left instructions with the receptionist that Michael was to work out of Jonathan Gage's office, at least until the matter of his disappearance was resolved. As he walked slowly through the hallway on the fifty-eighth floor, he read the nameplates on the large doors until he reached the one with Gage's name on it. He tried the handle, but the door was locked. He turned around and looked over the large wooden partition that delineated the secretarial station. Behind it he could see a thin, elderly woman working on the computer while she talked on the phone. "Gloria?" he asked, somewhat hesitantly.

She looked up at him from beneath the bifocals resting on her nose. Her face was a swirl of wrinkles, no doubt caused by the years she had spent chain-smoking. Her dark gray hair was straight and stringy, and her eyelids heavy with age. "Yes?" she said, still at a loss to recognize the young man or his voice.

"I'm Michael . . . Michael Elliot."

Gloria's eyes widened, and a smile came over her tobacco-stained teeth. None of her physical shortcomings mattered to him in the slightest. This worn-out woman in front of him was a saint. She had been the only thing that had saved his job. If she hadn't found the package that day and coordinated the filing, he would've been spending the rest of his life selling hot dogs at Dodger Stadium or something equally unpleasant. Gloria quickly hung up the phone and walked over to him. He wasn't sure why, but he set down his bags and hugged her. "Have they found Jonathan?" he said, before letting go.

She shook her head, and a tear began to fall down her cheek. She quickly wiped it away. "Look at me, will you. This whole thing is making a mess of me."

Michael didn't know what to say. Partners often forged strong alliances with their secretaries and were closer to them than to anyone else at the firm. It was no secret that a good secretary could make your career and a bad one could break it. The smart associates at Davis & White quickly realized this fact and even understood that a talented secretary had more power than they did. The law schools were filled with wet-behind-the-ears kids who were more than willing to work for the large New York sweatshops, but a bright and competent secretary in this city was a rarity. "Richard Montague asked me to come to New York," he said. "In light of Jonathan's disappearance, the firm wants me to go through his open matters to avoid any other mistakes like the one you saved us from making in the Global Network merger."

Gloria nodded. After thirty years with the firm, she was probably more familiar with this necessity than he was.

"They want me to work out of Jonathan's office until he comes back, if that's okay with you."

Gloria smiled. "What can I do to help?" she asked.

Michael paused. "Well, for starters you can bring me the files for any open matters that Jonathan was working on before his disappearance. Oh, and I'll need a key to his office."

"It's locked?" she asked, frowning. "That's strange; he normally kept it open." Gloria walked back around to her desk and opened the top left-hand drawer. "Here's a spare that I keep for emergencies," she said, handing him the key. "You can use it until Jonathan comes back. I'll call down now and get you a temporary access card for the building. It will let you get in after hours and let you access the internal stairwell. If there's anything else you need, just shout. I'll be right out here."

Michael thanked her and took the key. As he opened the thick wooden door and set down his bags, a strong sense of trepidation overcame him. Why had Jonathan Gage disappeared? For some reason, Michael hadn't given much thought to the possible reasons behind the young partner's disappearance, but now, alone in Gage's office, it was all he could think about. His own worries earlier that morning seemed insignificant by comparison.

Michael moved behind Gage's desk and sat down in his black leather chair. Except for its size it didn't look any different from his own office. There were the typical documents strewn over the desk, and a large leather day planner next to the phone. There was even a pad of the firm's time sheets, on which all attorneys were required to keep track of their billable hours in ten-minute intervals. The only real difference from Michael's own desk was the front second drawer. On it, he could see the splinter marks from where Gloria had jimmied open the lock. He smiled. Thank God for that woman, he thought again.

He turned his attention back to the top of the desk, and his eyes became transfixed on an antique silver picture frame resting on the left-hand corner. There, where he expected to see a picture of Gage's family, was a square of dull gray matting.

Someone must have taken the picture out. That was strange. Or maybe the frame had been a gift and he had never gotten a picture for it.

None of this really mattered much, Michael thought. He realized he knew very little about the young partner outside his professional life. Sure, Michael had worked with him on a number of transactions, but he had never even known if Gage had children. Michael shrugged and turned his attention back to the work in front of him. Sifting through the papers on the desk, he hoped he would find clues to what the young partner had been working on, but surprisingly most of the papers were administrative, firm-wide billing and expense reports, continuing education materials, and mail from the New York Bar Association.

Then he remembered the day planner, and he began to flip through the pages. There was one page for each day of the week. He felt the urge to check Thursday, the day of the Global Network merger. Below the date was a notation in big block letters reminding Gage to file the papers first thing in the morning. Michael then began to look through the subsequent pages, hoping there would be indications of any other filings that needed to be made or matters that needed to be handled. But there were no notations until he got to the coming Thursday. There he saw a strange item: *"Meeting with Robert Adams— Securities and Exchange Commission."* No client was identified. Michael reached over to the intercom and pressed the button.

"Yes, Michael. . . ."

"Gloria, do you know why Jonathan was meeting with the SEC next Thursday?"

The secretary paused. "I don't have that on my calendar. I'm not really sure. . . ."

Michael fell silent. He knew he needed to come up with a better way to figure out what Jonathan Gage was working on. Searching through the man's office and personal effects like some kind of grave robber was not going to get him anywhere. Then he realized that the answer was sitting right in front of him. The time sheets. All he needed to do was get a printout of

Gage's time sheets for the last month, then he would have a detailed chronology of everything he had been working on. "Gloria, I'd like you to do me another favor. Can you get me
Jonathan's time sheets for the last month? I want to see every
matter he billed time to. Also circulate a memo to all the attorneys in the office. Tell them to notify me immediately if they
were working on a matter with Jonathan Gage that was active.
Maybe someone will know what the meeting is for next week."

Michael spent the better part of the afternoon going through
the last month of Gage's time sheets, twenty-eight pages, each
representing a day of Gage's life. Somehow he couldn't help
but reflect that the last six years of his own life were similarly
represented. How could these scrawlings equate with the sacrifices that he had made? Somewhere in the bowels of the firm's
records center were notations of time spent on matters that he
could no longer remember, each of which had seemed so important when he was working on it. Michael shook his head and
turned his attention back to his notes.

From his review of the time entries, Michael had figured out
that over the last month Gage had worked on only three matters, all of which he knew had been completed. He had gone
over the files for each of these matters, but none of them had
involved the SEC. Each path Michael had taken to investigate
the strange entry in Gage's day planner seemed to lead to a
dead end. Maybe he was just being paranoid, he thought. For
all he knew, Robert Adams was merely a law school friend of
Gage who worked for the SEC. The two were probably just
planning lunch together to catch up. If this really had been
something important, Gage would have spent time preparing
for the meeting and even made a file for it. Surely there would
have been some kind of paper trail. Just when Michael was
about to give up, however, a strange thought overcame him.
What if the time sheets didn't reflect every detail of Gage's life.
What if there was something so confidential or sensitive that he
didn't want anyone else to know he was working on it?

Michael had often heard rumors about attorneys not billing
time to a matter because they didn't want their "fingerprints"

on the file. This usually meant it was a transaction that had gone bad and would end up in litigation. Whenever a client was sued over a deal, the other side's lawyer would get the firm's billing statements in discovery and find out which attorneys had worked on the matter. Once the attorneys were identified, they were subpoenaed as witnesses and forced to spend hours answering questions thrown at them by some pit-bull litigator trying to direct the blame and second-guess everything they did. Although Michael had never been in such a situation, he had heard enough horror stories to know that billing small amounts of time to a troubled deal was to be avoided at all costs.

But even if Gage hadn't billed time to a particular matter he was working on, he would have been required to open a new client account and provide the firm with certain basic information so they could run a conflicts check. Furthermore, there would likely have been at least some expense charges incurred. Michael quickly walked out of the office. "Gloria," he said, leaning over the wall of her station. "Did Jonathan open any new matters over the past couple months that were inactive?"

She began shuffling through the three-ring binders behind her desk that contained Jonathan Gage's client accounts. "No . . . but I remember there was a new matter that he opened up in June," she said, quickly flipping through the pages. "Here it is. On June fifteenth he opened a new client account, but nothing ever came of it."

"What was the name of the client?" Michael asked.

Gloria's fingers moved quickly over the page. "Yeah, now I remember. It was for Trinity Corporation."

Michael had never heard of them. For a moment he hovered over her desk, pondering whether to go any further. He knew he was reaching for straws, but he also knew if he left it unexplored it would haunt him. Something inside told him to go further. "Gloria, can you get me whatever we have in the files on Trinity Corporation? It's probably nothing, but I should take a look at it anyway."

Chapter 13

The decision to leave the Homicide Division of the New York Police Department hadn't been an easy one for Nico. He'd spent six years of his life with the unit and had been elevated two pay grades in the process. Although the money still hadn't been anything to write home about, it was enough for him to afford a small studio apartment on the edge of Hell's Kitchen. The old brick building was next to a home for unwed mothers, which tended to scare off most of the young professionals who were beginning to regentrify the area and kept the rent affordable. Most important to Nico was the fact that the building had a storage area deep in the basement where he could practice his saxophone. In this small concrete room, fifteen feet below street level, he could play as loud and as long as he wanted, knowing that the only people who could hear him were the tenants washing their clothes in the adjacent laundry room.

For the most part Nico hadn't minded the life of a bachelor, eating his meals out of paper bags and cardboard cartons and always running out of clean clothes by the end of the week. All this changed, however, when he met Kristina. She was in her residency at Columbia at the time and had stopped by the Blue Note after work with a couple of her friends. Nico was sitting in with the band that night and couldn't help but notice her. She was a tall and dark Latin woman, with a thick black mane of hair and deep ebony eyes that remained fixed on him as he played. Nico could barely concentrate on the music as he watched her body sway back and forth. At the break he sat down next to her and bought her a drink. Two years later they were married.

Although Nico enjoyed the fast-paced life of being a homicide detective, after he married Kristina he knew it was time for a change. He had seen firsthand the toll the job took on the other detectives' lives. Most of them were either divorced or on their second marriages, and he was determined not to suffer a similar fate. Above everything else Nico was a realist. He knew that it would be hard enough with one spouse working, not to mention both of them. To make matters worse, Kristina put in even longer hours than he did. If one of them didn't give in, sooner or later their marriage would suffer.

So when the next administrative assignment became available, Nico took it. It was chief liaison officer in charge of coordinating joint investigations between federal agencies and the NYPD. At the time there was still a deep-seated resentment in the department toward the Feds, primarily directed at the FBI. The detectives continually complained that the FBI agents were nothing more than glory seekers who took over their investigations, often excluding the locals completely or giving them only demeaning tasks. It was not surprising to Nico that there was little competition for the job with the Special Investigative Unit, not that he really cared. This job was his passport to a more stable nine-to-five life and the chance for a successful marriage.

As in any new job, bad parts came with the good. Most of his time was spent massaging officers' bruised egos or unruffling feathers, both within the NYPD and among the agencies they were working with. This was more tedious and time-consuming than anything else. The one thing Nico missed most, however, was having his own active investigations. Almost everything interesting that came into the SIU was assigned to detectives in the field. The only cases he handled directly anymore fell into two categories. The first were extremely sensitive and embarrassing investigations that had to be kept out of the media. These typically involved either politicians or foreign dignitaries caught with drugs or with male or female prostitutes. One time Nico had interceded in the investigation of the Japanese ambassador's son, who had gotten out of hand at a bondage club called Hellfire and sodomized one of the working girls while she was chained to a wall. Apparently this was against the club's rules—not that the young man had understood this, given the language barrier. Second, Nico handled routine matters that most of the other detectives didn't want to bother with. They usually involved petty crimes or favors for someone who had political clout. Following up on the missing-persons report for Jonathan Gage fell into this category.

After his meeting with Richard Montague, Nico had spent the morning following up on investigations he had delegated to other detectives. By the time he made it back to the station, it was well past lunchtime. He picked up a chicken pita and diet Coke from the street vendor outside the building and brought it to his desk. As soon as he set his food down, he noticed the computer printout lying on his chair. It was the list of charges from Jonathan Gage's American Express card that he had ordered the night before.

He began to read over the printout. He could tell the credit card had been used a number of times since Gage's disappearance. Under normal circumstances this would have been a good sign, but as Nico's eyes made their way down the page, a coldness began to pervade his body. "Damn it," he said. He had hoped to see charges for a plane ticket, a hotel, a restaurant, maybe even a bar that Gage had visited on a business trip out of town, something that might have innocently explained his disappearance. Instead the list contained charges for cameras and stereo equipment made at several electronics stores in Brooklyn Heights.

From this pattern, Nico knew the card had been stolen. He reached for the phone and dialed the number for the AmEx credit card fraud division. After only one ring a young man's voice came over the line. "American Express, how can I help you?"

"Hello, my name is Nico Fiori. I'm a detective with the New

York Police Department. I'm following up on a report you forwarded to my office earlier this morning. It's regarding a Mr. Jonathan Gage." Nico gave the card number and waited as the man pulled up the activity report on his computer.

"Yes, I see it here. What can I do for you?"

"Well, I wanted to know if you can check the signatures for the last three charges to make sure it's Jonathan Gage. You know, match them against the signatures you have for him in your files."

The young man hesitated. "Well, we could do that, but it normally takes a few days for us to get the original drafts back from the stores where the purchases were made. Is there something wrong? I could put a hold on the credit card if you think it's been stolen."

Nico hesitated. He knew that this would just spook whoever was using the card; then he might never find the suspect. He needed a way to track the thief down fast. "Let me ask you another question. Have there been any charges on the card since this morning?"

There was a moment of silence as the representative looked over the computer screen. "As a matter of fact there was," he said. "Someone used that card less than an hour ago at Universal City, an electronics store in Brooklyn Heights. The purchase was for seven hundred and eighty-nine dollars."

Nico took down the address of the store and told the young man not to cancel the card. Instead, he gave the representative his cell phone number and told the man to call him immediately if the card was used again. Nico then made a quick call to Frank Tortola, a detective in the Thirty-sixth Precinct in Brooklyn with whom he had worked a number of times before. Frankie, as he was known around the precinct, was a short olive-skinned man with a body as round as a fifty-gallon drum. A cheap cigar was never far from his mouth, and he would chew on it relentlessly until the end became dark from his spit. Although Frankie was pushing sixty, he knew more about Brooklyn than anyone Nico had ever met. "Frankie, it's Nico Fiori, downtown."

"If it isn't pretty-boy Nico. Hey, guys, I got Nick the Flower on the phone." Nico could hear the catcalls in the background. Given that Frankie was Sicilian, it wasn't surprising that he called everyone by a nickname, at least the people he liked. There was Tommy "the Tuna" Woods, who had gotten his name because his lips turned bluish whenever it got cold, and Jimmy "Shakes" McDonnell, who had a habit of shaking his dick a little too long at the urinal. When Frankie gave someone a nickname, it stuck like flypaper.

"So you calling up to tell us about another one of your gigs in Brooklyn?"

Nico laughed. "No, I wish I was," he said. "Look, I got a favor to ask."

Frankie became serious. "Sure, what you got?"

Nico quickly explained the situation and asked the detective to go to the electronics store with a couple of plainclothes officers. Whoever was using the card might still be in the area, he told him, and Nico didn't want to scare them off.

Five minutes later Nico was weaving his way through dense crosstown traffic to the bridge. By the time he made it to the store in Brooklyn Heights, it was a quarter past four and Frankie was standing in front of the building finishing a cigar. As Nico pulled up he flicked what was left of it into the gutter, then replaced it with an unlit cigar from his pocket, which he began to chew on.

"I already talked with the store manager," Frankie said, leaning down into the open window of Nico's car.

"Did you get a description?"

"I got better," Frankie said, pulling a videocassette out of his jacket. "The store has a camera behind the register. The manager already identified them in the tape, and one of the officers knew who they were. It's two local kids. Both of them live in the same building in Brooklyn Heights."

Nico shook his head. "Look, I can't go into all the details now, but we better go in with a full team as soon as possible. I'll have the warrant issued in less than an hour."

•   •   •

The tenants from the old apartment building on Battery Street were gathered on the sidewalk watching as Nico and the other police officers took the two kids out the front. With their hands pulled tightly behind their backs and their faces white as bedsheets, they were pushed past the crowd to the row of parked police cars. Upon recognizing one of the suspects, a man began to move forward and shout at Nico. "Come on, why don't you guys pick on somebody your own size? These are good kids. Don't you have anything better to do?" A uniformed officer next to Nico stretched out his baton and used it like a battering ram to push the man back toward the street. "Don't tell them anything, Jimmy," the man yelled. "Don't tell them anything till you get a lawyer."

Nico's thoughts were overtaken by the voices in the crowd, which were becoming louder. Trying his best to ignore them, he pushed his way forward with the first suspect and handed him off to a rather angry-looking officer standing in front of an open police car. The officer, who was as big and thick as a lineman, palmed the kid's head, then forced him into the backseat. Nico turned around and yelled at another uniformed officer behind him. "Put the other kid in a separate car and take them both down to the Thirty-sixth Precinct. Make sure you book them separately and put them in different interrogation rooms. I don't want them talking to each other under any circumstances."

While the second suspect was being loaded into the other police car, Nico could hear Frankie Tortola behind him trying to disperse the crowd. "The show's over . . . it's time to go back to your apartments." The crowd just ignored him and, after realizing the futility of his actions, Frankie turned around and walked over to the blue Crown Victoria where Nico was waiting for him. As the two drove away the tenants were still yelling obscenities and making New York's finest hand gestures. In the rearview mirror Nico could see the crowd become smaller and smaller, and he breathed a sigh of relief. "You know, people wonder why cops in this city are jaded," he said, shaking his head.

Frankie, however, didn't hear a word. He was already on the radio, calling ahead to the station to get the criminal records on each suspect. What he heard back, however, was surprising. The older suspect, Jimmy Dolan, was seventeen years old and didn't have a criminal record. The younger one, Anthony Scalini, who was barely sixteen, had only one prior conviction, for breaking into a car and stealing a radio two years ago. The idea that either of these kids would have rolled Jonathan Gage for his wallet seemed absurd.

When the detectives arrived at the station, they agreed that Nico would interrogate the older kid and Frankie the younger one. Nico checked his gun in the lockbox—not that he was particularly concerned that the boy would disarm him, but rules were rules. The guard then opened the door to the interrogation room. Nico entered and heard the door being locked behind him. It was just the two of them now, in a windowless ten-by-ten room. Before Nico could sit down at the table, the kid was on his feet. "I want to talk to a lawyer," he said, a smug expression on his face. "I know my rights. I have the right to an attorney, that's the Eighth Amendment."

Nico shrugged. "Yeah, close enough, kid," he said, pulling out the chair and taking a seat. "You know, it really doesn't matter. I don't want to ask you any questions anyway. I just wanted to show you something. You see this?" he said, holding up a black videocassette. "It's a tape made by a hidden surveillance camera above the cash register at Universal City, the electronics store you and your buddy visited earlier this afternoon. It shows you two clear as day using Jonathan Gage's stolen credit card and forging his signature. Now you can go call your lawyer if you want. It doesn't matter to me one way or the other. Right now I have a team of detectives going to the other three stores you and Anthony hit up. We're taking statements and will probably bring down a few people to identify you two in a lineup. The way I see it, you don't have to tell me anything. The videotape is going to be all the jury needs. I don't care if your lawyer is Johnnie Cochran, there isn't any way in hell you're getting out of this. I can play the tape back for you if you don't believe me."

The kid sat nervously back down, pulling his fingers through his curly blond hair. He wouldn't even look up from the table, and Nico continued. "Now your buddy, he's sixteen. He has one prior, but he'll probably go to juvenile. By the time your case goes to trial, you'll be eighteen. With mandatory sentencing guidelines, the judge will have to send you to prison. You'll be in there with the murderers and the rapists. I'm telling you something, you're a braver man than I am. If I were in your shoes right now, I'd be scared as hell."

Nico paused and took a sip from the can of diet Coke he had brought with him. Still there was no reaction, and he changed strategy. "You know, if you're expecting me to do this whole Sipowicz bad-cop routine, you got the wrong guy. That's Frankie, he's down the hall talking to your friend. That's not my style." He set down the soda and stared at the boy. "The difference between him and me is that I don't give a damn about the stolen credit cards. The only thing I care about is Jonathan Gage, the guy whose credit cards you took. He has a wife and two kids waiting for him at home. Any minute now they're expecting their dad to come walking in the door. None of them is going to get a minute of peace until they know what happened. All I want to do is put an end to their uncertainty. So I'm going to ask you just one question. . . . Did you kill him?"

The kid rose from the table shaking his head. "I didn't kill anyone," he shouted. "What in the fuck are you talking about?"

When a suspect broke down, he usually broke down hard. The tears were falling uncontrollably from the boy's face, and his whole body was trembling. It was like watching a wild animal being put in a cage for the first time. "How did you get the credit cards?" Nico asked.

"We found them. I swear, we just found them."

Nico's expression seemed doubtful. "Come on, you can do better than that."

"I swear to God, Anthony and I found them. We were on the Brooklyn Bridge Wednesday night, and we found a briefcase and a pile of clothes just lying there. There was a watch and ring on top. We hawked them both down at a pawnshop on Newburry Street," he blurted out.

"What about the credit cards?"

The boy wiped the tears from his eyes. "There was a wallet inside one of the suit pockets with some cash and credit cards inside. We figured the guy must have killed himself and wasn't going to miss them. I swear to God, we didn't kill him. I'm telling you the truth."

Nico felt sick to his stomach. For the next thirty minutes he went over the kid's story again and again, trying to catch him in a lie, but Jimmy Dolan wouldn't waiver. Finally Nico left the room. Frankie was outside waiting for him. The two compared notes, looking for inconsistencies, but both kids' stories were identical. "Do you really think either of these kids could have killed him?" Nico asked.

Frankie shook his head. "No way in hell," he responded. "Neither one has any history of violence. I'm telling you, these kids don't have the balls to pull something like this—"

Before he could finish, a uniformed officer interrupted them. "I've got two sets of irate parents outside. They want to know what in the hell is going on. They say they're going to call a lawyer if they don't see their kids."

The old detective just waved the officer off. "You think we got a jumper?" he asked.

Nico paused. "Do me a favor and send two uniformed officers to the bridge tonight to look for any evidence that corroborates their story. Maybe the clothing is still there. Also have them notify the Harbor Patrol. They can start searching the area, and I'll follow up with the coroner in the morning to see if they found a floater matching this guy's description."

Frankie nodded. "What do you want me to do with the kids?"

Nico shrugged. "Just show the parents the videotape; that'll change their attitude. Also see if you can get written statements from each of them; we'll take it from there. If they cooperate and their story checks out, the district attorney may be willing to cut a deal."

On the drive back to Manhattan, Nico used his cell phone to check his voice mail. There were two messages, both from Jonathan Gage's wife asking if he had any additional information. Nico struggled with the thought of calling her, but he knew she was probably asleep by now or at least trying to sleep. Besides, what would he tell her? He decided to wait until after he talked with the Harbor Patrol and the morgue in the morning. It always seemed easier delivering bad news in the daytime.

Chapter 14

Sunday, December 3

It was just after midnight, and the rain had finally stopped falling. Outside the revolving doors of the Chase Manhattan Bank Building, the streets of lower Manhattan shined like polished black onyx, and the lights from the storefronts reflected off the slick wet surface in a kaleidoscope of colors. Michael breathed deeply and felt the cold air fill his lungs. It was crisp and clean in the way it could be only after a storm had washed away all of the city's impurities. In front of him, the swishing sound of cabs could be heard passing on the wet concrete, and for a moment he thought about hailing one down but quickly decided against it. He had spent the entire weekend locked in the confines of Gage's office searching through boxes of documents until his eyes felt like they were going to explode. The walk would do him good, he thought.

As he made his way down William Street, however, his mind quickly began to wander. At first he thought about his friend Monehan and wondered what he would do with his life now that the firm had let him go. Then his thoughts drifted back to Raven as he debated over and over again whether the devious partner was manipulating him in the same way he had Monehan. Finally, when he had exhausted both subjects without any resolution, his mind went back to Karen. In the end it always came back to her, the smooth dark skin and soft full lips. He could still remember the way her body felt pressed against his and how the smell of her perfume lingered long after she was gone.

Although the firm frowned upon office relationships, she was well worth the risk. They would just have to be careful, Michael thought. As much as he had wanted to call her on Friday, in an abundance of caution he had decided against it. After all, Karen's secretary might have answered the line and put two and two together. Before he knew it speculation of their involvement would be whispered through the hallways. Besides, he didn't want to appear needy or overanxious. But it had been two days and he did have another reason to call her. He had left his briefcase at her apartment, and the last time they spoke he had completely forgotten to mention it. He would call her at home when he got back to the hotel. It was Sunday and still early on the West Coast. She was probably getting ready for bed.

Michael quickened his pace, but as he reached the next intersection, he couldn't help but stop. The enormous buildings lining either side of Wall Street made it a virtual canyon. To the east, he could see the waterfront. To the west, the spires of a large Gothic church rose solemnly into the darkness. Although Michael didn't know the name of the church, even if he had he would have probably dismissed it as mere coincidence. But there was no coincidence. This Episcopal church had been Jonathan Gage's sanctuary. It had been here in a dark wooden pew just inside the old bronze doors that the missing partner had prayed for his soul and asked God for forgiveness a thousand times. In the heart of Wall Street, one would have figured that Trinity Church would have been filled with young investment bankers and lawyers repenting their sins, but most hours of the day the church was as barren and empty as it was now.

Feeling the bite of the cold night air, Michael pulled the collar of his jacket shut and began to walk. Just past the Gothic church was an old graveyard filled with thick granite headstones, and Michael found himself walking in that direction, as if drawn there by some kind of unnatural force. Lower Manhattan was a strange place for a graveyard. In a city so full of life, it seemed out of place here. Two acres of prime real estate in the center of the financial district were lost on the dead.

However, before he could give it any further thought, an unsettling feeling suddenly came over him. It was as if someone was watching him, their eyes burning a hole in the back of his head. He quickly turned around, half expecting to feel the force of a lead pipe or some other blunt object come down upon him, but the streets were empty. There was no one else there besides him, but he couldn't help but feel that he wasn't alone. He was almost sure of it. Michael started to walk faster, then broke into a run. His heart began to pound erratically, and cold sweat fell rapidly down his forehead. He had to get out of there. Before he knew it he was running full throttle, his arms and legs pulling wildly at the seams of his suit.

Just as he reached the intersection, he saw a cab quickly passing by. He frantically shouted and waved his arms wildly. The yellow LTD screeched to a halt barely five feet in front of him, and Michael scrambled for the door.

"Where you going?" the driver asked in a thick Russian accent.

"Midtown . . . the RIHGA Royal," Michael said, closing the door behind him.

The cabdriver nodded and pulled into traffic. As Michael turned back, he could see the graveyard passing slowly through the window. He studied it one more time but again saw nothing. He was being paranoid, he thought. The city was getting to him. But just as he was about to look away, something on the far side of the street caught his attention. He could see the outline of a man hidden in the shadows. He was tall and thin, and wore a navy overcoat with thin black leather gloves. Michael tried to make out his face, but it was veiled in the darkness. A pit immediately formed in the base of his gut. Perhaps the man was a mugger. Crime in New York City had dropped off significantly in the last few years, but such things were still not uncommon. But the man was far too well dressed to be some kind of street thug. It was probably just someone walking home, he thought. That must be it.

"Is that on West Fifty-fourth?" the cabdriver asked.

Michael's attention was still back on the graveyard. "I'm sorry, what was that?"

"The RIHGA Royal, it's on Fifty-fourth, right?"

"Yes," Michael said, watching the church and the graveyard fade from his sight.

Midtown Manhattan was about twenty minutes away, and the farther Michael got from the financial district, the more relaxed he became. The streets of Tribeca, SoHo, and Greenwich Village soon passed before him as they made their way up West Broadway. When attorneys at the firm were in New York on business, they usually stayed at the Plaza and billed it to their clients, who rarely seemed to scrutinize the expenses. Michael, however, was on firm business, so there would be no fat client picking up his tab. Rather, he could expect the accounting department to crawl up his ass shortly after he submitted his expense report and scrutinize each and every charge like a forensic accountant. As a result he had made a reservation at the RIHGA, where the firm had a corporate rate. For the most part, Michael didn't really care. The RIHGA had recently been remodeled and was far nicer than any hotel he had stayed in before joining the firm. Besides, he always felt pretentious staying at hotels like the Plaza. These old-world establishments made him feel like a kid playing dress-up. He was much better off at a hotel where he wasn't constantly being sized up by every employee and guest. The RIHGA was perfect for him with its understated limestone lobby and nonjudgmental staff.

When Michael got to his room, he took off his jacket and looked at the phone, expecting to see the message light blinking. He was confident Raven would have called by now, just to make sure Michael hadn't fucked anything up. Surprisingly, however, there were no messages. He looked down at his watch. It was almost twelve-thirty, and he still hadn't eaten dinner. He ordered an eighteen-dollar cheeseburger from room service and thought briefly about the firm's accountants writhing in agony when they saw the bill. Screw it, he thought. He then went over to the minibar and took a quick inventory. Five dollars for an airplane bottle of Maker's Mark and three dollars for a can of soda water was extortion, but there were no alternatives. Twisting the cap off, he poured himself a bourbon and soda. He then took the glass with him into the bathroom.

Taking a large sip, he undid his tie and looked at his reflection in the mirror. The thick bluish black stubble was beginning to show on his face, and he looked more tired than usual. He reached over and turned on the faucet. After waiting for the water to warm, he dampened a washcloth and drew it across his face. The water made his forehead feel hot, or maybe it was the alcohol. He looked up at his reflection in the mirror one more time, hoping his appearance had improved. It hadn't. Although his body was still thin and muscular, he could see slight handles beginning to form around his waist, and his skin didn't look as taut as it had before. These were the scars of spending sixteen hours a day riding a desk, he thought. His eyes then drifted down to his hand, and when he got to the missing finger he stopped.

Michael remembered when he was four and his grandmother took him to the park by their house to play. He was so young back then that he didn't even realize he was different from the other kids. The pretty girl he was playing with that day wasn't much older than he was. She was chasing him around the monkey bars, and the two were laughing together. Then all of a sudden she turned pale as a ghost and began to cry uncontrollably. Her mother quickly ran over to her, asking what was wrong. "I want to go," she kept crying. "I want to go, Mommy." The mother didn't understand; then she saw Michael's hand. Trying to be polite, she quickly looked away and pretended not to notice. "I'm sorry," she explained to Michael's grandmother as she picked the girl up. "She must just be tired." But as the girl's mother carried her away, Michael could hear her crying. "He lost his finger, Mommy . . . he lost his finger in the sandbox."

Michael shrugged and turned off the faucet. If the missing finger had bothered Karen, she sure as hell hadn't shown it. After they had made love, she had even held his hand and wrapped her fingers around his. When he tried to pull it away, she simply kissed his hand and rested her head back against his chest. There was never any judgment or pity in her eyes.

Walking back into the room, Michael took a seat behind the desk and took the firm directory from his briefcase. The small green book contained home phone numbers and addresses for every attorney at the firm. "Karen Bauer . . . Karen Bauer . . . Karen Bauer . . . ," he repeated to himself as he drew his finger down the list of names until finally reaching hers. She should be home by now, he thought. It was almost ten in Los Angeles. Besides, he desperately wanted to talk with her. He would start off by apologizing for leaving his briefcase at her apartment. He would then confess how much he had thought about her today and ask to see her again first thing when he got back.

Michael quickly dialed the number and waited as the phone rang and rang. She must still be at work, he thought. Just when he was about to hang up, he heard her drawn voice come over the line. "Hello. . . ."

"Karen," Michael said. "I didn't wake you up, did I?"

"Who is this?"

"It's Michael," he said, smiling. For a moment he thought about her soft brown hair protruding from the sheets when he left. She was probably in bed early, getting sleep. "I'm sorry for calling this late. You see, I forgot to ask you about—"

Before he could say another word, he heard a man's voice far in the background. "Karen, who is that?" The voice sounded familiar, but she quickly covered the receiver with her hand. "I can't talk now," she whispered.

Michael didn't know what to say. He just sat there with the phone dangling in his hand unable to move.

"Look, I'm sorry. I'll call you tomorrow."

The bedroom was dark, save only for a sliver of light coming in from the bathroom. Karen quietly set down the phone. She could still smell his cigarettes in the room. He always had to smoke after they had sex, leaning his head back on the pillow like he had just run a marathon. It was never very long before he became hard again. He would then begin to kiss her. As he pressed his lips against hers, she would feel the heat of his mouth and the bitter taste of tobacco. There was something in the way he fucked her that made her feel cheap and dirty. He would grab her head and push it down onto him. She would then have to work him until he became harder. Then he would roll her over onto her stomach and ride her from behind, pounding relentlessly at her. He would grunt and thrust and grunt and thrust, until finally he would collapse onto her back. The whole process disgusted her. She no longer could remember why she slept with him in the first place.

The light from the bathroom grew brighter as Peter Raven opened the door. She could see him standing in the bedroom with one of her towels wrapped around his waist, a cigarette hanging loosely from his mouth, and a glass of whiskey in his hand. "Who was that?" he asked again with mild curiosity.

"None of your business," she said defensively. She was upright on the bed now and running her fingers through her hair.

Raven shrugged, then walked over to her and grabbed her by the jaw. "I asked who was it?"

His fingers were gripping her painfully. "Quit it," she shouted. "It's just one of the junior associates I have working for me. That's all. He's finishing a brief I have to file first thing next week."

Raven paused while he studied her expression. She was probably lying, but he really didn't care. After a moment, he let go. "What do you say we go again?" he responded, undoing the towel and letting it fall to the floor.

Karen sighed.

The middle-aged partner had become much more interested in sex last year after discovering Viagra. Now all he wanted to do was fuck. Half an hour from now he would be in his car, driving back to his pathetic wife and his two children who hated him. She had spent too much of her life with men who reminded her of her father, the same slicked-back hair, arrogant demeanor, and penchant for cigarettes and alcohol. The whole thing was pathetic. Her therapist told her it had something to do with a lonely childhood and a powerful father who was never around. As a result, she sought out older men, trying to find the father she never really had. Something like that, the therapist explained.

Poor Michael, she thought. How he had gotten involved with a woman like her was beyond her. "I can't do this anymore," she said, standing up and turning on the light. "You should go home."

Raven sneered in disbelief, but the look in her eyes convinced him that she wasn't kidding. "Suit yourself," he said, picking up his clothes. "You'll change your mind."

Chapter 15

By the time Nico made it into the police station Monday morning, it was already nine and there was another note waiting for him. It was from Mrs. Gage and had come in an hour ago. Nico picked up the message and placed it on top of the papers in his in box. After looking quickly through his Rolodex, he dialed the number for the New York County Medical Examiner's Office and asked for the duty officer. He was put on hold while they tried to locate him. After a few minutes the officer finally picked up.

"Hello, it's Nico Fiori with the NYPD. I'm wondering whether you recovered a body in the river over the last few days, a male Caucasian in his mid to late thirties. We think he jumped off the Brooklyn Bridge earlier last week."

The officer shuffled through his log sheets, but nothing matched the description. "Sometimes it takes time for the body to surface when the water is this cold, if it surfaces at all," the officer explained.

Nico gave the man the number for his cell phone and told him to call immediately if they found anything. Then he picked up Mrs. Gage's message and stared at it. He hated this part of his job more than anything, but there was no use putting it off. The passage of time wasn't going to make it any easier. He began to dial her number, but just before the phone rang he hung up. This wasn't the kind of news to give over the phone, he thought. He should go to her home and update her in person. She deserved at least that.

On the drive to Brooklyn Heights, however, Nico got a call from the duty officer. "Harbor Patrol just found a floater this morning, a male approximately thirty-five years old. The body didn't have any clothing. From what the Harbor Patrol told me, it looks like he'd been in the water for a number of days. The body's en route now."

Nico paused. "I'll be down immediately," he said, turning his car around.

The hallway on the second floor of the county morgue had the kind of fluorescent lighting one associated with only the most unpleasant of places. These were usually basements of tenement apartment buildings, underground parking garages, sterile hospital waiting rooms, and, on rare occasions like this, the autopsy facilities of the medical examiner. It had been over a year since Nico had been here, but the passage of time had done little to change the experience. As he moved closer to the large double doors, he could catch the familiar scent of formaldehyde, and his eyes and nostrils began to burn. Each time was the same, Nico thought. He took one last breath and stepped onto the rubber floor mat, causing the electric doors to swing open automatically. Inside a row of six stainless-steel tables were stretched out evenly across the floor, each with a coiled pink water hose, a sink, a vacuum drainage system, and a suspended scale. Only two of the tables were being utilized.

"Dr. Martinez?" Nico shouted, but there wasn't a response. "Excuse me . . . Dr. Martinez," he repeated, louder this time, until the examiner closest to the door raised his hand and motioned for Nico to come in. As Nico started to walk forward, he was again overcome by the acidic smell permeating the room. It was stronger this time, and the pain of nausea ripped through his body. He wrestled in his pocket for something to cover his nose, but it was empty. As if sensing Nico's discomfort, the examiner shouted over to him. "Get a mask out of the cabinet behind you."

Nico nodded and within moments was placing a gauze mask over his face. After finally getting it into position, he breathed deeply until the nausea passed. As he regained his composure, the examiner interrupted him. "Detective Tortola called just before you got here. He wanted me to tell you that they found a man's suit in a rain gutter on the far side of the Brooklyn Bridge. It had been run over and was torn up, but he said it matches the description of the suit Mrs. Gage said her husband was wearing the night he disappeared."

The examiner's words numbed Nico. It was time to bring the investigation to an end, he thought. He could see the black nylon sheet pulled away from the body, and he moved forward until he was standing at the edge of the autopsy table. Looking down into the man's cold blue eyes made Nico remember the first time he saw a dead body. It was when he was eight years old and his grandfather passed away. The priest had told his mother that it was important for him to see the body before it was cremated. So Nico found himself alone in the viewing room of the mortuary, staring down at the kind old man, with his thick gray hair brushed to the side in a way he never wore it when he was living. Nico remembered reaching down and placing his hand upon his grandfather's forehead. It had felt very cold to the touch, like the concrete sidewalk in winter. As he leaned forward, a tear that had welled up in his eye landed on his grandfather's brow, making the old man look like he was crying.

Nico suddenly shuddered. The investigation was getting to him, dredging up memories from his past that were buried deep within him. It was time to get it over with. Taking out the picture Gage's wife had given him, he held it next to the man lying on the steel table. Although the body was badly bloated and swollen, Nico could tell it was Gage.

"Damn it," he whispered under his breath.

The medical examiner's eyes remained fixed on the detective. "So this is the man you're looking for?"

"Yeah . . . it's him," he said. "What have you been able to come up with?"

The examiner looked back down. "Harbor Patrol found the body floating in the water at approximately nine thirty-five this morning. From the bloating, I believe he must have been in the water for some time, at least a few days. I spent the last hour going over the body. There are some bruises on his back and shoulders that must have been caused by the impact when he hit the water."

"How can you tell the fall caused the bruises?" Nico asked, still looking for the possibility of an assault.

The examiner adjusted his glasses. "Well, any impact to the body causes blood vessels to break. The white blood cells rush to the area of impact to contain the damage and throw off protein enzymes in the healing process, which changes the color of the bruise from dark reddish blue to brown, then from brown to a yellowish brown. See here," he said, pointing to the man's chest. "I can differentiate a fresh ecchymosis or bruise from an old one by the color." He pointed out the dark red bruises over Jonathan Gage's shoulders and back.

"How do you know he wasn't knocked unconscious and thrown over the side?"

The doctor shrugged. "Well, the size and location of the bruises rule against violence. Normally you find fresh bruises around a man's throat or skull when he's the victim of an assault. Also you would expect to see scratches or knuckle cuts on the victim's hands. There are none on him," he said, pointing to Gage's pale white hands. "I also checked under the fingernails for blood, skin, or any other foreign matter, but there's nothing. This man was definitely a jumper, and an unlucky one at that."

Nico was puzzled. "What do you mean?"

"Well, the Brooklyn Bridge at its lowest point is still over a hundred feet tall. Hitting the water from that height is like hitting concrete. Most people die instantaneously from the impact. It breaks their neck or their back, rendering them unconscious. This poor guy only broke three of his ribs, and he inhaled water. He must have struggled in the water for some time before he died."

Nico winced. "Do me a favor, don't tell this to his wife when she comes down to identify the body. She doesn't need to know."

The examiner nodded sympathetically.

"Did you find any evidence of alcohol or drugs in his system?"

"I sent blood and liver samples to toxicology for alcohol and drug testing. The results won't be available until Tuesday morning, but I doubt they'll find anything. There weren't any needle marks or other evidence of narcotics use. In addition, his stomach contained no more than thirty-two cc's of gastric fluid, and there wasn't any pill residue. I also made a smear from the gastric contents and examined it under the polarized microscope for refractive crystals. There was nothing. The contents of the duodenum and the intestines confirmed this as well."

Nico sighed. "Well, when you finish the autopsy, prepare the body so that it can be released to the family for burial as soon as possible."

An hour later, Nico found himself driving back to Brooklyn, trying to think of the best way to tell Mrs. Gage that he had finally found her husband.

Chapter 16

Michael sat in Jonathan Gage's office trying to concentrate on the work in front of him, but no matter how hard he tried, his mind kept drifting back to the phone call he had made to Karen's apartment, and the strange man's voice he had heard in the background. Those few words had set off a chain reaction in his mind, bringing with it a river of emotion he hadn't felt before. It was as if someone had taken a spear and impaled him deep in his heart. Then he would try to tell himself that he was just being ridiculous. After all, he didn't own her. They had only spent one night together. But in the end such feeble attempts at reason did little to comfort him. The jealousy had consumed him and there was nothing he could do to stop the bleeding.

The voice kept repeating again and again in his head as he racked his brain trying to place it. It had sounded so damn familiar. Maybe it was Steven White, the forty-two-year-old litigation partner who headed up Karen's department. Sure he was married, but this hadn't stopped him before. Everyone at the firm knew he couldn't keep his pants on. Two years ago he had become involved with one of the firm's secretaries after an office Christmas party. The next day, when he tried to pretend the whole thing had never happened, the woman became so angry that she sent an E-mail to the entire office detailing how the young partner had taken her back to the office that night and screwed her brains out in the fire stairwell. To make matters worse, the secretary had become so obsessed with making the partner's life hell that the firm eventually had to get a restraining order against her. But surely he had learned his lesson. Then again maybe it was someone younger, like the new litigation associate the firm had hired from Harvard. He was young, smart, and handsome, with the added advantage of not being scarred by any missing appendages, at least none that Michael could see.

The high-pitched sound of the intercom distracted him. As he picked up the phone, he could hear Gloria's voice. "Michael, I just got the files on Trinity Corporation from the records center," she said. "There's a problem. . . ."

The anxiety came back to him. What was he doing? He had forgotten all about what the firm had sent him to New York to do. He tightened his fist until it began to hurt, then chastised himself for being so foolish.

"What do you mean there's a problem?"

"Well, for starters, there are no files."

"How can there be no files?"

Gloria paused. "Well, I got the files back this morning, but the folders were empty. Either the files are missing or nothing was ever sent to the records center. I can't tell which. You can come see it for yourself if you don't believe me."

Michael shook his head. "Do you remember Jonathan ever sending any documents for Trinity Corporation down to the records center?"

Gloria hesitated. "Not that I can remember, but it was a while ago. You know he sent so much stuff to the files. I really can't be sure one way or the other."

"What about the billing statements, did he ever send out a bill on this matter?"

Michael listened to Gloria shuffling through the three-ring binders behind her desk. Moments later the wrestling was replaced with the sound of mumbling, as she read to herself. "Oh, here we go. He never sent out a bill for Trinity Corporation. The only thing that's here is a note from him to accounting to write off the expenses. They weren't much, just under five thousand dollars."

Michael shrugged. This was probably merely a personal matter. It wasn't uncommon for a partner to do some work for a friend or a family member and not charge for it. Partners had the prerogative to write off small receivables from time to time without raising any suspicion, but the same question kept going through his mind: Why weren't there any files? It didn't make sense. The tension hung over him like a dark cloud while he contemplated his next move. He knew that just because the bill had been written off didn't mean it wasn't traceable. He could still have the accounting department resurrect the breakdown of expenses from the computer system. At least this way he could get some detail about the work that was done.

"Gloria, have accounting generate another copy of the bill for Trinity Corporation."

"But Jonathan already wrote that bill off," she protested.

"I know that. I didn't say I was going to send it out. I just want to see it."

He was getting ready to go downstairs and get something to eat when the phone stopped him. He picked up the line; her voice paralyzed him. "Michael?" she asked.

At first he didn't know what to say. So many things had been going through his mind. Suddenly he was a deer caught in the headlights of an approaching car. All he could do was stand still, the phone pressed against his ear and his mouth as dry as cotton.

"I got the number from your secretary. I wanted to say I'm sorry," she said. "I should have told you I was involved with someone. I didn't mean for you to find out that way."

He tried to regain his composure. "That's okay," he said. "It was wrong for me to presume that you were . . . I mean . . . we were just together one night."

"No, it wasn't wrong for you to think that," she said, pausing. "Look, it doesn't matter. I'm not seeing him anymore. I should have ended it a long time ago. It was a bad relationship, but that's my cross to bear. I just didn't want you to think the night we spent together didn't mean anything. It wasn't like that. I want to see you when you get back. Maybe there's something we can build on. I'd like to try anyway."

Michael smiled. "I'd like that," he said. "I'd really like that."

Chapter 17

The entire office of Davis & White was stunned that afternoon when the news of Jonathan Gage's death was released. The memorandum distributed by Richard Montague was short and simple:

> *It is with our deepest regret that we inform you that Jonathan Gage was found dead this morning. Jonathan was a friend and respected colleague, and he will be missed greatly. The firm's thoughts and condolences go out to Mrs. Gage and their two children, Christopher and Jennifer. The funeral will be held this Wednesday at 9:00 at the Church of St. Ann in Brooklyn. The office will be closed in observance of this tragedy. All attorneys in the New York office are expected to be present.*

Although the circumstances of Jonathan Gage's death were not identified in Montague's memorandum, it wasn't long before rumors of the young partner's suicide jump from the Brooklyn Bridge echoed through the otherwise quiet hallways. Death always had a sobering effect on those around it, but this was never more evident than when someone willingly took his own life, especially someone as young and successful as Gage. His suicide left behind a thousand questions. Why hadn't there been any warning signs? Why didn't he reach out for someone? What could possibly have motivated him to do this? What about his wife and his children?

As Michael read the simple memorandum over and over

again, a painful realization overcame him. He had spoken to Gage the night before he had committed suicide. Maybe he was even the last person at the firm the despondent man talked to before committing this dreadful act. He had known there was something wrong in the young partner's voice that night, but he had carelessly dismissed it. If only he had talked to Gage, maybe he could have helped him. Before he could continue on, Gloria's frail figure appeared in the doorway. The tears were running down her face, and a white Kleenex was crumpled up tightly in her fist. Before he could say anything, the old woman let out an unnatural wail as if she were wounded, and he rushed over to her. She was bawling uncontrollably, and all Michael could do was hold her in his arms and watch as the black mascara ran down his shirt.

Two days later Michael found himself sitting alone in the hard wooden pew of the Church of St. Ann waiting for Jonathan Gage's funeral service to begin. Although he had heard rumors of the Davis & White death march, he had never seen it himself. It was, however, one of the firm's oldest traditions. Whenever a partner died, the other partners walked into the church lined up in the order that they had been admitted into the partnership, leaving an empty space where the recently deceased partner would have stood. The procession was designed to be a silent reminder to each of the attorneys that the firm was something that transcended any given individual and that even in the face of death the firm continues on. Of all Davis & White's traditions, this one now sickened Michael the most. Seeing it for himself that afternoon made him realize what an egotistical and arrogant display it was, drawing attention away from Gage's widow and children in their time of need and directing it to the firm.

Hadn't this man sacrificed enough? He had spent the last ten years of his life toiling sixteen-hour days in this inferno, and now, even in death, they were taking time away from his family. He couldn't bear to watch it. He began to search the room for someone he recognized. It wasn't surprising that Peter

Raven and the other Los Angeles partners hadn't flown back
for the services; they wouldn't have been expected to take two
days off. Still, it was strange that he recognized so few people.
Sure there was a handful of partners and associates he had met
over the years working on various deals, but there was no one
that he could call a friend or even knew on a personal basis. He
shook his head in despair.

At the front of the church he saw a woman dressed in black
and holding a young boy's hand. Although he hadn't met her
before, Michael guessed it was Jonathan's wife. Even in sorrow
she remained a beautiful woman, with deep brown eyes and
proud features. He could tell she was doing her best to maintain
her composure. The boy next to her was wearing a black suit,
and his curly brown hair rose unevenly off his forehead. He
couldn't have been more than four years old, and the expression on his face haunted Michael. It was as if the boy could tell
something very somber was happening, but clearly he didn't
understand the implications of it all quite yet. It seemed unfair
that death had a greater effect on the living than it had on the
dead. This event would scar the boy for the rest of his life, but
for his father it had been only a brief moment of pain. Michael
exhaled and tried to think of more pleasant things, but to no
avail.

When the death march finally finished and the last partner
sat down, the minister took his place at the podium and began
the eulogy. It seemed ironic to hear a man who knew so little
about Gage talk as if they were close friends. There was really
no one else, however, to speak for the deceased. The partners at
Davis & White never gave eulogies. This was another tradition.
Instead, this man who had met Gage only occasionally after
Sunday services gave a summation of the young partner's life.
The same words permeated his sermon. Gage was a "diligent"
and "hardworking" man who made countless sacrifices for
those around him. He was always willing to "go the extra mile"
for a client, no matter what the cost. His life was tragically cut
short, before he had reached the "prime of life" or "realized the
fruits of his labor."

The same thought kept going through Michael's mind. What was Jonathan Gage's life really about? Was his work all that defined the man? Michael quickly looked over the sanctuary to see if the minister's words were having the same effect on everyone else as they were having on him. Would each attorney return home that night and question his chosen path? Would this be a silent reminder to each of them just how fragile life could be? In the row in front of him, Michael saw a young attorney checking his watch nervously, and a feeling of emptiness overcame him. He realized that ten minutes after the sermon ended the words would be forgotten, and the attorneys would return to checking their voice mail and calling their clients on their cell phones. He should have known better.

At the end of the service, Gage's widow stood at the door of the church thanking people for attending the service. Michael waited as the line of people moved slowly toward her one by one until finally he reached her and shook her hand. "Mrs. Gage, I know you don't know me, but I was an associate who worked with your husband. He was a good man, Mrs. Gage. My condolences." She smiled and moved on to the next person. Michael could hear the partner behind him say virtually the same thing. It was as if even the firm's other partners didn't know who he was.

As he walked out of the church, Michael could feel a soft drizzle beginning to fall. Both sides of Clinton Street were lined with black Lincoln Town Cars and limousines waiting for the partners to leave. He looked up and down the street for a cab, but there were none. The only vehicle that wasn't black was a large white delivery van parked directly opposite the church. It had the best spot on the street, and the driver had arrived hours before the service began to make sure he had gotten it. From behind the black tinted windows, he had an unobstructed view of the church and could see everyone arriving and leaving perfectly. As Michael stood there, the driver focused his high-powered Nikon lens and shot off a rapid succession of pictures, but Michael was oblivious. He wasn't going to find a cab standing out in front of the church like this.

Besides, he felt awkward standing there alone. He would have better luck at the next intersection. He began to walk down Clinton Street and within moments was gone from view. The driver then quickly started the van and began to follow him.

A cold wind from the east blew through the city that afternoon, and as it wound its way through the narrow streets and alleyways, it made an unnatural sound reminiscent of the cries of old ghosts and spirits. Michael shuddered and pulled the collar of his raincoat tightly around his neck. He didn't have a winter coat. In Los Angeles, where the temperature never really got much below sixty degrees, he didn't need one. All he had brought with him was a thin navy raincoat he had found when going through his grandmother's belongings after she had passed away. It had been his grandfather's originally. Although it was old, it managed to keep the rain off and made the wind chill more tolerable. When he had first gotten to New York, Michael had thought about buying a new coat, but at the department stores on Fifth Avenue the cheapest wool coat ran close to a thousand dollars. At that price, he could bear the cold for a week or so. Besides, when else was he ever going to wear a wool coat?

Fortunately, it wasn't long before Michael found a cab, and thirty minutes later he was within the shelter of the warm lobby of the Chase Manhattan Bank Building. He quickly took off his raincoat and folded it over his arm, so as not to draw attention to the old garment, then made his way toward the elevator. When he got to Gage's office, a note was waiting for him on the chair. That was strange, he thought. He quickly picked it up and began to read it. The note was from Richard Montague, asking him to stay on for a few days to pack up Gage's personal things. Michael threw it onto the desk.

For the last five days he had gone through all of Gage's open matters, reporting to Montague and the other members of the executive committee daily. He had hoped to find some complicated matter that needed immediate attention, something that would have enabled him to prove to the committee that he was "partnership material." In the end, however, there had been nothing. After the Global Network merger, things had begun to slow down and responsibility for all of Gage's open matters had been assigned out to other capable partners in the corporate department. Michael realized that his chances of proving himself to Montague and the other members of the executive committee were falling hopelessly away. If all this wasn't enough, now he had been given the task of packing up the dead partner's personal belongings and delivering them to his wife like a porter. Michael sighed.

Few things he had done at the firm disturbed him as much as this one. It brought back memories of going through his grandmother's belongings when she passed away, every object bringing back the memory of a person who was no longer with him. It was better just to get it over with, he thought. He located some empty boxes and began to sift through the dead partner's belongings. He started first with the framed pictures lining the credenza. As he packed up the dozen pictures of Gage and his family, the same questions kept going through his mind. What could possibly have made him commit suicide? None of it seemed to make any sense. From all outward appearances, Jonathan Gage had the perfect life. He had a beautiful wife and family. He had a promising career. The man had far more than Michael could have hoped for. What would have motivated him to do such a thing?

After finishing the credenza, Michael moved on to the desk. As he reached into the front drawer, he could see a green ceramic paperweight that Gage's son must have made in preschool, along with some crayon drawings and brightly colored finger paintings. Pens, Post-its, and other office supplies were interspersed among them. Michael shuffled them all onto one of the pieces of construction paper and shoveled them into the box. Then, as he was about to shut the drawer, he noticed a small blue book pressed up against the side. At first it took him a second to recognize, but as he turned it around he saw the familiar silver eagle emblazoned on the front cover, along with two olive branches clutched in its claws. It was a cardinal rule for corporate attorneys at Davis & White to have a valid passport ready at all times.

No one ever knew when the firm would get an emergency call from some third-world country asking for assistance in renegotiating the schedule of payments on its foreign debt or in defending it against a hedge fund mercilessly buying up its currency on the open market. Maybe the call would be from a large multinational company fending off a hostile tender offer from a foreign competitor. It could be one of a thousand things, and time was always of the essence. In the world of Wall Street, such events weren't as uncommon as one would think. The firm had made a fortune off these and a thousand similar transactions, and Jonathan Gage's passport illustrated this fact.

Michael found himself flipping through the pages, starting first in the back then making his way to the front. There were stamps from every major country. The paper tigers of Asia were all represented, with stamps from Japan, Hong Kong, China, Korea, Singapore, Malaysia, and Thailand. Most of them were from the early nineties, when the Asian financial markets were experiencing phenomenal growth, Japan was flush with cash, and money was pouring into new developments in the region faster than anyone could imagine. Five years later, after the Asian financial crisis and Japan's economic hemorrhaging, the deals had dried up as fast as they had started.

Fortunately, the European commonwealth came into its own and took up the slack. Large resident corporations in sectors ranging from telecommunications to financial services were now on a buying spree. As a result, there were stamps from England, Belgium, France, Germany, Italy, and recently Switzerland and Luxembourg. Of course, no corporate attorney's passport would have been complete without the stamps of a dozen tax havens, including the Netherlands, the Netherlands Antilles, the Bahamas, the British Virgin Islands, the Cayman Islands, and Barbados, among others. There were enough stamps in Gage's passport to make any deal lawyer envious.

When Michael got to the front of the passport, he couldn't help but stop and stare at the picture. It had been taken almost eight years ago and the man looked strangely familiar, in fact too familiar. An unsettling feeling moved through Michael. He quickly looked at his own reflection in the empty glass picture frame on the desk and held the passport photo up next to it. The two of them could have been brothers. They were similar in height and weight. Even their hair, eyes, and skin color were the same. The picture was quite unsettling. He quickly closed the passport and put it into his pocket. He would return it to Mrs. Gage in the morning, along with the other personal effects.

Just before he finished packing, however, he took the brown leather day planner off the desk one last time and opened it. He began to sort through the pages, hoping there would be something that he had missed the first time, something that would give him some kind of insight into this tragedy. The book was a chronology of the last days of Jonathan Gage's life, but he had already been through it a dozen times. One more time couldn't hurt, he figured. As he began to flip through, the days passed quickly into weeks, but there was nothing. When he got to the day of Gage's disappearance, he stopped. The light coming in the office window made him see something he had missed before. In the margin on the left-hand side of the page were deep indentations. It looked as if someone had written something down on top of the paper, the pen leaving an imprint. He quickly held the page up to the light. Rotating it, he could make out a woman's name and phone number.

Sasha
212-555-7410

Michael tapped his pen against the edge of the day planner and wondered who this woman might be. It was probably some part of Jonathan Gage's life that was never meant to be uncovered, his mistress perhaps. Still, the question remained, why had this name and phone number been written on top of his day planner on the very day that he had disappeared. There was only one way to find out. Michael quickly dialed the number and listened to the phone ring twice before a woman's voice came over the line. It sounded like he had woken her. He looked down at his watch. It was nearly five o'clock. He paused, thinking that maybe he should just hang up, but instead found himself holding on. The woman's voice became harsher. "Hello, this is Sasha. Who am I speaking to?"

Michael couldn't help but wonder if somehow Gage was watching him this very moment. After all, weren't a dead man's secrets supposed to be carried with him to the grave? He should have known better than to dig this up, but he needed to reach some kind of closure. "My name is Michael . . . I . . . uh . . . I'm a friend of Jonathan Gage." As soon as he heard the words leave his mouth, he wished he could have retracted them.

The woman paused. "Referrals from Jonathan are unusual," she said. "Are you visiting New York or do you live here?"

Michael realized that she must have known from his accent he wasn't a native. "I'm just visiting," he confessed. "I'm from Los Angeles."

"What do you do for a living, Michael?"

She was asking too many questions, but he felt strangely compelled to answer her. "I'm an attorney. I work with Jonathan."

She paused again, as if making some kind of mental assessment. Finally she spoke. "Where are you staying, Michael?"

He hesitated. "At the RIHGA. . . ."

"Would you like me to come to your hotel, or would you like to come see me?"

Michael began to panic. So Sasha was a prostitute. "I'm sorry, I think there's been some kind of misunderstanding. Sorry to bother you," he said, quickly hanging up the phone. He took a deep breath, tore the piece of paper out of the day planner, and put it into his pocket. There was no use in letting Gage's wife find this paper trail. It would only upset her. Gage's indiscretions would lie buried in Michael's mind, never to be betrayed. The man's life was his own business. Who was he to destroy Jonathan Gage's memory?

So with that in mind, Michael closed the last box of Gage's

belongings and taped it shut. Walking outside the office, he set the box down on the floor next to the others. He would deliver them to Mrs. Gage in the morning. He then walked back into the office to turn off the light for the last time. Just before he reached for the switch, however, something struck him. Damn it, he thought. How could he have forgotten? With all that had happened over the last few days, the meeting Gage had scheduled with the SEC tomorrow morning had completely slipped Michael's mind. He knew that there was only one thing left for him to do. He would have to go to the SEC in Gage's place. There was simply no other choice.

Chapter 18

The cold wind coming off the East River cut across Nico's face with a fierce intensity. He was standing on the walkway of the Brooklyn Bridge, but he could no longer remember how he had gotten there or even why he was there. Below him the dark waters churned violently like a thousand withering snakes intertwined and coupled together, and staring into the turmoil somehow made Nico feel empty and alone. It was time to go home, he thought. His wife would be waiting for him, wondering where he was. His daughter had been waking up with nightmares lately, and he was the only one who could calm her. She needed him to protect her from the demons that interrupted her sleep. They both needed him. But before he could finish his thoughts, a man's voice broke through the darkness and reminded Nico why he was there.

Fifteen yards in front of him, Nico could see the man with his back turned to him. His clothes were lying in a pile on the side of the bridge, and he was moving slowly toward the railing. Nico felt the blood rush to his head as he tried to run to him, but all the muscles from his neck down were paralyzed with fear. No matter how hard he struggled, he couldn't move. It was as if he was frozen in a block of ice unable to free himself. All he could do was watch in terror as the man lifted himself onto the narrow steel scaffolding and stretched his arms out into the sky like a crucifix. Nico tried to scream, but his throat had constricted around his vocal cords, leaving him mute. All he could do now was listen. Over the shrill of the wind, he tried to make out what the man was saying. The voice sounded familiar. He had heard those words before, but it took a few moments to recognize them. Then it came back to him. The man was praying. Yes, Nico thought, he was saying the Lord's Prayer. Nico repeated the final words along with him as he had been taught as a child. "And lead us not unto temptation . . . but deliver us from evil."

When the man finished, the wind stopped for a moment and an unearthly silence filled the air. An inescapable feeling of weakness overcame Nico. His life's failures were passing before his eyes with a clarity that he had not witnessed before. He could see his father lying in the hospital bed dying from the cancer, while he sat beside him unable to do anything to ease his pain. He could see the disappointment in his mother's eyes the following year when he told her he was dropping out of NYU. Finally he remembered his brother's sadness when, after a string of bad jobs, he decided to join the NYPD like his father. Fate was a predator, Nico thought. When it came for you there was little you could do to stop it.

In the shadows Nico saw tension fill the young man's body as he contemplated what would happen next, the free fall through the night air and the harsh impact of the cold gray water below him. Before Nico could blink, a flash of light broke through the darkness. It was the headlights of an oncoming car. Surely this would cause the man to stop, he thought. He would realize the insanity of his actions and come down from the railing. But as the car moved closer, the young man just turned around. In the approaching headlights, his body became more and more visible, and Nico strained once again to see his face. Before he could do so, the man tilted his head up and took one last look at the lights of the Manhattan skyline. He then let his body fall back into the night—however, before he faded from view the illumination from the headlights made his face visible for a fraction of a second. When he recognized the man, all of the air left Nico's lungs. It was like he was looking into a mirror.

"No," Nico screamed. "No. . . ."

His wife began to shake him. "My God, Nico . . . what's wrong?" she asked. "What's wrong?"

He was upright now, his body tangled in the sheets and his forehead covered with sweat. His hands were shaking uncontrollably.

"Nico, wake up. You're having another bad dream." The damp cotton T-shirt was clinging to his chest, and he was trying to reorient himself. His heart felt like it was pounding a thousand times a minute, and he struggled to catch his breath. "You can't keep ignoring this," she pleaded. "It's beginning to scare the children."

He no longer knew what to say to her. She was right. He was drowning. "What is it?" she asked, brushing her hands through his hair, trying to calm him. He had seen her do the same thing with his son when the boy woke up from a nightmare. There was something calming in her voice and this simple gesture. The woman was a natural healer.

"This investigation has been bothering me from the day the Feds called," he said.

"The young attorney who killed himself?" she asked sympathetically. "I thought it was over."

Nico put his hands over his face. The sweat was heavy, and he felt like he had just come back from a run.

"Maybe you should go back there," she said, resting her chin on his shoulder and putting both arms around his waist.

Nico shrugged. "Now who's sounding crazy?"

"It won't go away," she said. "You have to go back to the bridge. There's something that's bothering you. If you don't do it, you'll never put these dreams behind you."

The port of New York had once been one of the largest shipping centers in the country, but that was before the mob had moved in. Now the harbor and the area surrounding it had largely become a source of blight and urban decay. The shippers all knew that cargo coming into New York was subject to a much greater risk of hijacking than anywhere else. Organized crime in the borough controlled the Teamsters union, and the dispatchers would regularly tip them off when anything valuable was coming in. Their thugs would then intercept the rigs en route. Most of the time the truckers simply rolled over without a fight. After all, no one could blame them. The ones who did fight usually ended up spending a month in the recovery ward of St. John's Hospital, pissing into a bedpan and relearning how to walk. Besides, it never did any good anyway. In less than twenty-four hours the goods were being sold on street corners or out of the backs of cars. It didn't matter whether the cargo was television sets, stereo equipment, watches, or clothing, its fate was always the same. The hijacking had become so prevalent that the shippers began to favor Baltimore as their port of choice. As a result, the port had fallen into a state of nonuse for most commercial shipments.

"Hey, what are you doing down here?"

Nico turned around and saw a large security guard coming toward him. The man was old, with thick gray hair and a weathered face. Probably a retired cop supplementing his pension, Nico figured. With what the city paid in benefits, most retirees were forced to work in menial jobs just to get by.

"It's okay," Nico said calmly. "I'm a cop." He reached into his jacket with two fingers and pulled out his badge. "My name is Nico Fiori. I'm a detective with the NYPD in Manhattan."

The guard studied the badge, then slid his nightstick back into its holder. "I worked thirty years with the Harbor Patrol before I retired," he said, as if to let Nico know that he had also been a cop. The old man then looked down at his uniform and shrugged, as if ashamed by where he had ended up. But there was no judgment or condemnation in Nico's eyes. "What's your name?" he asked, extending his hand.

"Clancy, they called me Clancy. It was my nickname back in the day," he said. "You know, short for Clarence."

Nico smiled. Everyone had a nickname.

"What brings you down to Brooklyn anyway?" the old man asked.

This was a good question and one for which Nico didn't have a ready answer. The dream had been coming back to him again and again. No matter how hard he tried there was little he could do to stop it. At his wife's insistence he had finally come down here to wrestle with the demons that were haunting him. He needed to reach closure. He needed to put an end to this.

"We found a floater in the East River on Monday. Harbor Patrol pulled him in down by Market Street. Apparently he was a jumper," Nico said. He looked back at the bridge, but a blanket of fog had already obscured it. All he could see were the large concrete and steel bases rising out of the water and disappearing into the gray. "We found his clothing on the Brooklyn Bridge walkway," he explained.

The old man stared back at him oddly. "Where did you say you found the body?"

"Down off Market Street," Nico repeated. "It was badly bloated and had been in the water for some time."

The old man shook his head. "You got your bridges mixed up. . . ."

Nico paused. Now it was his turn to look confused. "No, we found his clothing on the Brooklyn Bridge. I'm sure of it."

The old man walked over to the edge of the water. "Back in my day we had our share of jumpers off the Brooklyn Bridge. Most of the time somebody saw them jump, and we'd retrieve the bodies pretty quickly. Other times we'd just find them moving toward the harbor. You see, the current doesn't go in the direction you found the body, the current goes the other way. Whoever found the clothing must have found it on the Manhattan Bridge or further north, maybe the Williamsburg Bridge."

A rush of angst moved through Nico's body. He could feel the cold fog against his neck. "Are you sure?"

"Yeah, I'm sure," the old man repeated. "The current goes the other way."

Chapter 19

Thursday Morning, December 7

When Robert Adams joined the Securities and Exchange Commission, New York was his last choice of assignments. Even back then he knew his money would go further in places like Omaha, Kansas City, and Chicago. But the division wanted him here. After all, most of the attorneys who started in the Manhattan division of the SEC used it as a stepping-stone. They would put in a few good years to get the experience they needed, then leave for the high-paying jobs on Wall Street. As a result, the enforcement division had been gutted of its most experienced talent. Adams, however, was what the younger attorneys referred to as a lifer. After being with the SEC for ten years, he no longer knew of any other way of life, and he couldn't leave even if he wanted to.

His office was large by government standards, a wide oak desk in the center of the room and a big black leather chair behind it. On the wall above him, prominently displayed, stood the seal of the SEC. Through the window behind him he could see the twin towers of the World Trade Center, the orange sunlight reflecting brightly off their mirrored surfaces.

"Mr. Adams, I have a young man named Michael Elliot to see you. He says he's here for a ten o'clock appointment."

Adams turned his chair around and looked up at the woman, half squinting in disbelief. He was a short man, with a thin wiry frame and a narrow, hawklike face. His eyes were two tiny black beads peering at her as if she were some kind of target caught in his crosshairs. "Who?"

"He said his name is Michael Elliot. . . ."

Adams shook his head. "I know who he is," he said, his voice trailing off in frustration. "Did he say what he's here for?"

The woman paused. "He told me he's here for the meeting Jonathan Gage had scheduled."

Adams's head began to throb. Pressing his forefingers against his temples, he began to make small concentric circles, trying to relieve the pressure, but the pain only became worse. He looked up at his secretary, who was waiting for a response. "Is anyone with him?"

"No," she said. "He's alone."

Adams paused. "Give me a few minutes to gather my thoughts."

She nodded, then closed the door behind her. Once he was alone, Adams opened the top drawer of his desk. Inside was a stack of six-by-eight black-and-white photographs, which he took out and spread over it. The FBI in Los Angeles had done an excellent job on surveillance. There were pictures of Michael in his office taken from the building across the street. There were also pictures of him coming and going from his apartment in Hancock Park. Finally, there were the pictures of him in New York, by the graveyard at Trinity Church and then at Jonathan Gage's funeral. Although he had been able to obtain authorization for the wiretap on Michael's home phone, it had proved virtually useless.

To compound matters, the federal magistrate was unwilling to authorize a wiretap on the phone lines at Davis & White. There was too much concern about attorney-client confidentiality and interference with attorney-client privilege. Adams knew he would need more before the magistrate would permit him to go further. He glanced over the pictures lining his desk, then found a close-up of Michael and picked it up. "So what kind of game are you playing?" he asked as he studied the picture. "What kind of game are you playing?"

At fifteen minutes after ten, Adams's secretary opened the door again and poked her head inside. The pictures were now gone from his desk, and Adams motioned for her to bring Michael in. The woman nodded and turned around. "You can go on inside," she said, opening the door for him.

Michael entered the room and set down his briefcase. "Hello, Mr. Adams, my name is Michael Elliot. I'm an attorney with Davis & White," he said, walking forward to shake his hand, but Adams's hand remained firmly fixed at his side.

"Why are you here, Mr. Elliot?" he asked, as he stared at Michael's left hand. Something was wrong, but he couldn't quite tell what it was. Then it struck him; the young man was missing a finger. That was it, the third finger, his ring finger, was gone. Adams couldn't believe he hadn't noticed it in the pictures. He quickly diverted his eyes away from the deformity, then stared back up at his visitor. "I asked why you are here, Mr. Elliot?"

Michael looked at him blankly, as if caught unwillingly in a mess that wasn't his own doing. This wasn't going at all as he had expected. "Mr. Adams, I'm not sure if you know this, but Jonathan Gage is dead. The funeral was yesterday. I've taken over all of Jonathan Gage's open matters. . . . I'm familiar with most of the things he was working on. If there are any problems, I'll do my best to provide you with the information that you need. Now, may I ask what this meeting is regarding, Mr. Adams?"

Adams's anger increased. "Are you here representing Davis and White? . . . Did they send you down here?"

"I'm not sure what you mean. . . ."

"Listen, don't think for a goddamn minute that this is going to stop with him. I've been working on this investigation far too long."

Michael looked perplexed. "What are you talking about?"

"Don't play stupid with me," Adams responded harshly. "We already know that Gage was the partner in charge of a number of transactions in which there was extensive insider trading . . . Transatlantic Insurance . . . United Financial . . . Consolidated Semiconductor . . . Global Network. It was just a matter of time before we traced it back to him. He knew that, didn't he?"

Michael suddenly felt unable to breathe. Never had an attorney at Davis & White been accused of such impropriety.

"Mr. Elliot, were you involved in any of these matters with Mr. Gage?"

Michael began to panic. "Mr. Adams, I think you should be speaking with someone more senior at the firm regarding this investigation . . . I mean . . . I don't think I should be saying anything further until one of our senior partners is here. Something like this has never happened."

"Mr. Elliot . . . let me ask you again . . . were you working on any matters with Jonathan Gage?"

"Mr. Montague," his secretary said, poking her head inside his door. "I have Michael Elliot on the phone for you. He says it's urgent."

"I'm just about to head out to the club for lunch. Tell him you tried to catch me, but I was gone. Tell him I'll call him back this afternoon."

"Yes, Mr. Montague."

As he walked down the hallway, he could hear his secretary passing the message on to Michael. Anything the associate needed to talk about with him could surely wait. Besides, if it involved substantive matters, there were other partners the young man could call who were far more capable. He had done his part by helping the boy once.

When Montague returned from lunch, however, he was surprised to find Michael sitting in his office. The associate's face looked pale and drawn, and he was staring blankly out the window. Before Michael noticed him in the doorway, Montague walked back outside and gave his secretary a stern look. She just shrugged her shoulders. "Mr. Montague . . . I told him that you had an important meeting at one-thirty, but he said it was urgent. He said he wanted to wait for you."

Montague scowled and walked back into the office. As soon as he made it through the door, his face changed like a chameleon. "Hello, Michael, I thought you would be in Los Angeles by now. What can I do for you?" he asked, feigning interest.

Michael looked up at Montague's weathered face. "Mr. Montague, I think we have a problem."

Montague's demeanor changed instantly. "What is it now, Mr. Elliot? I really don't have time for this. I have an entire firm to manage," he said, lying through his teeth as he sat down at his desk. The firm had been on autopilot for years, and every time he said such things he half expected a bolt of lightning to come down from the heavens and strike him dead.

"I know, Mr. Montague, but I was going through Jonathan Gage's calendar last week, and I discovered he had a meeting scheduled with the Securities and Exchange Commission this morning. The entry in his calendar didn't indicate what it was for, so I figured I would just go to the meeting in his place."

Montague rose as he was talking, took his gray pin-striped jacket off, and hung it up in the large cabinet against the wall. As his suit coat rested on the hanger, he ran his hands over the lapels to smooth out any creases. He seemed uninterested in what Michael was saying, but after all, as managing partner, his job was mostly thinking of creative ways to shift his problems to other people. "I'm listening," he said, turning around and walking back to the desk.

"They told me that Jonathan Gage was the subject of an insider trading investigation . . . they said it involved a number of matters that the firm was working on."

Montague abruptly turned toward Michael. The muscles in his neck tightened around the two thin jugular veins, and he scowled. "What do you mean?"

Michael paused. "They said Gage was engaging in insider trading in connection with four mergers he was working on . . . Transatlantic Insurance, United Financial, Consolidated Semiconductor, and most recently Global Network. That's the one we just finished."

"I know which deal it is," Montague barked. He proceeded to fall down in his chair and put his hand over his mouth.

"I told the investigator that Gage had committed suicide. I tried to explain that I was just filling in for him, but he started asking me more questions. He said the SEC was going to conduct a full-scale investigation into Gage's dealings at the firm and anyone else who was working with him on these matters. Mr. Montague, I worked with him on a number of those matters."

Montague's face had become pale. "Have you spoken to anybody else about this?" he asked, lowering his voice.

"No, Mr. Montague. . . . You're the first person I've told."

The managing partner walked to his door and shut it softly behind him. "Now listen to me. I don't want you to tell anyone else about this. This is to remain strictly confidential. If something like this ever got out, it would destroy this firm, do you hear me?"

Michael nodded.

"Regardless of whether it's true or not, clients would be quick to make judgment. For all we know, this is just speculation or misinformation. I'm going to call Bill Vernon. He's one of our senior litigation partners and was the former director of enforcement at the SEC. I'm going to ask him to handle this. I'll have him pull some strings and slow them up." Montague hesitated and looked back at Michael. "When you were going through Gage's office, did you notice anything unusual? I mean, was there anything that might have indicated something was wrong?"

"You have to understand, I wasn't looking for anything like that," Michael exclaimed. "The only thing I was looking for was active client matters that needed attention, not evidence of insider trading."

Montague frowned harshly at him, as if there was only one right answer. "I want you to go back through all of his files." He stopped for a moment and looked directly into Michael's eyes. Suddenly his demeanor changed, and he placed a hand on the young attorney's shoulder. "Michael, you know you will be the only one who knows what's in these files. If something were to be taken, let's say something that might be incriminating, you would be the only person to know. Now, I'm placing a lot of trust in you. I'm highly confident that when you finish going through everything, you will end up finding nothing to implicate Gage or this firm. Do you understand?"

Michael stared back into the old man's eyes, wondering whether he was somehow being asked to make a deal with the devil himself. Montague's cold black pupils had gripped him and left him unable to say a word. All he could do was nod helplessly. Suddenly a crooked smile came over Montague's thin lips, and he patted Michael hard on the shoulder.

"You did the right thing coming to see me. You did the right thing. Just remember, the firm has a very long memory for things like this. It returns its favors, Michael," Montague said, escorting him to the door.

For a moment Michael stood silently in the doorway. He was in a fog now, trying to take it all in. As he opened the door he could hear Montague return to his desk and begin talking loudly into the phone. "I don't care who Mr. Vernon is with, you tell him that I need to see him in my office immediately." Michael then shut the door softly behind him so that no one else would hear the conversation taking place inside.

Chapter 20

The office seemed smaller now. The walls were closing in on him, making him feel claustrophobic and confined. What had Montague meant by his implication that Michael would be the only one who knew what was in Gage's office? Was he really asking him to destroy evidence implicating Gage or the firm? In the wake of a federal investigation, such actions were clearly criminal. Maybe he was simply misinterpreting the managing partner's message. After all, Montague hadn't come right out and asked him to do it. But Montague wasn't an idiot. He would never come out and directly instruct the young associate to obstruct justice and interfere with a federal investigation. The message was one that would have to be read between the lines. "The firm has a very long memory," Michael whispered to himself. "The firm has a very long memory."

His mind drifted back to a conversation he had had with James Monehan when he started with the firm. Monehan had warned him that over the course of his career he would be confronted with a number of situations in which he would have to make what Monehan called the "hard" decision. There were only two types of lawyers in this world, his friend explained. There were the ones who never compromised their own morals or integrity to better themselves or their clients. Then there were the ones who would lie, cheat, steal, cajole, and manipulate just to gain the slightest advantage. There was a thin line that separated the two. If you crossed that line once, each time after that became easier. There was no halfway point, no gray area, no crossing over merely on occasion. Each attorney had to make the decision for himself. Michael knew that this was much easier said than done. He wondered what Monehan would do in the same circumstances. Would he cross that line just to make partner?

Suddenly Michael caught himself. What was he doing? He hadn't found anything incriminating yet. There was still a good chance that he would find nothing at all, making the whole point moot. He was simply letting his mind run wild again. He would just have to go through Gage's files one more time. If he didn't find anything, Montague would simply think Michael had been a team player after all. If he did find something, he would deal with it then.

Michael shut the door to Gage's office and locked it behind him. The banker's boxes were stacked up against the wall, each filled with the files for all of Gage's open matters. He began to take the boxes down and go through their contents carefully. It was a long and torturous process. If Gage had been involved in illegalities, there would surely be signs here. After all, Gage spent most of his waking moments in this office. Furthermore, no matter how smart he was, it would have been virtually impossible for him to hide all of his actions. Somewhere along the line he would have made a mistake or left a paper trail.

At the end of the afternoon, however, Michael had still found nothing. All of the matters Gage had been working on could be accounted for, with the exception of one: Trinity Corporation. For this particular matter, Michael had been unable to find anything. An unsettling feeling crept through him. What had once looked relatively innocent was becoming more and more troubling. He leaned over the desk and pressed the intercom. "Gloria," he said, his voice floating into the ether. He looked down at his watch. It was almost five o'clock. "Gloria," he repeated.

After what seemed like eternity, her voice came over the line. "Yes, Michael," she said, half out of breath. "I was just coming down the hallway when I heard you."

"Gloria, I was wondering whether accounting ever retrieved a copy of the bill for Trinity Corporation."

"My God, you still haven't gotten that," she exclaimed. "Hold on, let me check." She put him on hold.

Michael knew he was grasping at straws, but there was little else he could think of. After a few minutes Gloria returned. "Michael, this is odd. I just spoke with Vince down in accounting. He told me that the billing records for this matter were deleted from the hard drive several months ago. He didn't know how it could have happened."

Michael was silent. If he could just see a copy of the bill, he could put his mind at ease. Now it would continue to eat at him, like a splinter caught under his skin, digging deeper and deeper.

"I told him you needed the bill desperately," Gloria explained. "Fortunately, the computer hard drive is backed up onto magnetic tapes daily. They sent a person down to archives and are pulling it up right now. Someone will be up with a hard copy shortly."

Michael breathed a sigh of relief. Once again Gloria had saved him.

"Do you want me to stay around?" she asked. "It wouldn't be any trouble."

"No, you've already helped out enough. I think I can take it from here."

At half past seven Michael was distracted by a knock on the door. "Come in," he shouted. The handle to the large wooden door jiggled back and forth in response but didn't budge. Michael had forgotten that he had locked it and suddenly felt embarrassed. Attorneys at the firm rarely locked the doors to their offices unless they were working on a sensitive matter. "Just a minute," he replied, rising from the desk.

When he opened the door, a clerk was waiting for him, holding a large brown interoffice envelope. In the sender column he could see the words *Accounting Department* stamped in dark blue ink. "Here's the bill for Trinity Corporation," the young man said. "It's the last delivery of the day."

Michael thanked him and shut the door. On his way back to the desk, he opened the envelope and began reading through the printout. Firm bills were usually in two parts. The first part contained a summary of attorney and paralegal time charged to the matter, and the second part contained a listing of the out-of-pocket costs and expenses. The Trinity Corporation bill was only one page long, since there was very little time charged to it. The only entry was for an S. Villanueva, who spent twelve hours working on the project. Although Michael didn't recognize the name, from the billing rate he knew it must be a paralegal. He immediately looked adjacent to the name for the description of work performed. There were just two words: *Incorporation Matters.*

Michael felt his heart sink. If Gage had simply bought or sold the stocks in his own brokerage account, the SEC would have discovered it long ago. They had sophisticated computers that could trace large purchases and sales made right before pending merger announcements. They would then check to see if the buyers or sellers had any relationship to the company or its advisers that gave them access to inside information. It was quite simple. And Gage surely would have known this. If he was going to engage in insider trading, he would have created a shell company, something that would be difficult to trace back to him. Most likely it would have been an offshore corporation with a trading account set up with one of the brokers. The words *Incorporation Matters* on the Trinity Corporation bill suddenly made the SEC accusations seem far more real.

Michael's hands were shaking. He had set up a number of such offshore corporations as acquisition vehicles or for financing transactions. It was commonplace, or so the tax attorneys at the firm had often told him. Profits derived offshore were rarely taxed. Furthermore, banking and brokerage secrecy laws made them difficult to trace. Every few years the tax havens would change when the federal government's scrutiny of such practices intensified. At first the Bahamas and the British Virgin Islands were the jurisdictions of choice, but now the Netherlands Antilles was preferred because it still had favorable tax treaties with the United States and strong bank secrecy protection.

Michael looked down at the list of expenses for further confirmation of what he had feared. On the third line he saw a charge for $2,500 from Corporate Services International. For a small fee CSI would set up foreign corporations and act as a managing agent. The service had correspondent offices in over twenty foreign countries, most of which were tax havens. Hundreds of companies would use the CSI address as their mailing address and appoint CSI as agent so that they could take advantage of the tax treaties. For the most part, the office was just a clerk and a secretary, who would file the charter documents, maintain the scant corporate records, and forward mail. Michael knew he could contact CSI to get the details on Trinity Corporation, but that would take days. They were usually slow to respond and suspicious of outside inquiries. He needed a quicker answer.

He pulled out the firm directory and found the listing for the paralegals in the New York office. He searched for the name Villanueva but couldn't find it. That was odd, he thought. He picked up the phone and dialed the number for Natalie Petrone, the paralegal coordinator. Natalie had been with the firm for over forty-five years, and any time attorneys needed a paralegal they had to clear it with her first. Although it was late, Natalie often worked as hard as the attorneys, and he knew he had a good chance of getting her. Luck was with him, and the phone rang only once before she picked up the line. "Natalie," she responded, her voice rough from years of smoking.

"Hello, it's Michael Elliot. I'm glad I caught you. I've got a small emergency on my hands that I'm hoping you can help me out with."

"Not another helicopter flight to Albany for a corporate filing," she said, half joking.

"Not exactly," Michael said, pausing. "I'm following up on a different matter that Jonathan Gage was working on. It was for an entity named Trinity Corporation. I believe a paralegal with the name S. Villanueva was working on it with him, but I wasn't able to find that name in the firm directory."

"That's because she's no longer with the firm."

Michael paused. "No longer with the firm," he repeated. "What do you mean?"

"Well, Sandy left at the end of summer to go back to Columbia Law School. You know how it goes, most of these college kids do this for a year or two to see if they like it. If they do, they move on to law school."

Michael hesitated. "Do you have a number where I can reach her? It's kind of important."

"Hold on a second, let me see." Michael could hear the shuffling of papers, then silence. "Here we go, I've got her number at school. It's 212-555-3981. By the way, tell Sandy I said hello."

Michael wrote the phone number down quickly. "Thanks, Natalie, I really appreciate it."

"Do you need another paralegal on the matter? I can get someone to help you out with it tonight if you need it."

"No, that's okay. Thanks again," he said, hanging up the phone.

Michael stared back down at the phone number. Something was wrong. The pieces were not fitting together as he had hoped. For a brief moment he thought back to Montague's admonishment. The words kept repeating again and again in his mind: "The firm has a very long memory . . . the firm has a very long memory." The investigators from the SEC would probably never uncover the Trinity Corporation files, he thought. All he had to do was throw away the printout and forget he ever came upon this information. But something held him back. As much as he wanted to, he couldn't do it. He slowly dialed the phone number and waited until he heard a young woman pick up the line.

Chapter 21

The sky was a dark, billowy gray that morning, and the clouds hung heavy over downtown Los Angeles. They had gotten little rain this year, and the clouds looked as if they were going to make up for it. When she reached into the closet for her long winter coat, she discovered the briefcase and remembered that she had never gotten it back to him. She had found it the morning after they slept together. It had barely been light out when he left, and in his rush he had forgotten it. Men were a strange species, she thought. After she slept with them, they often acted like little boys, leaving their things behind or becoming overly possessive of her. She had wanted to give it back to him that morning, but she knew she couldn't take it into the office. It would be too hard to explain and people would start asking questions. Besides, if Raven ever found out about the two of them, he would make Michael's life miserable.

It was absurd that a man with a wife and children would be so possessive of her, but that was his nature. Raven viewed people as property and didn't like lending them out. Her mind kept going back to the night Michael called her apartment. She wondered whether he had recognized Raven's voice. Had he put it together? Would he hate her for it? She knew she couldn't blame him. She hated herself for becoming involved with a man like Raven, so why wouldn't he? If it had been anyone else, she wouldn't have cared, but, for some reason, with Michael it was different. She felt guilty for hurting him, and it bothered her in a way she hadn't anticipated. She told herself she would tell Michael about Raven, but with him in New York and her in Los Angeles, there really didn't seem to be much point to bringing it up now. Besides, she wanted to explain it to him in person.

While she had gotten the notice about Jonathan Gage's death just like everyone else, she had never worked with him and didn't really know much about him. The secretaries had been gossiping about the suicide for days, but for the most part she had remained uninterested. It was hard to get emotional about someone you knew so little about. Besides, she didn't care much for office gossip. The thought that Michael in New York was somehow tied to this matter didn't even cross her mind. She had shifted her attention back to her work and tried to distance herself from all the firm's politics.

When she returned home that night, however, she was surprised to find Peter Raven waiting for her. She had made the mistake of giving him a key weeks ago, and he was now sitting on the couch with his tie hanging loosely around his neck. His shirtsleeves were rolled up, and a half-full bottle of Chivas Regal was resting on the coffee table. The room reeked of whiskey and cigarettes. She hated it when he smoked in her apartment, but he never seemed to care. Raven didn't say anything when she walked in. Then she saw the briefcase lying at the base of the couch.

He had found it the same way she had. He had taken off his coat and gone to hang it up in the hall closet. At first he hadn't recognized it. Raven was a self-absorbed man who paid little attention to anyone but himself. Even when he saw the initials beside the handle, it had taken him a while to figure out. He had repeated them in his head—MSE, MSE, MSE, MSE—trying to match them with the initials of the other partners. He'd seen the briefcase before, he was sure of it. It occupied a familiar space in his mind, but where?

Raven went to the bar and poured himself a stiff drink. He tried to open the briefcase, but it was locked. He took another long pull from the glass as he decided what to do. It was a three-combination lock, which meant there were only a thousand permutations. He had nothing better to do, so he set the three numbers to zero, then moved each one up a number at a time. With each try he became a little drunker and a little angrier. When he got to the number 213, he heard the click. Raven smiled. The sequence was the area code for downtown Los Angeles—in hindsight it seemed obvious.

When he opened the briefcase, he found Michael's day planner. His business card was in front—Michael S. Elliot. The *S* was for Salvatore, the name of his grandfather, although Raven didn't know this. He held the briefcase and shook his head. His anger built for another fifteen minutes before Karen came home. He was now halfway through the bottle of whiskey and was on his last cigarette. Raven was not a particularly even-tempered man. Even cold sober he was prone to quick and sudden outbursts, but when he drank his anger only became worse.

Karen was used to dealing with men with bad dispositions and a penchant for alcohol. "Go ahead and make yourself at home," she said sarcastically, taking off her jacket and throwing it on the love seat. She went behind the bar and poured herself a large glass of vodka. A friend had once told her that litigation was much like the art of self-defense. To be effective, one had to match force with force. If your assailant drew a knife, then you drew a knife. If he drew a gun, then you drew a gun. If he was getting drunk, she would get drunk. She would go head-to-head with him without batting an eye. This was her apartment. He was sitting on her couch. He was drinking her booze, and he had gone through her closet. If anyone had a right to be pissed off, it was she. She filled her glass again and took another sip.

Raven finished his cigarette and instinctively reached for another before realizing that the pack was empty. He crumpled it up and threw it on the floor. He didn't even give her a chance to explain, not that she would have lied. It was pretty obvious what had transpired. "So you're fucking one of my associates," he said, kicking the briefcase onto the floor, where it made a loud thud.

"Who I choose to spend my time with is none of your goddamn business. You seem to be forgetting something," she said, raising her hand and pointing to her ring finger.

Raven sneered and took another drink. "I would've expected you to sleep with another partner," he said, as if she were some kind of whore. "Someone who could have helped your career . . . at least that I could have understood."

"Yeah," she sneered. "Because sleeping with you has done wonders for my career."

Raven ignored her. "Did you tell him about us?" he asked, fearful that if Michael knew about his indiscretions, it might give the young associate leverage. He hated anybody having something on him.

"Of course, we talked about you all night long as we fucked."

Raven stood up. Then, without the slightest warning, he backhanded her hard. Her skin stung from the impact. This was the first time she'd ever been hit. Her face was beginning to throb, and her eyes filled with tears. A smug and condescending smile came over his face as he moved closer. Suddenly her body filled with rage, and the instincts came back to her. Without the slightest hesitation she fired off a combination with the full weight of her body behind it—jab, cross, hook, and uppercut. The first punch caught him by surprise but landed short of its target. With the second punch, however, he wasn't so lucky. The cross hit him square in the nose, unleashing blood down his face in a stream of red. The hook caught him in the eye. He screamed out in pain, but the uppercut that came next was by far her best shot. She put all of the force she could muster behind it and aimed low. Her fist hit him square in the groin, causing him to double over in pain. Now she knew what it was like to hit a heavy bag so hard that it came clear off the hook.

"You bitch," he shouted. "You bitch, are you crazy?"

She went over to her purse and took out her Mace. "Get out of my apartment, and don't ever come back again or I'll call the police. Do you hear me?"

"You're crazy," he screamed, crawling to the door. "You're fucking crazy."

Chapter 22

Columbia Law School was on the main campus, just opposite the corner of West 116th Street and Amsterdam Avenue. The directions her roommate had given him were easy enough to follow. He was to go to the law library, and Sandy would be in the far cubicle on the northeast corner of the third floor. The library was large by conventional standards and lined with shelves of statutes, cases, and administrative codes from each of the fifty states. Interspersed between them were rows of treatises, journals, and serials, some more than a century old. It was practically enough to discourage one from the practice of law, Michael thought. He quickly made his way past them until he reached a low hutch of cubicles. "Hello, Ms. Villanueva," he said, directing himself to a young woman with her head buried in a large casebook.

The woman looked up at him, startled to hear her name. On most occasions Sandra Villanueva was considered a beautiful woman, with long blonde hair and girl-next-door features. Tonight, however, she had the disheveled appearance characteristic of so many students in law school. Her blue jeans were old and faded, and the oversized sweatshirt she was wearing was chosen more for comfort than for appearance. She had pulled back her hair with an old beret, and she wore no makeup. An empty cup of coffee was resting on the desk, and her eyes were swollen and red, no doubt from reading the fine print of a dozen law cases.

"Hello, my name is Michael Elliot. I'm an attorney with Davis and White."

Her curiosity quickly turned into a frown. "How did you find me?"

"Your roommate told me you would be here. She said you always study in the same place, third floor . . . far cubicle . . . northeast corner."

"Great," she said with faint enthusiasm.

Michael quickly tried to break the tension. "So, what are you studying?"

She looked down at the casebook. "Criminal law," she replied, marking the place she had left off and capping her yellow highlighter. "Something you Wall Street types never really have to worry about."

Michael paused. Her comment was a little too close to home, but he brushed it off as best he could. "Yeah, I guess you're right."

"They make you learn so much stuff that is totally irrelevant in the real world. Like I'm ever going to need to know this stuff."

Michael shrugged. It didn't seem that long since he was in the law library reading arcane cases, the names of which he could no longer remember. Just like her, he had stayed away from study groups, preferring to study by himself. Most people in law school studied intensely not because they enjoyed the material but rather out of the raw fear of looking like imbeciles in class when the professor called on them. This back-and-forth questioning was called the Socratic method, but as far as Michael could tell it more closely resembled a cruel game of intellectual dodgeball. One student would be called upon to recite the facts of a case and the issues presented; then the professor would hurl questions at him like a bully throwing a large rubber ball at the small kid standing against the wall. Everyone else would watch nervously and laugh as the poor student was humiliated question after question, but it was the uncomfortable laughter of watching someone get hit in the testicles. The most unsettling part was knowing that it was just a matter of time before your name was called. Come to think of it, Michael thought, his entire time at law school could pretty much be summed up as three years of fear and a few times of getting hit in the testicles with a large rubber ball.

One time he had seen a fellow student suffer this humiliation in front of his fiancée. Paul Kouros had invited his fiancée to sit in on one of his classes because she was thinking of going to law school herself. Visitors weren't uncommon; however, before class one of Paul's friends decided to play a practical joke and left a note for the professor purporting to be from Paul. The note explained that Paul's girlfriend was sitting in on class, and he really wanted the professor to call on him to impress her. The professor, a particularly vindictive man, was more than up for the challenge. In the course of an hour, he tore Paul apart in what could only be described as a bloodletting. Not surprisingly, Paul's fiancée decided not to come to law school that fall.

Sandy interrupted his thoughts. "What brings you all the way up to Harlem? Let me guess, the firm wants to make me an offer to come back as a summer associate before grades even come out."

Michael smiled. "I wish that was it. Unfortunately, I was hoping that I could have a couple minutes of your time to talk to you about one of the matters you worked on for Jonathan Gage before he died."

The young woman's face became pale. Michael suddenly realized she must not have heard the news. After all, a law student's life was largely spent in a vacuum. One never had the time to watch television or read the papers. "Oh, I'm sorry. You haven't heard, have you? Jonathan passed away."

Her lips trembled. "Passed away, what do you mean?"

As soon as he heard himself say it, he knew he had made a poor choice of words. He felt almost cowardly for trying to hide the truth from her. "He committed suicide a week ago," Michael confessed.

"Oh my God, that's terrible!"

Michael gave her a moment before continuing. "The firm brought me out from Los Angeles to take over his affairs.

That's why I'm here. I'm hoping you might remember doing some work for a client called Trinity Corporation. I believe Jonathan may have set up an offshore entity for them."

"He was so young," she said, oblivious to his question. She took off her glasses and sat silently. "I'm sorry, what did you say was the name of the matter?"

"Trinity Corporation," Michael repeated.

She shook her head. "I'm sorry, that doesn't ring a bell."

"Please, Ms. Villanueva," he pleaded. "It's really important. Can you think hard? Is there anything you remember about it?"

"Trinity Corporation . . . Trinity Corporation . . . Trinity Corporation," she repeated, as if probing her mind. Suddenly she stopped and squinted at Michael. "Come to think of it, I do remember doing some corporate formation work for Jonathan. It was about a year ago, wasn't it?"

"Yes," Michael said.

"I remember setting up a Netherlands Antilles company, along with a few offshore accounts. He was working with another attorney on the matter, but I can't remember his name."

"Do you remember what office the attorney was in?"

"I believe he was in the Los Angeles office."

Michael felt the wave of anxiety come back to him. Who in the hell could Gage have been working with in Los Angeles? The only logical person besides himself would have been Arturo, but Arturo told him he hadn't worked with Gage before.

Sandra's voice interrupted his thoughts. "Why don't you just get the files from the records center? They should have all this information."

Michael hesitated. "I wish it was that easy. I already checked, and the files were missing."

Sandra shook her head. "That records center is a black hole. Half the stuff I sent down there never made it back out."

Michael nodded in agreement. "The only reason I was even able to figure out you were involved on the matter was through a copy of the firm's billing statements taken off the computer backup. I saw you billed time to the matter, so I tracked you down. There were also some charges for Corporate Services International. You don't remember who at CSI helped you with this?" ·

"No, I'm sorry. It was a while ago. I really can't remember."

Michael shrugged. "It was a long shot," he said. "Well, I appreciate your help. If you remember anything, please give me a call. I'm working out of the New York office for another few days."

As he walked back to the elevator, the unsettling feeling came back to Michael. What was Trinity Corporation, and who was the attorney Gage had been working with in Los Angeles? The further he delved into this matter, the less it all looked like some kind of mistake. The SEC's allegations now felt like a noose around his neck. Had Gage really set up this corporation as a vehicle to hide his insider trading activities? None of it made any sense. Gage had a life any attorney would envy. What could have possibly motivated him to risk all of this? Had he become so egotistical that he thought he wouldn't get caught? Michael shook his head. As he pressed the button for the elevator, he heard footsteps coming toward him. Quickly turning around, he saw Sandra rush around the corner.

"I'm so glad I caught you," she said, out of breath. "I just thought of something. Why don't you just get a copy of my chron files?"

Michael looked at her blankly. "What do you mean?"

"I kept a personal file of everything I worked on at the firm. You know, kind of a backup record in case of emergencies. I sent it all to storage in the basement, and the boxes are dated. Just call my old secretary in the morning. She'll know how to retrieve it. Hopefully there's a copy of the information you need in there."

Michael paused for a moment. "Did anyone know you kept this backup file?"

Sandra shook her head. "No, I don't think so."

"Please do me a favor and don't tell anyone else about this until you hear from me, okay? There's been a lot of stuff disappearing lately, and I don't want you to get in the middle of it. If anyone calls you asking questions about Trinity Corporation, let me know as soon as possible."

Chapter 23

The large white van pulled to an abrupt stop in front of the Chase Manhattan Bank Building. Inside a carefully gathered team of federal officers waited for their instructions. Special Agent Robert Adams could feel his adrenaline pumping. This was the moment he had been waiting for. Reaching into the pocket of his jacket, he removed his enforcement badge and clipped it onto his lapel. He then took the small handheld radio off the dashboard and plugged in his headset. One piece fit neatly into his ear, allowing him to monitor the open channel, while a small microphone came down over his mouth, allowing him to communicate with the other agents while keeping both hands free.

He looked down at his watch. It was almost time for the show to begin. In the rearview mirror he saw the second van pull up behind him. Nico Fiori was sitting calmly in the front seat, waiting for his signal. Between the two vans there were eight officers, four from the enforcement division of the SEC and four from the New York Police Department.

"Nico, is your team ready to go?"

"Yeah. Do you really think we need all this hardware?"

There was nothing but silence. The two men clearly had different agendas. Adams wanted to march into the offices of Davis & White with all the subtlety of a sledgehammer smashing through a plate-glass window, while Nico preferred a less offensive approach. After not hearing a response, he realized he had probably undermined Adams's authority and quickly tried to rectify the situation. "Well, it's your show," he said, opening the door and stepping out onto the street.

Adams looked back at his team. "Okay, let's go in."

The van doors opened in unison, and the men marched through the lobby with Adams in the lead. There was only one bank of elevators servicing the top floors of the building, which meant there was only one way up and one way down. As a precaution Nico suggested leaving one of his plainclothes officers downstairs in front of the elevators. Adams agreed. The remaining officers quickly commandeered the first available elevator, asking the people who were waiting to take the next one.

The ride up to the fifty-eighth floor was solemn. Adams reached into his jacket one more time, making sure he had brought the search warrant. The other agents would never let him live it down if he left it in the van. When the doors opened onto the pristine lobby of Davis & White, Adams pushed his way forward to the receptionist and handed her the papers. "My name is Robert Adams. I'm a special agent with the enforcement division of the Securities and Exchange Commission. As I believe you already know, this is Lieutenant Nico Fiori with the NYPD. We have a search warrant for the offices of Jonathan Gage, one of your partners."

The young receptionist stared at him with her mouth hanging open as the phones on her switchboard rang unanswered. In the last four years, she had never seen anything like this happen.

"If you could just show us where Jonathan Gage's office is located, we can get started."

The woman turned pale as a ghost, and the panel of lights below her lit up like a Christmas tree. "I . . . uh . . . can I bring somebody out to talk to you?"

Adams smiled. "Sure, why don't you see if the managing partner is available?"

The receptionist quickly pressed the button for Richard Montague's direct line. "Rose, this is Rachel at the receptionist's desk. I have a large group of men out here from the SEC

and the NYPD. They say they have a search warrant for
Jonathan Gage's office. Can you send someone out here immediately to talk to them." There was a long moment of silence
before she continued. "Okay, sure." The receptionist looked
back at Adams. "Someone will be right out. Would you please
have a seat?"

Adams noticed that two men wearing neatly pressed suits
were sitting on the lobby couch staring attentively at what was
happening. They were clearly clients waiting for a meeting, but
the looks on their faces were of sheer horror. The younger man
quickly leaned over and began to whisper something in the ear
of the older. Adams wondered how long it would take for word
to spread through the city. It was just a matter of time, he
thought. News had a tendency to disseminate quickly in the financial community. Those who didn't hear about it by word of
mouth would read about it soon enough.

Tomorrow morning an article would appear on the front
page of *The New York Times* reporting that the SEC had exer-
cised a search warrant upon one of New York's most prominent
law firms in connection with a widening insider trading investigation. The story would also indicate that the NYPD was
looking into ties between the insider trading ring and the murder of one of the firm's partners. Adams had leaked the information to the paper's managing editor just to make sure
nothing would be left out. Of course it was just a matter of time
before the law firm tried to get an injunction challenging the
search warrant and narrowing the scope of the government's investigation. This was only natural.

"Gentlemen, you might as well make yourself comfortable,"
Adams said.

One of the larger federal agents took a seat on the corner of
the couch next to the two conservatively dressed men. Their
conversation immediately ceased, and one of them walked up
to the receptionist. "You can tell Mr. Rudolph that we've decided to cancel our meeting this morning," he said, nodding to
the other man, who rose. The two clients then moved toward
the elevator. The receptionist called after them, "Excuse me,

Mr. Rudolph will be right out. Really, there's no reason to leave." But it was already too late. They were gone.

Richard Montague was in the middle of a conference call with the firm's finance committee when his secretary interrupted him. Upon seeing her enter the room, his face instantly filled with anger and his eyes narrowed. She knew better than to disturb him during such calls. He placed his hand over the receiver. "Can't you see I'm on the telephone?" he shouted.

The elderly woman just looked at him sternly. "Mr. Montague, put down the telephone. We have a problem."

Her reaction surprised him. He paused for a moment, then took his hand off the receiver. "Excuse me, gentlemen, can I put you on hold for a moment?" He pressed the button on his phone, and the light began to blink. "Yes," he said. The tone in his voice had changed from one of anger to one of concern.

"Mr. Montague, there's a man out in the lobby. He's from the Securities and Exchange Commission. He says he has a warrant to search Jonathan Gage's office. There's a team of people with him, including that detective from the NYPD you spoke to last week."

Montague's face filled with tension. "Goddamn it," he responded. "Ask Bill Vernon to meet me in the lobby immediately. I don't care what he's doing. You just get that useless piece of shit up here, you hear me."

Montague then watched his secretary walk quickly back to her desk. He took a moment to think. He'd almost forgotten about the phone call he had placed on hold. He pressed the button. "I'm going to have to reconvene this meeting tomorrow. We've had a little problem that I have to deal with."

Montague hung up the phone, walked over to his wall cabinet, and took down his jacket. He often chastised young attorneys for walking around the office without coats. After all, they weren't accountants. After putting the jacket on and straightening his lapels, he headed to the reception area. He was surprised by the number of men who had taken over his lobby. It was practically a vigilante mob. "Gentlemen," he said, looking immediately for the man in charge. "My name is Mr. Montague, and I'm the managing partner of this law firm. Is there something I can help you with?"

Adams rose. "My name is Robert Adams. I'm a special agent with the enforcement division of the Securities and Exchange Commission. I'm here to serve you with a warrant to search the offices of one of your attorneys, Jonathan Gage. If you could direct me to his office, I'd appreciate it. In addition, we have an arrest warrant for one of your associates, Michael Elliot."

Montague tried to keep his best poker face. "Mr. Adams, we're always willing to cooperate with the government, but we are in a very sensitive situation here. We can't just open up a partner's office to you. We do work for a number of important clients, and to do so would be a breach of our duty of confidentiality to these clients. We're willing to provide you information which is proper, but certain types of communications are protected by attorney-client privilege, and it will take us time to go through them."

Adams had anticipated this response. "We don't want any information pertaining to his clients, at least not at this point in our investigation. We'd just like to take a look at Mr. Gage's office for any personal files and any files pertaining to entities he may have created for himself." Before Adams could continue, another man entered the room. His thick gray hair was combed neatly back, and he had the appearance of a statesman. Adams recognized him as Bill Vernon, the former director of enforcement for the SEC. The rumor was that he had left the public sector several years back to take a lucrative job on Wall Street, but Adams hadn't realized it was with Davis & White.

The man walked over to Adams and put his hand on his shoulder. "Hello, Robert. It's good to see you. What seems to be the problem here?" Adams looked surprised that Vernon remembered who he was. Before he could say anything, Vernon went on. "Why don't we continue this conversation in the conference room down the hall. I'm sure we can come to some kind of agreement that will be satisfactory to everyone involved and permit you to carry out your search in the least disruptive manner possible."

Michael was sitting quietly in Jonathan Gage's office when there was a knock on the door. He was surprised to see a messenger holding a thick red interoffice mail envelope. "My supervisor told me to bring this to you," he said, setting it down on the desk. "He said it was important." Michael took the package and thanked the clerk. There were two columns on the front of every interoffice envelope, one for the recipient and the other for the sender. Every time the envelope was reused, the names of the last sender and recipient were scribbled out and new names were written in the row beneath it. He glanced down the long list of scratched-out names until he finally reached the last name on the bottom. The package had been sent from Sandy Villanueva's secretary and no doubt contained the paralegal's backup files. For a moment Michael hesitated. His mind drifted back to his conversation with Montague and the managing partner's admonishment that he would be the only one who knew what was in Gage's office.

Michael knew the investigators from the SEC would probably never uncover the Trinity Corporation files. All he had to do was throw them away and forget this whole thing had ever happened. But he had gone too far down the road to turn back now. He needed to know what Gage had gotten himself into and why the young partner had ended his life so tragically.

Michael undid the string holding the envelope shut and pulled out the documents. The file was quite extensive, with an index in front and numbered tabs. He began to flip through the papers. The first tab contained the paralegal's correspondence with Corporate Services International. Sandra's instructions to CSI had been relatively simple. She had reserved the name Trinity Corporation and had appropriate charter documents prepared and filed in the Netherlands Antilles. This was not uncommon in and of itself. However, the next series of letters gave Michael reason to pause.

The correspondence was directed to two banks, one in Luxembourg and the other in Belgium, each requesting account applications and signature cards for numbered accounts. In his entire career Michael had come across a numbered account only once. It was in a transaction for a wealthy Swiss national. At the time the partner in charge of the matter had explained that numbered accounts were simply bank accounts that were identified by a number rather than by a name. Clients often established them for no reason other than to afford themselves a certain level of protection and privacy, especially if bank records or passbooks were lost, stolen, or obtained under duress. While Michael believed many people did set up numbered accounts for legitimate purposes, he was by no means ignorant of the primary reason for such accounts. Most were conduits for drug dealers, money launderers, arms traffickers, and covert intelligence agencies in the U.S. and abroad, who used them to shield their activities from outside scrutiny. Why would Trinity Corporation have needed to set up a numbered account? The whole matter was becoming quite unsettling. There could be only one reason for all the secrecy. The SEC's allegations must be true. But why had Gage gotten himself into this mess. And who was the mysterious attorney in the Los Angeles office who had helped him? Michael then remembered that paralegals usually sent copies of their correspondence to the other attorneys working on the matter. He quickly leafed through the letters looking for a name on the bottoms of the pages, but there were none.

Michael then flipped to the last tab of the file that contained copies of the corporate charter documents for Trinity Corporation. Surely there would be copies of the resolutions issuing the stock and establishing a managing director with the power to control the corporation and sign on its behalf. Just past the memorandum of association and bylaws, he found what he was looking for. When he got to the second page of the resolutions, his body froze. Next to the title Managing Director was the name *Michael Elliot*.

The signature beside it was his own, duplicated perfectly. "Jesus Christ," he said. He stood up and backed away from the desk like it was some kind of bomb getting ready to detonate. His heart was racing a mile a minute, and he began to hyperventilate. Suddenly there was a knock at the door. Before he could respond, Gloria's face appeared in the doorway. She looked as if she was in shock herself. She must have seen the files, he thought.

"Michael," she said. "You're not going to believe this. There's a team of officers from the SEC and the NYPD in the main conference room."

The blood was rushing to his head, and the room felt like it was spinning out of control. This wasn't happening. This couldn't be happening. His eyes drifted back down to the document on the desk in front of him. "Do you know what they want?"

"They have a search warrant for Jonathan's office. Mr. Montague just went to meet with them," she said, starting to cry. "They want you to come down to the conference room immediately. . . . Michael, they said they have a warrant for your arrest."

Part II

Chapter 24

There wasn't much time. He felt as if he was stuck in a room that was filling up with water. He could see it rising inch by inch around him, but there was nothing he could do to stop it. He knew the longer he stayed the more likely it was that he would never escape. How had this happened? How had things spiraled out of control? The evidence he was holding in his hand was damning. How could he possibly convince them that he had nothing to do with this? Michael cursed out loud, and his hands began to shake. He was having an anxiety attack. For a moment he felt as if he was going to faint. He needed to gain control over himself. Michael closed his eyes and took a deep breath. When he reopened them, the room stopped spinning and a strange calmness pervaded him. Only a month ago he would have thought himself incapable of such cool deliberation at a time like this. He turned to Gloria. "Tell them I'll be right down," he said, ushering her out the door and closing it behind her. He took another deep breath and gathered his thoughts. On the back of the door he could see his jacket hanging, as if it was calling out to him. He knew he had to get out of there. After putting it on, he reached for the door handle, but something stopped him. The documents—how could he just leave them? He rushed back to the desk and picked up the files. He had to get rid of them. For a moment he thought about throwing them in the trash can, but that would be the first place they would look. They probably had a team searching through the Dumpsters right now. He looked around the office for another place to hide them, but there was nothing that would suffice. Just when he was about to give up, he saw the large red envelope. The interoffice mail, why hadn't he thought of it before?

Michael undid the flap and slid the documents inside. He picked up a black felt-tipped pen, crossed his name off the list, and scrawled "JAMES MONEHAN—LOS ANGELES OF-FICE" in large letters. He opened the door and walked into the hallway. For a moment he expected to see Gloria waiting for him, but fortunately she was on the other side of the carrels, busy talking to the receptionist.

Michael started down the hall. The interoffice mail drop was only two offices away, but it seemed like a mile. As he made his way toward it, his mind began to wander. What if someone saw him? He was hiding evidence and obstructing a federal investigation, but there was no choice. When he got to the shute, he pulled open the door without the slightest hesitation and dropped the envelope inside. The sound of the package sliding down the mail drop made him breathe a sigh of relief.

His calm, however, was short-lived. Michael knew they were waiting for him in the conference room at the end of the hall—a team of investigators from the SEC along with members of the NYPD. He had to pass right by them in order to get to the elevator. Fortunately the firm occupied eight floors in the building, the one he was on now and another seven below him, each of which was accessible by an internal stairwell. Michael turned left into the back hallway and walked toward a large metal door. Using his temporary access card, he opened it and began to run down the stairs. His footsteps echoed loudly in the narrow corridor, sounding as if someone was chasing after him. He began to move faster. When he'd gone down two flights, he used his access card to reenter the offices.

The fifty-sixth floor held the firm's library, and attorneys and paralegals regularly used the interoffice stairs to access it. People were sitting at the carrels or meandering through the stacks. Most were preoccupied with their work and ignored Michael as he passed through. When he got to the elevator, a woman was waiting. Her face was buried in a book, and she had already pressed the down button. Michael pretended nothing was wrong. He wasn't sure how much time he would have. Five minutes, maybe ten, then they would begin to look for him. First in the building, then the search would be expanded to the airports and train stations. New York was a big city. With so many millions of people it was easy to get lost. He needed time to think.

When the elevator arrived, he waited for the woman to enter, then followed her in. She had pressed the button for the lobby, and he stood behind her while the doors shut. He felt the familiar pull as the express elevator began its descent. Then a horrible thought came to him: What if they had someone in the lobby waiting for him? There was only one way in and out of the offices. Chances were they would have posted an officer at the elevator banks. He lunged at the button for the last floor the express elevator stopped at. For a moment he felt the anxiety return. Had they already passed it? Was it too late? Then the descent slowed and the number fifty-one lit up. Michael let out a sigh of relief.

The woman was staring at him oddly. "I'm sorry," he said. "I forgot to press my floor." She shrugged and turned her attention back to the book.

Michael quickly got off the elevator. The fire stairs were his only option. They went all the way to the lobby and were far from the elevator banks.

Michael raced to the stairwell. He opened the door with his access card and started down, counting each floor as he passed. In no time the sweat was rolling off his forehead, and his shirt became damp. He cursed himself for not staying in shape. In high school he had been a distance runner. With his missing finger, running was one of the few sports that didn't place him at a disadvantage. His best time in the mile had been four minutes and twenty-two seconds, but those days were long gone. Now he was twenty-five pounds heavier and couldn't break six minutes if he had to. At the twenty-fifth floor, he could feel his heart racing and his breath becoming heavy. He was hitting a stride, but his legs were beginning to ache.

He looked at his watch. Two minutes had passed. He pushed

harder. As he got into the single digits, he could feel the adrenaline kicking in. Nine-eight-seven-six-five-four-three-two-one. At the last floor he stopped. Bending over he tried to catch his breath and brushed the sweat off his face. All he had to do was make it out of the building. He took one more breath and placed his access card over the sensor. When he heard the electronic lock release, he pushed the door open.

The uniformed NYPD officer was waiting at the express elevator. He had studied Michael's picture the night before and scrutinized each of the men coming on and off the elevator. When Michael came out of the stairwell, the two of them were less than twenty feet apart, but the officer's attention was focused in the other direction. Michael breathed a sigh of relief. He walked unnoticed toward the revolving glass door and didn't look back.

The legalities of executing a search warrant on a law firm were quite complex, but Robert Adams was well aware of this. He had been through it with the federal magistrate when he sought the search warrant. The scope had been narrowed from what he had originally requested, but this wasn't surprising. Given Davis & White's reputation and political connections, no judge would want to be second-guessed in what was sure to be a controversial and well-publicized matter. For the most part, Adams had anticipated all of this. What he hadn't anticipated, however, was running into Bill Vernon. Under no circumstances was he going to open up the firm's file room to Adams or anyone else without a fight. "We are more than willing to cooperate," Vernon explained "But I've got to make sure that everything is in order here. I just can't turn over the keys to you gentlemen, as much as I'd like to. There are a number of interests that have to be balanced. We have to consider our clients' right to attorney-client confidentiality. But I'm sure you already know that," he said, smiling.

Vernon put on his glasses and began to slowly read through the two-page search warrant. The fact that there were seven federal and local officers in the conference room didn't seem to bother him in the slightest. Instead he remained calm, maintaining all the composure of a master card player in the world tournament of poker. If there was any anxiety it didn't show in the slightest. After he had read through the warrant twice, Vernon set the papers on the table. Taking off his glasses, he glanced back up at Adams. "Let's talk about the warrant," he said.

Adams's impatience got the better of him. "Why don't we talk about Michael Elliot first? Where is he?"

Vernon seemed unconcerned and waved off the question. "His secretary said he was on his way. I think we should give him a few minutes."

Adams reluctantly conceded. The two men then spent the next five minutes debating what could and couldn't be turned over to the federal officers. Neither wanted to go back to the judge for clarification—Vernon didn't want to be seen as obstructing a federal investigation, and Adams didn't want to lose any time. Finally, after both men had made concessions and a satisfactory resolution had been reached, Adams again became cognizant of the fact that Michael still hadn't joined them. "Where is Elliot?"

Vernon looked at his watch. The associate should have been there by now and he was losing his confidence. He walked over to the speakerphone and had the receptionist connect him to Gage's office. The phone rang twice before Gloria picked it up.

"This is Bill Vernon. I'm down in the main conference room," he barked. "Elliot was supposed to be here ten minutes ago. Tell him to get his ass down here."

There was a long silence.

"Do you hear me?" he demanded.

Gloria didn't know what to say. "Mr. Vernon, he left for the conference room ten minutes ago."

"That's impossible!" Vernon shouted. "He's not here." Vernon's confidence was now completely gone. As he looked back over at the team of officers in front of him, he could see Adams's face become red with anger and the muscles in his neck constrict.

Adams slammed his fist on the table. "Where is his office? Take me to his office."

"He's on this floor," Vernon said.

The men began running down the hallway. When they got to Gage's office, Gloria was standing in the doorway with her hand over her mouth.

"Where is he?" Adams shouted.

Gloria was shaking and tears were running down her face. "He should have been there. He told me ten minutes ago that he was going down to the conference room to join you."

For a moment Adams didn't know what to do. His investigation was quickly turning into a disaster. He was not experienced in search and containment. He was a prosecutor by training, a man who spent most of his time in an office following paper trails and chasing down money. For the first time he felt out of his depth. Suddenly he heard static behind him. He turned around and saw Nico Fiori taking the radio off his belt and calling down to the guard in the lobby.

"Elliot is missing. . . . I repeat, Elliot is missing. . . . Have you seen him come off the elevator?"

There was more static, then the officer responded. "No, I've been down here the whole time. He hasn't come off."

"Call for more backup," Nico said. He looked up at the officers behind him. "Form two teams and search the building floor by floor. Start here and work your way down." The teams headed off in different directions.

"Is this Jonathan Gage's office?" Adams blurted out.

Vernon nodded, and Adams began to rifle through the room. "Do you have a log of files that Elliot accessed?"

"Yes, our records center keeps track of all our files."

"I want to see a list of everything Elliot got his hands on. I'm also going to want to search his office in Los Angeles. We'll give you two days to make sure the documents don't contain any confidential communications. If you believe any information we've requested is privileged, we'll have an ex parte hearing to determine whether the documentation is protected. Do we have an understanding?"

For the first time in his career, Vernon was at a loss for words. His face was now a pale shade of gray, and he looked like he was going to vomit.

"Do we have an understanding?" Adams repeated.

"Yes," Vernon mumbled. "We have an understanding."

Nico turned his attention back to Gloria, who was still sobbing. "It's okay," he said. "Do you know where he's staying?"

"I believe he's at the RIHGA. . . ." As soon as the words left her mouth, she felt like Judas. She began to cry harder. "My God, what has he done?"

Chapter 25

It had been over a year since Karen Bauer had been back to the Federal Building. As she walked through the hallways, memories of cases began to come back to her. She couldn't have asked for a better training ground. But as at any other workplace, the office proved to be filled with petty politics and gamesmanship. In the end she realized she had gotten all she could out of the job, and it was time to move on.

Her meeting had been scheduled for two o'clock with Susan Felding, a staff attorney whom she didn't recognize. This wasn't unusual. The U.S. Attorney's Office was a revolving door. However, when she got to the conference room on the eighth floor, she was surprised to find a ghost from her past also waiting for her. Rick Smith was ten years older than she, but he had remained thin and taut. His family had been from the Midwest, giving him his fair skin, light brown hair, and All-American features. He had been a guard on the University of Kansas basketball team but was too short to play professionally. Instead he had gone to law school, then joined the Department of Justice, where he had risen to become the U.S. attorney for Los Angeles. She hadn't expected to see someone of his stature at this meeting. From the expression on his face, he clearly hadn't expected to see her there either.

Their relationship had been brief and, in hindsight, just another in a series of mistakes she had made with the opposite sex. His innocent looks had been deceiving. When they started working together, she thought he was different from any other man she had known. This was largely why his advances caught her off guard. One night after they had successfully tried a case together, they went out for a drink to celebrate. One drink turned into two and then three. Before she knew it they were in his car with their hands all over each other like high school teenagers.

She was never mad at herself for sleeping with him. After all, she was as much at fault as he was. What bothered her about the relationship was her not having seen him for what he really was. At the time she thought she was the first woman he had been with since he married. He had told her his marriage was falling apart, and he was going to divorce his wife. Their relationship lasted for several months before he told her he didn't want to hurt his children and was going to give his marriage another shot. He even told her that if he had two lives to live he would have wanted to spend one of them with her. It wasn't until several months later that she realized he had taken up with an attractive young woman in the civil division soon after they broke up and there had been others before and after her. Now here they were, face to face.

"So you've gone to the other side," Smith said.

Susan Felding seemed surprised by his comment. "You two know each other?"

"Yes," he said, pausing. "Karen was an assistant U.S. attorney before she decided to go into private practice."

Karen looked at the young woman standing next to him. She was petite, with long auburn hair and deep blue eyes. Smith had always surrounded himself with the prettier women in the office, and there was no doubt that he was sleeping with her. Karen looked back up at him and smiled. "Well, it doesn't seem like you've had any difficulty finding new talent in my absence."

Smith's face became pale. "Will Mr. Faud be joining us shortly?" he asked abruptly.

"Mr. Faud had to leave the country for a family emergency," she explained. "He wanted me to meet with you anyway. So why don't we get down to business?" She took a legal pad from her briefcase and uncapped her Mont Blanc pen. "Now, you requested that my client, Mr. Faud, turn over his personal financial statements in connection with a pending federal investigation involving two satellites. Is my client being accused of any wrongdoing at this time? Is he the subject of this investigation?"

Smith folded his hands in front of him and looked over to Felding. "Susan, can you do me a favor? I left the export licensing file in my office. Can you get it for me?"

She began to protest. "But I thought you didn't want—"

He held up his hand to stop her. "I've changed my mind," he said.

The young woman looked miffed as she stood up and walked out the door. The expression on Smith's face went from anger to feigned concern. "Do you know who your client is?" he asked. "Do you have any idea what you're involved in?"

Karen capped her pen. "Why don't you tell me?" she said, leaning back in her chair.

"The State Department has a file two inches thick on this guy. He's been linked to everything from political assassinations to selling arms to the third world."

Karen shook her head. "Come on, Rick," she said, rolling her eyes. "The major defense contractors didn't seem overly concerned when he was buying five hundred million dollars' worth of satellite equipment from them. Neither were the congressmen from the district where the satellites were made. I believe my client has already explained that he had no idea of any modifications allegedly made to these satellites. He was simply a broker facilitating the negotiations."

"He knew goddamn well what these satellites were going to be used for. The National Security Agency should never have approved the export licenses in the first place."

"But they did," Karen said calmly. "So now you're on some kind of fishing expedition. If you're concerned that someone may have made payoffs to have people look the other way or expedite the licensing, then I suggest you subpoena the records of the politicians involved in the matter. My client has done nothing wrong or even remotely illegal. Before you make wild accusations, I suggest you do your homework."

"He's in on this," Smith said, shaking his head. "He's in on it up to his eyeballs."

"You and I both know that you don't have any grounds to subpoena this information from my client. If you did, you would already have gone into court. So I'm expecting this to end here and now." She closed her folder and rose from the table.

Before she could leave, Smith grabbed her by the arm. "Karen, listen to me. Stay away from him," he said. "He's dangerous. You have no idea the things he's involved in."

"Let go of my arm," she said, pulling away. "It's a little late to protect me."

"I'm telling you, stay away from him."

His order just seemed to anger her. "Find your information somewhere else, or I'm going to make sure that it gets painful for both of us. I don't think you're going to want to explain to the federal judge why you should recuse yourself from this matter given your prior sexual relationship with defense counsel."

Smith turned pale as a ghost as she picked up her briefcase and marched out of the conference room.

Driving back to the office, Karen couldn't help but revisit what Smith had told her. She knew Faud had a bad reputation when she got involved in the matter, but what was Smith referring to? In her mind she tried to dismiss it. There were two sides to every story in litigation. If the client was really dangerous, the firm wouldn't have taken him on. Smith was simply posturing. Litigation had a tendency to bring out the worst in people. It was probably just rumor and innuendo. Nonetheless, there was something about Faud she found disturbing.

Karen tried to think of other things as she made her way back to the office. She had a settlement conference in federal court later that afternoon. There would be just enough time to call Faud and update him before she had to leave again. As she drove onto the freeway on-ramp, she was completely oblivious of the black Mercedes sedan following her. It had been there from the moment she left the U.S. Attorney's Office. The driver's instructions were simple. He was to remain unobserved at all times and update them on her position every hour.

When Karen got back to her office, she immediately called Faud at the private phone number that he had given her. "Mr. Faud," she said, pausing. "I wanted to give you an update."

"How did the meeting go?"

"As well as can be expected." There wasn't any reason to share the gory details with him. As far as she could tell he had a short temper. "I told them while we wanted to be cooperative, we weren't prepared to open personal and confidential financial information to facilitate a baseless investigation. I explained that they have other means of obtaining the information they need, and that I would challenge any subpoena in court."

"How did the attorney respond?"

"He didn't," she said. "He likes to play his cards close to his vest, but I'm pretty sure he's got nothing on you. Otherwise he would have put the pressure on."

"Very well," he said, pausing. "I trust you will keep me apprised."

"Absolutely, but I expect it to end here."

"Ms. Bauer," he said. "Do you know this man, Rick Smith? I understand you worked at the U.S. Attorney's Office."

Karen paused. So that was the reason they had brought her into this, she thought. But how would Faud have uncovered such a thing? He must have a mole deep inside the U.S. Attorney's Office. "Yes, I know him," she said. "We worked extensively together."

"Well, Ms. Bauer, I strongly suggest you use every means within your power to persuade him to forget about this." Then the dial tone came over the phone.

There was something about his voice that made her sick to her stomach. She felt like a marionette with someone pulling the strings above her. Faud knew more about her relationship with Smith than he was letting on, and she didn't like to be played.

Chapter 26

The financial district was filled with men in dark suits and black wing tips making their way down busy streets. Against the cold, gray backdrop of the buildings, the traffic formed a monochromatic river of motion, and Michael tried to blend in quickly. His heart was racing. Small beads of sweat formed on his forehead and quickly fell like threads against his neck until coming to rest on his collar. He kept trying to tell himself that this was all a bad dream. Any moment he would wake up in his bed, the sheets drenched with sweat and his body tangled in them like an insect caught in a spiderweb. But no matter how hard he tried to pinch himself, he didn't wake up. Whoever had done this had gone to great lengths to set him up. And his running would only make him look guiltier.

Still, he knew his odds were far better on the streets than in jail. At least this way he would have a chance to figure out who had framed him, rather than having to rely on a defense attorney without the slightest clue where to start. The case against him was compelling. He had worked with Gage on each of the transactions in which the SEC had found evidence of insider trading. To make matters worse, it was just a matter of time before they recovered the corporate records and bank statements with his name and signature on them.

His head began to throb. He needed more time to think, but time was the one thing he didn't have. The federal agents surely had realized he was gone by now. They were probably sealing off the building and bringing in more officers to search floor by floor. Maybe they had even checked with building security and discovered that his access card had been used to unlock the door to the fire stairs. Perhaps they were circulating his picture at this very moment. He couldn't think about it. He just had to go on.

The only thing he had going for him was that it would take the agents time to uncover the paper trail. The Trinity files had already been purged once from the firm's records center. When they searched Gage's office, they would find nothing. It would take them a few more days to track down Sandy Villanueva. Even then, they would be unable to locate the Trinity files. The only incriminating evidence was now in the mailroom en route to Los Angeles. Still, it was only a matter of time.

Michael quickened his pace. Once he had made it a safe distance from the building, he checked his wallet. He had taken three hundred dollars from the ATM the night before, but that wouldn't last long. To make matters worse, he wouldn't be able to use his credit cards because they would allow him to be traced in a matter of moments. He would need cash, a lot of it. Fortunately, the downtown branch of Bank of America was near the World Trade Center. He had more than fifteen thousand dollars in his savings account. He didn't think they could have frozen his account this quickly.

Michael pulled open the large glass doors of the bank and made his way to the raised desk with its cubbyholes filled with deposit and withdrawal slips and its pens fastened by long silver chains. He took a withdrawal slip and filled it out as best he could. Then he waited in line for a teller. There was one guard at the front entrance and a row of tellers behind the thick wooden counter. The first available teller was a woman who didn't look more than twenty-five. That was the only thing he had going for him. A withdrawal of this amount would surely draw some attention, but the woman seemed indifferent. If she asked why he was making such a large withdrawal, he would just tell her he was buying a car. It was his money, and he could do what he wanted with it. Then again, there was the possibility that the Feds had anticipated he would do this. Maybe they had already frozen his accounts. How culpable would he look now? The federal investigators show up at his office with a search warrant, and he runs, only to get caught less than a mile away in a bank withdrawing a sizeable chunk of his savings. There would be no getting out of it. Hell, there was probably no getting out of it anyway.

"Next," the young woman called.

Michael studied her closely. If she showed the slightest hesitation when accessing his account, he would run for the door. The old security guard didn't even have a gun. Besides, he wouldn't shoot an unarmed man.

"Can I help you?" the woman repeated.

"Yes," Michael replied, handing her the withdrawal slip. "I would like to withdraw fifteen thousand dollars from my savings account."

"What's your account number?"

"I actually forgot my number. I was hoping you could check with my ATM card."

The woman looked annoyed, but she took the card and began punching at the computer. She then took the withdrawal slip and filled in the number. "I'm going to need to see some identification."

Michael reached into the pocket of his jacket and pulled out the first thing he could find. It was Jonathan Gage's passport, and for a moment he felt as if his heart would stop. The woman looked up at him, and Michael hesitated. Fumbling, he reached back into his pocket and withdrew his wallet.

"I can use your passport," she told him.

"No, that's okay," Michael responded, taking out his California driver's license.

The young woman paused for a second, then picked up the withdrawal slip. "Hold on a second," she said. "Steve," she shouted.

Michael began to panic. A young man in a tie came over and consulted with the teller out of Michael's earshot. After a few moments, the woman came back with the manager. Michael looked for the guard. He was no longer by the door. Maybe the woman had triggered some kind of silent alarm; maybe he had gone for the police. Before Michael could think any further, the young man spoke. "Excuse me, Mr. Elliot. . . ."

Michael froze. "Yes," he stammered.

"I noticed you are withdrawing a rather large amount of cash from your savings account. I hope you're not closing your account with us. I mean, I could suggest a certificate of deposit to provide a better rate of return if that's what you'd like."

Michael sighed with relief. "No, I'm not closing the account. I'm just putting a down payment on a car."

"Oh." The young man smiled. "I could put that in a cashier's check if you'd like. It might be safer."

Michael hesitated. "No, that's okay. It'll be easier with cash."

The man nodded, seemingly appeased. When he got five feet away, he stopped again and turned around. "So what kind of car is it anyway?"

Jesus Christ, Michael thought. "It's a Volvo station wagon," he replied, doing his best to kill the conversation.

"Oh," the man responded with faint enthusiasm. "Have a good day."

The teller returned to the window. "How would you like that?"

"In hundreds," Michael said. He watched her count out fifteen stacks of ten one-hundred-dollar bills. Then she put them all together and handed them to him. He didn't even bother recounting. He simply slipped the bills into an envelope and placed them in the top pocket of his jacket. He smiled and walked out of the bank.

As the federal agents moved through the hallways of the Chase Manhattan Bank Building, the secretaries whispered and stared. Before the floor-by-floor search was finished, the rumors were running rampant through Wall Street. No one could believe that a prominent lawyer from Davis & White had been murdered. Even more disturbing were the allegations that a young associate from the same firm was now a suspect in the crime. To make matters worse, Michael Elliot was nowhere to be found. The surveillance tapes and computer records confirmed that he had used his access card to go down the fire stairs and exit the building. There was even video footage of him walking out behind the officer posted at the elevator.

Now there was only one alternative. Nico called his secretary and instructed her to have pictures of Michael faxed to every precinct in the city, along with a brief description. "WANTED—Michael Elliot—for federal securities fraud and for questioning in connection with the murder of Jonathan Gage, a prominent Wall Street attorney. Suspect was last seen wearing a dark gray suit, white shirt, and red tie. He is five feet eleven inches tall, with dark skin, dark hair, and medium build. Suspect is in his early thirties and has fled arrest once. He may be armed." By the time the third watch came on, there would be five thousand police officers looking for him. With any luck they would pick him up by nightfall. But New York was still a big city. With over ten million people living in just a few square miles, it was an easy place to get lost. Nico knew that the more time passed, the less his chances would be of finding Elliot.

"So where do you think he's going?"

"I don't know," Nico said, rubbing his temples. His head was beginning to throb. "Elliot's secretary said he was staying at the RIHGA on Fifty-fourth Street. Maybe he's gone back to get his things. I think it's unlikely, but we should check it out anyway."

Adams nodded, and the two left the building. The ride to the hotel was quiet; neither wanted to discuss what had happened. Nico used the time to study the picture of Michael he had with him. Truth be told, he didn't know much about the young attorney other than what was in the SEC file. There had been a brief description of Michael's background, along with the surveillance pictures the FBI had taken in Los Angeles and New York. But from what Nico could tell, Michael seemed like a perfectly normal young man. He had no prior arrests or convictions. There wasn't the slightest sign he was remotely capable of these acts. Still, appearances were often deceiving. Going through the NICA rap sheets each morning served as daily confirmation of this fact. The pictures that came over the transom rarely seemed to match the crimes. On one side would be a photo of a kind-looking man and next to it a description of the alleged crime—murder, rape, torture, disfigurement, assault, mayhem.

But no matter how hard Nico tried to dismiss them, the doubts kept coming back to him. What could have possibly been the motive for Michael to kill Jonathan Gage? Had the two been partners in crime and Michael double-crossed him? After all, Gage knew that the Feds were close to bringing him in. Maybe he had decided to run and Michael came to New York to help him. Then something happened. Maybe Michael got greedy. Instead of splitting the profits down the middle, perhaps he planned to go for it all. Money often had a strange effect on people. In his years as a detective Nico had seen men do a lot worse things for a lot less cash. But something didn't seem right with this theory. He reached up and began to run his fingers through his thick black hair. He needed a few days to piece things together, but time was running out.

Michael's room was on the twenty-eighth floor. After Nico explained the situation, the hotel manager was more than happy to give him a master key. Nico now held it in his left hand. With his right he reached for his service revolver. The Glock nine millimeter felt strange to him. He could disassemble and reassemble the gun in the dark, but now it felt awkward. He didn't think Michael would be there, although there was always a chance. He had already underestimated the suspect once; he wasn't going to make the same mistake twice.

He slid the card key into the electronic lock and waited until the green light flashed. "Police," Nico shouted, pushing open the door. His gun was pointed straight in front of him. For a moment he listened for motion—footsteps, the rustling of clothes, the release of a safety catch—but there was only silence. After checking the bathroom, Nico holstered his gun and called in for two undercover officers. He would post them on twenty-four-hour watch in the lobby in case Michael came back. But he knew that was unlikely. Then Nico took out a pair of latex gloves and began to go through Michael's belongings. In the closet he found another suit, along with several dress shirts, ties, socks, and underwear. There was even a pair of jeans, an oxford shirt, and a pair of loafers. It was what Nico didn't find, however, that was most disturbing.

When he had reopened the investigation of Jonathan Gage's death, Nico thought he would have to exhume the body. This required family consent or a court order, neither of which he had the time to obtain. Fortunately, the medical examiner had the discretion of preserving blood and tissue samples in autopsy cases where foul play had already been ruled out, and Dr. Martinez had had the foresight to retain the samples on this case. When Nico told him of the inconsistencies between where the victim allegedly jumped and where the body was found, Martinez retrieved the samples from cold storage.

Detailed blood workups were costly, and in cases where suicide was the most likely cause, the medical examiner often didn't go to the additional expense. The initial screenings in the Gage autopsy had been only for common drugs—barbiturates, cocaine, heroin, and similar substances readily accessible on the streets. They hadn't screened for drugs that were less common or more difficult to trace. With foul play now suspected, however, Dr. Martinez was authorized to conduct far more comprehensive testing.

There were a number of ways to make Gage's death look like a suicide. The most likely was that Gage had been rendered unconscious and his body thrown into the river. Chloroform and ether were common possibilities, but both had strong smells easy to recognize on a body, even one that had been in the East River for some time. There also weren't any signs of struggle or suffocation often associated with inhaling either of these substances. However, when Dr. Martinez finished more detailed screenings, he found something unusual. There were traces of Rohypnol, a drug banned in the United States but still accessible abroad and on the black market, in the victim's bloodstream. Rohypnol was often called the date-rape drug;

one or two drops placed in a drink would have been enough to render Gage unconscious.

Jonathan Gage had been drugged and his naked body thrown into the East River. The victim had still been breathing at the time and had inhaled a good amount of water before drowning. Whoever had killed Gage had dumped his body into the river at a remote location where it was unlikely he'd be seen. The killer had then gone back to the Brooklyn Bridge and laid out Gage's clothes, wedding ring, and briefcase to make it look as if he had been a jumper. With the weight of the federal investigation on his shoulders, suicide would have been a natural reaction.

Searching Michael's hotel room, Nico had hoped to find something incriminating. Perhaps a bottle of Rohypnol in the medicine cabinet, a suitcase full of cash, a Brazilian passport. But he found nothing even remotely suspicious. He would have the crime scene investigative unit send over a low-priority dispatch that evening to pack up Michael's belongings and check for soil or fiber samples that might tie him to the East River. Nico then tried to think of what else the room could tell him. He walked over to the desk looking for some kind of note on hotel stationery, but there was nothing. He looked into the wastebasket. There were a couple of crumpled pieces of paper inside, a receipt from the Carnegie Deli and another from the gift shop downstairs. He turned his attention back to the phone. He made a note to ask the manager for a printout of phone calls made. Maybe that would give him some clue about where Michael would run.

Chapter 27

Penn Station was filled with people waiting to take early trains home to the suburbs of New York, New Jersey, and Connecticut. Most of the people working in the financial district who had families eventually moved out of the city, riding the trains into the city in the morning and back out again at night. Although it was only midafternoon, the station was filled with people, rushing out to soccer practice or home to pick up their children after school. It was nothing like what the place would look like at five o'clock. Michael had heard that being there at rush hour was akin to being stuck in an ant farm, people climbing over each other and fighting for the first chance to get home.

On the platform in front of him Michael saw two NYPD officers in their navy blue uniforms and black polished shoes. Each had an earpiece plugged into a walkie-talkie on his belt. They were watching everybody coming in and out of the station. Michael suddenly wished it were rush hour. It would have been easier to fall in among the crowd. Nonetheless, he tried his best to look inconspicuous. There was a middle-aged woman walking next to him. He asked her for the time, then engaged her in small talk until they had made their way past the officers. Any second he expected the men to come after him, but they remained still.

In the center of the station Michael found a board listing all the departing Amtrak trains. Trains to Washington, DC, left every hour, and the next one was in less than twenty minutes. Michael walked up to the first available ticket window. "I'd like to buy a ticket on the two o'clock train to Washington, DC." The ticket agent didn't even look up at him. Her hands just typed his destination on the keyboard in front of her. She was old, and her smoker's wrinkles and silvery hair reminded him of Gloria. Poor Gloria, he thought. They were probably putting her through the third degree this very moment. There was no one left to protect her. It didn't seem fair.

"That will be eighty-six dollars," the woman said, interrupting his thoughts.

Michael handed her a hundred-dollar bill and waited for his change and the ticket. The woman passed them to him with barely a glance. "Next," she called.

As Michael walked away from the booth, he looked back to where the two police officers had been standing, but they were gone, and their absence sent a wave of anxiety through him. Were they looking for him? Maybe his picture had already been circulated throughout the train stations and the airports. Damn it, he thought. He couldn't keep doing this to himself. He just had to continue on.

His train was departing from the sixth gate, and he still had twenty minutes to kill. He walked slowly toward the platform. The screeching of the brakes on an arriving train filled the station. Michael suddenly felt the need to hear a friendly voice, even if it was just for a moment. The only person he could think of to call was Arturo. Maybe his friend would be able to help him out. Surely he would have some idea about who had set him up. Maybe he could even retrieve the interoffice package going to Monehan's office. Michael rushed over to the wall of pay phones and instinctively reached for his calling card. Once the dial tone came, he punched in the number for Arturo's office. It was almost eleven o'clock in L.A., and he hoped Arturo would be back from his regular morning run to the coffee stand downstairs. The phone rang four times, but there was no answer. "Come on, Arturo," he said to himself. "Pick up the goddamn phone."

The phone continued to ring. Just when he was about to give up, he heard Arturo's voice over the line.

"Art Rollins," the voice said, half panting.

"Arturo," Michael said, then paused. For a moment he was at a loss for words.

"Jesus Christ, I heard the phone ringing and ran down the hallway." Arturo struggled to regain his breath.

Michael could almost picture his friend standing behind his desk, the disheveled sandy brown hair hanging in his face, the poorly tied knot in his necktie, and his shirt coming untucked in the back. Arturo was a complete and utter failure as a lawyer, but as a friend he was loyal and unquestioning. "Arturo, I need your help. I don't have a whole lot of time to explain. . . . You're going to hear about it soon enough. Please, just promise me you won't believe anything you read in the papers or hear through the rumor mill."

"What are you talking about?" Arturo responded, as if this was some kind of practical joke.

"Somebody set me up," Michael whispered into the phone. "The partner I was working with in New York, Jonathan Gage, he was involved in insider trading. They think I was helping him."

"Quit joking around," Arturo said. "I'm not buying it."

"Look, I don't have much time. I need you to do me a favor. One of the associates in our office was working with Sandy Villanueva, a paralegal in New York, on a matter called Trinity. He helped her set up an offshore corporation in the Netherlands Antilles with one of the corporate services. I need you to figure out who was helping her. Whoever it was pretended to be me. They even forged my signature. Check the phone records. Check the computer system. Maybe you can trace the documents and figure out who was doing this."

"You're not joking, are you?" Arturo asked. Michael could hear him fumbling for a pad and scrawling down the instructions. "Where you gonna be, the New York office?"

Michael played with the coin return on the pay phone as he tried to gather his thoughts. "I'm not coming back to the office," he said, then paused. "Look, there's one other thing I need you to do for me. There's—" He stopped. Jesus Christ, what was he doing? He looked down at his hand. He hadn't used any change to make the call. He had used his calling card. "Damn it," he said out loud.

"What's wrong?"

How could he have made such a careless mistake? They would trace his calling card and find out that he had called Arturo. They would question Arturo until he folded like a cheap metal chair. A trial attorney had once told Michael that examining a witness was like playing cards. Everyone had a tell, a gesture or sign that he'd repeat whenever he was bluffing or lying. Unfortunately Arturo had his own tell. When Arturo tried to lie, he would stutter uncontrollably. As a matter of fact, he was quite possibly the worst liar Michael had ever encountered. They would tear him apart. Thank God he hadn't told Arturo about the package in Monehan's office.

"What do you need me to do?" Arturo asked again.

"Just find out who Sandy was working with on the Trinity matter. Someone was giving her instructions and pretending to be me. I'll call you when I can," he said, hanging up the phone.

Michael opened his wallet and took out the calling card, along with his other credit cards. He wasn't going to make the same mistake again. He walked over to the trash can and was about to throw them out when something stopped him. He took out his Visa card and walked back to the ticket booth, making sure he was at a different window from the first time. "When's the next train to Chicago?" he asked quietly.

The man typed in the destination and studied the screen. "Next train leaves from gate seven in ten minutes. You barely got enough time."

"I'd like to buy a ticket on that train," Michael said, handing over his Visa card.

The man looked up at him. "I'll have to see some identification."

Michael took out his driver's license and passed it under the partition. The man wrote down his DMV number and processed the card. There was a long moment of silence before he heard the computer printing the ticket. Michael signed the receipt. The paper trail would now lead the federal agents to Chicago. He had bought himself some more time, but at what cost? He had just put his best friend in the middle of all this. As he began walking toward the Washington, DC, train, he spotted the two police officers making their way down the stairs. Another two officers were standing by the gate behind him. Something was happening.

He turned quickly into the newsstand and pretended to browse through the magazines. Any moment he expected to feel their hands on his shoulders, his arms being thrust behind him, and handcuffs being placed around his wrists. He heard their shoes on the concrete coming toward him. They became louder and louder, echoing above the voice on the loudspeaker announcing the departing trains. There was a shuffling behind him and the sound of barking. Then the footsteps broke into a run. Michael turned around just in time to see the officer coming at him. There was no time to react. He braced himself for the impact. The man's shoulder hit Michael so hard he fell back. This is it, he thought. It's over.

"Freeze," one of the officers shouted.

Michael didn't make a move. The voice was somewhere behind him. He opened his eyes expecting to be staring down the barrel of a gun, but all he saw was the backs of the officers as they ran past him. The dog was barking furiously now, his nose pressed against two large pieces of luggage. A man was on the ground, two officers above him. Michael's heart was racing. He didn't know what was going on, but he wasn't going to wait to find out. He turned around, walked back up to the Washington, DC, train, and gave the conductor his ticket.

It was late afternoon when the news first reached her. She had been out of the office meeting with the U.S. attorney in the morning, then behind closed doors for the remainder of the day in a settlement conference, and was completely oblivious to everything that had happened. Returning from the federal courthouse, she decided to get a cup of coffee from Starbucks before heading back up to the office. The night that they had made love, Michael had told her how he had bought coffee there each day hoping to see her. Every day she went for coffee she thought about what he had confessed—how much he had wanted to ask her out and how much he had wanted to hold her. It wasn't just the attention she found flattering. Men often undressed her with their eyes. The ones who approached either were full of themselves or figured they had nothing to lose. Michael Elliot was neither of those. The thing she liked most about him was the thing Michael hated about himself, his shy and quiet manner. In his eyes she could see pain and loneliness that were not unlike her own.

Karen still felt bad about not telling him she was involved with Raven. Truth be told, she was ashamed. The relationship with Raven had been a mistake from the beginning. She was glad he had found out about Michael. In hindsight, maybe she had become involved with Michael knowing it would end this way. Regardless, one thing was clear. It was time for her to move on.

Karen was oblivious to the conversation in front of her until she heard his name. It rang out like the sound of pots and pans being dropped on a kitchen floor. She listened closer this time, pretending not to pay attention to their conversation yet concentrating on each and every word. The two women were secretaries in the corporate department. Although she couldn't remember their names, she had seen them in the office. They were chatting like schoolgirls. Neither could believe he had done it. Both kept saying it again and again. Karen felt her heart drop. Done what? she thought. What in the hell had happened? Why were they talking about him this way?

She felt like shaking the women and screaming at them, but she kept her eyes fixed straight ahead. They were looking for him in New York, but he wasn't in the office. Who was looking for him? For God's sake, what had happened? It was like watching a Spanish-language television station. She could pick out bits and pieces of what they were saying, but she couldn't follow the substance.

She finally lost her patience. "Excuse me," she said, tapping one of the women on the shoulder. "I couldn't help but over-hear your conversation. What's going on?"

Both women looked up at her in surprise. Karen Bauer rarely ever spoke to other women in the office. She made it a habit not to gossip, and most of the women hated her for it. Both women were in shock she was talking to them.

"You didn't hear?" the short, chubby one asked. "Every-one's been talking about it. I got a call from a secretary in New York. They said a team of federal officers came into the office. They had a search warrant for Jonathan Gage's office, and they wanted to arrest Michael Elliot and bring him in for question-ing."

Karen froze. "What for?"

"That's what's strange, nobody seems to know for sure. Ap-parently he just disappeared before anyone could find out."

"What?" Karen asked again, hoping she had misheard.

"When the police came looking for him, he was gone. The whole office is in an uproar . . . and there're rumors."

To have Karen Bauer listen so eagerly to anything this woman had to say was almost overwhelming. The secretary began to overflow like a teapot filled with boiling water. Once she had started, Karen couldn't shut her up. It was pitiful, this woman trading on Michael's misfortune for a few moments of attention. God, she hated the rumor mill. Nonetheless, she needed to know what had happened. "What rumors?" she asked.

The woman paused. "That he's somehow tied to the death of Jonathan Gage."

Karen shook her head. "Jonathan Gage committed suicide," she stated firmly.

"That's what we all thought. But apparently they've re-opened the investigation."

The ring of smog that had hung wearily over the Los Ange-les basin earlier that afternoon now created a sand painting of deep orange, red, and purple streaks over the horizon. Art Rollins, however, was oblivious to the display as he shuffled outside the building along with everyone else fleeing for the weekend. Instead of heading to the parking garage, he turned the corner and proceeded to Nick's, the downtown watering hole. Inside the restaurant he could see the suits hovered over the bar and the secretaries chatting in packs and eyeing everyone who entered. A couple got up to leave, and Arturo rushed over to their table and sat down. If Michael had been in the office, he would have come down with him. Without his friend, however, Arturo looked like a lost dog. As he sat by himself, he searched the crowd, but he didn't see anyone else from the firm. Eventually the waitress came by, and he ordered a beer.

Laura was working downtown that afternoon, and she had told him she would meet him here at seven. It was now ten after, but she was never any good at keeping track of time. Laura was a court reporter who spent most of her days traveling the city, attending depositions and making transcripts. She had been working at a deposition in the Davis & White conference room when they met. During a break Arturo had bumped into her in the hall, and the two had begun to talk.

Laura was a full-figured girl, with curvy hips and large, round breasts. Her hair was dirty blonde, and her face smooth and alabaster. She was always smiling and had warm, kind eyes. While some men preferred tall, skinny women, Arturo had always been a breast man, and that was what had drawn him to her. Everything else proved to be a bonus.

They had now been going out for two years, and it was apparent that Laura was becoming restless. Women in their late twenties all viewed relationships as a series of progressions. If they weren't moving forward then they were moving back. Recently she had begun saying things like "I just don't know where this is going" or "I need something more." Other times she would just cry uncontrollably. When he asked her what was wrong, she wouldn't tell him. Then there would be the stories about how her friends had just gotten engaged, always with a slight hint of trepidation, as if she would be the old maid of the bunch. It wasn't that Arturo didn't love her. He was simply scared of, well, he wasn't quite sure of what. But things seemed fine; he saw no need to fix something that wasn't broken. With each passing month, however, he could see her wanting more.

Laura's thick blonde hair appeared above the crowd. She was looking for him, and he raised his hands to get her attention. She smiled and bounced her way over. Throwing her briefcase on the floor, she leaned over and gave him a big kiss. Arturo sheepishly turned his head away. He hated public displays of affection, which only seemed to make her want to kiss him more. Without hesitation she reached over and took a sip from his pint of Sierra Nevada. While most women drank wine or martinis at Nick's, she ordered a beer. The calories never bothered her, and it showed. Nonetheless, she had a pretty face, and men couldn't help but stare at her. Laura took off her jacket and set it down, drawing attention from several men at the bar. "So where's your mate?" she asked.

"He's still in New York," Arturo replied, not wanting to go into the details. She would find out soon enough, but this wasn't the time or the place. He wondered what Laura would say if she knew that he had spent the last three hours in the file room searching for anything that might exonerate his friend. Unfortunately he had found nothing, but he was planning on doing some more digging over the weekend. It would be easier with the office empty.

"So how was your day?" he asked, trying to change the subject.

She shrugged. "Eight hours stuck in an office with defense counsel staring at my breasts."

Arturo suddenly became conscious that he was doing the same. "Well, I guess I can't blame him."

She took another sip. "What about you?"

He winced. "Raven's been on the warpath all day. Something must have crawled up his ass and set him off. He got this first-year so flustered the kid just quit. Can you believe it? I think he must have had a fight with his wife. There were bruises on his face."

"That one sure has a temper." She reached up and brushed Arturo's hair away from his eyes.

Arturo pulled back. "Why do you always do that?"

"Afraid your friends are gonna see you?" she asked. "Poor baby, don't worry, I'll make you forget all about your bad day," she said, smiling. She looked at him with mischievous eyes and then whispered in his ear, "I've been incredibly horny all day."

Arturo's eyes widened. He wanted to finish his drink as soon as possible and rush her home.

"I have a little surprise for you," she said.

Arturo's thoughts began to wander. Laura discreetly unbuttoned her blouse one notch and quickly leaned over so that he could see the black lace bra underneath. "That's all I'm showing for now," she said, smiling. "But it gets better down below."

Arturo flushed. He imagined the black thigh-highs and garters she was wearing under her skirt. She often surprised him with different lingerie. He took a quick slam of his drink. As he laid a twenty down on the table and got up to leave, his face suddenly became pale.

"What's wrong?" she asked.

"Speak of the devil, here comes Raven. Damn it," he cursed under his breath.

Raven's eyes fixed on him, then shifted to Laura. After quickly surveying the other women, he made his way over to them. "Hello, Arturo," he said, shaking his hand. He looked over to Laura, as if waiting for an introduction.

"Hey, Peter," Art said through clenched teeth. "This is my girlfriend, Laura."

She extended her hand, and Raven held it for a little too long. "I thought you might be down here. I was hoping you could do something for me quickly."

"Uh . . . sure . . . ," Arturo replied. What was he going to say?

"I need you to pull the closing documents for Con Semiconductor. I need a memo summarizing the key covenants for a meeting tomorrow morning with the client. I want to walk the board through their ongoing obligations. The meeting just came up. I wouldn't ask you to do it, but it's important," he said, doing his best to look serious.

Arturo felt his stomach drop. He would have to sift through two boxes of documents, then type a memo that would take hours. "Sure, Peter," he said. Any prospect of spending the night with Laura had disappeared. "Well, I better get started," he said, the anguish heavy on his face. "I'll give you a call tomorrow."

Laura stood up and gave him a hug while Raven watched. "I'm just gonna finish my beer," she said.

Raven looked up at the waitress. "I'll take a Scotch on the rocks," he said, looking back at Arturo. "I'll make sure no one bothers her."

"Great," Arturo said under his breath as he walked to the door.

Raven leaned over and stared at the break in the top of Laura's blouse. The smell of her perfume intrigued him. "So how long have you and Arturo been going out?" he asked.

"Two years," she said.

"I don't think I've seen you at any of the firm's functions. Surely I would remember someone as pretty as you," he said, smiling.

The waitress handed him his drink. He swirled the ice with his finger, then put it in his mouth. He would move slowly, he thought. He would bring down her guard with fifteen or twenty minutes of conversation. After he had gotten her to agree to one more drink, he'd put his hand on her shoulder. Then he would say, "Arturo's gonna be late, why don't we go back to your place for a drink?"

Chapter 28

The following morning the front page of *The New York Times* contained the headline "SEC Investigates Wall Street Law Firm" in large block letters. As soon as he read it, Montague knew these six small words would prove deadly. Although he had tried his best to suppress the story, in the end it had been too little, too late. Now the country's most prominent newspaper was describing in excruciating detail the ongoing SEC investigation into insider trading involving "several" Davis & White attorneys. To make matters worse, the article discussed the death of Jonathan Gage, the apparent suicide that had now been ruled a homicide, and the pending search for a young attorney named Michael Elliot who had been implicated in the crime. They had even included sketches of Gage and the missing associate. The only mitigating disclosure was a single sentence at the end of the article indicating that the firm was cooperating with federal and state authorities and was conducting its own internal investigation. It was a small concession that had been inked out at the last moment, after the firm's lawyers had threatened to bring suit for libel and slander. Of course Montague had tried to call a friend on the board of directors of the venerable paper, but in the end, like almost everything else, his effort had proved futile. It was imperative for the integrity of the paper that reporters not be compromised by outside business interests, Montague's friend told him. The liar, Montague thought. The paper had done it a thousand times to protect their own. It was already happening; everyone was starting to abandon him.

Montague knew he didn't have much time. On Wall Street a law firm lived and died by its reputation. Clients often hired attorneys for their political connections and the perception of what the firm could do for them. A name like Davis & White lent credibility to a transaction. With a scandal like this, however, clients would begin to abandon ship. Before long every relationship that had been built over the last century would crumble. Sure, he would try his best to contain the damage, but how long could he hold it together?

Fortunately, none of the firm's clients would pull their business immediately. Changing attorneys on a pending engagement was costly, and a new firm would charge a fortune just to get up to speed. But deals in the pipeline were a different matter. The law firms on Wall Street were a carnivorous pack. They would all use this scandal to gain competitive advantage. First they would try to steal the firm's clients one by one, then they would move in on its attorneys. A partnership was a fragile alliance. One or two key defections could create a panic. The headhunters were probably already circling.

Friday afternoon as he had made the rounds, Montague had seen the closed doors and heard the whispers that stopped when he approached. The partners were all probably talking to their headhunters or directly to the managing partners of other firms. It was mutiny, fair and simple. Bastards, each and every one of them. He wasn't going to let it happen, not on his watch.

Montague summoned the emergency meeting of the partnership for ten o'clock Saturday morning in the firm's largest conference room. Each of the partners in the satellite offices was tied in via conference line—Los Angeles, Hong Kong, Tokyo, London, Paris, Brussels, and Moscow were all represented. He dispensed with the roll call, then cleared his throat. "I've convened this emergency meeting of the partnership to inform each of you of the status of the SEC's investigation into two of our attorneys for insider trading, as well as the murder of Jonathan Gage. For those of you in our foreign offices who have not had an opportunity to see the article in this morning's *New York Times,* let me outline what we know and what we don't know."

Montague began with the recitation of the facts—the disappearance of Jonathan Gage, the apparent suicide turned homicide, the role of Michael Elliot, who was believed to have been working with Gage and potentially involved in his death, the firm's recent cooperation with federal authorities, and, last, the search for the missing associate. The investigation had not involved the firm itself, Montague explained. The SEC, however, could still claim that the firm's procedures to monitor such breaches of confidence were grossly inadequate and that Davis & White had created an environment in which these activities were likely to flourish. Such a proclamation would be the final nail in the coffin for them all. There had been insinuations, but nothing more. Still, rumors could kill the firm's reputation, Montague explained. Now it was incumbent upon each and every partner to try his best to control the damage.

Montague then outlined his strategy for survival. The firm would retain the city's best public relations firm. They would play up the fact that the firm was heavily involved in the detection of the problem and was cooperating with federal investigators. They would also create rumors that such problems were rampant at every other firm on Wall Street. They would do the underhanded and duplicitous things that one did to survive. All the firm's clients were to be contacted immediately and personally by the responsible billing partners. Attorneys were to be instructed to explain the situation and minimize the potential exposure.

Relations with the SEC and the U.S. attorney were as strong as ever, Montague lied. The government appreciated the firm's assistance. If anything, their relationship with the U.S. government was stronger. This firm was still politically connected and had pull with anyone who mattered. He stressed the importance of everyone working together through this difficult period. There must be no loss of clients. Profitability would continue, he assured them.

In conclusion, Montague took the firm's partnership agreement out of an old maroon record binder. It had been written almost a century ago and, despite the passage of time, had changed little since its creation. Every attorney admitted into partnership at the firm had been required to sign it, although, truth be told, no one really knew what it said. That was, no one but Montague.

"I must remind each of you of the emergency powers clause in Article Twelve of the partnership agreement," he said. "In times of emergency, the managing partner has the authority to take all steps necessary in his sole discretion to preserve the safety and financial viability of the partnership, including the right to unilaterally amend this partnership agreement." His listeners had become silent. "I think we can all agree that we are now facing a severe emergency, one that has the potential to destroy the firm as we now know it. We must all stick together. There will be no defections. It is for this reason that I am now adopting a penalty provision. Any partner engaging in acts harmful to this firm's reputation or trying to divert business away from the firm will be fined five million dollars. This meeting is now adjourned."

The planes taking off from Dulles Airport awoke him. At first it took Michael a few moments to remember where he was. The light was coming in through the old curtains, and the room reeked of a blend of cigarettes and mildew. Slowly it came back to him, the train ride to Washington, DC, and the old seedy hotel he had found the night before. It was so close to the runway that as the planes passed overhead, the room would begin to shake and the dresser drawers would begin to rattle. From all visible appearances, the hotel hadn't been updated since it was built some fifty-five years ago, but at sixty-nine dollars a night, what did he expect? Besides, they took cash without asking for identification.

The clock radio on the nightstand read 11:15 in bright green numerals, and Michael turned it around so he wouldn't have to stare at it. He put the pillow over his face and tried to steal back a few moments of sleep, but his efforts were in vain. As he sat in the cold bed, he couldn't help but wonder whether they had traced his credit cards and found the train ticket to Chicago. He knew it would buy him only a little bit of time, but every moment counted. His mind drifted back over the events of the last week, his conversations with the paralegal and the missing files he had recovered. How long would it take them to retrace his steps? The Feds were probably already interviewing everyone in the office. They would find out about Sandra Villanueva quickly enough, but the files would be much harder to locate. With any luck they would sit unattended in Monehan's in box until he returned from vacation.

Michael remembered what Sandra had told him. She'd been working with someone in Los Angeles on the Trinity matter. Somebody had gone to great lengths to lead her to believe it was him. Whoever was behind this must have intercepted his correspondence and pretended to be him. Sandra had never met him before and wouldn't have known the difference. He was just a voice to her. The documents she had sent by interoffice mail to Los Angeles had simply come back with his signature. It was all so damn confusing. He knew only one thing for sure—he had to make it back to Los Angeles. He needed to find the files before the Feds did.

The room suddenly began to shake and the drawers began to rattle, but this time it was louder. The plane seemed like it was right on top of him. Michael couldn't take it anymore. Resting on the dresser was a remote control for the television that was chained down by a long, thin cable. He fumbled for it and turned on the TV. He couldn't imagine why anyone would want to steal a remote control, especially one as beaten up as this. But everything in the room was either chained down or so old it wasn't worth stealing. The place was a mess, the shag rug so badly stained that he couldn't bring himself to walk on it in bare feet for fear of what might poke at him or bite him. He had a nagging suspicion he wasn't the only fugitive residing here. The place was a haven for grifters, drug dealers, addicts, and prostitutes. Now he was one of them.

Michael began channel surfing to take his mind off his present state. When he got to the news, however, he stopped. There was a reporter standing in front of the Brooklyn Bridge, then a picture came on the screen that caused Michael to shudder. It had been taken from the Davis & White directory. All attorneys were required to have their pictures taken for the book. Michael was fresh out of law school, wearing his navy blue suit and conservative tie. He looked much younger, full of ambition and drive. Little had he known then that the photo would appear on national television as part of a manhunt. Michael turned up the volume. The reporter was recounting the story of the disappearance and purported suicide of a powerful corporate attorney on Wall Street. Then he described how the apparent suicide was revealed to have been murder.

Michael couldn't believe it. This was the first he had heard that Jonathan Gage's death was anything other than a suicide. More shocking was what followed. A young attorney named Michael Elliot was now wanted for insider trading, as well as for questioning in connection with the murder. Michael felt sick to his stomach. If someone had created a paper trail tying him to Trinity Corporation, there was probably a trail of evidence linking him to the murder. Damn it, he thought.

Another wave of nausea moved through his body. This time he ran for the bathroom. He was gagging, and his stomach was convulsing violently, but nothing would come out. His head fell forward and his eyes began to water. This is insanity, he thought. He breathed deeply, gasped for air. After a few moments, the nausea passed enough for him to stand up and pull himself to the sink. Cupping his hand, he rinsed out his mouth and looked in the mirror. He had been on the run now for thirty-six hours, and it had already changed him in ways he could have never contemplated. Things that had seemed so important on Friday now seemed utterly meaningless. He was a fugitive wanted in connection with a murder. Even if he was eventually found innocent, his chances of ever returning to the firm, making partner, or even practicing law were remote at best.

He wondered what his grandmother would think. This

wasn't what she had worked so hard to raise, a fraud artist and murderer. Then there was Carl. It would take a while for the news to reach him at Lake Arrowhead, but when it did he would be equally disappointed. The newspapers and CNN reports were damning. Maybe he should have stayed, he thought. Maybe then he could have explained what had happened and taken his chances. But there was no way they would have believed his story. Hell, if he didn't know the truth, he wouldn't believe it either. In any event, there was no use dwelling on the past. He couldn't change it even if he wanted to. He could not let them do this to him. He would keep going until he vindicated himself or they caught him, whichever came first.

Michael quickly showered and got dressed. His suit was wrinkled, and he was desperately in need of a shave, but it would have to wait. He had to get back to Los Angeles quickly. The picture the police were using was old. His hair was much shorter now, and his face looked older. With a little work and a change of clothes he could disguise himself so no one would be able to recognize him, but still there was a problem. To buy a plane ticket he would have to show identification. The Feds had undoubtedly alerted the airlines to look out for anyone traveling under the name Michael Elliot. When he tried to buy a ticket, the computer would send a warning to airport security and he would be arrested on the spot. He could try to take a train or a bus to Los Angeles, but that would take days.

Michael walked to the sink and splashed water over his face. As he looked at himself, it suddenly came to him. He ran back to his jacket and fumbled for the passport. How could he have forgotten it? He had meant to give it back to Jonathan Gage's wife, but it had completely slipped his mind until he found it Friday at the bank. He went back to the bathroom mirror and held it up next to his face. The two men could have been brothers. They were the same height, weight, and coloring. The only difference was that Gage was graying at the temples and had small round glasses, but a quick trip to the drugstore would remedy that. He would pay cash for his ticket and book it for tomorrow night under Gage's name. The airport would be empty late on a Sunday and no one would be looking for a dead man.

The fluorescent lights of the Columbia Law School library flickered once before going completely off. It was closing time. The staff regularly used this signal to let people know that they had only fifteen minutes left and that it was time to start packing up. Sandra Villanueva set down her casebook and began to rub her eyes. When she reopened them, the lights were back on, and she could hear the rustling of papers in the cubicles around her. Everyone was putting on their backpacks and heading for the door. She decided to wait another ten minutes to finish the case she was reading. After all, she knew she wouldn't be able to get anything done back at her apartment. There were too many distractions, not to mention her roommate.

Sandra turned her attention back to the remaining few pages. Once she had finished them, she packed her books into her blue nylon backpack. There were four books in total, *Contracts, Torts, Criminal Law,* and *Property.* Each one weighed close to ten pounds and made the backpack feel like it was filled with dumbbells. As she threw it over her shoulder, she heard a creak behind her. She turned around toward the stacks of books and froze. Several years ago a woman had been raped in the library. Although no one ever talked about it much anymore, the incident still remained a haunting memory in her mind. Sandra reached into her pocket, grabbed her keys and clenched them tightly in her fist.

"Hello," she said in the direction of the noise. She listened for the sound of someone moving, but there was nothing. As far as she could tell she was the only person left. She repeated herself again, but there was still no response.

She had been drinking too much coffee, she thought. It had given her the jitters and she was hearing things that weren't really there. She walked to the front of the library. Normally there was a clerk by the door checking out books and stocking the shelves, but tonight no one was there. She turned around one more time and looked down the hallway, but it was still empty.

She scolded herself for being so paranoid. She then walked over to the elevator and pressed the down button. When the doors opened, she hurried inside and pressed the first floor. Her mind drifted back to her pending midterms. She still needed to prepare outlines for two of her classes and time was running out. The day had come and gone, and Monday would soon be upon her.

Just as the elevator was about to close, a hand jutted inside, causing the doors to stop. Suddenly she felt herself jump. She remembered the keys and clenched them tightly in her fist. When the doors opened again, she was relieved to find a third-year law student staring at her. He worked at the front desk on Saturday nights, and she had seen him there earlier.

"I almost missed it," he said, stepping inside. "You must have been the last one in there. I just made the rounds and locked up."

Sandra exhaled. "You startled me," she said, putting her keys into her pocket. She could still feel her heart pounding.

"Sorry," he said, pressing the button again. He quickly tried to change the subject. "Are you going to bar review tonight?"

Bar review was what the law students often referred to as their night out drinking. They would meet at a bar close to the law school campus and drink themselves into oblivion. She had gone once or twice to this event, but being around all those law students usually just stressed her out. "Nah," she said, pausing. "Maybe another time."

He raised his eyebrows and shrugged it off, as if he had been shot down a hundred times before. When the elevator door opened, the two headed in opposite directions. Secretly she wished he was walking her way. Although security had tried to rid the campus of the homeless, there were often vagrants who would panhandle or shake down students for change at night. It was the Vietnam vets that scared her the most. They often wore fatigues and talked to themselves out loud, as if they were haunted by demons. Sometimes they would even make violent motions, striking in the air at some unknown foe.

Sandra zipped the collar of her jacket shut. She could feel

the cold air against her face, and her skin felt dry and parched. She wanted to get home to her apartment, turn on the heat, and make herself some hot tea. She hadn't eaten since lunchtime and her stomach was beginning to make noises. Suddenly she felt the strange sensation of someone watching her. She quickly turned around and stared into the darkness, but it was impossible to make anyone out. Then she heard the sound of the wind rustling through the trees and a footstep. "Who's there?" she said. "Is someone there?" She squinted, but couldn't make out anyone. She looked around for help. There was a couple standing outside one of the buildings smoking cigarettes, but they were a good distance away. She turned around and began to walk faster. She kept listening for footsteps behind her, but she heard nothing. She cursed herself again for drinking too much coffee.

The intersection wasn't much farther. As she picked up speed and stepped into the street, she suddenly heard the sound of a car starting. Then, without the slightest warning, the black sedan came barreling down at her. Sandra's back was turned to it. Before she could react, the headlights had fixed on her. They were moving too fast for her to move out of the way. The backpack filled with books was an anchor around her neck, dragging her down. She expected to hear brakes screeching, but there was only the sound of the car accelerating faster. Oh my God, she thought. She screamed and held her hands out in front of her. The car just picked up speed. Events from her past began passing before her eyes like pictures from a slide show. She remembered her eighth birthday, the smile on her mother's face at her high school graduation, the way her first boyfriend used to look at her, the feeling of the sun on her face in summer, it was all coming back to her and there was nothing she could do. She didn't feel the impact, only the strange sensation of weightlessness as her body flew uncontrollably over the hood. The force was too strong for her to correct it. She was spinning. That was it, she thought. Then she came back down and felt her head slam into the cold, hard concrete. An ungodly cracking sound filled the air, and everything went black.

Her body was lying on the concrete, contorted in an unnatural position. The car stopped twenty feet in front of her, and the man inside stared at her listless body in his rearview mirror. He was looking for any signs of life, the twitch of a finger or the rise and fall of breathing. But her spine had been snapped in two like a branch being stepped on, and he knew there was nothing more for him to do. When he was sure she was dead, he sped off in the direction of downtown Manhattan.

Chapter 29

Monday, December 11

It was just before dawn, and the sun was beginning to rise over the San Gabriel Mountains. The two FBI agents waited in front of the old Spanish house in Hancock Park until the rest of the team had arrived. The federal forensics unit was the best in the nation. Their technicians were well trained in collecting evidence and preserving a chain of custody that couldn't be questioned at trial. When the van arrived, they all began to unload the tackle boxes. Each was filled with plastic bags, glass jars and receptacles, and tags to identify exactly where each item of evidence was found. With their hands covered in thin latex gloves, the men had an almost ghostlike appearance that morning. Their shoes had been covered with surgical boots, and their bodies had been draped in sterile white overalls to eliminate any claim that they had tracked foreign material into the crime scene.

The search warrant had been issued late Sunday night by a federal magistrate, and the instructions were clear. The team was to do a thorough search of Michael Elliot's apartment. His computer hard drive was to be bagged and sent back to Washington for further analysis by the white-collar-crime team. Any personal records, bank statements, or similar documents were to be held in the Los Angeles office pending Adams's arrival. The agents had been briefed on the murder of Jonathan Gage and were told to pay particular attention to any evidence linking Elliot to the crime. He had motive, he had opportunity, and right now he was their leading suspect. Within a short time of arrival, the team began to methodically take apart the apartment.

It wasn't until noon that Nico got the call. Robert Adams wanted to debrief him on the outcome of the search. "I called you right away," he said. "They found a bottle in the medicine cabinet. They think it's Rohypnol."

"Jesus Christ," Nico said.

"The forensic unit is sending it to the lab for chemical breakdown to see if it matches the drug found in Gage's bloodstream. Once we confirm it, we'll have a new arrest warrant issued. With the charge elevated to murder, we should get more resources devoted to the manhunt. Maybe we'll even get him on the most wanted list."

Nico paused. Something didn't feel right. His instincts were telling him that it was too neat, too clean. The suspect had been smart enough to avoid arrest, yet he had left evidence directly implicating him in the murder. "Did they find his prints on the bottle?" he asked.

There was silence, and he repeated himself. "Did they find his prints on the bottle?"

"No," Adams said. "But that doesn't mean anything."

There was more silence.

"You don't think that it's strange?" Nico asked.

"There could be a million explanations," Adams responded defensively. "Maybe he was wearing gloves . . . maybe he wiped the bottle down. Anything could have happened."

Nico closed his eyes and took the phone away from his ear. Why would he have gone to such lengths to make Gage's death look like a suicide, then keep the one piece of evidence tying him to the crime in his medicine cabinet? Maybe he thought there was no chance anyone would catch him, but then why go to the trouble of wiping his fingerprints off the bottle? It just wasn't right.

"What was he like when you met him?" Nico asked, changing the subject.

The question caught Adams off guard. "What do you mean?"

"You told me that he came down to your office. How did he respond when you questioned him?"

"I don't know," Adams said, trying to think back. "He acted the way you would have expected him to act. He tried to pretend he didn't know anything about the investigation. He said he was just filling in for Gage and had seen the meeting scheduled in his day planner. When I started asking him more questions, he got defensive. He pretended like he didn't know what I was talking about and said he would have to talk to the managing partner."

"Did you ever think that maybe he was telling the truth?"

"Then why did he run?"

"I don't know, maybe he was scared."

"Come on," Adams responded. "This kid is anything but scared. He's a professional if you ask me. Last night I had the FBI trace the charges on his credit card. They discovered he bought a ticket on the two o'clock train to Chicago. When I had them intercept the train en route, he wasn't on it. Amtrak had him down in the computer as checking in, but he must have gotten off the train before it left or en route to throw us off. So I went back to Penn Station this morning and interviewed each of the employees working the ticket booth. One of them said she thought she remembered a young man who fit the description buying a ticket to DC around the same time for cash, but she couldn't be sure. I'm telling you, this kid is good. Now we don't know whether he's in Washington, DC, Chicago, or still in New York."

"Has he got any friends or relatives in the city?" Nico asked.

"No, we did a background check. He doesn't have any family."

"You mean in New York, right?"

"No, he doesn't have any family at all . . . period . . . end of story. His mother had him when she was seventeen, then abandoned him. No one even knows who the father was. Apparently, his grandmother raised him. She passed away when he was still in college."

"What about friends or girlfriends?"

"The kid was a loner. There's only one person in Los Angeles I'm supposed to contact. His name is Art Rollins. The people I interviewed told me the two worked together and are supposed to be pretty good friends. Maybe this Art Rollins can give us some more information."

Nico didn't say anything.

"So what do you do if you're him? You've got fifteen thousand dollars in cash that you've taken out of your savings account. Where do you go?"

Suddenly it came to Nico. "He's going back to Los Angeles."

"Oh yeah? What makes you think so?"

"Because it's familiar to him. New York, Washington, DC, Chicago, they're all big cities, especially if you don't know your way around. He's got no ties to those places. I would want to get back home if I were him."

Adams seemed skeptical, but he was willing to go along. "We have to go through his office and belongings anyway. And there's not much more we can do here. I guess we have nothing to lose."

"I'm telling you," Nico repeated. "He's going back to Los Angeles."

It was almost midnight, and downtown Los Angeles was empty. The rain had fallen sporadically that evening, and the air was charged with static electricity. Any moment she expected to see lightning. As she held out her hand from underneath the alcove, she felt a drizzle. She knew that before long it would turn into a full-scale rainstorm. Karen opened her umbrella and pushed her way into the darkness. She hoped to get home before it started pouring, but it was too late. As soon as she made her way up the stairs and onto Hope Street, the rain began to come down hard. She walked faster, trying her best not to slip on the wet sidewalk.

As she passed the First Interstate Bank Building, a voice called out from the darkness. "Karen," he said, softly. His voice was barely audible over the sound of the rain coming down on her umbrella. She looked behind her, making sure the wind wasn't playing tricks. "Karen," he said, this time louder. She edged forward. In the shadows she could see a man in a dark suit. He was hiding like some kind of homeless vagrant. Suddenly she became conscious that she was alone. Her hands began to tremble. She reached for the pepper spray she kept on her key chain.

"Who is it?" she shouted.

The man moved forward until his face became visible in the streetlight. It was Michael. His hair was matted, and his clothes were sopping wet. He looked like a stray dog that had been standing in the rain too long. She wanted to reach out for him, but something held her back. "My God, what are you doing here?" she asked, lowering her voice. "You know they've got half the damn world looking for you."

"I know," he said. The rain just streamed off his forehead and beaded down his coat. There was a sadness in his eyes that seemed to take hold of her. "I don't want to drag you into this. . . . I just needed to see you one last time."

Karen shook her head. She didn't know what to do. Suddenly she saw a man walking in their direction. He looked like a homeless vagrant, but she couldn't tell for sure. "It's dangerous for you to be here."

"I know," he said, looking down. She was the only one he could turn to now.

For the first time in her life, Karen was at a loss for words. He had risked so much coming here. She couldn't just leave him standing out in the cold. Damn it, she thought. "Follow me back to my apartment," she whispered. "I'll leave the door ajar. After I've made it inside, come on up. If anyone sees you, you'll have to get out of there."

She didn't wait for a response. Instead she just turned around and began to walk back up the street toward her highrise, the umbrella clenched tightly in her fist. He let her get about a hundred yards in front of him, then followed quietly behind her. When he got to the front door, it was ajar just as she'd said it would be. He pulled it open and quickly walked to the elevator. When he got to her apartment, she was waiting for him. She had drawn the drapes and turned down the lights. She had been scared that someone would see him, but fortunately the hallway was empty. She pulled him inside and stripped off his soaking jacket. For a moment they just stared at each other. Then she dropped his coat on the floor and held him. She could feel his tears against her cheek and his cold, wet hair against hers.

They made love with the sound of the rain against her window. There was a sense of finality in the way he touched her. Everything—her eyes, her lips, her skin, her touch—seemed more beautiful and vivid to him that night. When they were done, he fell asleep in her arms. She listened to him breathing, his head resting on her breasts. She ran her fingers through his short brown hair and wondered what would happen in the morning.

He woke up at three o'clock. The thunderstorm was raging over the city, and he could feel it shaking the bed. His heart was pounding wildly. She wrapped her arms around him and tried to calm him, but to no avail. It had been a brief reprieve. Soon everything would start coming down on him like a heavy rain.

"You can't sleep, can you?" she asked. He shook his head. He had slept only sporadically in the last two days, a few hours back at the hotel in Washington, DC, and a few hours on the plane to Los Angeles. She never asked him whether he had done it. Probably her training as a lawyer prevented her from doing so. Never ask a question unless you already know the answer.

"What are you going to do?"

"I don't know," Michael said. His voice was filled with desperation. For the first time since all this had happened, he felt like giving up. "I thought about turning myself in."

The words hung in the darkness. He thought she would agree, tell him it would be the prudent thing to do. After all, he was innocent. Surely they would figure that out. Besides, he was ill equipped to continue running. It was just a matter of time before the authorities found him. He was naïve to think he could figure everything out on his own.

Karen's reaction, however, startled him. She was upright in the bed, tying her hair back in a knot. She wanted him to tell her everything that had happened. He obliged, recounting the evidence he had uncovered, the documents with his name and signature on them, to how he had used Gage's passport to fly back to Los Angeles.

She was determined not to let him make a mistake. "Whoever did this, they want you to get caught. They planned it this way. They want the Feds to find the documents. If you give up now, you'll be doing exactly what they want you to do," she said. "This is like a trial, Michael. You have to anticipate your opponent's next move. You've got to think four or five steps ahead of them. Try to figure out what they're going to do next so you can counteract it. The one who wins is the one who makes a move that's not expected. You've got to take control of the game."

Michael walked over to the window and pulled back the curtain. He could see the First Interstate Building in front of him rising taller than any other building in downtown Los Angeles. Karen was right. There was still one last thing he could do. Two days ago he would never have contemplated such an act, but now it was his only chance.

Chapter 30

Tuesday, December 12

The kitchen was quiet that morning. The kids were still in bed, and his wife was in the bedroom getting ready for work. Nico sat alone at the table, his jacket on the chair opposite him. He was making sandwiches for the kids' lunches when he heard the sound of his wife behind him. Her silk blouse was tucked neatly into her dark wool skirt, and her hair was pulled away from her face. She always looked her best on the way to the hospital. It made him think that she was far too smart and beautiful for someone like him. Their children had gotten their mother's looks and intelligence, although he would never admit it. As she passed by him, Nico grabbed her around the waist and pulled her toward him. At first she tried to pull away, she always did. But upon realizing the futility of her efforts, she threw her white hospital coat on the chair and kissed him. "I made you some coffee," he said, turning his attention back to the pieces of bread staring up from the table.

"What time does your flight leave?" his wife asked, hugging him.

"Ten o'clock." He sighed. He didn't want to go. He had taken this job to avoid being away from home.

"Don't worry, the kids and I will be fine. The nanny is going to stay over until you get back."

"I know," he said, and paused. "It's me I'm worried about."

She smiled and ran her fingers through his hair. "I've never seen you this way," she said. "You're going to find him. I know you will. I just hope you can help him."

The United Airlines flight to Los Angeles lifted off the tarmac of JFK Airport just after ten. Nico and Adams had booked seats together so that they could discuss the case during the five-hour flight. The plane was virtually empty, and they had the entire back row all to themselves.

Nico settled in and began reading the forensic report from the FBI field office in Los Angeles. It covered the search of the suspect's apartment, along with the analysis of the drug found in his medicine cabinet. It was verified as Rohypnol and matched the substance found in Jonathan Gage's bloodstream. They had also traced Michael's credit cards and uncovered the train ticket to Chicago. The FBI had intercepted the train and interviewed all the passengers, but no one could remember the suspect ever being on it.

When they traced his calling card, they had better luck. They uncovered the call to Art Rollins and planned to interview him late that afternoon. Other than that, however, they had come up with little. There were no other credit card purchases or calls to signal his location. His hard drive and telephone records revealed nothing even remotely relating to the insider trading allegations or the murder. They had even set up a hot line for tips, but all they got had proved useless.

"How did you first find out Elliot and Gage were involved in insider trading?" Nico asked, setting the reports down.

Adams took off his glasses and marked where he had stopped reading. "It wasn't easy. You see, after the eighties we got real good at tracking down insider trading. We had computer programs set up at the NASD that let us monitor the daily trading activities in almost every exchange-listed and over-the-counter stock. Whenever there was a big merger announcement or other event that moved the price of a company's stock, we'd review the trading history for someone buying stock options or equity right before the merger announcement. When unusual activity was identified, we'd contact the brokers who'd executed the trades and get information on the underlying buyers. Then we'd look for any possible connection between the buyer and anyone who had access to the confidential information," he said, shaking his head.

"When we first started doing this, it was amazing what we found. Most of the time it was the wives, brothers, fathers, friends, or other relatives of insiders. Usually the insider had gotten drunk and let it slip to someone who traded on the information. Other times it was pillow talk, someone would tell his mistress about a deal he was working on, then she would buy the stock in her personal account. It was quite simple. What these guys were doing, however, took it to a whole different level."

"What do you mean?" Nico asked.

"When we developed the computer system, we left out only one thing. The system looked for key announcements about a company, then looked for unusual trading in its stock. What we didn't realize was that these types of events affected not only that particular company's stock but also the stock prices of other companies in the industry, usually competitors or key strategic partners. Our computers weren't set up to track this.

"Take the Global Network merger that was announced recently. There are only a handful of manufacturers of optical-fiber switches. When the merger was announced at a large multiple to Global Network's current trading price, the stocks of the other companies in the industry jumped. Let's say that instead of buying stock in Global Network, you bought calls on the stock of its competitor. No one would have been able to detect it. The plan was brilliant, really. We would have never uncovered it if Gage hadn't screwed up."

"What do you mean?"

"About two years ago the computer picked up an account with a pattern of unusual trading. It belonged to a young woman named Tatiana Kirischev, who was living in Manhattan. Over three months she had purchased the stock of several acquisition targets within days of the mergers being announced. We knew it had to be more than a coincidence, but we couldn't find an immediate relation to any of the insiders. So on a hunch we cross-referenced the lists of insiders for the transactions to see whether there was a common thread.

"The only person common to all three transactions was their lawyer, Jonathan Gage. So we started surveillance. It turned out Tatiana was a very-high-priced hooker operating under the name Sasha. I mean, you should have seen this woman. She was from Czechoslovakia and had long, blonde hair and a perfect body. It turns out Gage was one of her regulars. To make matters worse, she was tied to a Russian organized crime family that was penetrating New York, and she was on the U.S. Attorney's list of undesirables. When we confronted her and threatened to arrest her, then send her back to Prague, she agreed to cut a deal."

Nico's mind went back to Jonathan Gage's wife and family. They had no idea about any of this. "What did you get from her?"

Adams smiled. "She told us Gage had made a lot of money in the stock market. He knew about many transactions before anyone else did, and he had used this information to make millions of dollars that he had hidden offshore. She began to use the information he gave her to make her own trades. But she wasn't sophisticated enough to realize how easily things could be traced. When we confronted her with the evidence we had compiled, she rolled over on him to avoid a prison sentence and eventual deportation. He never knew she was doing any of this."

Nico shook his head. "Did you ever confront him directly?"

"No," Adams admitted. "After she told us all this, we began to look at every merger and acquisition in which Gage was involved. We then looked back at the trading history for unusual activity surrounding any of these transactions. The strange thing was, there wasn't any. Either she was lying or he was doing something else we couldn't trace. My hunch was the latter. It took weeks of racking my brain to finally figure it out. It turned out he wasn't trading in the stocks of his own clients after all. He was using the inside information to trade in the stock of competitors in the same industry.

"It required a lot more work. He had to know the companies and guess how a particular piece of information would affect the industry in general. When we started digging deeper, we found a company named Trinity Corporation that had set up accounts with a number of brokers. It had a history of buying or selling the stock of certain competitors right before each of Gage's clients made a big merger announcement. It was ingenious really. Trinity Corporation had a seven-hundred-percent annual internal rate of return off its investments. When we finally got the account records from the clearing brokers, we discovered that it was a Netherlands Antilles company, and there was only one signatory. Michael Elliot, its managing director. That's what led us to him," Adams said.

"We uncovered all of this just a few days before Jonathan Gage disappeared. We had set up a meeting with him at our office. We told him we wanted to talk about his ties to Trinity Corporation and certain trading activities we had uncovered. We already had Michael Elliot under surveillance in Los Angeles. The meeting was scheduled for the seventh of December, but Gage disappeared before then. A few days later Elliot shows up at my office for the meeting I had set up with Gage. It was strange," Adams said, then hesitated. "This kid just shows up and tells me he's filling in for the dead partner. When I confronted him, he pretended he didn't know a thing about any of this."

After a pause Nico asked, "What if he really didn't know anything about this? What if it's a setup?"

"You want to know what I think?" Adams responded, looking over at Nico. "I think this kid was in on it from the very beginning. I think he and Gage were partners in crime. The two just thought they were smarter than everyone else. They never thought anyone would be able to uncover their plan. Then Gage screwed up with the hooker. When he finds out we're on to him, he begins to run scared. I think Elliot was worried. . . . Gage was going to turn himself in, so he took matters into his own hands. He drugged Gage and dumped his body into the East River to make it look like a suicide, hoping the investigation would end with his death. When it didn't, he ran. It's that simple, end of story."

Nico remained unconvinced. There were still too many pieces of the puzzle that didn't quite fit together. "I'm telling you, I don't think this kid is our murderer."

"Why else did he run?" Adams asked.

"I'm not sure," Nico said, shaking his head. "Maybe he was scared. I just hope we'll have the chance to ask him, before it's too late."

He could see the line of traffic forming along the Harbor Freeway. It was still early in the morning, but the veins and arteries into downtown were already beginning to clog with cars. Los Angeles was like no other city in this respect. Rush hour began in the morning around seven o'clock and didn't end for three hours. In the afternoon it could start as early as three and not let up until eight. The city was choking itself, Michael thought. A few days ago he would have been out there with them, stuck in traffic and checking his voice mail, making calls on his car phone, even dictating letters to his secretary, but now that seemed like a lifetime ago. Beyond the freeway he could see the sprawl of South Central, where all the houses had bar-covered windows and were spray-painted with graffiti. The old neighborhood had decayed years ago. As a result the financial center had moved north, toward the freeway and away from Broadway and Hill Street. Carl had told him that the shift of the financial district was largely a by-product of the LA riots in the sixties. People became scared, and the new buildings downtown were built like fortresses. Whereas in most cities storefronts lined the downtown streets, in Los Angeles there were just tall concrete walls and parking garages. People would come into work through gated entries, then take elevators four or five stories up to the lobbies of their buildings. On this level there would be several small restaurants, coffee stands, and stores. There was never any need to go beyond the concrete-and-steel enclave. It was a city above the city, a place where the poverty on the streets below wasn't visible. If the transients, panhandlers, or other undesirables ever found their way onto the upper levels, they were quickly escorted away by the security guards.

Michael suddenly found himself banished to the street level, an outsider and a fugitive. He knew he had to find a way back into the First Interstate Bank Building. Lying somewhere inside James Monehan's office were all the documents he needed— the corporate records, the bank statements, and the correspondence for Trinity Corporation. It was all there in an interoffice envelope. He needed to find it before the Feds did, but there was a problem. Surely the FBI had notified the guards at the front desk to keep an eye out for him, and his access card would have been deactivated. When anyone was fired or otherwise determined to be a security risk, the firm deactivated his access card so he could no longer enter the building or parking garage. You didn't need a card in the daytime, but attempting to sneak in then would be suicide. The federal agents were probably still going through his office. No matter how hard he tried to disguise himself, someone would surely recognize him. He knew there was only one way for him to get inside. It would have to be at night, and he would need a new access card.

In order to preserve attorney-client confidentiality, the firm had adopted a number of security measures, including restricting attorneys' access to the offices in other departments. A litigator couldn't enter the corporate department and vice versa. There were also firewalls in the computer system that restricted access to servers and computer records. Michael would have to steal an access card from someone in the corporate department. For a moment he thought about Arturo, but this would just implicate his friend further. Besides, after the phone call he had made to his friend, the FBI probably already had him under surveillance. It would have to be someone else, but who?

Suddenly it came to him. "Peter Raven," he whispered. The senior partner was a man of routine. Every time he left the building, he put his access card on top of the visor of his Porsche 911. Oftentimes when Michael had driven with him to client meetings, he had observed this same pattern. Now he just had to figure a way to get Raven out of the office.

From the pay phone on Bunker Hill, Michael dialed the number. He had called it so many times he knew it by heart. It was just after eight o'clock, and chances were Raven wouldn't be in for another hour.

The phone rang once before his secretary picked it up. "Peter Raven's office."

Michael covered the receiver with his T-shirt and did his best to disguise his voice. "Hello, this is Robert Hawthorne," he said softly. Hawthorne was one of Raven's most notorious clients, an eccentric financier who had made a fortune buying and selling troubled companies. His deals were often difficult, but the fees reached upwards of seven figures. He hadn't used the firm for over a year, but his call would surely cause Raven to start salivating over his share of the potential billings. "You may have trouble hearing me," Michael said, trying to make up excuses for his voice. "I'm calling from my cell phone, and I'm going through the hills and may break up. I flew in from New York yesterday and was hoping that Peter could have dinner at L'Orangerie at seven o'clock this evening."

"Hold on a second. Let me check his schedule." Raven's secretary put him on hold, then checked her calendar. She knew Mr. Hawthorne was an important man. Given the recent turmoil, Raven had been scrambling to keep hold of his existing clients and defuse the rumors. Some new business from Hawthorne was just what he needed. "It looks like he's free. I'll tell him to be there at seven. If there's a problem, where should I have him call you back?"

Michael thought fast. "I'll be unreachable in meetings all day. Just tell him it's imperative I meet with him. Tell him that it's extremely confidential. No one else must know about it."

"I understand, Mr. Hawthorne," she said, hanging up the phone.

Chapter 31

His office was reminiscent of a ball of fishing line that had been found washed up on the beach, all wound up, tangled and knotted with occasional pieces of debris caught in between. There seemed to be no order to any of it. Papers were scattered like a whirlpool over one credenza, and banker's boxes of documents littered the floor amongst crinkled food wrappers and empty coffee cups. It was Robert Adams's worst nightmare and made him dislike Art Rollins from the start. Adams was from a military family, and his life was predicated on routine and discipline. He'd spent his career as a federal prosecutor trying to bring order out of chaos, following paper trails and wire transfers, and doing his best to untangle messes. He had the feeling this office could be a two-year project in and of itself.

"So you're Art Rollins," Adams said, staring at the disheveled man in front of him.

The young attorney's sandy brown hair was hanging in his eyes, and the collar of his jacket was turned up in the back. He appeared uncomfortable and fidgeted back and forth in his chair. His eyes kept shifting to things around the room, the deal cubes on the shelf, the volumes of books behind him, the silver-framed picture of him and his dad, the two diplomas on the wall, and finally back to the eyes of Adams, whose gaze had made him so nervous. Arturo didn't know what the prosecutor and the detective wanted. He had never been questioned by a law enforcement officer. But this was not an interrogation room. There were no bright lights, just Adams's black eyes focusing on him.

Adams let the silence build, studying the young attorney's mannerisms. "Your father is Art Rollins, Sr., isn't he?" Adams asked, looking over at the picture of Arturo and his father. God had played a cruel joke on the man, Adams thought. Art Rollins, Sr., was the head of one of the largest investment banks on Wall Street and was highly respected in the financial community. Clearly the boy had been shoved under the carpet, sent where he would have little chance of embarrassing his father's sterling reputation.

"Yes." Arturo nodded, swallowing hard. The mere use of his father's name made him wince.

"He's got to be proud of you. I mean, having a son who's an attorney at a prominent Wall Street law firm like Davis and White."

"Yeah," Arturo said, raising his eyebrows sarcastically.

Adams reached in his jacket pocket for the green-and-white pack of Kool cigarettes. "Do you mind if I smoke?" he asked.

"I think this is a nonsmoking building." Arturo stopped as soon as the words left his mouth. "But I guess they're not going to arrest you," he said, wincing at the stupidity of his comment.

The cigarette was hanging loosely from Adams's mouth. The dry paper from the wrapper had absorbed a small drop of saliva and adhered to his lip. He looked up at Arturo, then took the cigarette out of his mouth. "You're absolutely right. The receptionist told me this was a nonsmoking building."

Arturo knew his comment would come back to haunt him. "I mean, I really don't care."

"No, that's okay," Adams said. "I'll just hold it for later." Restraint filled the prosecutor's face as he continued. "You and Michael Elliot were friends, weren't you?"

Arturo nodded.

"We're investigating his ties with insider trading involving a number of deals the firm was working on. You probably already know that, don't you?"

Arturo nodded his head.

Raven had told Arturo that he was to cooperate fully with the authorities. The firm would have an attorney present if he

wanted, but Arturo had decided against that. He explained that
he knew nothing about the allegations and had no material that
would bear on the investigation. He swore again and again that
Michael was incapable of such things. He had been friends with
him ever since the two were summer associates. Michael had
been the one attorney who had befriended him when no one
else would. The fact that he came from a prominent family and
his idiosyncrasies never infringed on their friendship. Nonetheless, Raven stressed again that the questioning should concern
only his relationship with Michael and anything that would
help them find him. On no account was he to discuss any matters relating to other firm business. If Adams started asking
questions along these lines, Arturo was to call Raven immediately. This was the deal that the firm had cut.

"Let me ask you a couple questions about Michael Elliot,"
Adams said. His attention again became fixed on the cigarette
between his fingers. Knowing it was so close but that he
couldn't have it created an aching in him that began to grow
and grow with each moment. It had become a game of will. He
would get this over with quickly, then he would light the fucking cigarette.

"When was the last time you spoke to him?"

"The-the-the-the . . . week he left for New-New-New . . .
York," Arturo said, stuttering.

"Did he seem strange to you? Was he acting unusual?"

Arturo looked out the window. On the mirrored glass of the
adjacent office building, he could see the entire skyline. The
way the sun caught it created a reflection that burned his eyes.
He looked away, then to the carpeting and his brown leather
shoes. The argyle patterns on his socks didn't match. He had
been in a rush that morning, but it didn't seem to matter much
now. He looked back up at Adams. "Nnn . . . nnn . . . no," he
responded.

"Has he tried to contact you at any time since he disappeared?"

Arturo avoided the question. "I don't know exactly what
you think he did, but Michael would never do anything to harm

his clients or the firm. He isn't like that. I've read what they've said in the newspapers—that he's implicated in Jonathan Gage's death somehow. I don't believe he's capable of such a thing."

"You 'don't believe' he did such things? How much do you really know about your friend?"

"I know enough about him to know he wouldn't do something like that. He isn't motivated by money. He's one of the few in this profession who isn't."

Adams reached into his briefcase and took out a large manila file, which he set on the desk. "We have evidence that Elliot set up an offshore corporation in the Netherlands Antilles under the name Trinity Corporation. He then set up a number of brokerage accounts in its name in the U.S. and traded on inside information. It's all here in black and white. You can read it for yourself if you want. We believe he also set up a number of offshore accounts that he used to wash the money. We're still in the process of tracking them down." After a pause Adams went on. "We also know that Jonathan Gage was found dead, floating in the East River. It turns out he was drugged with Rohypnol. We found a bottle of that drug in Michael Elliot's apartment. Now how well do you think you know your friend?"

Arturo couldn't believe what he was hearing. He felt as if ice water was being pumped through his veins. His hands were trembling, and his eyes began to water. He shook his head.

"Did Michael Elliot try to contact you after he left last Friday?"

Arturo froze like an animal caught in headlights. "Nnn . . . nnn . . . nnno," he said. "I haven't talked to him since he left for New York."

Adams moved forward in his chair until he was inches from Arturo's face. "He didn't call you? He didn't ask for any help?"

Arturo was caught. There was no place to go. He shook his head no.

Adams pounded his fist on the desk. "I know he called you. We traced the calls on his phone card. He called you from the pay phones at Penn Station, right after he bought a train ticket. I know he called you, Art. You're helping him, aren't you?"

"Nnno," Arturo cried. "He called me, but I didn't . . . I'm not . . . I mean . . . I . . ."

Adams couldn't bear to see this grown man crying. He shook his head in disgust. "What do you think your father would say?" he asked, standing up. "For God's sake, something like this could ruin his career . . . the son of a prominent investment banker, aiding and abetting a fugitive and tied in with an insider trading scam."

"I didn't do anything." Arturo began to wail. "Keep my father out of this. He has nothing to do with this. I have nothing to do with this. I didn't know anything about any of this."

Adams could tell he had touched a nerve, and he continued to probe at it like a dentist working a cavity. "Then you've got to help me, Art. You've got to help me bring him in."

Arturo closed his eyes and winced. He had his arms folded across his chest and was slumped in his chair like a jellyfish. "No," he shouted. "No. . . ."

Adams knew he had him. "You've got to help me bring him in, otherwise I've got no choice. Will you help me?"

Finally, Arturo broke. "Yes," he screamed. "Just keep my father's name out of this . . . keep him completely out of this."

The sun was blood red as it set over the Santa Monica Bay. From his corner office on the forty-second floor, Peter Raven could see it fade slowly behind the blue-gray ocean until there was only a sliver of color floating on the horizon. It was getting late, he thought. Hawthorne was not a man to be kept waiting. Raven quickly called down to the valet to make sure his car would be waiting when he got to the parking garage. He put on his jacket and reached for his briefcase. His secretary was already gone, but the lights were still on in the associate offices lining the hallway, which pleased him to no end. Any other time he would have made the rounds to check on what each of them was working on and which had time to take on more projects. But tonight he would just have to call them from his car phone after dinner. The ones who had gone home before he called would get new assignments in the morning. It seemed only fair, he thought.

The bright red Porsche 911 was waiting in the valet station. It had been washed, detailed, and filled with gas, all as he had instructed. As he got into the car, he noticed a small watermark on the hood. He got out and began shouting at the valet. "You see this," he said, pointing at the hood. The valet just looked blankly at him. Raven walked around to the front of the car. "Come here, look at this," he said. "Right there, it's a watermark. I pay you guys a small fortune to detail this car and you miss this. You tell Raul I want him to clean the hood in the morning, you hear me?" The valet spoke little English and kept looking at the car, trying to see what Raven was pointing at. He could neither see any damage nor understand the man's hand gestures. Raven gave up. He would have to convey the message to the manager himself in the morning. He got into his car and tore out of the parking garage.

Traffic on Interstate 10 was stop-and-go all the way to La Cienega. By the time he pulled up to the valet at L'Orangerie, it was five minutes after seven. Raven got out of the car and waited impatiently for the valet to hand him the ticket. Across the street Michael sat outside the small coffeehouse watching him. It was amusing to see the partner scurry around at his direction for once. He was going to go ballistic when Hawthorne ostensibly stood him up. Michael just prayed he had left his access card in the usual place. Within moments Raven disappeared inside the restaurant, and the Porsche pulled behind the building. Michael got up and quickly made his way across the street. By the time the valet came running back around, Michael was standing in front of the restaurant. "Excuse me," he said politely. "My boss was just here a few moments ago in a red Porsche 911. He forgot some papers in the car and wanted me to get them." The valet looked up at him and then back to the two cars that had just pulled up. "If you walk me to his car, it will only take a moment."

The boy made the quick assessment that he wasn't a car

thief. "I'll tell you what, it's parked in back. I left it open. You can get it yourself if you like."

Michael thanked him, then walked to the parking lot behind the restaurant. Raven's car was parked in the corner. Michael opened the door and pulled down the visor. It was dark, and at first he couldn't see anything. "Please be there," he whispered. He began to feel for the access card, but there was nothing. Damn it, he thought. His eyes remained fixed on the back door of the restaurant. Michael had called the hostess that afternoon and made a reservation under the name Hawthorne. He hoped Raven was inside waiting for his host, but what if he came out? He frantically searched again for the card. Suddenly he felt the ridge of a pocket lining the visor. He reached inside, and touched the thin plastic card, and breathed a sigh of relief. He removed the card and put the visor back in its upright position. With any luck Raven wouldn't know the card was missing until the following morning. Michael slipped it into his jacket, then faded back into the darkness.

Inside the elegant restaurant, Raven was waiting for Hawthorne to arrive. If it had been any other client, he would have left long ago, but the prospect of a seven-figure fee gave him an amazing amount of restraint. Forty minutes later the manager approached the table with a message. "Mr. Hawthorne just called," he explained. "Unfortunately he has been delayed and will have to take a rain check." Raven cursed to himself as he thought about the money slipping through his fingers.

The Chevy Impala was over ten years old, and the primer spots from an earlier collision were clearly visible on the driver-side door. Michael had found it that morning through an ad in the *Los Angeles Times* classified section. It was run-down and in need of bodywork, but at least it ran. For eleven hundred dollars it was a bargain. He turned the ignition over and held his breath until it started. As he revved the engine, he could hear it struggle to turn over, and smoke spit out the tailpipe.

Thank God he wasn't going to own it long enough to require a smog check, he thought.

As he drove down Olympic Boulevard toward downtown, the city seemed quiet and tranquil. The lights in the office buildings had formed a mosaic pattern on the skyline, and the urban blight that normally surrounded the city had disappeared. When he got downtown, he parked in an empty lot near Pershing Square. At this time of night the stores were all closed, and the streets were empty. The only people walking around were either homeless or the janitorial staff who worked in the highrises. Before he got out Michael removed a gray industrial shirt from a duffel bag and unfolded it. He had bought it at a uniform shop in the garment district that afternoon. It matched the ones he had seen the cleaning crew in his office wearing. All the buildings downtown contracted with outside cleaning services, which usually hired illegal immigrants from Mexico and Guatemala and paid them less than minimum wage.

Michael changed into the shirt and a pair of black chinos and sneakers. Tonight he would be one of them, working through the building floor by floor, cleaning out trash and vacuuming. In the six years he had been with the firm, he couldn't remember the faces of any of the people who cleaned the building at night. It was almost as if they were invisible. He could remember people shuffling through while he was working, but he had never paid much attention to them. This was the one thing he now had going for him. With any luck no one would notice him.

Michael pulled down the rearview mirror and looked at his reflection one more time. He hadn't shaved, so a dark shadow covered his face. If anybody looked at him for more than a few seconds, they'd know it was him. It was simply a chance he would have to take. He had to get back in the building. Who would be waiting for him there was an open question. Maybe the Feds had found the documents in Monehan's in box and knew he would come back for them. Even if the Feds hadn't found the documents, the firm itself might have taken precautions. Would they have a guard posted outside the office?

Would one of the associates recognize him? There were a million things that could go wrong. To make matters worse, once he was inside the building it could easily be closed off, making escape impossible.

Michael tried to remember whether the cleaning crew checked in with the security guards. Normally visitors had to sign in, but he had never seen the cleaners do this. He decided he would just take his chances. He opened the glass door to the lobby, and walked past the guards to the elevators. If he was going to run into anyone from the office, it would most likely be here. Michael kept his eyes fixed on the floor. A radio was playing the Dodgers game while the two security guards talked. It was the bottom of the ninth, and the Dodgers were up two to nothing. Michael waited to see if the guards would call out to stop him, but there was only the sound of the announcer. He quickly walked into the first open elevator, inserted his card, and pressed the button for the forty-second floor. Michael looked at his watch. It was eight o'clock, and there were bound to be a few corporate attorneys left in the office. He had thought about waiting another hour or two, but then there was the risk that Raven would realize his card was missing and alert the guards.

As the elevator came to a stop, Michael heard two voices outside in the firm's lobby. He thought for a second about pressing the door-close button, but it was too late. The muted tone of the doors opening resonated through the small confines of the elevator. He told himself not to panic, but his heart was racing, and he could feel the blood rushing to his head. As the elevator opened he saw Nico Fiori and Robert Adams standing in front of him. They were going back and forth about the investigation and debating their next course of action. The two men were so involved in their conversation that they just walked past him into the elevator. Michael kept his head down and held the door as they got on.

He then withdrew his hand and let the doors close behind him. When the elevator had gone, Michael breathed a long sigh of relief. This was far too close for comfort. Looking down at his hand, he suddenly saw the watch. Damn it, he thought. The vintage Rolex Carl had given him would be a dead giveaway. How many men on the cleaning crew had gold watches like this? What if they had seen it? The wave of anxiety swept through him. He inhaled deeply and hurried to the door to the interior offices. Using Raven's access card, he opened it. He would just have to get in and out as quickly as possible.

Michael listened again for voices as he walked down the hallway. The lights in several offices were still on, but he couldn't hear anyone. He knew better than to look in, for fear of making eye contact. After making it past four offices, he saw the door to Monehan's office in front of him. He quickly opened it and turned on the light. The desk was filled with stacks of paper, each with an index card on top indicating the transaction to which it pertained. Michael shut the door behind him and began to search for the interoffice envelope. He doubted Monehan's secretary would have opened his mail. Chances were she would have just put it in his in box for him to sift through when he got back, but Michael didn't see an in box. He looked on top of the credenza, but there was nothing but deal documents. It had to be here somewhere, he thought, it just had to be here. He moved from stack to stack until finally he saw a box on the floor filled with papers. As he began to sift through it, he realized it was what he was looking for. The box was filled with mail. Monehan had been gone so long, his secretary must have just thrown it all into a box and left it on the floor. There were dozens of interoffice envelopes inside, interspersed with copies of *The Wall Street Journal,* legal updates, and junk mail.

Within a few moments he came upon a thick red envelope with his own writing on the front. It was the documents he had sent Monehan, and he began leafing through it. Then he heard a shuffling outside the door. Michael felt his throat tighten. He knew there was no reason for a cleaning person to be looking through an attorney's files, but he was too close now to let go of it. He wouldn't have another chance. Then he heard the door opening. Michael saw a trash can two feet away. He took the entire envelope and threw it inside, then picked up the plastic bag and drew it up in his hand.

As he turned around, Daniel Goldberg was standing behind him. Daniel was a pasty-faced, pale-skinned first-year fresh out of Yale Law School. Michael pretended to be emptying out the trash and looked down so that the young attorney couldn't see his face. With the trash bag in hand, he excused himself and began to move to the door until he heard the sound of Goldberg's voice. "Excuse me . . ." the first-year whined. "Aren't you forgetting something?"

Michael stopped. He didn't know what to say.

Goldberg finally exhaled loudly. "You missed my office," he said. Only a first-year attorney who was completely powerless at the firm would feel the need to exert this kind of control over someone else, Michael thought. For a moment he wanted to kick the crap out of Goldberg and duct-tape him to the chair, but he restrained himself. Instead he nodded, walked subserviently into the office next door, picked up the trash can, and took the plastic bag from inside. Goldberg smiled.

There was no one else in the hallway, and Michael quickly made his way along the row of offices. When he passed his own he could see that the light was on and no one was inside. Opened files were strewn over the floor and credenza. They must have been going through everything, he thought. In the corner of his eye he saw the silver frame with the picture of him and Carl. There were very few things he would have cared about losing, but the picture meant a great deal to him. He paused, then moved quickly toward it. He took the picture, placed it in the trash bag, and headed straight for the elevator. When he got inside he took out the Trinity files and the picture frame, tucked them both under his belt, then pulled his shirt over them. Within moments he was outside the building, making his way to the car.

Chapter 32

A stillness pervaded her office that morning. It was as if she couldn't hear the phone ringing or the voices of people passing in the hallway. Although he had been gone for only one day, her mind couldn't escape him. She wondered where he was and, more important, if he was safe. She hoped he was far away where they couldn't find him. When she had woken up and found him gone, she'd felt as if she had been hit hard in the stomach. Normally she prided herself on being strong and unemotional, but she found herself crying like a child that morning. She desperately wanted to help him, but he had departed as quickly as he came, leaving only a note on her kitchen table.

Karen,

I'm sorry for bringing you into this. I've already asked far more from you than I ever should have. As I watched you sleeping, I realized that you mean more to me than almost anything else in my life. It's for this reason that I must go.

Please forgive me for leaving so suddenly, but I have only one chance and time is running out. You've been more helpful to me than you will ever know. Promise me whatever you hear, whatever they tell you, you won't believe it. I love you. Wherever I may be, you won't be far from my thoughts.

Michael

She had read the note over and over, not wanting to let it out of her hands. She had even called in sick, hoping he would try to contact her and come back to her apartment, but he never did. The next day she tried to get on with her life, but it was a dismal failure. Sitting at her desk that morning she tried to concentrate on her work, but her mind kept drifting back to him. She was staring out the window, wondering where he was and how she could find him, when she heard a voice.

"Karen Bauer?"

She turned around and saw a strange man standing in her doorway. He was in his early forties, with black eyes and gray streaks at his temples. She wondered how long he had been watching her. "Can I help you?" she asked.

The man didn't say a word.

"Can I help you?" she repeated, this time more firmly.

"I'm sorry," he finally responded. "My name is Nico Fiori. I'm a detective with the NYPD."

Karen tried not to panic, but the questions began to race through her mind. Had Michael been caught? Was he in jail? She struggled to maintain her composure. As a trial attorney she had taken a hundred witnesses through cross-examination, but this was the first time the tables had been turned on her. Everything she had learned, everything she had been taught, fell back into the recesses of her mind. "What can I help you with?" she blurted out.

"It's about Michael," he said, studying her reaction.

Karen wondered how much the detective knew about them. "Michael who?" she asked, but as soon as the words left her mouth, she realized she had made a terrible mistake. Something in his eyes looked sad and pained.

"Michael Elliot," he said.

Karen stopped. He could see through her lies. How had he found out about her? No one else knew about their relationship. Had Michael lied to her about that? Then it came to her, the call he had made that night from the hotel in New York. That was the only possible explanation. They must have checked the phone records and found her number. The detective then must have put two and two together and realized they were involved. It seemed futile to continue lying. "Do I need a lawyer?" she asked.

Nico looked up at the wall of diplomas behind her. "I thought you were a lawyer," he said, smiling.

"A lawyer who represents himself is a fool."

"Well, I don't think you're a fool," Nico said.

Something in his eyes made her want to trust him. "Is he okay?" she asked.

"I don't know," Nico responded. "The longer he stays on the run, the harder it's going to be for me to help him."

So he wasn't in custody, Karen thought. He was still on the run, but they were getting closer. "I don't know where he is," she said, truthfully. "But even if I did, I'm not sure I would tell you."

"I understand," Nico said. It was the first honest answer he had gotten out of her. He decided to lay his cards on the table. "If it helps, I don't think he did it."

Nico's response surprised her. "That's not what the papers say, and last time I checked there was still a warrant issued for his arrest."

"You're a trial attorney, aren't you?" he asked.

She nodded.

"Well let me tell you what's bothering me. The SEC and the FBI are convinced that Elliot and Gage were involved in an insider trading scheme. They think Elliot turned on his partner and killed him to cover up his own involvement. But there's a problem with their theory," Nico said, pausing.

"The FBI forensic team searched Elliot's apartment and didn't find a single piece of evidence linking him to Trinity Corporation or the insider trading. The only thing they found linking him to the murder was a bottle of Rohypnol, the drug found in Gage's bloodstream. Now it doesn't make any sense to me that Elliot was careful enough to make sure everything in his apartment and office tying him to the crime was gone, but then he's careless enough to leave the one most damning piece of evidence in his medicine cabinet. Why weren't there any fingerprints on the bottle? He was careless enough to leave it in the cabinet but careful enough to wipe off his fingerprints?

"I think this has setup written all over it," he said. "Then there's a gap in time. Gage was missing for several days before Elliot flew to New York. Where was he? What did he do? Who'd he meet with? For all we know Gage was dead before Elliot got to New York. Hell, no one could really be sure how long the body had been floating in the river. I'm telling you, I don't think he's the murderer. I think he's just running scared."

"Then why the arrest warrant?"

"When he ran, we didn't have any choice. We never heard his side of the story and couldn't corroborate it."

She was still doubtful.

"Look, I know this is a lot for you to take in right now. I want you to keep this," he said, handing her his card. "It has my pager number. I want to help him, but I need to bring him in. Please, think about it. If he calls, convince him I can help him," he said. "You have my word on it."

Nico left Karen's office not sure whether he had done the right thing. What if Adams and the others were right? Maybe Elliot had simply been arrogant or careless. Still, it was all too neat, too clean. Someone must have set him up, but only Elliot could help him figure it out. He needed to find Michael, and he needed to find him quickly. If he was right, the person who killed Gage was still out there. Chances were he was trying to get to Elliot first. With Elliot dead no one would ever be able to uncover the truth.

When Nico got back to Elliot's office, Adams was still packing up boxes and sifting through files. He had already taken the hard drive from the computer and sent it to DC for analysis. So far they had found nothing incriminating, not even any correspondence with the paralegal in New York regarding Trinity Corporation.

As Nico walked in and took a seat, Adams looked up at him.

"What did she tell you?" he asked.

"Nothing."

"Do you think she's involved in this?"

"I doubt it," he said. "She's too smart. I think the two of them were seeing each other, but I don't think she knows anything about Trinity Corporation. I gave her my card and told her to call me once she had a chance to think about it."

Their conversation was interrupted by Raven's voice cutting through the air like fingernails on a chalkboard. After having been stood up last night, he was fit to be tied. "Goddamn it, just get me another access card," he barked. "I don't know where in the hell it is. I had to wait in line at the guard station this morning and sign in. Just get me a new one ASAP."

Nico looked up at Adams. "Are you thinking what I'm thinking?"

"Yeah," Adams said.

The two men bolted into the hallway just as Raven was walking into his office. "Excuse me. Did you say you're missing your access card?"

Raven turned around and squinted at Nico. Over the last few days he had been more than accommodating to these guys. He had given them free access to Michael's office, and they had practically taken over the conference room at the end of the hall. By now they had sifted through so many files they could have filled a room with boxes, but he really didn't care. The closer they got to tracking down Michael the better. He'd give them anything they wanted at this point.

"Did you say you're missing your access card?" Nico repeated.

"Yeah," Raven responded.

Nico looked over at Raven's secretary. "Can you do me a favor and call down to building security? I want to know if your access card was used to enter the building last night. What time did you leave?"

Raven still didn't realize what they were getting at. "I left at seven to meet a client for dinner," he said. Then it struck him. "Oh, shit!" he shouted.

"What?" Nico asked.

"The client never showed up," Raven said, looking down at his secretary. "Call Hawthorne's office right now. That little fucking prick, I bet he set the whole thing up. Hawthorne probably wasn't even in town."

Nico knew he was on to something. Elliot was in Los Angeles, and he had been close enough to touch. He had come into the office last night using Raven's access card, but why hadn't they seen him? Then it struck him. How many people on the cleaning crew would have a gold Rolex watch? They had passed right by Elliot and not even realized it. Damn it, he thought. Now only two questions echoed through his head: Where would Elliot run next? And would they get to him before Gage's killer did?

The air was heavy with the smell of pine and cedar. Winter had come early this year to the San Bernardino Mountains. The leaves on the dogwood trees were already changing to bright shades of red, orange, and gold, and a cold wind was blowing in from the north. As he drove up the steep mountain pass, Michael could hear the sound of the engine on his old Chevy struggling. For a moment he wondered whether the car would make it up the steep incline, but he had already pulled over twice to let it cool down. He checked the engine light one more time, but everything was normal. As he turned his attention back to the road, he could see the thick forest passing in front of him. It felt like a different world up here. The thought that Los Angeles was just a few hours away seemed almost incomprehensible.

Michael unfolded the map and traced the spidery veins that ran along the side of the mountain past Lake Arrowhead. Carl's house rested at the end of an old gravel road off Highway 173. Out of an abundance of caution, Michael parked on an abandoned fire road a mile away and watched the house for an hour before approaching. He could tell Carl was there. There was a cord of freshly cut firewood stacked against the porch, and a plume of gray smoke was rising from the chimney. As he walked around the perimeter, he could see his friend's old Jeep Cherokee parked in front, but there were no other cars anywhere.

When he finally thought it was safe, he walked around to the back of the house, where he saw Carl through the kitchen window. He was by the sink washing vegetables and chopping them on an old wood block. All Michael could hear was the running water and the pounding of the knife. He listened for another voice, but didn't hear anyone else. When he was sure Carl was alone, Michael walked back around to the front door and knocked. Within moments the faucet turned off and the porch light came on. Michael didn't imagine Carl had many visitors. The closest cabin was a good mile away.

Carl was wearing a checkered flannel shirt, jeans, and hiking boots. His hair was grayer than Michael remembered, but otherwise he looked healthy and strong, his body toned from outdoor activity. "I had a feeling you might come here," he said, pulling Michael inside and hugging him.

Carl was the first man he'd be able to look in the eye since all this had happened. "I'm sorry, but I didn't have anywhere else to go."

He had seen Carl only sporadically since his grandmother had passed away and suddenly felt ashamed for letting so much time pass. When Michael had returned to Los Angeles after law school, Carl had already moved away. He had traded his house in Hancock Park for this old A-frame cabin on the hills overlooking Lake Arrowhead. Every so often he would call Michael and tell him there was a room available for him anytime he wanted. But Michael rarely accepted the invitation. In hindsight it was a terrible mistake, but going to Carl's cabin and seeing the pictures of his grandmother always made him feel sad and empty. "How did you hear?" he asked.

"It's all over the news. They even had a picture of you in the *Los Angeles Times*."

Carl heard the splatter of grease and walked quickly back into the kitchen, motioning for Michael to follow. "You must be famished," he said. "You look like a prisoner of war. I was just cooking some lake trout. There's more than enough for both of us."

The fire burning in the stone fireplace filled the house with warmth, and Michael took off his jacket. As he sat down at the small table, Carl fixed him a plate of scrambled eggs, fried trout, vegetables, and toast. It was his first meal in a week that hadn't come from a drive-through window, and Michael devoured it. Carl scrambled up some more eggs and placed another filet into the frying pan. He'd caught them that morning, he explained. Once Michael finished his second serving of trout, Carl poured him a cup of coffee from the pot on the stove. It was the same steel coffeepot Carl had when Michael was growing up, and the coffee was as strong and thick as he remembered. It would be hard for them to track him down here, Michael thought. He had shared the details of his personal life with very few people, but eventually they would find him. He had a day, maybe two.

Michael sat on the couch with Carl and recounted what had happened. He told him about how he had met Jonathan Gage and worked with him on a number of transactions. He told him how the young partner had disappeared, and he had gone to New York to take over for him. Then he described the meeting with the SEC, the missing files and, finally, the Trinity documents with his name on them. He tried to explain why he had run and how he had gotten the files back. He told Carl about Karen and her advice. He now had only one advantage, he said. Michael took the folders from his backpack. The two men began to read them page by page, trying to untangle the web of financial transactions.

It appeared that Trinity Corporation had set up numerous brokerage accounts in the United States that were capitalized with initial investments totaling twenty-five million dollars. All the account statements from them were forwarded to a management company in the Netherlands Antilles, and all profits from the trading activities were forwarded to a bank account on Grand Cayman Island. The bank there had standing instructions to transfer the money in equal portions to five banks across the world, in Panama, the Isle of Man, Barbados, the Netherlands Antilles, and Switzerland. Each of these banks in turn had standing instructions that all funds were to be swept to a master account in Luxembourg at Banque Commerciale du Luxembourg. From there, the management agreement with Alan Schrager, vice president of private banking, provided for half of the proceeds to be held in a managed account under the name of Trinity Corporation. The other half of the proceeds were to be transferred to numbered account 80888 in the British Virgin Islands with BVI Holdings Bank. There were no details in the file with respect to the identity of the account, but for some reason the numbers looked vaguely familiar to him. He had seen it somewhere before, but he couldn't remember when. Whoever was behind this account was clearly the funding source for Trinity Corporation's initial capital, and they were now sharing in half of the profits of the illegal enterprise.

Michael shook his head. He could not believe what he was reading. It was all there in black and white. In the files were dozens of account documents and instructions, each signed by him. It was quite ingenious, he thought. The Feds would be able to trace the money to the Grand Cayman bank, but once they did they would be sent on a chase around the world to find it. The bank secrecy laws of each of these countries would make it costly and difficult to trace. By the time they could subpoena the bank records, the money could be moved a hundred times. As Michael sipped the strong black coffee, he tried to make sense of the documents. There was clearly enough evidence here to send him away for the rest of his life. Coupled with the drug found in his apartment, it was even probably enough to convict him for murder.

When he was done going through all of the evidence he knew he only had one chance left. "I don't want to get you involved in this," Michael said, backing away from the table.

"Look," Carl replied, staring him squarely in the eye. "I may be old, but I can take care of myself."

After a moment of quiet deliberation, Michael began to lay out his plan.

Chapter 33

Thursday, December 14

They had met only once. It was a few years back, as best Arturo could recall. Carl had come into the city to visit Michael, and they had asked him to have lunch with them at the central market. Arturo had accepted their invitation, but somewhere through lunch began to feel like an outsider. Although they tried their best to include him, the conversation soon began to drift to the Dodgers and the baseball games they had attended together on Sunday afternoons. Arturo had smiled and pretended to follow along, but the truth was he didn't really know much about baseball. In fact he had never been to a game with his father, or anyone else, for that matter. The one thing he was able to garner, however, was that there was something special about the relationship between Carl and Michael. Although they weren't related by blood, the two men had a general fondness and affection for each other that was far different from the relationship he had with his own father. As the two shared stories, Arturo couldn't help but feel slightly jealous of his friend, as much as he hated to admit it.

When he got back to the office that afternoon, he had tried to call his own father to see if he could mend their tattered relationship. Not surprisingly, his father's secretary told him he was on a conference call and would have to call him back. Arturo left a message that it was important they talk, but the message was never returned. Looking back on it now, Arturo realized he had always been a failure. After being caught shoplifting at the age of thirteen, his father sent him away to boarding school to get rid of him. At the time he had committed the childish prank more for attention than anything else. His father was never around, and he was being raised by nannies, while his mother wallowed in vodka tonics and played bridge. It had been his feeble attempt to reach out for help, but it had gone unanswered. From that point on, Arturo and his father rarely spoke, other than at the obligatory Thanksgiving and Christmas dinners.

In hindsight his father's response shouldn't have surprised him. The man was always more concerned about other people's perceptions of him than he was about his relationship with his own children. When Arturo was caught stealing that day, he had brought shame and dishonor to his father's reputation. His father had chosen work over his family long ago, so it was only natural for him to effectively write Arturo off. After a poor liberal arts education, Arturo's mother pulled some family connections to get him into a bottom-tier law school. When he graduated his father was fearful that he would return to New York and further sully the family's name, so he interceded and arranged a job for his son on the other side of the country. He had figured it was unlikely that young Arturo could get himself into trouble in the Los Angles office of Davis & White, but somehow he had.

As Arturo listened to Adams's questions that morning, he couldn't help but feel he was still paying the same price over again. History was somehow repeating itself, but now the stakes were much larger. With each question, Arturo told Nico and Adams everything he could about his best friend. He described in detail how they had started together as summer associates and worked together for six years. He told them all about the deals Michael had worked on and his work habits. The only thing Arturo didn't tell them about, however, was Carl. When they asked about Michael's family or girlfriend, Arturo simply told them he didn't have any. Michael's job was his life, he explained. The questions seemed to go on and on that morning. With each answer, Arturo felt more and more ashamed. He was betraying his best friend, and the mere thought of it sickened him. It was getting to the point where he could no longer stand to look at his own reflection.

There was just so much coming at Arturo from so many different directions. He thought about his father and how he would react to all this. Arturo being implicated in an insider trading conspiracy would ruin his father's career, and Adams knew this. Each time Arturo began to waiver, he plunged the threat like a knife deeper in between his ribs, then turned it and turned it until Arturo winced in pain. "For God's sake, we've been doing this for two days, and you haven't given me anything remotely helpful. I need to find him. I need to bring him in. If he's innocent like you say he is, he's got nothing to hide from. The longer he stays out, the more guilty he looks. He was in the offices, we know that now. He's got to be close. I want you to tell me where he is."

"I don't know," Arturo repeated. "I told you, he doesn't have any family here."

"There has to be someone, maybe a girlfriend."

"He wasn't seeing anyone," Arturo repeated.

"What about Karen Bauer?"

Arturo looked up at Adams like he was crazy. "Yeah, like that's ever gonna happen," he said, sneering.

Adams shook his head. It was apparent Arturo knew nothing about Michael's relationship with the woman, but there were probably a lot of things he didn't know about his friend. Adams looked back up at the credenza. There was a thin layer of dust covering the deal cubes on the counter, all except a long thin rectangle. Adams looked over at Arturo, then walked up to the credenza. "There was a picture here," he said to Arturo. "It was a picture of Michael with a man. The two of them were fishing at a lake. Who was it?"

Arturo shook his head. "I-I-I . . . don't knowwwww," he said, doing his best to lie.

"Who was it?" Adams repeated. "Look, I'm telling you. This is the last time I'm going to ask you."

"No . . ." Arturo shook his head.

Adams dug the knife deeper. "I'm done with this, you hear

me," he shouted. "I'm going to call the *Wall Street Journal* tomorrow and tell them all about how the son of a prominent Wall Street banker was involved in an insider trading scheme. That should be good for the headlines. Your dad will love it."

"No," Arturo shouted. He was standing up in the chair pulling his fingers through his hair. He felt like jumping out the window, anything to end it.

"Where is he? . . . I'm not going to ask again."

Arturo closed his eyes. He was at the end of the line. The room was closed, and there was nowhere else to go. After a long moment of silence, he finally said the name. "Carl . . . Carl Ford."

Adams was scribbling the words down on a legal pad.

"Who is he?"

"He was Michael's next-door neighbor growing up. I've only met him once."

"Where does he live?"

"In the mountains," Arturo said. "Big Bear Lake or maybe Lake Arrowhead, I don't know which. It's a couple of hours away from here. That's all I know," he said in final resolve. "That's all I know."

Michael woke up late that morning. By the time he got out of bed, Carl was already gone and a note was lying on the kitchen table. It was from Carl and said he had gone into town to pick up a few things. For a moment Michael wondered whether Carl had gone to the authorities. Suddenly he heard a sound at the back door. Expecting to see a team of investigators, he was surprised to find only Carl with a bag of groceries under his arm. The guilt quickly overcame him. He was becoming paranoid.

"Look," Michael said. "I can't stay here much longer. They'll find someone who can put us together. They always do."

Carl nodded and reached into his vest pocket and pulled out an envelope. "I want you to have this."

Michael pushed his hand away, but Carl was adamant.

"Look, just take it. It's the least I can do. When you get there, call me. I'll send you more money. I'll do whatever I can, but you've got to go. We may not have much time."

Before Michael could respond, the phone rang. The two men stopped and stared at each other. Michael suddenly got a bad feeling, and his eyes widened.

Carl quickly ran over to the phone and picked it up. A frantic voice came over the line. "Carl, it's Art Rollins. They're on their way . . . the Feds are on their way."

When the authorities got there, Carl was in back of the house splitting wood. In his red flannel shirt, jeans, and worn leather gloves, he looked more like a man out of a cigarette ad than a retired lawyer. He was in far better shape now than he'd ever been living in the city. Lifting the fifty-pound block of pine in one hand, he placed it on top of the old sawed-off stump, then came down on it with the ax, splitting it into halves. The bite of the winter was heavy in the air. Soon the snow would come. He wasn't surprised to hear their cars pull up. He knew they'd be coming eventually, but he was surprised by the number. There were two black-and-whites from the San Bernardino Police Department, along with a blue Crown Victoria with U.S. government plates. Carl set down the ax and brushed the wood chips off the stump. He sat down and watched them get out of their cars. The two San Bernardino police officers approached him first.

"Hello, Jake," Carl said, shaking his head.

"Carl," the older officer responded, tipping his hat.

Lake Arrowhead was a small town. The two had seen each other often over the years, mostly at the usual local functions—the high school pancake breakfast, the Chamber of Commerce fish fry, and of course at the local bar and grill. There was a pained look on the officer's face, as if he was being forced to do something he would regret. "This gentleman, he's with the SEC," he said, looking over to Adams. "His friend is with the NYPD. They're looking for a young man who's wanted for murder. They think you might be harboring him."

Carl took off his leather gloves. "Michael Elliot isn't here," he said. "But you're more than welcome to look around."

The young officer walked inside to search the cabin, but he would find nothing. The sheets had been taken off the guest bed and washed. The bed had been remade and the house cleaned. There wasn't the slightest trace that Michael had been there. Before long the officer came out shaking his head. "If he was here, he sure isn't here now," he yelled, walking back to where they were all sitting.

Carl smiled. "What did I tell you," he said.

Before he could get cocky, the old San Bernardino officer cut him off. "Carl, you were the talk of the diner this afternoon," he said, taking off his hat. "Jenny said you came by the bank and took out twenty thousand dollars in cash. That's a lot of money to be taking out for no reason. I wouldn't have thought anything of it, however, until these gentlemen came by the office asking me where you lived. They say they're looking for a fugitive, someone wanted for murder. Now, I don't suppose you can show me what you did with the money."

Carl shook his head. "Last time I checked, it was a free country, Jake. What I do with my own money seems like my own business."

"Well, not if you're aiding and abetting a fugitive."

Carl didn't flinch. "Well, it seems to me you don't have much proof of anything. All you have is a bank teller saying I took out some money. As far as I can tell, no one has even seen him up here. Hell, I doubt you guys even have enough to justify a search warrant. You can try to arrest me, gentlemen, but frankly you don't have shit."

Adams was livid. "I know he was here, and I'm going to find him," he said, pointing his finger at Carl. "When I do I'm going to arrest your sorry ass for aiding and abetting a fugitive. That will bring you ten to twelve at San Quentin. We'll see how you like spending your golden years in a maximum security prison."

Carl eyed his ax and looked back up at Adams. "Well, until you get yourself some kind of search warrant, why don't you get the hell off my land? Good day, Jake," he said, turning and placing another log on the old stump.

They had missed him three times now. The first time had been in New York when they executed the search warrant. The second time was in Los Angeles at the offices of Davis & White. This was the third time and it was becoming harder and harder for Adams to take. For Nico it was different. He still had his reservations. There was the unexplained gap of time from when Gage had disappeared to when his body was found. There was also the bottle of Rohypnol without any fingerprints. It was too clean a setup, but Elliot's running hadn't helped him. There were two FBI agents in the Netherlands Antilles this very moment trying to obtain subpoenas for the management company that had set up the corporation. They were also trying to gain access to the Trinity Corporation bank records in Grand Cayman to trace the money, but the laws made it difficult.

Nico knew that Elliot must have flown to Los Angeles—there was no other way he could have gotten there so fast. He must have had fake identification or a forged passport. The fact that he had gone to this trouble just made him look guiltier. Then again, maybe he wasn't traveling under an assumed name. Maybe he was just using somebody else's passport. At first the idea seemed absurd. Whose passport would he have used? Art Rollins's? It was unlikely. Art had been in Los Angeles and wouldn't have had a way to get his passport to Elliot. Besides, the two looked nothing alike. Then he remembered seeing the sketches of Elliot and Gage in *The Wall Street Journal,* one right above the other. At the time it had caught his attention. Gage had looked older, but otherwise the two could have been brothers. Elliot had taken over the partner's affairs. He had gone through his belongings. Maybe, just maybe, he was using the dead partner's passport.

The idea was absurd. Still, Nico couldn't let it go. He turned to Adams. "How quickly can the FBI check the passenger lists on all domestic flights for a particular name?"

Adams looked confused. "We have access into their booking

computer from Quantico. When the country was worried about terrorism, the FBI set up direct links so that they could check the passenger logs almost instantaneously. We already flagged Elliot's name in the database. If he tried to use his passport, airport security would have been alerted, and they would have arrested him."

"I don't think he's traveling under his own name."

"Well, whose name do you think he's using?"

Nico paused. "I know this is going to sound crazy, but I think he's using Jonathan Gage's passport."

Chapter 34

A thick gray haze hung over Mexico City that afternoon. Through the linenlike veil Michael could make out the outlines of tenements and shantytowns stretching for miles before they disappeared into the horizon. At first he thought the haze was fog, but when he got out of the airport and felt the wall of heat, he realized it was smog caused by years of unchecked air pollution. The highways here were the resting homes for every old and dilapidated car and truck that failed the emission control and environmental standards in the United States. Novas, Impalas, Thunderbirds, and Pintos littered the streets. They even passed a rusted-out Pacer with big aquarium windows and white smoke spewing from the tailpipe. It reminded Michael of the wreck he had bought a few days ago in Los Angeles, which spewed the same garbage into the air. He had abandoned the car at Ontario Airport several hours ago, but before long it would also find its way down here.

He had taken the first flight out of the country he could find. It was a United Airlines flight out of Riverside, bound straight for Mexico City. Going back to LAX would have been far too dangerous. The federal agents were just hours behind him, and chances were they had alerted airport security. In Mexico City he would buy himself some time. There were still a number of things he needed to do before going on to Luxembourg. As he waited in traffic, his mind drifted back to Arturo. The federal agents would surely trace his call to Carl and realize he had tipped Michael off. What would happen to him now? He had risked everything for his friend. Now he was an accomplice.

They would arrest him and ruin his career and life. Carl had also taken these same chances. They were both in trouble because of him. What had he done?

Michael tried to think of other things. As he drove toward the center of the city, he could see young kids in tattered clothes playing on the street. They were all shoeless and in need of baths, but fresh water was a luxury. The pollution was everywhere he looked. As he breathed in, he could feel his lungs begin to ache, as if he were breathing in a smoke-filled room. He had read that in Mexico City a child's lung capacity was half that of a child in the United States. We have exported our ills to the third world, he thought. Now he was feeling the pain of it.

Upon seeing Michael hyperventilating, the cabdriver looked back and smiled, revealing a mouthful of silver-capped teeth. "You get used to it," he said in a thick accent. Michael turned away. They passed a beautiful stone church with colorful stained-glass windows. Its arched doors and Gothic features contrasted starkly with the concrete slab apartments and liquor stores around it. If there was ever a place that needed God, it was here, he thought. Mexico City was as close to hell as he ever wanted to come.

After a few more blocks the streets became cleaner. Michael could see men and women in suits. They were getting closer to the financial district, he thought. Michael knew his Spanish was rough. He had the basic skills that anyone growing up near downtown Los Angeles possessed. He had taken four years of Spanish in high school and another two in college. At one time he could even read *Don Quixote* in its native language, but that time seemed like an eternity ago. He tried to remember the words for things they passed—*carro, escuela, machina, factoría.* Some words were familiar, but most escaped him. Fortunately he could still remember the basics. He could get a hotel room, buy a plane ticket, order a meal, but he had no illusions of fitting in among the natives. He wondered how long it would take the FBI to find him. With twenty-five million people living in greater Mexico City, the authorities here had their own problems. Drug cartels and the corruption seemed far more important than a young man from the United States wanted in a fraud investigation, even if it did involve murder. Life was cheap here. For five hundred dollars you could have someone tortured and killed. Nonetheless, he wasn't going to take chances. He would leave tomorrow afternoon for Luxembourg.

At the cabdriver's suggestion, Michael checked into a small hotel on the fringe of the Zona Rosa. The red zone was one of the cleanest districts in the city, and all the best hotels and restaurants were there. After checking in he hung up his clothes. He had put half his money inside one of the suitcase compartments and the other half in a money belt he'd purchased at the airport. There was about twenty-seven thousand dollars left. There was a small metal safe in the base of the closet, but the manager probably had a master key and would go through it when he was gone. Michael took out a thousand dollars and put the rest into an envelope. He pulled out one of the dresser drawers, set the envelope inside on the baseboard, and slid the drawer back inside. He then walked out to the main boulevard.

The Zona Rosa was beautiful at dusk. The streets were filled with tourists, and people were eating and drinking in open-air cafés and restaurants. The architecture here was different than he had anticipated. It was European, not the California adobe and red tile to which he was accustomed. They could have been in Spain or Portugal, if it weren't for the abject poverty and pollution. He saw two formidable officers dressed in dark green uniforms at the corner, but neither seemed to pay him any attention.

Michael walked past them toward a small outdoor restaurant with dozens of couples eating and drinking on the patio. He sat at the bar and asked for a shot of tequila. They gave him Patrón Añejo, a sipping tequila, which was smooth and filled with the taste of aged oak barrels. He looked over the crowd. Everyone seemed to be happy, engaged in conversations or eating. The moon was beginning to rise over the buildings, and the night air remained warm. He could no longer feel the tightness in his lungs. His body was adapting.

Suddenly he smelled cigar smoke and looked behind him. A Mexican man close to three hundred pounds was lighting a large madura-wrapped Cohiba. Michael could always tell a good cigar from a bad one by the smell. Most cheap cigars turned his stomach, but the aroma of a good cigar was sweet and rich. There were two teenage women with the man; each had long brown hair and was dressed stylishly. The man had the air of money about him, and the women wore expensive gold jewelry.

"My friend," the man said in a thick accent. "You're an American, no?"

Michael nodded. It must have been obvious.

"Where in the states are you from?" he asked, waving his cigar in a broad welcoming gesture.

Michael sipped the Patrón. There seemed little reason to lie. He doubted whether this man could have possibly recognized him. "California," he responded.

The two women became animated. "Do you live on the beach?" one asked.

Michael smiled. Their only experience with California was probably from watching Spanish-dubbed versions of *Baywatch*. "No," he said. "I'm from Los Angeles."

"I have family from Los Angeles," the man said, becoming animated.

Michael nodded, as if they now had something in common. He looked down at the long gray ash forming at the end of the man's cigar.

"My cigar, it bothers you?"

"No," Michael said. "It actually smells good."

"Then you'll join me," the man said, reaching into his vest pocket and withdrawing a leather holder. He opened it and passed Michael a large cigar.

"That's okay," Michael replied.

The man took his hand and placed it inside. "No, I insist. Please join us."

A waiter appeared behind Michael with a pair of silver clippers and cut the tip of the cigar for him. What the hell, he thought. He was tired of being alone, and no one knew who he was down here. He lit the cigar. "Señor Cordova, another drink for your friend here?"

The fat man smiled at the waiter and waved for two more drinks. He was drunk, and the rolls of fat seemed to be poking out all over when he gestured. "This is my wife," he said, smiling at the young woman next to him. "And her sister, Christina."

Michael drew in the cigar smoke and sipped the tequila. For the first time in a while he could feel himself relaxing. They spent the next hour drinking tequila and smoking cigars. As the night progressed, the young women became friendlier. They talked about California and Mexico and the differences between the two. The man's name was Salvador, and he was a banker. Surprisingly, he was a progressive from what Michael could tell. He was disdainful of the government of Vicente Fox and seemed to favor economic and political reform. When they exhausted politics they returned to smoking their cigars and stared at the moon. "I can't help but think that you look familiar," Salvador finally said, exhaling a large plume of smoke. His pencil mustache disappeared beneath his round cheeks. "I travel to the States on business often."

Michael felt a lump form in the base of his throat.

"Are you famous? Maybe in the television or papers, CNN perhaps?" he said, raising his cigar to his lips and studying Michael.

What had he been thinking? He had to get out of there. "I don't think so," he replied, forcing a smile and shaking his head. "Unfortunately, I'm no one famous."

"Still," Salvador said, the words slurring, "you look like someone I know. Christina, who does he look like?"

"Don't be silly, Salvador," she said, brushing his arm. "You're embarrassing the man."

Salvador continued to study him. Michael quickly rose.

"Ladies, it was a pleasure. I have an early morning." He reached for his wallet, but Salvador stopped him.

"Don't be silly," he said. "We can't persuade you to stay? Two lovely women."

"I wish I could," Michael said, reaching for his jacket. "I really must be going. Maybe we'll run into each other again," he said, shaking the man's hand. Heading for the street, Michael looked back at the table one more time. He saw Salvador's eyes widen. It was as if he had seen the Holy Ghost. His mouth opened. Michael began weaving through the crowd. He swore he heard Salvador's voice rising above the others. He ran in the opposite direction of his hotel. Suddenly he remembered the Federales; they were all over the Zona Rosa. He turned down a long, dark alley, then another left and another left.

Suddenly he was in the tenements. The line between abject poverty and wealth was clear, and he had crossed over. The people in the streets were eyeing him suspiciously. It was obvious he was a foreigner who had strayed from the Zona Rosa. He might as well have put a target on his back. He had to get out of here quickly.

On the next corner he saw a bar with bright lights and heard loud music coming out of it. Two old yellow cabs were parked in front, but no one was inside either vehicle. He tried to remember the word for cab in Spanish, but it escaped him. He walked inside and waved at the bartender. *Manejar* was the only word he could manage to get out of his mouth. He motioned to the two cabs outside. *Manejar.* One of the old men drinking a Tecate at the bar looked up from behind two slits for eyes and nodded.

"He's not working," the bartender said in broken English.

"Tell him I'll make it worth his while."

The man was half drunk, and getting in a car with him was probably suicide, but there was no other choice. The man stood up, wobbling at first, then holding on to the bar to steady himself. *"Cuánto?"* he asked.

"Fifty dollars. It won't take you long."

The old man's eyes opened wider. "Another fifty and you

take one of the girls for the night," the bartender said, looking for his own way to cash in on this opportunity.

At first Michael didn't understand what he was saying, then the man pointed to the back of the bar. Under the colored lights of the dance floor was a row of women. On second glance, Michael could see they were girls, none could have been older than seventeen. They were dressed in short skirts and glittery tops, like little girls playing dress-up. Michael shook his head no, but then something came to him. Salvador had probably alerted the Federales. But they would be looking for a single man, not a couple. Michael nodded to the bartender that he had changed his mind. A few of the men at the bar laughed, and he walked back to the dance floor.

As Michael approached, the girls all began to look up at him, smile, and fawn. He walked toward a shy young girl at the end of the bar. She wasn't dressed like the others. She was wearing a simple flowered dress that looked like it was her mother's. She wore no makeup. It looked as if this was her first night. Michael grabbed her hand, and she stood up and followed him. The men at the bar were staring as he took a fifty from his pocket and handed it to the bartender. He then motioned for the cabdriver to come along.

Michael had no intention of touching the girl, but just being with her made him feel guilty. On the drive to his hotel she tried to force a smile, but this only made him feel worse. If she had been born in the United States, she might have been spared this life. Instead she had been born in this sewer, with no chance to better herself. She had probably been forced into prostitution to support herself or her family. It was virtually slavery down here.

When they got to his hotel, Michael handed the cabdriver a fifty. "Come back tomorrow," he said. "Wait for me. I'll be down at eight o'clock. I'll pay you another hundred."

The old man nodded and looked at the woman one more time. He laughed as he drove away.

As Michael walked her toward the hotel entrance he kept looking for sign of the Federales. Fortunately, there were no police cars or officers anywhere. Still, it was better not to take chances. He put his arm around the girl as if she were his wife and walked her through the lobby into the elevator. No one gave them a second glance. He hit the number for the third floor and rode up quietly. She held his hand awkwardly as they got out and walked to his room. "It's okay," he said, "I don't want to sleep with you."

She looked confused.

"Have you eaten? *Comida?*" he asked, motioning with his hands.

She shook her head no. When they got inside he ordered room service—a steak for her and a couple of beers for himself. He watched as she devoured her food. In the light she was much prettier than he had thought. She had high cheekbones, full lips, and dark brown eyes. When they were done eating, she picked up a beer and began to sip. Giving alcohol to a minor seemed to be the least of his problems right now. Besides, it was comforting not to be alone. Just having someone in the room with him seemed well worth the money.

When she was done she stood up and reached around to unzip her dress. But Michael shook his head no. She looked confused again. He assured her everything was okay, then took two hundred dollars from his wallet and gave it to her. "Just stay the night," he said. He sat back on the bed and watched her as his eyes became heavy. He lay down and drifted into sleep.

Chapter 35

Friday, December 15

The morning light came in through a break in the curtains and awoke him. He was lying naked in the bed, the sheets hanging loosely over his body. Suddenly he became conscious of the woman next to him. Her head was resting on his chest, and her long black hair was swept away from her face. It slowly came back to him. He remembered the episode in the restaurant, running into the bar and bringing the woman back to his hotel. He couldn't remember much else, just lying down on the bed and sipping a beer, then being overcome with fatigue. He prayed to God he hadn't had sex with her. He must have fallen asleep. She had undressed him and put him under the covers.

As she rolled over he saw her dress was still on. He breathed a sigh of relief. She was far too young for a life like this. He wished he could find some way of helping her, but he had his own problems to deal with. It was less than eight hours before his flight, and there were so many things left to do.

For the next few minutes he went over the events of the last few days in excruciating detail. It seemed as if he was living someone else's life. He had been forced to do things he never thought he was capable of. When would it all catch up to him? It wouldn't be long before the U.S. authorities expanded their search beyond U.S. borders. The federal officers would notify their counterparts abroad, and the State Department would organize a search for him. He needed to get to Luxembourg. There were no direct flights, but he could catch an afternoon

flight to Havana and from there take the morning flight to Luxembourg.

The shuffling in the bed distracted him. The girl was stretching out like a cat. It took her a second to realize where she was.
She went to use the bathroom, and he waited for her to return.

"Would you like some breakfast?" he asked.

The girl shook her head and instinctively looked for her
purse. It was resting on the table, and he had left another hundred beside it. She looked at the money and back at him. "You
don't have to give me this," she said. She handed it back.

"No," he said. "Please take it. The cabdriver will be coming
soon. We can give you a ride home."

She pulled her hair back and clipped it with a barrette from
her purse. She looked as pretty in the morning as she had last
night. She had breathed new life into him. He had been given a
full night's sleep, which was more than he could have hoped for
under the circumstances.

"Will you stay in Mexico City another night?" she asked.

"No," he said. "I'm leaving this afternoon."

She frowned in disappointment.

He walked her downstairs. The cab was already waiting for
them. The old man was in the front seat, his eyes still slits of
red in the warm morning sun. He looked parched and dried out
like a turtle on its back in the desert. Clearly hung over and
spent, Michael thought.

"Where do you go?" he asked, looking at the girl and smiling.

She gave the cabdriver her address.

"Let's drop her off first. Then I need you to take me to a tailor. I need a suit and some dress shirts."

The driver nodded. Ten minutes later they dropped the girl
off in front of a tenement apartment. She thanked Michael
again and kissed him softly on the cheek. As the taxi drove
away, he didn't look back. The driver then took him to the old
garment district. "My cousin, he is a tailor. He will take care of
you." Michael looked skeptically at the old man but followed
him into a long narrow store with bolts of fabric lining the

walls. A short fat man with glasses approached the driver, and the two began talking in Spanish. Michael had never had a suit custom-made for him, but there was a first for everything.

"May I help you?" the man finally asked.

"I need a suit. Gray, preferably. Nothing fancy. I need it by this afternoon."

"I no can do," the tailor said, protesting. "A suit takes time."

"I have to be on a flight this afternoon. I'll pay extra."

The man looked at his assistant in the back room. She was making chalk imprints on a long cutting board covered in fabric. She marked her place and sized him up. "I can do it," she said.

"And I'll need two shirts."

Within moments he was standing in front of a dressing room mirror while the two of them took measurements—his inseam, his waist, his chest, his sleeves. The tailor barked out numbers, and the seamstress made notes as he fitted a measurement jacket over him.

"What do you do, señor?"

Michael paused. "I'm a banker. I want it conservative."

The man nodded and brought out several bolts of pin-striped fabric. Michael picked the one in the center, not too dark and not too light. He then chose simple Indian white cotton for the shirts. When he was done he decided to walk the streets to purchase accessories. At a shoe store on the corner, he purchased a pair of black wing tips and a matching leather belt. A little farther down he found a pair of silver cuff links and two silk ties. It was an expensive day, but it was important that he dress the part. Now there was only one thing missing. He needed a briefcase.

Two blocks away he came upon a shop filled with briefcases made of black, brown, and maroon dyed leather. Suddenly he remembered the very first deal he had worked on as a corporate associate. As usual Raven had put him in far over his head and had provided little assistance. The deal was relatively small, only twenty million dollars. At the time, Michael had no idea what he was doing, so he did what most young lawyers did, bluffed his way through it. He was too inexperienced to know what points were important and what weren't, so he negotiated each point as strongly as possible.

He remembered seeing the opposing counsel's briefcase resting on the table the first time he walked into the closing room. It was a big, old, brown leather accordion briefcase with a large tear in the center. Its hinges were on the verge of breaking, and the flap that held it down looked like it had been chewed raw by a dog. But the handle was the most remarkable thing about it. It was scarred and scraped on one side, and held to the clasp by gray duct tape wrapped around and around like a sprained arm in gauze. When the deal was over and they were all patting each other on the back, Michael asked the attorney why he didn't buy a new briefcase.

The man was a gray-haired southerner with a permanent scowl on his face. "You see, son, this briefcase is a badge of honor. This has seen more closings than you can even imagine. A briefcase like this should strike the fear of God in you. Now, when I come into a closing room and see a shiny leather briefcase like that one you got there, I know I'm dealing with some kid straight out of law school who doesn't know his ass from a hole in the ground. Son, it will be years before you realize the way I just screwed you in this deal."

The old man's client started laughing, and Michael laughed uncomfortably with them as if he was joking, but he knew the man was probably telling the truth. He didn't sleep for days afterwards, wondering how his inexperience had disadvantaged his client. Now that all seemed like a lifetime ago. Nonetheless, he wasn't about to make the same mistake twice.

"Do you have any used briefcases? I need one that's broken in, a briefcase that looks like it's seen better times."

The man looked at him as if he was crazy. Nonetheless, he called to one of the craftsman in the back. "I'm sorry," he said, shaking his head. Michael headed for the door, but before he reached it he heard the man's voice again. "Señor," the old man said. Michael turned around. The man was holding up a worn

leather briefcase with scuff marks and scars. It had the initials
JS painted on the front.

"How much is it?"

"Two hundred dollars," the man replied. It was true extortion, but there weren't a whole lot of other choices.

"Can you take off the initials?"

The man looked at the craftsman, who nodded.

"Do you want us to put on new initials?"

Michael thought for a moment. "No, that's okay."

They had taken the first flight out of LAX that morning. The
FBI had told them he was in Mexico City, but his precise
whereabouts was unknown. After extensive deliberation, the
U.S. Attorney's Office was now heavily involved. They had extensive experience with the Mexican authorities, but most of it
was related to controlling the trafficking in narcotics. Over the
last ten years the Drug Enforcement Administration had
worked closely with the federal and state police in Mexico, but
the rampant corruption made it difficult and their efforts had
yielded few results. Most of the police were on the payrolls of
the drug cartels, and the leads the DEA were given usually led
to dead ends or proved to be of minimal value. To compound
matters, the Mexican federal and state police were often at war
with each other. Feuds routinely arose in the border towns, not
over jurisdiction but over who was entitled to the large payoffs
for ensuring uninterrupted shipments into the States. One such
dispute even resulted in a gun battle on the streets of Tijuana,
killing several officers as well as two innocent people. On another occasion, the identity of a DEA informant who infiltrated
one of the cartels was inadvertently disclosed to senior officers
in the Mexican federal police. Less than twenty-four hours
after the incident, the mutilated and tortured body of the DEA
agent was found in a riverbed near Calexico. Although relationships had gotten better since this incident, they still weren't
strong.

Cooperation in Mexico was tied to only one thing—money.
Although the government often changed hands, the corruption

never did. Payoffs and bribery were a way of life down here. As a result the U.S. authorities had been forced to use covert operations and develop their own network of informants. Employing methods developed by the intelligence agencies, they had become quite effective at penetrating the drug cartels, which just made the tension between U.S. and Mexican authorities worse.

After a number of phone calls, the head of the criminal division for the U.S. Attorney's Office gave Adams the name of someone at the U.S. embassy in Mexico City who would help them. Jon Finch was a thin, pale-complected man in his mid-thirties, with prematurely gray hair and small wire-rimmed glasses. Although his card identified him as an officer with the State Department, he had CIA written all over him. Everyone knew that intelligence officers held most of the diplomatic posts down here.

Finch introduced himself, then explained the situation as delicately as possible. As a matter of protocol, they would meet with the Mexican police. However, they shouldn't expect much cooperation. If there wasn't any money in it for them, they were unlikely to devote any real resources to the search. Furthermore, by alerting the federal police that Elliot was in Mexico City, they risked the Mexicans finding him first. The thought that they might torture him, then track down the money themselves, wasn't beyond reason. Adams was told that under no circumstances was he to indicate how much money had been made as a result of the insider trading. This would only put a bounty on the young man's head.

Their meeting with the deputy chief of police and his staff was virtually useless, as anticipated. As they were leaving, Finch took Adams and Nico aside. "This is to be expected," he said. "You're operating in the third world. . . . That all being said, I still may be able to help. We maintain our own sources here in the city. If I had to go through the government anytime I needed something, it would cost me a bloody fortune. Are you sure he's still here?"

"We don't know," Nico said. "He could be in South America by now."

Finch shrugged. "Well, I suggest you go down to the Zona Rosa. It's the tourist district. If he's in Mexico City, chances are he's there unless he's very, very adventurous. You can split up. I'll send two of my men to drive each of you around. Both speak perfect Spanish. Maybe someone's seen him. Meanwhile, I'll do some checking of my own."

Nico and Adams spent the better part of the afternoon in the Zona Rosa showing Michael's picture. As Finch had suggested, they divided the district between them. Finally, Adams had some luck. At a small outdoor restaurant, a manager recognized the picture.

It was the young man who had come in last night and joined Salvador Cordova. The two sat for an hour drinking tequila and smoking cigars, then Salvador got belligerent. He was shouting at the young man as he was leaving, but the manager had simply written it off as Salvador being drunk. His wife and her sister had practically thrown the drunken Mexican into a Town Car to get him home. Adams asked the manager if he knew where the young American was staying, but the manager shook his head no. He had run off, and he hadn't been seen since.

Adams didn't know why Michael had come to Mexico City. He could be procuring a new passport or a new identity. Everything was for sale down here. But one thing was abundantly clear—they were getting close.

While Adams was questioning the restaurant manager, Nico was making his way from hotel to hotel. He had started with the major American hotels, but he knew he was doing this all backwards. Michael would have never stayed at a large hotel. There was too much risk of someone recognizing him. He would have picked some out-of-the-way place where there were few Americans. Nico asked his companion where the nationals stayed. The man took him to the fringe of the district, and they began stopping at the independently owned Mexican hotels, where there were no fax machines or satellite televisions. At a small five-story hotel, Nico showed the picture and watched the manager's eyes widen. It was clear he had seen the associate. Nico's driver began speaking with the manager in Spanish, and the manager pointed upstairs and across to the foyer. "What's he saying?" Nico interrupted. "What's he saying?"

"Apparently the American stayed here last night, but he wasn't alone. He was with a young Mexican woman. They checked out this morning."

"Does he know where they were going?"

"No. He thinks he was leaving the country."

Suddenly the manager began speaking again.

"What's he saying?" Nico asked.

"The American asked where he could find a tailor. He said he needed to buy new clothing."

"How long ago was that?" Nico asked.

"Five, maybe six hours."

Nico quickly called Adams's cell phone. Before Adams could tell him about the manager at the restaurant, Nico began talking. "He was here, but he checked out this morning. The hotel manager said he was going to the garment district to buy some clothes. My guess is that he's heading back to the airport. Call Finch and tell him to meet us there immediately. Tell him we need to check all flights leaving Mexico City for the name Jonathan Gage. Tell him to notify the airport police. There's a chance he hasn't left. Even if he has left, he might still be in the air. We can divert the flight or have authorities waiting for him when he gets off the plane."

Thirty minutes later Nico and his driver pulled into the Mexico City airport. It wasn't hard to find Finch. He was standing in front of the loading zone with three police cars behind him, their lights flashing. The deputy police chief was with him, his badge prominently displayed on his lapel and several armed officers in tow.

Nico jumped out and approached them. "Did you find him?" he asked.

Finch shrugged. "Well, I've got some good and some bad news."

Nico felt his stomach drop. Before he could ask anything else, Adams pulled up.

"What happened?" Nico asked Finch.

"He was here all right," Finch said. "We checked the flight itineraries and discovered he purchased a ticket on a flight out of Mexico City an hour and a half ago. The plane is still in the air, but you're going to have a hard time meeting it."

"What do you mean?" Adams shouted. "We've got officers all around the world. We can coordinate with local law authorities and have them waiting for him when he comes off the plane."

Finch shook his head. "Not on this flight, my friend. It's an Air Cuba flight bound for Havana. It's already in Cuban airspace. There's nothing we can do. We've lost him," he said. "We've lost him."

An hour later they were still at the airport. They had searched the terminal one more time on the off chance Michael missed the plane, but there was no trace of him. Nico stood at the curb looking into the darkening sky. The roar of the plane engines overhead made their voices almost inaudible. It was like a movie running in slow motion. He could see himself reflected in the windows of the black-and-white police car; he looked thin and worn out. He hadn't spoken to his wife in twenty-four hours, and he suddenly longed to hear his son's and his daughter's voices. He was thousands of miles away from his family, in a place where everything seemed dirty and corrupt. It was time to go home, he thought.

A sense of loss overcame him. There was nothing more he could do. Michael was on his own. They had tried very hard, but in the end they had lost. Adams sat on the curb with his head in his hands, cursing. There was no way in hell the U.S. Attorney's Office would let him follow Elliot to Cuba. Tensions were high enough after the Elián González matter. Elliot was in a country without a U.S. embassy or any U.S. jurisdiction. The paper trail would be impossible to pick up.

Nico suddenly heard his cell phone ringing. It may have been the second or third time, he couldn't tell for sure. It blended almost indistinguishably with the sounds of the planes overhead. He picked it up and walked back under the alcove. Adams remained at the curb with Finch. When Nico returned to the two men, he was as pale as a ghost.

"What's wrong?" Finch asked.

Nico shook his head. "I know where he's going."

Adams looked up at him with his mouth open. Another plane roared overhead, and the buildings began to shake.

Nico shouted loudly over it, *"I know where he's going."*

Chapter 36

Luxembourg was as good a place as any to die. The events of the last two weeks had changed him so much that he no longer knew who he was. In his heart he felt scared and alone. Just a short while ago he had known exactly what he wanted to do. If he continued to work hard, he would become a partner at Davis & White, maybe even a member of the executive committee. Raven would champion him in Los Angeles, and Montague in New York. The firm remembered those who were loyal to it. His hard work would finally pay off. The world was wide open and full of possibilities. Now that all seemed like a child's dream. He was too tired and worn down. He had led federal and state authorities on an international manhunt spanning two continents. He had fought hard, but now it was time to bring it all to a close.

The appointment with Alan Schrager, vice president of private banking for Banque Commerciale du Luxembourg, was scheduled for ten o'clock. From the airport in Mexico City, Michael had faxed Mr. Schrager detailed instructions. All investments in the Trinity Corporation account were to be liquidated immediately and the proceeds converted from Luxembourg francs to U.S. dollars. Amounts representing the principal originally deposited were to be used to purchase United States bearer bonds, which he would pick up at their morning meeting. Interest that had accrued on the amounts wired into the numbered account, less the bank's management fees, were to be wired to a trust account in New York.

Michael had arrived early Sunday evening on a flight directly from Havana. The airport was only six kilometers from the capital, and he took a bus straight to his hotel. After checking in, he walked through the city streets in an attempt to calm himself before he went to bed, but it was to no avail. Luxembourg City was a stark contrast to Mexico City and Havana. The population of the entire city was less than ninety thousand, and poverty seemed almost nonexistent. At one time the country had been rich with iron ore and steel exports had made up the majority of its export trade. However, when the industry slumped in the mid-seventies, the government had reacted quickly by enacting favorable banking and tax laws, making it an emerging financial center. As confidence was lost in Swiss secrecy laws, Luxembourg rapidly evolved into an appealing alternative. With such surrounding wealth in France, Germany, and Belgium, the influx of capital far exceeded government expectations. Now there were over one hundred twenty banks crowding the Boulevard Royal, a small and picturesque version of Wall Street.

The city itself rested high on a rocky outcrop overlooking the Pétrusse Valley on one side and the Alzette Valley on the other. His hotel was in the Grand, or lower town, an archaic cobblestone quarter. The commercial center was across the Pétrusse Valley to the south, connected by two bridges, the Pont Adolphe and Pont Passerelle. Fortunately, everything was within walking distance. The locals spoke mostly French and German, neither of which he knew. Most citizens, however, were multilingual, and the hotel concierge told him he wouldn't have a problem speaking English.

Michael left the hotel early that morning, deciding to stop for a coffee at a small café down the street from the bank. As he walked along the Boulevard Royal, however, an unsettling feeling returned to him. Someone was watching. He could feel it. This was Mexico City all over again. When he got to the door of the café, he turned quickly around but no one was there. He thought again about what Karen told him—think a step ahead, always a step ahead. As he sat in the café he watched the

bank and the buildings around it for signs of their presence, but
he could see no one. Finally, it was time to go. He paid his bill,
took the briefcase and headed for the bank. The building was
old, nineteenth century, with a carved stone entrance and marble floors. Two guards were standing in the lobby, checking
each person who came and left.

"Bonjour, puis-je vous aider?"

Michael didn't understand. "Do you speak English?" he
asked.

The two guards looked at each other. "Of course," one said,
disparagingly. "Who are you here to see?"

"I have a ten o'clock appointment with Alan Schrager—private banking division."

"Please wait one moment," the guard said, dialing to the office. He spoke with someone on the other end of the phone,
again in a language that Michael couldn't recognize. He studied the man's facial expressions for any sign of hesitation or
doubt. Both guards were armed, which was unusual in this
country. Since coming off the plane he hadn't seen one officer
who was armed. The guard finally set down the phone.

"Mr. Elliot," he said, "please take the elevator to the fourth
floor. Someone will meet you there."

Michael tried to remain calm. So many things were going
through his mind. How much had been accumulated in the account? Would it be this easy? Could he simply walk into a bank
with his passport and signature and walk away with the money?

An attractive woman met him on the fourth floor. Her
blonde hair was clipped behind her head with a barrette, and
she was wearing thick black-framed glasses in an effort to look
more businesslike. "Mr. Elliot," she said. "Please come this
way."

Michael followed her down a corridor lined with meeting
rooms. They were all in the interior of the building, each with
only one way in and one way out. The woman opened a door
for him and directed him to a chair. "Mr. Schrager will be with
you momentarily," she said, closing the door behind her.

The room was starkly decorated. A large wooden conference

table stood in the center with a few chairs around it, but there were no pictures or other artwork. Luxembourg bankers were known for their pragmatism. Most important, there were no windows; privacy was to be maintained above all else. What went on in the confines of these rooms was never to be disclosed. This had been the code of the Swiss bankers, and was what had made them the bankers of war criminals, dictators, drug runners, organized crime, and, last but not least, the foreign intelligence agencies of almost every G7 country. Luxembourg had adopted the code and improved upon it.

Michael was startled by a knock on the door. The man who entered was not at all what he anticipated. Alan Schrager was thin, with a pale complexion, black hair, and a broad nose. Michael guessed that he couldn't have been much older than himself. Wearing a gray suit, black shoes, crisp white shirt, and simple silk tie, Schrager was the model of conservatism. "Hello, Mr. Elliot," he said, extending his hand. Michael stood up and shook it. The matter-of-factness in his voice said this was something he had done a hundred times before. "We received your instructions by fax and have liquidated the account of Trinity Corporation as you requested. One of my assistants will be bringing by your bearer bonds momentarily. I first wanted to go over the particulars of your account with you."

This was it, Michael thought. Now he would learn the answers to the questions that had been running through his head for days. The banker opened a file folder and set it down next to him.

"Over the course of the last two years, you deposited an aggregate of one hundred twenty-six million dollars in U.S. currency into your account. Pursuant to your original instructions, we wired half of these funds to the numbered account you specified in the British Virgin Islands. The rest of the proceeds were converted into Luxembourg francs at the then prevailing exchange rates and invested in conservative value funds managed in our fiduciary account. Given the capital appreciation and beneficial fluctuation in the exchange rate, your account earned an additional twelve million in U.S. dollars. We have taken the original sixty-three million dollars and purchased U.S. Treasury bearer bonds as you requested. The appreciation, less our standard management fees, totaling one-point-nine million U.S. dollars, was an additional ten-point-one million dollars. Upon consummation of our meeting, we will wire-transfer these amounts to the account in New York you have designated."

Michael looked at the statement. It was a careful breakdown of deposits over the last two years. He was sure each one corresponded with a deal he had worked on, but he could no longer remember. At the bottom were the interest computation and the currency exchanges. They had made a huge amount of money, even after deducting the large management and liquidation fees.

"Now with respect to the account in New York, we wanted to make sure we had the name correct. What does FBO mean?"

"It's an acronym," Michael explained. "It's a trust account—for the benefit of, FBO, Laurel Gage and her children."

"Oh," Schrager said, nodding. "If you will please sign at the bottom of this letter to acknowledge receipt of the account statement."

Michael signed the paper and passed it back. The banker then took out another paper. "We will need your signature beneath the wire-transfer instructions and a cross-receipt for the bearer bonds. And of course, last but not least, we will need your five-letter password."

Michael froze. "I beg your pardon," he said.

"Your password. When you set up the account with us, you instructed us that any withdrawals must be accompanied by the five-letter password."

Michael felt his stomach drop. The walls of the small room seemed to be closing in on him. He tried to remain calm. "Sure," he said, fumbling through his briefcase. "I wrote it down just so I wouldn't forget it." He opened the briefcase fully and began to sift through the papers. He had read the account statements a dozen times on the plane, but there was never any mention of a password. Schrager was studying him.

He smiled that wry, confident smile that only a banker could muster at a time like this. For a moment Michael thought about pushing him out of the way and running for the door; then he remembered the two guards downstairs. He would never make it out alive. He tried to remain calm.

Five letters, he thought. It wasn't in the papers anywhere. Gage must not have trusted his partner in Los Angeles. He must have set up a secret password that would prevent his partner from absconding with the money without him. Five letters. It would have to be something simple, something only he would have known. He thought about the names of Gage's wife and two children. None were five letters. He again wondered what would happen if he ran. Each guard downstairs had enough firepower to support a small rebellion. Five letters.

He thought about Gage's office and his belongings. What would he have chosen? Suddenly it came to him, the woman's name in his day planner. It was Jonathan's secret. What was her name? What in the hell was her name? Schrager was looking nervous. He was beginning to stand up. Suddenly it came to Michael. "Sasha . . . S-A-S-H-A," he said.

The young man looked down at him. A long moment of silence filled the air, then a crooked smile broke across the banker's lips. "For a moment you had me worried," he said, laughing. "We'll be right down with your securities. Once again, it was a pleasure doing business with you."

The sky over the Place d'Armes was a weathered gray that afternoon, and a mist had left the old cobblestone streets shiny and black. As he walked back to his hotel, Michael kept looking over his shoulder to see if he was being followed, but the streets were empty. Nonetheless, he clenched the handle of the leather briefcase tightly in his fist. He kept repeating the words in his mind—"sixty-three million dollars . . . sixty-three million dollars . . . sixty-three million dollars." He had never held so much money so close to him; the mere thought of it was almost overwhelming. It would be so easy for him to disappear. He could catch a plane back to Havana and spend the rest of his life on the white sand beaches, drinking silver daiquiris and smoking cigars. Such things, however, were often easier said than done. There were his friends back home. Arturo and Carl had risked so much to help him. Now they were as much involved in this as he was. There was also Karen. The thought that he would never see her again was more than he could take.

After making one quick stop, Michael returned to his hotel and walked up the lobby stairs to his room. Using the magnetic card, he released the electronic lock and pushed open the door. The curtains were drawn, and the room was dark. He walked blindly forward and set down his briefcase. A voice startled him.

"Hello, Michael. . . ."

Every muscle in his body froze. The voice was so familiar to him. It was the same voice that had been haunting him for the past two weeks. Damn it, he thought. He hadn't expected this. The light suddenly came on, and Michael could see the cigarette smoke hanging in the air. As he turned around he saw Raven's narrow eyes fixed on him. He was holding a black revolver with a silencer in one hand and a Benson & Hedges in the other.

"You were always so predictable," he said, shaking his head.

Michael didn't know how to respond.

Karen had never told him who she was with the night he called, and he had never asked. Some things were better left unsaid, but now he couldn't help feeling betrayed. He had fallen in love with her, and she had been sleeping with Raven all along. He was a fool. She was probably in on this from the beginning. She had convinced him to go for the money just to make it easier for them. Michael had gotten the money out of the bank, now Raven would kill him. All the loose ends would be taken care of, and she and Raven would live off the money.

"You set me up from the very beginning. All those years that I worked for you, busting my ass," he said, pausing and shaking his head. "But why did you kill Jonathan?"

Raven took another drag from his cigarette. It seemed harmless to explain it now, so he indulged Michael's curiosity.

"They would never have been able to trace the insider trading to Gage if he hadn't become reckless. He got involved with a Russian whore and passed confidential information to her. She was trading on it, and the idiot never even realized it. When the SEC traced the leak to him, he got scared. He thought they knew everything."

"So you killed him," Michael said, his voice filled with contempt.

"My God, we're all going to die at some point. You make it sound so terrible."

Michael felt sick to his stomach. "Jesus Christ, don't you have a conscience? The man had a family. He had a daughter and a son."

Raven shrugged. "Gage brought this on himself. It didn't have to end this way."

"So how were you planning to get the money out? The accounts were all set up in my name."

Raven smiled. "Originally we were going to use your passport. I knew you kept it in the front drawer of your desk. Gage and you looked so much alike that no one would have suspected. I told him that I would bring your passport to New York with me. With it he could then travel on to Luxembourg under your name and retrieve the money. The paper trail would point directly to you."

"But you never intended on sharing the money with him, did you?"

Raven paused. "I might have. But after he screwed up and got the SEC involved, he left me no option. He was a wanted man. Eventually they would find him, and he was the only person who could implicate me. There was really no other choice, but after I killed Gage I needed a new plan to get the money. Fortunately, you made it easy for me. When you came back to the office, I realized that you must have found the account documents. That was the only possible explanation. You came back for them because you were planning on going for the money yourself. You see, deep inside we're really not that different. It was too tempting. So instead of figuring out a way to get at the money myself, I simply waited for you to get it for me."

But that was where he was wrong, Michael thought. Now there was just one other question. "What about Karen? Was she in on this with you?"

Raven shook his head. "She never told you about me, did she?"

"No," Michael confessed. "I had to figure it out on my own."

Raven paused. There was no need to lie anymore. "Well, if it makes you feel any better, she didn't know anything about this. But with you out of the picture, I think things may change. I'll have to make amends, but that should be easy. When you're found dead, she's going to need someone to comfort her."

"You bastard," Michael shouted. He thought about lunging for the gun, but he knew he would be dead before he could get it. For the moment there was nothing to do except listen to the rain pounding gently on the window. Raven undid the safety. "Michael, since we've worked together for some time, I'm going to give you a moment to pray before you die."

Michael breathed deeply. "Before you pull that trigger, you might want to check the briefcase."

Raven hesitated. "What do you mean?" he asked. Still aiming the gun at his chest, he walked over to the briefcase and unlatched it. He pulled out a large thick envelope with his free hand and tore it open. Inside was a Luxembourg telephone book. Raven became agitated and pointed the gun at Michael's head. Before he could say anything else, there was a knock on the door.

Raven paused. "You better not do anything stupid, or I'll blow your fucking head off."

Michael nodded. He just needed Raven to stay calm. He didn't want any accidents. "Who is it?"

In a thick German accent, a man said, "Mr. Elliot, this is Gerd from the front desk. I have a package here from the Banque Commerciale du Luxembourg. It's marked urgent. They wanted me to hand-deliver it to you."

Raven looked at him suspiciously. "What's in the package?"

It was now Michael's turn to smile. "Keys to a safe-deposit box," he said. "You didn't think I'd be stupid enough to bring the money back to the hotel with me? Kill me and you get nothing."

The knocking again filled the room. "Mr. Elliot, the bank said I must give this to you in person."

"I hate to disappoint you. I know how much you wanted to kill me, but, like it or not, we're going to have to strike a deal. This shouldn't be hard for two seasoned deal lawyers like us. Of course, you could go ahead and shoot me, but then you'll never get the sixty-three million, and we both know how much you want it."

Raven hesitated. His back was up against the wall. Time was running out. "Just get rid of him," he said, impatiently. "Then we can talk."

Michael nodded and walked to the door. By the time he opened it, Raven had already taken a seat beside the window. The revolver was hidden under a pillow but easily retrievable. A man in a blue crested jacket walked in with a large padded envelope. "I'm sorry to interrupt you, Mr. Elliot. I didn't realize you had company, but the bank said it was urgent." He reached inside the envelope. When his hand came out, it was holding a Smith & Wesson .38 caliber revolver. "Nobody move," the man shouted in perfect English. "Put your hands where I can see them."

Raven looked down at the pillow. The gun was just six inches away. "He's got a gun," Michael shouted. Before Raven could reach for it, the man lunged at him and brought him down to the floor.

The next person through the door was Nico Fiori. His gun was drawn and he was shouting. "Down on the floor. . . . Get down on the floor." There were voices in the hallway. It seemed as if a dozen officers had descended on the room. Everything was moving too fast.

Nico moved over to where Raven was lying. He grabbed the partner's right hand and pulled it tightly behind his back. The left hand quickly followed, then the handcuffs were clamped around both wrists.

Raven wore a look of complete shock as Nico grabbed the back of his jacket and pulled him up. Michael turned to Nico and exhaled. "It's about time," he said, standing up. The Interpol agents in their dark fatigues were speaking in languages Michael couldn't understand. They were moving quickly through the hotel making sure that no one else was with him.

Facing Raven, Michael unbuttoned his shirt to show him the wireless microphone that was duct-taped to his chest. He looked at his boss one last time, anger and contempt filling his eyes. Then Michael slammed his fist into the base of the aging partner's abdomen, causing him to crumple in pain. "That was for Karen," he said, turning away. "That was for Karen."

Chapter 37

Tuesday, December 19

In a small conference room in the basement of the U.S. embassy in Luxembourg City, Michael debriefed Robert Adams and Nico Fiori. He described in detail the deals he had worked on as an associate with Peter Raven and Jonathan Gage, and how he had been asked by the executive committee to fly back to New York to take over for Gage when he disappeared. In hindsight he realized his stint in New York had been set up by Raven to make him look more culpable. He recounted into a tape recorder the last conversation he had with Gage the night before he was murdered. The worry in the partner's voice that night had remained permanently etched in Michael's memory. Gage had known the SEC was on to him and he was going to run, Michael explained. Raven had met him in New York to stop him the only way he knew how.

Michael then told them about the day planner he found in the dead partner's office, the meeting with the SEC noted inside, and the strange entry for the woman named Sasha. He talked about the funeral and about tracing the missing files for Trinity Corporation through a paralegal. He explained how he had found the backup files the day of the search and why he had run. Finally, he explained why he had called Nico from Cuba and struck a deal to turn himself in, in return for the chance to exonerate himself. He laid it all out for them in detail.

The only things he left out were the night he spent with Karen in Los Angeles and how he had sought refuge with Carl at Lake Arrowhead. When they asked him about that missing

time, Michael refused to answer. It was a condition of his cooperation that neither friend be implicated in any wrongdoing.
Furthermore, Art Rollins's name and that of his father were to
be left out of the record entirely. In the end these were small
concessions, and Adams agreed to them in return for his cooperation. As for the interest accrued in the Luxembourg bank account, that was a different matter. After extensive negotiation,
the U.S. attorney finally agreed that these amounts could be re-
tained by Michael as a reward under the "whistle blower"
statutes to do with as he saw fit. In the end placing the proceeds
in trust for Mrs. Gage and her family seemed only right.

When they were done the three men shared a cigar on the
roof of the embassy overlooking the old city. Adams finally admitted that he had misjudged Michael. "It was Nico who was
the believer in you," he said, smiling.

Michael shrugged. He bore neither man any ill will. They
were only doing their jobs.

"So, what will you do next?" Nico asked.

Michael paused. "I don't know," he said, taking a long pull
from his cigar. They were smoking Cuban Monte Christo No.
4s, clearly contraband, but no one seemed to care. The following afternoon Adams would hold a press conference. He and
the bureau chief for the U.S. Attorney's Office would go
through all the details of the case, and the story would make the
front pages of newspapers around the world. The Department
of Justice had unraveled a complicated insider trader ring and
solved the murder of one of New York City's most prominent
merger attorneys. Investigations were still continuing into the
death of Sandra Villanueva, a former paralegal with the firm,
and the identity of the person behind numbered account 80888
in the British Virgin Islands. In time they would unravel these
mysteries as well. Adams knew it would be a great moment for
his career, and for Nico's as well. But Michael's life had been
inexorably changed.

"Do you think you'll go back to the firm?" Adams asked.

"That would be extremely difficult," Michael said.

Suddenly he realized that there was something else he had

left out of his testimony. It was the managing partner of Davis & White, instructing him to destroy evidence and obstruct justice. Maybe it was for the better, Michael thought. It was a chip he could use to his advantage later.

The private Gulfstream jet landed on the tarmac of Findel Airport shortly after ten o'clock. A black limousine was waiting on the runway for him. As the managing partner of Davis & White, Richard Montague had been informed by the Justice Department that Michael Elliot was under federal custody and was cooperating with the authorities. However, another partner, Peter Raven, was under arrest, and they were seeking to extradite him for the murder of Jonathan Gage.

It was bad enough when an associate was implicated in this, but to have one of his partners involved was far more damning. To make matters worse, the partner in question had until recently been a member of the firm's executive committee. What would people think? For the past week he had been waging a personal war to save the firm's reputation. He had spent a small fortune on public relations firms and media trying to minimize the damage. But with Raven going down and the investigation widening, he knew the whole organization was at risk. The balance now hung in the hands of one man, Michael Elliot.

Montague needed to talk to the young associate immediately. What had he said to the authorities? Montague remembered all too well his conversation with Elliot little more than two weeks ago. Would he tell the authorities that Montague had instructed him to destroy evidence? Would he otherwise try to implicate him? Of course he would deny it. Any such conversations were simply the figment of a young and fertile imagination. Still, the allegations alone would probably be enough to destroy the firm. And what about Raven? God only knew what he would say to save his own skin.

There was only one solution. Montague would have to cut a deal with Elliot. The Feds still needed Elliot's cooperation and testimony. Of course, he'd agree, but it was only fair that there be something in it for him. He was still a member of the firm.

Montague would make him a partner, and together they would present a united front. He would use Michael to get the Justice Department to narrow the scope of their investigation away from the firm and its clients. In the meantime, the papers would tell the story of how a young associate worked hand in hand with the SEC to ferret out the corruption within the Wall Street firm. He would then become a partner as a sign of his faith that everything at the firm had been restored to normal.

Hell, Montague would slot him into Raven's position. Elliot could have Raven's office and Raven's secretary for all he cared. He needed someone to fill the spot anyway. Then, a few years from now, when this was all behind them, he would call Elliot into his office and tell the young man that he hadn't matured into the lawyer Montague hoped he would and maybe it was time he found a new home. He would push him out quietly just like the others for whom he had had to make accommodations.

They met that night in the hotel bar. Montague sat at the small table opposite Michael and ordered a gin and tonic. "You had us all scared there," he said, slapping Michael on the shoulder like they were old friends. "I tried to explain to the authorities that you were never capable of involvement in such things. This firm always thought highly of you. We recognize your talents. You were a star from the day we recruited you." His delivery was polished. He had rehearsed it on the plane, refining it to sound more and more sincere. "As soon as I heard what happened, I wanted to come to Luxembourg myself and make sure you were all right. It must have been a hard week. You led the authorities on quite a chase," he said, snickering. "Although I can't condone what you did, I surely understand it. Hell, I'd like to think I would have done the same if I were in your position."

If one thing rang true, this was it. Montague would have eaten his own young to save his skin. But Michael didn't say a word. He just let the old partner continue groveling.

"We want you to come back, Michael. We want to stand behind you in this difficult time. We want to make you a partner. We'll need somebody to take over for Raven—to manage the clients he left hanging out there in the wind. He betrayed a lot of people's confidences. However, we believe that you can restore their faith." Montague expected Michael to glow like a schoolgirl asked to the prom by the captain of the football team. They would slap each other on the back and drink Scotches to celebrate. Then Montague would go back to his room, have another drink by himself, and call for a hooker. Michael's reaction, however, surprised him.

"I'll need a few days to think about it," he said.

Montague sat upright. "Well, I . . . uh, sure, I understand. You've had an awful lot on your mind. Why don't you sleep on it? I'm sure things will seem a lot clearer in the morning." He shifted to the topic that was foremost in his mind. "Michael, the SEC has some notion that the firm created an environment in which this type of thing was bound to flourish. They've threatened to seek sanctions against us," he said. "It's ridiculous, really. But did they ask you any questions about our own internal investigation?"

"What do you mean?" Michael responded.

"Well, did they ask if we tried to sweep this away or cover it up? Something like that would look terrible for the firm."

It was always the firm, Michael thought. The old man was still trying to save his own skin. "Not yet," he said, standing.

"What about this numbered account I've heard about? Have they found out any of the details of who was behind it?"

"It's not fair for me to comment on that," he said, shaking Montague's hand weakly. "Now, if you'll excuse me, it's late, and I've got an early morning meeting with the Luxembourg authorities. They need to take my deposition for the extradition hearing." Michael walked out, leaving Montague alone with his half-finished drink.

A cold wind blew through the streets of Luxembourg City that night, bringing with it the memories of those who were no longer with him. Michael drew the collar of his jacket shut and put his hands in his pockets. As he walked back from the hotel, his mind drifted to Jonathan Gage and his family. He wondered what they would do. In the end there was little to feel good about. One man was dead and another would spend the rest of his life in prison for murder. With Raven, it was relatively easy to understand. The man's whole life had been predicated on the pursuit of money and power. Eventually it had consumed him. With Gage, however, it was a different story. Where had he gone wrong? Why had he taken that first chance? He was a young man with a beautiful wife and adoring children. His whole life was in front of him. Now he would never see his son hit his first T-ball or be there to comfort him when he came home after his first fight. He would never know what it was like to see his daughter dressed up for her first day of school or have the chance to strike fear in the boys who eventually would come to pick her up for the winter formal or the prom. Sixty-three million dollars seemed almost trivial when compared with what he had given up. Finally there was Sandra. In the end he couldn't help but feel that her death was somehow his fault. If he hadn't brought her into this, she would be alive. This was something that would weigh on his conscience for the rest of his life.

Michael took the cold night air into his lungs. There was one thing he could still do. He would use the ill-gotten gains to make sure Gage's family was well taken care of. Some good had to come out of this, he thought, but it would never be enough. As for himself, he was still left feeling empty and alone. He had spent nearly all his lifetime chasing partnership at a firm like Davis & White. Now that it had finally been offered to him, it no longer seemed important. His mind returned to his grandmother and all she had sacrificed for him. She had wanted desperately for him to become a law partner, and it seemed almost unfathomable for him to give it up. Still, there was no resurrecting the dead. He just hoped she was in a better place. Perhaps she was playing bingo with St. Peter, winning bottles of Scotch that she'd pass on to him the next time they saw each other. It was a pleasant thought.

Finally, his mind drifted to Karen. In the end it always came back to her. When he called her from the embassy earlier that afternoon, she started to cry as she explained her prior relationship with Raven. In hindsight it had been a mistake for her not to tell him about it, but she was only human. Besides, Michael knew it wouldn't have changed the way he felt about her. As he walked back to the hotel, he wondered where she was that moment and what she was doing. It was still very early in the morning in Los Angeles, and she was probably in bed, her brown hair flowing over the soft white sheets. He remembered the way she looked as he watched her sleeping the first night they made love. If he could somehow have stopped time, he would have lived in that moment. She had instilled in him the drive to continue on. Now all he could think about was getting back home to see her.

Chapter 38

Wednesday, December 20

The following morning Michael testified in the extradition hearing. Two days later the U.S. attorney general would be granted the right to take Peter Raven back to New York to stand trial for murder, but Michael wouldn't be there to witness it. He and Nico had decided to take the first flight home. There was no longer any need for either of them to stay. They sat next to each other on the plane, sharing stories about their childhoods and how different it had been growing up on opposite coasts. Over drinks, however, the differences faded and they realized they had more in common than either would have imagined.

"Have you given any more thought to what you're going to do?" Nico asked.

Michael shook his head. "I don't really know," he said. "They've told me I can go back to the firm if I want. They'll even make me a partner."

Nico smiled. "Are you going to take it?"

Michael paused. He really didn't know. All he had to do was sign the partnership agreement, and he would guarantee himself the Holy Grail for a corporate attorney, a seven-figure salary and the respect and admiration of his peers. Turning it down seemed almost unfathomable. In the hundred-year history of Davis & White, no one had turned down such an offer. But the events of the last month had changed him in ways he would never understand. "What about you?" he asked. "Did you always know what you wanted to do with your life?"

Nico laughed. "Are you kidding? At one time I wanted to be the world's greatest saxophone player," he said. "But sometimes you reach a point when you realize what you really want just isn't worth the sacrifice. It would have been a hard life—always on the road and scraping just to get by. I wouldn't have had a family either. Now I have a beautiful wife and two kids who love me. I never look back. Sometimes things just work out differently for a reason."

The two went on talking until Nico fell asleep. Michael thought again about everything that had happened. Then he took out a sheet of paper and began writing. By the time he finished, the flight attendant was asking passengers to prepare for landing. The skyline of New York appeared outside the small window. The sun was just beginning to rise, and the sky was turning from black to a beautiful shade of violet. Below him he could see Manhattan, the East River on one side and the Hudson on the other. The lights were still on in the buildings along Wall Street, and the Brooklyn Bridge was beyond them. New York was a beautiful city, but it wasn't his own. He knew he didn't belong here. He would catch the next flight back to Los Angeles. But there was one thing he needed to take care of before he left.

When Michael and Nico cleared customs, there was a beautiful woman with two children by her side waiting at the terminal. They had a white paper sign with the words *Welcome Home, Dad* written in crayon and felt pen. Nico's wife was holding one end of it while his son held the other. This was a crowning achievement for Nico. His name would appear in a hundred newspapers before the day was up, but all he wanted to do was spend a night at home. He wanted to eat a home-cooked meal, give the kids a bath, and put them to bed. Then he wanted to spend the night in his own bed in the arms of his wife. Nico's daughter ran over and jumped into his arms. He picked her up and leaned to kiss his wife.

Michael stood awkwardly beside him. He had never had a

family, but he was going to make sure that he didn't miss out on one in the future. He had been given a new life and he wasn't going to let it go.

Nico suddenly became conscious of Michael standing next to him. "Honey, this is the man I told you about, Michael Elliot."

She smiled and shook his hand. In her eyes was the understanding of everything he had been through. "Do you need a place to stay?" she asked.

"No," he replied, extending his hand to Nico. In the coming months he would spend more than his share of time in New York. He would return once for the preliminary hearing and again for the trial. Raven would be convicted in the Supreme Court of Manhattan, the jurisdiction where Jonathan Gage had been killed, but that wouldn't be for a while. For the time being Michael had been given a reprieve, and he intended to use it.

"If there's anything I can do for you," Nico said without hesitation, "let me know."

Michael paused. "There is one thing," he said. He handed Nico the letter. "I'm gonna catch the next flight to Los Angeles. I was hoping you could have someone drop this off at Richard Montague's office."

Nico looked at the envelope with the words *PERSONAL AND CONFIDENTIAL—TRINITY* written on it. He knew what it contained. "Good luck, Michael," he said, shaking his hand. "Good luck."

When the Federal Bureau of Investigation finally showed up at the Bel Air mansion, they found the place empty. All signs that Mohammed Faud had ever lived there had been completely destroyed hours before. Looking at the address on the pillar of the front gate, Adams couldn't help but smile—80888. It suddenly seemed ironic. He was surprised that it had taken so long for them to put it all together, but eventually they had. Faud was the seed money for Gage's and Raven's illegal enterprise. When they traced the identity of the numbered account in the British Virgin Islands they uncovered his management company. Unfortunately, however, when they got to the account it was already empty. The funds had been moved and by the time they traced the wires all that was left was a series of dead ends. When they ran the names of Faud's management company through their computers, however, they had better luck. They found out about the U.S. attorney's ongoing investigation into Faud's management company, which eventually brought them here. But Faud was one step ahead of them. Adams knew that chances were he would never see nor hear from Faud again.

As for Richard Montague, however, it was a different story. In order to cut himself the best deal he could, Peter Raven rolled over on the managing partner and told federal authorities that Montague had been involved in this all from the start. He described how Montague had first introduced Raven to Mohammed Faud and how the three of them had come up with the scheme. He also told them about how Montague had enlisted Jonathan Gage's help several years earlier and how he and Montague had planned his death and that of Sandra Villanueva in order to protect them all.

It was a dreary Tuesday morning when they finally came to arrest Montague. He was sitting at the head of the boardroom ranting and raving when Adams entered with his team of officers. The room was filled with partners. If Adams had known that a meeting of the executive committee was under way it would have only made him happier. The receptionist had tried to stop them from going in, but Adams wasn't about to make the same mistake twice. "Richard Montague, you are hereby under arrest for the murders of Jonathan Gage and Sandra Villanueva." The old man kicked and screamed when they handcuffed him and began to read him his Miranda rights. He was yelling obscenities and telling them they would all be sued. No one listened. Ten minutes later the executive committee voted unanimously to remove Richard Montague as managing partner.

Epilogue

Life seemed to move more slowly for him now. The worries that had once hung over his head like a cloud were finally gone. He had traded in his gray wool suit for a pair of khakis and a white linen shirt. The dark circles that had hung under his eyes for the past several weeks were finally gone, and he had put on a few of the pounds he had lost. After avoiding it for as long as possible, he had come into the office to pack up his belongings. It was time to move on, he figured. He had spent too much of his life making promises to himself that he hadn't kept. Maybe sometime in the future he would get bored, but for the time being it seemed healing. He would take it day by day, forgetting about the alarm clock for a while.

The door behind him opened. He turned around to see Arturo's shaggy brown hair and round face poke inside his office. "You've decided to leave, haven't you?" Arturo asked, the disappointment heavy in his voice.

Michael smiled and shook his hand. "What gave you that idea, the boxes or the lack of a suit?"

"Neither," his friend said solemnly. "It's the peace about you. For the first time in your life you look like you've finally come to rest."

A silence filled the office.

"Do you know what you're going to do?" Arturo asked, raising his eyebrows.

So many people had asked him this question over the last

week. "Well," Michael said, looking out the window toward the mountains. "For starters, I'm going to go up to Lake Arrowhead and spend a couple of weeks with Carl. Then I signed on with a relief agency down in Mexico for a month to build houses for the poor. I figure it's about time I did something to wash away the sins of the last six years," he said, smiling, but there was seriousness in his voice. "After that I really don't know. I just can't go too far away. They want me to be available for the trial."

Arturo nodded. "Do you think you'll ever practice law again?"

"I don't know," Michael said, finishing the last box.

He walked behind his desk and reached into the bottom drawer. He took out the bottle of Scotch, set down two glasses, and poured one for himself and the other for his friend. As the two sipped their drinks, they reminisced about what things were like when they started at the firm and the people who had come and gone. They talked about what would happen after the trial and how the Los Angeles office wouldn't be the same now that he was gone. "You know, it's crazy. They're going to make Monehan a partner. They practically begged him to come back. Now they want him to take over Raven's clients. Can you imagine that?" Arturo said, shaking his head.

Michael smiled. It had been the last chip he played. In return for his cooperation, the firm would make Monehan a partner in his place and give him a long-term contract. It was almost unheard of, but in the end the firm had little choice.

"Yeah, I heard that," Michael responded, taking a long sip. "If anyone deserved it, it was him."

When they finished their drinks, Michael gathered up his belongings and started to leave. At the door, however, he stopped. Reaching into the box, he took out the bottle of Dewar's and tossed it to his friend. Arturo looked horrified as the bottle sailed through the air toward him. He barely managed to get both hands up and catch it. "Are you crazy?" he shouted.

"You might need this from time to time," Michael said, shutting the door behind him.

As he rode the elevator down for the very last time, he

couldn't help but feel as if a door to part of his life was being closed behind him. He had spent six years here, some times good and others not so good. In the end it had taught him what was important in life, and he wouldn't look back on it with regret. Things happen for a reason, he said to himself. When he got to the lobby, Karen was waiting for him. She was wearing jeans and a plain white T-shirt. Her face was devoid of makeup, and she looked more beautiful than ever.

"It's about time," she said, rolling her eyes. "You're not going to get teary eyed on me, are you?"

She had agreed to take a week off and come with him to Lake Arrowhead. They would stay at Carl's house, maybe try a little fishing. They would take long hikes among the pines and the creeks. The first snow of the season was already upon them. She told him she couldn't make any promises. They'd spend the week together and take it from there, but he wasn't about to let her go. He brushed a strand of hair from her face and kissed her. He would marry her that spring, he thought. That was the only plan he was going to make now.

As he walked out of the building, he could feel the warm air against his cheeks. There was always something strange and mystical about the Santa Ana winds. They could change direction at a moment's notice and begin and end just as suddenly. Michael looked up at the First Interstate Bank Building one more time. The lights were on in the firm's main conference room. There must have been a closing going on, but the excitement of the deal no longer had any allure for him. Younger attorneys would come through the ranks to take his place, and he knew he wouldn't be missed for long. For the first time in his life, however, he was comfortable with this thought. Life was a succession of doorways, he thought. While some closed, others would open.

Karen's voice came back to him.

"Are you all right?" she asked, taking his hand.

He looked into her eyes and smiled. "You know what, I think I am," he said. "For the first time in my life, I really think I am."

L.A. JUSTICE
CHRISTOPHER DARDEN
& DICK LOCHTE

"EXCITING." —*Chicago Tribune*

"A STORY THAT TWISTS AND TURNS."
—Laura Lippman, *Baltimore Sun*

"GRIPPING." —*Sunday Oregonian*

World-famous prosecutor Christopher Darden and award-winning novelist Dick Lochte return with Deputy DA Nikki Hill and a high-profile murder case that takes hold of her life—and won't let go.

"[A] FRENZIED PAGE-TURNER...Darden's legal smarts and Lochte's sure prose touch work well in tandem."
—*Publishers Weekly*

0-451-20541-3

To order call: 1-800-788-6262

A KISS GONE BAD

Jeff Abbott

"A BREAKTHROUGH NOVEL."
—*New York Times* bestselling author Sharyn McCrumb

"Rocks big time...pure, white-knuckled suspense. I read it in one sitting."
—*New York Times* bestselling author Harlan Coben

A death rocks the Gulf Coast town of Port Leo, Texas. Was it suicide, fueled by a family tragedy? Or did an obsessed killer use the dead man as a pawn in a twisted game? Beach-bum-turned judge Whit Mosley must risk everything to find out.

"Exciting, shrewd and beautifully crafted...A book worth including on any year's best list."

—*Chicago Tribune*

0-451-41010-6

To order call: 1-800-788-6262

S425/Abbott

PENGUIN PUTNAM INC.
Online

Your Internet gateway to a virtual environment with
hundreds of entertaining and enlightening books
from Penguin Putnam Inc.

*While you're there, get the latest buzz on
the best authors and books around—*

Tom Clancy, Patricia Cornwell, W.E.B. Griffin,
Nora Roberts, William Gibson, Robin Cook,
Brian Jacques, Catherine Coulter, Stephen King,
Ken Follett, Terry McMillan, and many more!

**Penguin Putnam Online is located at
http://www.penguinputnam.com**

PENGUIN PUTNAM NEWS

Every month you'll get an inside look at our upcom-
ing books and new features on our site. This is an
ongoing effort to provide you with the most
up-to-date information about
our books and authors.

Subscribe to Penguin Putnam News at
http://www.penguinputnam.com/newsletters